PENGUIN BO

The Guilty

P. J. Tracy was the pseudonym for the mother-and-daughter writing team of PJ and Traci Lambrecht. Together PJ and Traci were authors of the bestselling thrillers *Want to Play?* (a Richard and Judy Book Club pick), *Live Bait*, *Dead Run*, *Snow Blind*, *Play to Kill*, *Two Evils*, *Cold Kill* and *Nothing Stays Buried*. PJ passed away in 2016, but Traci is continuing the series with *The Guilty Dead*.

By the same author

Cold Kill

Two Evils

Play to Kill

Snow Blind

Dead Run

Live Bait

Want to Play?

Nothing Stays Buried

The Guilty Dead

P. J. TRACY

PENGUIN BOOKS

PENGUIN BOOKS

UK | USA | Canada | Ireland | Australia
India | New Zealand | South Africa

Penguin Books is part of the Penguin Random House group of companies
whose addresses can be found at global.penguinrandomhouse.com

Penguin
Random House
UK

First published by Michael Joseph 2018
Published in Penguin Books 2018

001

Set in 12.01/14.25 pt Garamond MT Std
Typeset by Jouve (UK), Milton Keynes
Printed and bound in Great Britain by Clays Ltd, Elcograf S.p.A.

A CIP catalogue record for this book is available from the British Library

ISBN: 978–1–405–93602–6

To PJ, always. You are in every word I write.

Prologue

Gus Riskin sipped from a bottle of water as he surveyed Trey's living room. What he saw infuriated and disgusted him. The priceless Persian rug beneath his feet was filthy, pockmarked with cigarette burns and littered with the castoffs of a dissolute life: pizza and take-out boxes of indeterminate age now housed skittering colonies of roaches; empty beer bottles and martini glasses had drooled out their meager remains, leaving crunchy spots on the expensive silk pile; drug paraphernalia and detritus were scattered around the room like grotesque confetti. Something somewhere was putrefying, or maybe the whole house was so fetid with human decay, both physical and moral, it had permanently saturated the air. None of this was his problem, but he still found it deeply offensive.

'Okay, Gussy boy, let's bang.' Trey's voice was croaky and manic as he bounced into the room on spindly, scabrous legs, his margarita glass sloshing more effluent onto the rug. He sank into a sofa, drained what was left of his drink, then bent over the coffee-table and snorted a hearty noseful of coke from a snowy pile. He let out a pleasured sigh. Then his waxen face twisted into an expression of warped mirth. 'One last party before spin-dry, right?'

Gus smiled, wondering if Trey was asking for validation or just stating a fact. 'What could it hurt?'

'Let's make it a good one. Hey, you sure you don't want a drink? A bump?'

'No, thanks.'

'You're a clean liver with a clean liver, Gus.' He laughed at his own bad joke, then rubbed his fingers together in a frenzied, greedy gesture. 'Gimme, gimme, Mr Sandman, whatcha got for me tonight?'

Gus tossed four glassine packets of heroin onto the coffee-table. 'Something special. For your last party.'

Trey fondled one of the packets with shaking hands, scrutinizing its contents. 'Looks good. Not south-of-the-border street shit.'

'I wouldn't do you like that, man. This is pure number four, just came in this morning. You don't even have to heat it up.'

'You're the boss.' He pulled a thick bundle of cash from between the sofa cushions and tossed it over. 'There's a little something extra for you this time. You never let me down and that's worth a lot.'

If there was any genuine sentimentality in that statement, it was quickly forgotten as Trey began his ritual with desperate fervor: dissolve the heroin salt, load the syringe, tie off the arm, wait for the stairway to Heaven to open up.

Gus was mesmerized, watching the liquid rise into the plastic body of the syringe as the needle greedily sucked it up, like a honeybee with nectar. He winced when Trey stuck the needle into a partially collapsed, infected vein, then sagged in ecstasy as the syringe and the surgical tubing fell to the floor.

'Can you stick around for a while, Gus?' Trey asked, in a syrupy voice. 'You know, just in case.'

'Sure, I can do that.'

'I forgot to put on some tunes. I've got a soundtrack all cued up.'

'I'll take care of it.'

'You're the boss,' Trey repeated, his voice scarcely a mumble now.

Gus took his time turning on the sound system, tweaking the treble and bass, adjusting the volume. When he was finally satisfied with the levels, he checked on Trey. He was unconscious, but still breathing, which was a god-damned miracle, considering the amount of high-quality dope he'd just pushed.

He sat down on a velvet-covered chair and gazed up at the hideously ugly painting hanging above the fireplace, thinking that beauty truly was in the eye of the beholder. But did anyone *really* think that that painting was beautiful, or was it only beautiful because it was so valuable? Trey had hinted on more than one occasion that it was worth twice as much as the house, which was a notable claim, since the current market value of the place was at least four million dollars, maybe more. He also had some very cool pictures hanging in other rooms, so they probably weren't as valuable, but Gus liked them. In his opinion, one of them should be hanging above the fireplace instead.

He closed his eyes for a moment and imagined himself living up here in the West Hills above Sunset Boulevard. Not with a depraved waste of skin and air like Trey, but with a few nubile young ladies. They'd spend sun-kissed days sipping margaritas by the pool and continue the party until the sun came up. Movie stars and rock stars would drop by to gush about his exquisite taste in art and the amazing sound system. Gus would modestly deny any credit for the shitty artwork, explaining that it had come with the house, but he would take undeserved credit for the sound system because it *was* truly amazing, the best part of the place, as far as he was concerned. It was an audiophile's wet dream, and right now it was piping in Johnny Cash's cover of the Nine Inch Nails song 'Hurt.' A paean to heroin addiction. An oldie but goodie that would never go out of style.

He was startled out of his unattainable fantasy when Trey stirred a little on the adjacent sofa and started making unpleasant retching sounds. Gus jumped out of the chair and touched his neck. His pulse was weak and thready.

'Are you in there, Trey?' He shook him, sloshed some water on his face, slapped him a few times. His eyes sprang open, empty and unfocused, but not entirely without a remedial understanding of his dire situation.

He watched as Trey's arm moved spasmodically toward the cocaine-dusted coffee-table, toward a Narcan syringe, the overdose antidote he always kept close at hand. Right now, it was impossibly out of reach. In the background, Johnny Cash's voice narrated abject desolation in a dark, warbling bass, opining about an empire of dirt.

Gus saw genuine fear and desperation in Trey's face, and he snatched the Narcan and held it up. 'I think you need this.'

There was a pathetic flicker of hope in the rheumy eyes, and Gus committed that to his scanty list of precious

memories as he flung th...
explosive rage. 'Oops! Sorry...

The flicker of hope died, ...
betrayal. Trey made some more u...
arm dropped.

Gus knelt close to him and watched...
back and forth in their sockets as they t...
face into focus, tried to comprehend. 'You...
ber me, do you? No? Well, I guess it's not ...ant
anymore.'

Trey wasn't looking so good. In fact, Gus was pretty
sure he was finally dying, so he sat down on the sofa next
to him, placed his hand on the bony shoulder, and waited to
feel it. It wasn't exactly peaceful – no death was, because
the true purpose of life was fighting death at all costs
and the body did it right up until the bitter end – but it was
still far better than he deserved. Fortunately, Hell would
balance the scales. That was why it was there. And, really,
there was no reason to unduly torture someone bound for
Hell.

'Trey?'

Gus jumped off the sofa and gaped at the scrawny,
bruised ghost of a girl careening against the walls as she
emerged from the hallway that led to the bedrooms. She
paused, trying to steady herself against the arched doorway that led to the living room, and gaped back at him.
'Who the fuck are you? Where's Trey?'

Gus wondered how long she'd been there. A few hours?
A week? Even if Trey had still been alive, he wouldn't have
remembered how this dope-sick waif had gotten into his
house, whether he'd invited her or if she'd just slipped in

roaches that had taken up residence.

a nap,' he said, suppressing the urge to laugh picked up a glassine packet and waved it at her. Maybe you want to take a nap, too.'

Her hard, suspicious face softened with the purest lust Gus had ever seen and she took a few halting steps forward. 'You got some?'

'I've got plenty.'

She licked her sore-covered lips hungrily.

'What's your name?'

'Lucky.'

'No kidding? Well, I'm not so sure about that.' He gave her a lascivious smile. 'Come here, Lucky, and I'll take good care of you, like I took good care of Trey. Pure number four.'

An hour later, Gus was jogging down the dark, narrow, labyrinthine streets of the West Hills toward Sunset Boulevard, Johnny Cash's voice still loud and clear in his head.

Minneapolis, Minnesota

Detective Leo Magozzi was sitting at his desk in Homicide, watching the local morning news on the ancient relic of a television set that perched on top of an equally ancient relic of a metal filing cabinet. Everybody in the department complained about it, grumbled about upgrading to a newer model, like something that had been manufactured in the twenty-first century, and some voiced the obvious argument: why have a TV at all when you could stream anything you needed off your computer in higher fidelity? And why have a filing cabinet full of moldering paperwork that had already been digitized around the time dinosaurs walked the Earth?

But Methuselah would not be forsaken. And his stalwart companion and pedestal, the obsolete filing cabinet, would never get ditched, either – the two belonged together, and the doddering pair was a locus of solidarity, showering the senior members of Homicide with warm, fuzzy nostalgia from a bygone era and amusing the juniors with its charming kitsch.

There was a healthy dose of superstition involved, too – there would never be an outright confession of such irrationality, but they all harbored a latent fear that messing with the antediluvian TV and filing cabinet would translate into seriously bad juju, like an 80 percent spike in the homicide rate overnight.

His partner, Gino Rolseth, ambled into the office, slightly favoring his left foot. He tossed his briefcase onto the floor next to his adjoining desk and dropped into his chair, stifling a yawn. 'I hate Mondays.'

'Rough night on the town?'

'Yeah. Angela and I took the kids to a grandstand show at the State Fair. I spent two hundred bucks on deep-fried food, visited a walk-in cooler to look at a bunch of sculptures carved out of butter, then capped off the night listening to some pre-pubescent boy band whine about girl problems they can't even begin to imagine yet. Five hours after the show was over, we finally got out of the parking lot.'

'And you had the time of your life.'

Gino got a goofy look on his face, just like he always did when his family was the topic of conversation. 'Pretty much.'

'Plus you got some hardened arteries out of the deal. Win-win.'

He leaned back in his chair and patted his ever-expanding paunch fondly. 'There is that. It's the one time of the year I can eat absolute crap with impunity and not get the stink-eye from Angela.'

'It took you five hours to get out of the parking lot?'

Gino shrugged. 'Well, maybe half an hour. Good interrogation technique, by the way. I like how you distracted me, got me in a happy place, then backtracked and called me out on my patently false statement.'

'Thank you, but I'm not finished yet. What happened to your foot?'

'A delinquent tween with a nose ring, an attitude, and a foul mouth. She was jumping up and down like a spring during the concert and landed on my foot. She felt bad about it after I suggested a little course correction of her life. A kid that young with a mouth like a sailor and a nose ring? That can't be going anywhere good.'

'Probably not.'

Gino looked up at the TV curiously while he gulped coffee from the travel mug that was never far from his right hand. The slogan 'YOU HAVE A FRIEND IN TEXAS' circled its perimeter in bold red letters. As far as Magozzi knew, Gino had never been to Texas and didn't know anybody who lived there, but he'd never asked about it. Some mysteries were richer left unsolved.

'Did I miss something, Leo? You've got Methuselah on and you never fire up that cranky piece of junk unless the chief is giving a press conference.'

'Breaking news. Trey Norwood is dead from a suspected heroin overdose.'

'That's breaking news? The kid was a total high-ball. It was only a matter of time before he OD'd.'

'Spoken with the profound sensitivity of a true fatalist.'

'Life's fatal. We're all going into the ground eventually, it's just a matter of how and when.' He leaned forward, set his elbows squarely on the desk, and propped his chin in his hands, suddenly hypnotized. 'Turn it up, Leo. Nothing like the smell of *Schadenfreude* in the morning.'

Magozzi did so, and they both listened to the media soundbite, delivered by a young male anchor just cutting his very white teeth on the early-morning news. His delivery was robotic, but he'd figure out the teleprompter after

9

some more air time, learn to construct a believable façade of genuine feeling. Sociopaths were able to learn that skill, too, and if they could do it, this kid could.

Gregory 'Trey' Norwood the Third, son of legendary Minnesota businessman and philanthropist Gregory Norwood the Second, was found dead in his Hollywood Hills home early this morning at the age of twenty-eight. An unidentified female was also found deceased in the home. No official cause of death has been determined at this early stage in the investigation but, according to the Los Angeles Police Department, drugs and paraphernalia were present at the scene.

Trey Norwood's struggles with substance abuse over the years were very public and plagued him throughout his short life, although sources tell of his recent commitment to sobriety. He was scheduled to check into a rehabilitation facility in Malibu later this week . . .

'What a waste, makes me sick,' Gino decreed gloomily. 'The kid had everything going for him, including a brain, which he just didn't use. One last whirl around the smack carousel before he hit the cleaners and, boom, he's just another dead junkie. Where the hell was Papa Norwood when his only kid was turning himself into a pin cushion?'

. . . A family spokesperson has asked that everyone respect the Norwoods' privacy during this difficult time . . .

'This is depressing.' Magozzi got up and turned off the TV. Methuselah didn't have a remote with a mute button. Neither did Gino. 'Papa Norwood is the Minneapolis Police Department's biggest booster and an old friend of Chief Malcherson's. We should go offer our condolences.'

'Yeah, you're right.'

'And keep our opinions to ourselves.'

'Don't I always?'

Magozzi didn't answer.

One

One year later

The early birds had just begun to sing their garrulous summer songs as the rising sun traced the horizon with showy hues of ochre and lavender. The cardinals were always the last to bed and the first to wake, and also the most tuneful of Gregory Norwood's avian friends. The blue jays were much louder, and didn't possess the cardinals' gift of song. They just screamed. Especially the juveniles. But that was all right – the birds kept him company, allayed some of his loneliness, and reminded him of a normal life, which he hadn't lived for a long time in spite of appearances.

It was very early, but sleep was impossible on this day of all days. He got out of his soft featherbed and went through the usual ritual of a morning at home. It consisted of a brisk shower, a precise shave, some judicious application of a lightly scented tonic to his face, then the closest attention to detail as he dressed. Everything perfect, down to the medium-starched shirt that was as white as fresh snow and without a single crease, the crisp Savile Row suit, a pair of custom-made Italian shoes.

He did a final check in the mirror to make sure he hadn't missed a single whisker or a slight razor nick that might bleed. His face hadn't weathered nearly as well as his clothing over the years, but the deep lines and creases didn't bother him as they would have had they been on his clothing. They were a topographical map of life's hard truths and tragedies, the first and foremost being the loss of his only son a year ago today. The terminal diagnosis he'd received last week was a distant second – laughably irrelevant in the scheme of things. He'd already lived a full life. Trey's had barely begun.

He stared at his reflection. He didn't look like a man who had less than a year to live. Funny how something so deadly could grow in silence as it slowly ate you from the inside without betraying its presence. Cancer was such a cunning disease.

He finally emerged from the bedroom suite and walked downstairs, unassailed by the sounds and aromas of a normal morning in his household. There was no coffee brewing, no breakfast being prepared, no murmurs of the staff or his wife Betty as she briefed them on the plans for the day. He was all alone. He'd made certain of that.

They were at the Aspen house now, preparing for Trey's anniversary memorial down at the gazebo. It squatted next to the Roaring Fork River, equidistant from the main house and the guest cabins. The gazebo had been Trey's favorite place growing up – as a child, he'd sit there for hours and watch the trout negotiating the pristine water that cascaded over multi-colored rocks as it made its magical journey to someplace else.

They look just like agates, Dad, like the ones we get at Lake Superior! Only they're HUGE! They're boulders!

Such a sensitive child, so aware of the tiniest details of everything around him. He'd loved nature more than anything, and you couldn't keep him inside no matter what the weather was like. He saw magic everywhere and inhabited his own little worlds, different ones each day. But something had gone terribly wrong. And it was his father's fault.

Failure. The word hadn't been in his vocabulary until Trey.

Tonight, he, Betty and daughter Rosalie would finally release Trey's ashes into the Roaring Fork so he could hitchhike with the trout over the agate boulders and make that magical journey to someplace else, someplace better.

Gregory paused in the doorway of the empty, silent breakfast room where he normally seated himself every morning after coming downstairs. As always, there were flowers in a crystal vase centered on the big black walnut table. Today the vase was filled with lush August roses from Betty's garden. A full place setting was waiting for him at the head of the table, and Chef had put out a platter of pastries and fruit before he'd left last night, but no food or beverage would be served or swallowed here today.

It felt strange to close the doors on the deserted room without even setting foot inside, but it also felt liberating. He'd lived a life of obligations, both large and small, but there were none today.

He retreated promptly to his study and disabled the security system and surveillance cameras, which also felt liberating. He hated being watched and recorded by his own cameras twenty-four hours a day, but Betty insisted on it. She had a pathological fear of intruders and dishonest help. She also had a pathological fear of unfaithful husbands, although he'd never once betrayed her or their marriage vows.

He drew down the shades and mixed himself a pitcher of martinis at the wet bar. This morning belonged to him, and he would indulge his clandestine thirst for gin and oblivion with no consideration for anything else, except positioning his long-deceased father's most beloved Frank Sinatra LP on the same turntable he remembered as a child. He gently dropped the needle into the well-used grooves and closed his eyes as music filled the room, instantly transported to a different time, a different place, just like Trey would experience tonight.

There were occasional pops and hisses as the needle encountered the scratches in the vinyl on its slow track down the shiny black disk, but it didn't bother him. Some people wanted to experience nostalgia through an idyllic lens, but he wasn't among them.

Everything gets scratched up with use, he mused, as the gin started to enter his bloodstream. Just like his life, just like everybody's life. The old record and the old turntable were poignant reminders of that.

Time passed as he listened to Frank and drank martinis with the same abandon the singer and legend had shown back in his prime days. He was alone, but felt like he had a friend and compatriot in Frank.

After a certain point, things blurred into a mesmeric stew: the music stopped as the record ran its course; the olives bobbing in his glass looked like disembodied eyeballs; the shuttered gloom of his office cooperated nicely with the gin to dull his vision. But his mind and body were alive, itching with a buzzing electricity that fed a spectacular recklessness.

He unlocked the top drawer of his mahogany desk and

withdrew a Colt Peacemaker from its coffin of cherry-wood and velvet. As he gazed upon it, he suddenly realized what a conundrum he held in his hand. The name alone boggled the mind. When had death ever brought peace, or solved anything at all? You could kill your enemies, but they would always return, like angry ghosts, in one form or another, haunting you, tormenting you.

And for a perfectly tooled instrument of death, it was such a beautiful thing, so exquisitely crafted of the finest materials. Or perhaps there wasn't such a puzzle here: death and beauty were two of the most powerful forces driving humanity and often went hand in hand.

The grip felt slimy in his sweating palm as he pressed the cool barrel against his temple. This could be the Colt Peacemaker's finest moment – it could finally do its job as advertised and actually bring peace through death. At least, Gregory Norwood II's final peace. In a millisecond, he could be liberated from his guilt and regret, from the slow, agonizing crawl to the grave as his body was ravaged by disease. But, as tempting as the prospect was, it wasn't his time yet. He had one last thing to take care of, one last mystery to solve.

And then his phone chimed, shattering his focus, shattering his perfect moment. His hands were shaking as he placed the gun back in its velvet nest and reached for the phone. Funny, the whole time he'd been holding the gun and ready to use it, his hand had been steady as a rock. Steady as an agate boulder in the Roaring Fork River. Now that he was about to answer this call, it was quaking like aspen leaves in the autumn, when their stems were getting weak and they were about to fall to the ground in a shower of gold coins.

'Yes?' he snapped.

A hesitation at the other end of the line, then, 'Gregory?'

'Oh. Oh, Robert. Sorry to be curt. I was expecting another call, so I didn't even look at the ID before I answered.'

'Can I help you with something? You shouldn't have to deal with any external annoyances today.'

'No, that won't be necessary, but thank you. We're just having some problems with our new caretaker in Aspen,' he lied. 'There were some issues when Betty arrived last night. A broken faucet, dead mice left in traps and so forth.'

'Well, I hope you get it sorted out. Listen, Gregory, I'm sorry to disturb you today, but I just wanted to let you and Betty know you're in our thoughts and prayers. Louise and I went to mass last night and lit candles for Trey.'

'That was kind of you. And kind of you to call.'

'I hadn't expected you to answer. It's good to hear your voice.' He heard Robert sigh anxiously. 'Are you all right?'

Gregory deflected the question because he couldn't give his old friend the answer he wanted to hear. 'I'm flying to Aspen this evening to meet Betty and Rosalie. We'll be spreading Trey's ashes.'

'I think that will be a good thing. Perhaps it will bring you some closure.'

A word that should be struck from the language, Gregory thought, feeling bitterness rise in his throat, partly from gin, partly from regret. 'There is no closure for something like this, Robert. My actions, my inactions, are responsible for Trey's death. I killed my son.'

There. He'd finally said it out loud to the one person who would understand. It felt so good. But then Robert's stern warning at the other end of the line fragmented his joy.

'Gregory, we've spoken about this. You must *not* go down that path. Do you understand? It's dark and dangerous and it will never put right a tragedy. It will only bring more.'

'Tragedy. There's plenty of that to go around, isn't there?' He took another sip of his martini while he waited out Robert's silence.

'Have you told Betty yet?'

'You mean, did I tell her she would be a widow soon, just days before she said her final goodbye to Trey? Of course not, Robert. There's only so much grief a person can endure at one time.'

'Have you been drinking?' he asked.

'Excessively. Drinking like Frank.'

'Frank?'

'Frank Sinatra,' he explained, no longer bothering to modulate his voice or the sudden belligerence welling up in him. Whiskey courage, they used to call it in his day, but in this case, it was gin blessed with a little vermouth. 'I've recently discovered that it's a wonderful thing, being drunk. It gives you strength and freedom. You lose all inhibitions. All fear.'

'I'm coming over.'

'Please don't. I prefer to be alone.'

'Listen to me –'

'Tell me something, Robert. When you go to confession, do you feel cleansed? Does it help your soul when it's so sick that it's dying inside of you, poisoning you?'

'Uh . . . well, yes, of course. God forgives.'

'Everything?'

'If you confess your sins, God will forgive you.'

17

'But I'm not Catholic. I'm just a boring Episcopalian without a priest or a confessional booth. I don't think I'm eligible for unconditional amnesty.'

'God is merciful. There is grace everywhere, Gregory. We may not see it, but it's there.'

'That's comforting to know. Thank you, Robert. I appreciate the call. I'll let Betty know.' He hung up, wishing he hadn't answered.

When the phone rang again a few minutes later, he looked at the ID. He'd been expecting a frantic callback from Robert, but he was wrong. This was an unknown number, most likely the call he'd been dreading and the one he'd been waiting for. Even Robert couldn't help him with this.

Two

Gerry Stenson had found a nice bank of shrubbery behind the Norwood estate to conceal himself. He couldn't get close enough for a shot, not without trespassing on private property, but if Gregory Norwood II decided to take a dip in his pool on the one-year anniversary of his son's death, his Canon 600-millimeter zoom would be able to catch it from this angle. Not that such a photo would be a scoop, or even marketable to any mainstream outlet – that was painfully obvious from the lack of other paparazzi present – but a local rag had an interest in the Norwood story and they would pay for good shots of him or his family. Not much, but it was something, and something was better than nothing when you were three months behind on the rent, buried in debt, and desperate.

In his line of work, he'd been called a maggot and much worse. But maggots had their place in the food chain, too. Unfortunately, it was at the rock bottom of it, exactly where he was now. He was just another maggot, looking for a scrap of meat.

He felt sweat gathering on his brow as the rising August sun worked like a convection oven, heating the damp ground beneath him, coaxing the humidity higher and higher, fogging up his lens. Damn hot, sticky day in store. A scorcher. Just wait until two o'clock – people would be melting in the streets. Maybe he should be taking shots of that instead.

He lowered his camera, swabbed his brow with a bandana, and pulled an energy bar out of his bag. This particular one was a self-proclaimed miracle bar that promised instant nirvana, a lifelong hard-on, and a mansion on Jupiter Island through sustainable, fair-trade organic ingredients fortified with outrageous amounts of refined sugar.

That was Kris – she always put little snacks and beverages in his kit before he left for a job, and always from the New Agey co-op she devoutly frequented, happily oblivious to the fact that some so-called health food was exactly the opposite. They were always accompanied by notes, carefully written on Post-its. Today's read: 'Love you to the moon and back, Sugar Bear.'

Suddenly he felt a sickening guilt creep up on him. His sweet, thoughtful, loving Kris didn't know about the financial troubles yet, but he couldn't keep them from her forever, especially if his luck didn't change soon. He had to catch a break.

Gerry was washing down his energy bar with the last dregs of a vitamin water drink – courtesy of Kris, of course – when he heard the gunshot and jumped like a grasshopper.

He swore out loud, clambered to his feet, then froze as he worked through potential scenarios. There had been only a single shot, and that shot had come from the Norwood estate, he was sure of it. Suicide was his first thought – the normally media-savvy old man had become a virtual shut-in since his son's overdose. He also hadn't accompanied his wife last night to their Aspen compound.

As a full-on epic tragedy filled out in his imagination, he started running for the security fence, stumbling through the underbrush. There was no worry about private-property issues now because he would just be doing a welfare check. Good Samaritan and all that. Maybe he'd even save the life of Minnesota's beloved benevolent patriarch and become an instant hero. And if he got a juicy shot in the process, well, so be it.

Maggot.

The word was ringing in his head as he jumped the fence and ran across the Norwoods' manicured back lawn, past a formal rose garden, past the pool toward the main house, all the while his weighty camera rig swinging from the strap on his neck, digging into his flesh. Of course he'd call 911 if he found something bad, but the cops were probably already on their way – in a wealthy, peaceful enclave like this, a gunshot would be called in immediately.

He'd laid out the scenario so clearly in his mind, knew exactly how it would unfold, but in his version, there wasn't a man coming at him from his right flank, taking him down and smashing his face into the lawn.

Three

Harley Davidson's Summit Avenue mansion was dark except for the pair of Tiffany lamps that glowed amber and green and projected art-nouveau lilies onto the windows of the third-floor Monkeewrench office. From the street, the sight might have looked charming and whimsical against the backdrop of the forbidding, red-stone estate, but it was still too early for anybody to be walking the boulevard to appreciate it.

Harley was wide awake and at his desk, mindlessly playing bridge with his computer while he waited impatiently for the chamomile tea – *Nature's Sleep Aid!* the box proclaimed – to take effect. He had no idea what had jolted him out of a sound sleep an hour ago – maybe a bad dream that had fragmented before he could commit it to waking memory, a strange sound his subconscious had registered, or just old-fashioned insomnia from working too many long, intense hours lately.

But, whatever the reason, it had unnerved him, and more troublesome still was that this had been happening with alarming frequency lately. Up until a few weeks ago, he was the guy who could fall asleep in the mosh pit at a heavy-metal concert, and now he was haunting his own mansion in the wee hours, like a displaced ghost.

He'd checked the doors, the windows, and the alarm systems on all three floors, but everything was buttoned up tight, as it always was, and if there was a boogeyman out there somewhere, he was messing with the neighbors.

He suddenly thought of Grace MacBride, one of his dear friends and partners in Monkeewrench Software. She was eight months pregnant now and probably sleeping like a log. She had a burgeoning new life in her womb, an awesome dog named Charlie, which was probably hogging half the bed, and the baby's daddy, Leo Magozzi, hogging the other half. The irony lifted his mouth a little – Grace, the most devoted loner and outcast he'd ever known, was now lovingly cocooned in the safety and comfort of things she'd always eschewed – or, at least, the things she'd never allowed herself to want.

It made perfect sense to Harley that a homicide cop had been the one ultimately to breach Grace's titanium shell – they both had very complicated relationships with death, and if that wasn't the foundation of a solid bond, he didn't know what was.

He played another game of bridge and felt none of the drowsiness the chamomile tea's colorful packaging had promised. He finally decided that herbal nightcaps were for hippies, amateurs and recovering alcoholics. It was time to hit the wine cellar for something a little more reliable, like a good port.

Years ago, when he'd been given the opportunity to buy the historic estate on Saint Paul's most coveted boulevard, the basement had almost been the deal-breaker – decades of neglect, unchecked water damage, and massive colonies of microbial evil-doers had nearly rendered the entire home uninhabitable. But in the end the place had spoken to him, and such a grand old dame deserved to have a custodian who could afford to take the restoration seriously, which he had. And once the deep basement had been gutted, revealing stone walls beneath moldering wood panels, he realized he had the makings of a perfect, naturally climate-controlled, wine cellar, and the deal-breaker became the most cherished feature of his home.

As he descended into the dark heart of the cellar on a spiral staircase, he took deep breaths, drinking in the dusky aromas of wine-saturated cork and wood, stone, and the mushroomy undertone of earth. There was no smell like it in the world, and there were times when he would spend hours down here among his racks and casks, until the scent of his subterranean paradise had permeated his hair, clothes, and skin.

He aimed a remote and clicked on a toggle that lit the wall sconces. Once his eyes had adjusted to the sudden light, his gaze seemed to drift of its own accord right past the racks of port to the old wine crate he kept stashed in a corner all by itself, a crate he hadn't thought about in years. In it was a sparse collection of childhood mementoes – a pathetic assortment of trinkets and all that remained of his distant past, before Atlanta, before Grace, Annie, and Roadrunner, before the four of them had fled from a killer, resettled in Minneapolis, and built Monkeewrench into a modest software empire. It was the entirety of a sorry, ephemeral young life reduced to the size of a box meant to hold twelve bottles of wine – nine liters. Nine liters of life, if that.

He moved toward it reluctantly and knelt down, placing a hand on the cool pine lid, feeling as apprehensive as if he was about to open Pandora's box and unleash evil spirits into the world. But the spirits in the crate weren't evil, just sad, and he finally lifted the lid and exposed a scuffed-up baseball, some plastic figurines left in a field by a traveling carnival, a few old coins, and a railroad spike – things a scared, troubled, runaway boy had found of value while on the run among the back roads and woods of rural Georgia.

At the very bottom of the crate a battered, dog-eared book of poetry was sealed in a plastic zip-top bag. It produced an instant smile. Jesus, he'd forgotten all about it.

He removed it from its sheath and cradled the wrecked spine in his big hand while he carefully opened the cover. Inside was a faded inscription, written in a painfully neat hand: *Property of Miss Elizabeth Daltry.* Miss Lizzy.

His memories made the trek back to his eighth year of life. He'd been on the run for three days, fleeing the hell of a foster home where there was never any food, only drugs, alcohol and cruel strangers, who thought it was funny to use him as a punching bag. Sometimes he was left alone for days at a time. His only friends were rats, mice and cockroaches, and his only nourishment was what he could scavenge from other people's trash.

Hiding out in the Georgia woods, starving, overheated, and exhausted, he'd miraculously stumbled upon a clearing that seemed like Heaven. There was soft, silky grass to lie on and a small pond with purple flowers along the shore. Miss Lizzy had found him there, sound asleep. She was the oldest person he'd ever seen, with long gray hair tied back in a pink ribbon and a face so wrinkled he could barely see her eyes among the folds of skin. But she had a young smile and an open heart. She'd taken him to her little house on the edge of the clearing and fed him roast pork and pickles, then peach cobbler. When he'd started crying silent tears of relief, she'd told him about poetry, how it was salve for sorrow and lonely souls, like the two of them, and she'd read to him while he drank lemonade.

His phone interrupted his reverie and he felt a writhing panic in his stomach: good news never came early in the morning. Unless it was Magozzi, ready to share what they'd all been waiting for. The possibility soothed him as quickly as the buzz of his phone had agitated him.

But there was no signature on the caller ID, just 'unknown number.' It was a call he'd normally never take, but the odd timing was enough to pique his curiosity. Maybe it was the boogeyman, and this would be his opportunity to tell him to go to Hell once and for all.

'Hello?'

'Mr Davidson?'

The voice was generic male and vaguely familiar, but he couldn't put a name to it. 'Who's asking?'

'This is Special Agent Dahl . . .'

'Dahl? Are you shitting me? It's the crack of dawn.'

'I had planned to leave a message.'

'Well, you got me now. What's up?'

Dahl cleared his throat in hesitation. 'I'd prefer to meet in person.'

'Hey, I'm flattered you think so highly of my company, but I need a little more to go on. I don't like cloak-and-dagger bullshit and neither do my partners.'

'It's sensitive.'

Harley grunted. 'Are you calling from the office?'

'No.'

'You're calling from a burner phone?'

'Yes.'

'Okay, then. You're secure on your end, I'm secure on mine, so give me a hint.'

'It's an issue of national security. Does that interest you?'

Harley heard a pained sigh at the end of the line, as if Dahl had just thrown himself on a pike. As far as his upward career mobility was concerned, maybe he just had. Monkeewrench operated in the shadows, always skirting the fine gray line between justice and illegality, and feds weren't supposed to inhabit the same domain. But Dahl was a true patriot – if you cut him, he'd bleed red, white, and blue. He'd taken a lot of career risks in the past to serve justice and his country and, for that, Harley admired him. 'Hell, yes, of course I'm interested. In fact, we're finishing up a little freelance project somewhere along those lines.'

'Excellent. I'd like to meet as soon as possible.'

Harley grabbed a bottle, one of his best. 'We're both awake, so how about now? I was just about to open up some port.'

'You're opening a bottle of port *now*?'

'I've gotta sleep sometime and port is better than a pill any day.'

'At your place, then.'

'No place better, unless you want to meet at an all-night convenience store or a strip club. Isn't much else open.'

'I'll be there in half an hour. Try to stay sober.'

'You don't get drunk on port, you savor it.'

'That was an attempt at a joke, Mr Davidson.'

'I figured. But you need to work on your delivery. See you soon.' Harley hung up and rehashed the short conversation. Monkeewrench had worked with Dahl a few times before, never officially, and Gino and Magozzi were always the intermediaries – the ones who contacted him first and brought him on board in the course of a homicide case that would benefit from federal assistance. This was different. For Dahl to deviate from established protocol and contact Monkeewrench directly meant he was desperate and there would be a good reason for that, which was unsettling.

As he ascended the stairs with a bottle of Niepoort Old Tawny, he tried unsuccessfully to shake the feeling that the boogeyman was getting closer.

Four

Harley had always thought Dahl looked a little too California surfer to be taken seriously as a federal law-enforcement officer. His blond hair, perfect white teeth, and perennial tan just didn't synch with the generic blue suit, the gun, and the rigid, charmless demeanor.

But Dahl wasn't so pretty right now. Whatever was on his mind had taken its toll on his good looks. He still resembled a surfer bum somebody had cleaned up and dressed in a suit for church, but one who'd been on a beach bender all weekend.

Harley let him in and led him to the main-floor library. 'You look a little roughed up, Dahl. You slept much lately?'

Dahl eyed the bottle of port sitting on a side table. 'No.'

'I'd offer you a glass, but since you're always on the job and alcohol is *verboten*, can I interest you in a wheatgrass shot? Some kale ginger carrot juice?'

Dahl took his time looking around the room, then leveled a shrewd gaze at Harley. 'I'll take a wheatgrass shot.'

'I'll have to go out back and get some grass clippings from the compost bin.'

'Then I'll take a port.'

Harley grinned and poured him a glass. 'So you're really going rogue, are you?'

'Temporarily. By the way, I don't own a Vita-Mix and I

don't drink my vegetables. I prefer them intact, as God intended.'

'Well, then, we've got more in common than I thought.' Harley examined his glass of port. 'When you come to think of it, this is fruit juice. What's the difference?'

Dahl took a sip and closed his eyes. 'The miracle of fermentation.'

Harley cradled his glass between his two big hands, more suited to wrenching at engines than precision typing on computer keyboards, but he was equally at ease with both. 'So tell me what's going on.'

'Nothing specific, actually. And that's the problem.'

'So, no crime?'

'Not yet. But I don't have a good feeling about the immediate future. Which is why I called you. We could use your expertise. Monkeewrench's expertise.'

'Dahl, it's just you and me, no eyes or ears. Spit it out.'

'Plain English, the Bureau is inundated with terror threats, many with actionable intelligence. Even if we tripled our manpower and resources, we still couldn't keep up. We need to find a way to streamline the process, eliminate some of the eyes-on work, and bring in local law enforcement to follow up on what we can't, or what we've had to mothball on a federal level. We simply don't have enough people. The levee is breaking.'

Harley went to great lengths to keep his expression neutral, because the freelance project they'd been working on fit that description exactly. 'I won't argue with you on any of the above. So you're looking for intelligent software. Maybe a new database overhaul.'

'That was my thought. Beyond that, we're having some

issues with security breaches that are further impeding our work.'

'Hacking, you mean.'

He nodded.

'Well, no shit, that's a given. Have you been able to isolate a source?'

'Not exactly. Right now, we're focusing on the usual suspects: Eastern Europe, Russia, North Korea, China . . .'

'Islamic State?'

'We haven't found any direct links yet.'

'Of course you haven't. ISIS has the oil money to hire the big dogs from hostile countries to get that shit done for them. Hackers are the new mercenaries, Dahl, so you and your people better start paying attention to that battle front. Computers are on the verge of becoming weapons of mass destruction without the plutonium-239.' Harley took a sip of port and let it linger on his tongue. 'So, not only do you need some new software to help streamline and restructure your domestic cases, you need better firewalls, more strategic than tactical. Which is smart, by the way.'

'In a nutshell, yes. Not a lot to ask.'

Harley snorted. 'You're getting funnier by the minute. Maybe I should pour you some more grape juice. Look, Dahl, I'm not going to promise you anything without input from my partners, but we've spent the better part of the past year working on a program just like the one in your fantasies.'

Dahl blinked at him. 'Really? That's . . . fantastic.'

'But it's still a baby. We're going to run the first beta test this morning, so we don't even know if it'll work yet. And if you want to implement something like this, it can't be under the radar. We're talking massive renovation here and it'll have to go all the way to Washington.'

'I understand that.'

'So what are the chances your ideas are going to fly?'

Dahl bowed his head and rubbed his eyes. 'Truthfully? Slim to none. I've come to realize that government bureaucracy is a quagmire mostly inhabited by people with no imagination or ambition beyond their own personal enrichment, so nothing substantive ever gets done. But if something gets presented that looks like it might solve some problems for them, and help their careers and their paychecks, the wheels can move. It's all about the packaging.'

'Man, you're almost as cynical as me.'

'Maybe more so.' He held out his empty glass. 'I'll take a refill, if you don't mind. This is excellent.'

Harley freshened his glass. 'You've stuck your neck out before, but this is a whole new level of crazy. First off, you're going to make your superiors look stupid for not thinking of something this obvious in the first place.'

'Don't worry, they'll find a way to take full credit for it if it's successful. If it gets implemented at all. And I'm fine with that.'

'But if it does get implemented and it's not successful, you'll go down in a spectacular ball of fire.'

'That's the way things work in my world.'

Harley watched Dahl methodically swirling his glass counter-clockwise. He seemed hypnotized by the shimmying liquid, or maybe it was just a place to rest his eyes while he pondered more onerous realities. He was a good soldier and, like all good soldiers, he carried a heavy burden the average person probably couldn't even imagine. But there was more to Dahl, some layers he hadn't seen before, or maybe that he hadn't allowed himself to see until now, prejudiced as he was by his appearance. 'You think you'll last until mandatory retirement?'

'I sincerely doubt it. I might be looking at the end of my career, but at least I'll be able to live with myself if the chips don't fall the right way and people die.'

Harley rose from his perch on the hearth and clinked glasses with him. 'I don't have a problem with a whole new level of crazy. So what else is on your mind?'

'What do you mean?'

'Come on. A long-term software overhaul is a fantastic idea but it doesn't synch with your early-morning out-of-the-blue phone call or the fact that you showed up ten minutes later and are now polishing off your second glass of port. What's really lighting your fire?'

Dahl dragged his hands down his face, displacing the puffy purple pouches that had taken up residence under his eyes. 'We're getting metadata and limited intelligence that suggest Minneapolis might be a terror target.'

'Jesus Christ. So why are you here drinking my booze instead of busting your ass tracking down the bad guys?'

Dahl glowered. 'We have twenty-four-hour surveillance on all local suspicious persons known to us. But they're not the source of the chatter. There's a new breed out there, the kind of wolves that run in small packs, often rag-tag and without previous terror affiliation. Major overseas terror organizations are providing these individuals with financial and material support and giving them orders. We've seen this model in attacks in Europe, and it's migrating here because it's effective. And their greatest tool is the level of cyber sophistication.'

'I take it your wolf-hunting in Minneapolis isn't going so well.'

'You know as well as anybody that the terrorists are going dark. Everything is end-to-end encryption now, the dark net, onion routers that bounce our cyber divisions all over the globe before they dead-end in a church computer somewhere in Bulgaria. We need to isolate the players, crack their encryption, and find them.'

Harley scoffed. 'Come on, Dahl, the government has the best cyber surveillance and warfare capability in the world, and you're telling me you can't find some weaknesses to exploit? It's a bitch to get through an onion router like Tor, but it's almost always doable because human error is going to be a factor eventually. And you might not be able to crack encrypted messages mid-stream anymore, but you can hack the software at either end and get into their shit that way.'

'With over a thousand active cases nationwide, how long do you think that will take? We've had to divert existing personnel to new divisions that deal exclusively with this phenomenon. Which illustrates my earlier point – we're drowning.'

'And you think we can help?'

Dahl held his gaze for a moment. 'I know you can. First of all, you might be slightly less encumbered in your methods. And you would have the luxury of focusing solely on Minneapolis. Where is Minneapolis in the national triage right now? I can tell you, it's far down on the list. We can't pursue this further without warrants, and that's not going to happen with what little information we've been able to collect.'

Harley's brows inched up his forehead. 'Oh, I get it. You want us to break federal and international laws because you can't.'

Dahl shook his head. 'I'm only asking that you take a look and see if you can help avert a potential disaster in our city. Preferably without breaking any laws.'

Harley let his eyes drift over the thousands of volumes sitting on his library shelves, all filled with vast amounts of important knowledge, none of which would help him right now. 'I need to talk with Grace, Annie, and Roadrunner about this. And before we can give you an answer, we need whatever information you have to see what we can do.'

'I'll work on that.'

'Work hard, because it sounds like the Doomsday clock is ticking a little faster.'

Five

The sun was low in the sky, sinking fast behind the mountains, and he pushed his aching legs harder, pumping on the bike pedals like his life depended on it. And it did – if he got home after dark, Mom and Dad would be so mad they might even take away his Nintendo for a while, and what kind of a life would he have without it?

He started to panic when the sun slipped behind the peaks of the Maroon Bells. It was still sort of light, so he had time, but not much. At the last minute, he veered off the main road and jumped onto the shortcut path through the woods. He and Clara used to play here when they were little, and now it was where she sometimes came to make all kissy-face with her boyfriend. Yuck. He hoped he wouldn't run into them.

He saw movement up ahead in the shadows between the trees, and as he got closer, he saw something lumpy on the ground and two men kneeling over it. He squeezed the brakes hard and felt his rear tire skid in the gravel, almost dumping him. The men must have heard him, because they looked up, startled. Then one stood and started jogging toward him.

He tried to turn around and pedal away, but his entire body felt frozen, like he was stuck in a big ice cube. He didn't recognize the man, but he looked really mad.

'It's a little late for a young boy to be out, isn't it?' the man said menacingly, like the neighbors' German shepherd that growled at him sometimes.

'I – I'm on my way home.'

'You'd better hurry. But first I want you to listen to me – really listen, very carefully. Can you do that?'

He bobbed his head up and down.

'Good. If you tell anyone – anyone – that you saw me here, something really bad is going to happen to your family. And then something really bad is going to happen to you. I'll make sure of it. Do you understand?'

Tears stung his eyes and started rolling down his cheeks.

'DO. YOU. UNDERSTAND?'

'Y-y-yes,' he stuttered, through chattering teeth.

'Go home. Remember what I said. Don't ever forget.'

Gus Riskin jerked awake in bed, his sheets damp with sweat and tangled around his torso. He took deep breaths until his heart settled into a normal rhythm, then groped on the nightstand for his glass of water and drank what was left. He'd had the dream for most of his life, but it'd been plaguing him almost every night lately. It had to end. And it would, soon.

He got up, turned on the bedside lamp, and cued up his favorite CD. When the ominous first movement of Gustav Holst's *The Planets* began – Mars, the Bringer of War – he dropped to the floor and started doing push-ups. He didn't stop until he hit one hundred and sweat was sluicing off his body.

After he'd showered, he started a pot of coffee, then made himself a breakfast of fried eggs and toast in his tiny apartment kitchen. As he ate, he watched an orange puck of sun rise unromantically over the highway a few hundred yards from the building. He often wondered if the apartment complex had existed before the highway, or if some developer had thought that putting residential housing right next to a busy thoroughfare was a good idea.

The road was clogged with morning commuters on their pilgrimage to the daily grind. There was something comforting about witnessing the sameness of other people's routines: the reliable ebb and flow of morning and evening traffic Monday through Friday, the weekend respite when weary workers stayed at home and off the roads. It was a modern communal ritual where the participants never actually communed with one another, except through the blast of a horn or the raising of an offensive finger.

It was pathetic, really, how isolated people had become even when they were in the midst of many others, and they didn't know it. They were in their cars or in front of their computers or on their phones, and never thought for a minute about engaging the person next to them in face-to-face conversation. Gus never felt more alone and dehumanized than when he was in a city with thousands of people swirling around him, like uncaring extras in a movie scene. But the knowledge that some of those zombies wouldn't survive the day for any number of reasons cheered him.

He used to watch people and imagine what their lives were like, where they were going, what their hopes and fears were. He'd stopped doing that when he'd realized that none of them were wondering about him, and because of that deficit in character and intellectual curiosity, very few would ever make an impact or even a ripple in the world. They would just live their lives, unaffected and unaffecting: some would trudge along and carry out their mortal sentence in a purgatory of anonymity; some would become victims; and a few would victimize. Eventually they would all die and be forgotten. But nobody would forget Gus Riskin, even after he was dead.

He cast off his dark introspection and washed his dishes in the sink, then placed them carefully in the drying rack. He wasn't the best housekeeper, but it was important to keep things tidy – a place for everything, everything in its place, his mother had always told him. When he was satisfied with the kitchen, he gathered what he needed for the day and placed the items by the door, then made his daily visit to the strongbox in the bedroom closet.

Today would be the last time for this private ritual, which was a shame, because it was the part of the day he'd always looked forward to most. But you had to learn to let go of even the most cherished things eventually as they came to their ordained terminus. There was always something better ahead.

He inserted the old key into the lock and turned it slowly, closing his eyes when he heard the soft click as it disengaged. He always felt a surge of panic just before he opened the lid, then rapture when he saw the beautiful green bills packed almost to the top. It was all still there, of course it was. It couldn't walk off on its own, now could it? And the best part was, every single bill represented the suffering of those who deserved it.

For a brief moment, he pondered what his life would be like if he abandoned his work and just disappeared with the money. He could get himself a nice little place in the desert – Arizona or New Mexico – where there were no highways, no self-absorbed people; a place where nobody would bother him. Maybe he'd settle down with a lady, get a dog, maybe even some chickens. He could have a nice, normal life.

He pulled out some of the precious stacks of bills from his private ATM, stuffed them into a duffel bag, then reluctantly closed the lid and relocked the box, pocketing the key. He'd come back later for the rest.

He suddenly felt a sense of lightness, of freedom, as he walked toward the door. A burden had finally been lifted and he understood with perfect clarity that he wasn't meant to have a normal life. It wasn't his destiny to go through his time here without making a ripple. An impact.

He locked up, took the stairs down to Abdi's third-floor apartment and rapped sharply on the door. Footsteps thudded within, and the door cracked open, showing Gus a sliver of the little man's ferret face and suspicious, darting eyes.

'Let me in, man. I've got a busy day.'

Abdi unhooked the security chain and opened the door, releasing an acrid wave of burned onion and bitter coffee. 'Come in, come in, hurry.'

He eyed the duffel bag with the same kind of fierce lust Gus had seen in Lucky's eyes when he'd shown her the packet of heroin, right before he'd killed her with it. Kindly. She'd been headed in that direction anyhow, and Gus felt like he'd done her a favor by saving her from the protracted suffering and indignity of her life. Maybe Lucky hadn't been such an inappropriate moniker for her after all.

Abdi pointed at the duffel urgently. 'What I asked for?'

'As long as you have the rest of what I need, it's all yours.' He partially unzipped the duffel and gave him a glimpse of green.

Abdi hemmed in a smile and shuffled into a bedroom,

while Gus looked around the quiet apartment. It was a dump, like the rest of the units in this building, but he did like the colorful woven rug hanging on the wall. All the geometric shapes in bright primary colors reminded him of a Rubik's Cube.

A few minutes later, Abdi came back with a cardboard shipping box and placed it gently on a folding table. 'This is it, friend. The rest of what you need.' He smiled and showed the shiny gold cap on one of his front teeth. 'Be careful. Otherwise – KABOOM!' He threw up his hands dramatically, then started laughing. 'Just joking.'

'Yeah. Kaboom. You're hilarious.'

'You remember how to do? What I showed you?'

Gus nodded as he sorted through the box bristling with wires and laden with electronic components. All he needed to do was add the juice. 'I remember.'

'Schematics in the bottom, in case you forget. But don't finish your work here. Put them together someplace else.'

'No shit. I'm not a dumbass, I've got a place.' He looked around the apartment. 'Where is everybody this morning?'

'Doing their jobs for today. Every day we work. You, too. We're a good team. Mutually beneficial, yes?'

'Yep, very.' Gus smiled. 'Everybody gets something out of this.'

Abdi suddenly became very serious, which always heralded a tiring, mindless platitude. 'The Almighty Prophet will reward you for your holy work in his service.'

'Seventy-two virgins when I get to Paradise, right?'

'Oh, yes.'

'You know, I never really got that. Shit, I'd rather have seventy-two whores in this life, wouldn't you?'

Abdi's face screwed up in disbelief, then rage. 'How dare you mock –'

'You take yourself way too seriously, Abdi. You've gotta loosen up a little. Don't forget, you need me to make things happen, so I've kind of got you by the balls.' He chuckled and gestured to the bag of money. 'When you think of it, you should be paying me, not the other way around, so I think it's time to negotiate.'

The little fucker was fast and the dagger seemed to appear out of nowhere, but Gus was faster. He heard the satisfying sound of bones snapping as he wrenched it out of Abdi's hand. To his credit, he didn't scream. He didn't make any sound at all, except for a pained grunt. 'I don't think your friends are going to call the cops if you go missing, do you?'

Abdi was skinny, so it wasn't hard to crush his trachea and send him to Paradise to meet his seventy-two virgins, although he did put up a decent fight. Gus thought about taking his gold tooth for a little extra spending money, but ultimately decided the mess it would make wasn't worth it.

The killing had been easy, but stuffing him into a Hefty trash bag and carrying him out to the Dumpster was a bitch. It took all of his strength to make it look like he was casually tossing in an everyday bag of rubbish, just in case anybody was watching. But he didn't think anybody was. This building had two kinds of tenant – the ones who had jobs and were long-gone by now, or the unemployed losers who lived off welfare, drank all night, and slept until noon.

Actually, now that he thought about it, there were three kinds of tenant, the third being a small terrorist cell with great connections overseas and a broad knowledge of important things, like bomb-making and operational cyber security. Too bad they were one man down today.

His timing was perfect, just as he'd planned. As he ambled to his car with his duffel full of money, a Waste Management truck rolled up to take out the trash.

Six

Magozzi had never been able to tear his gaze away from Grace MacBride, or not for long and only when absolutely necessary to preserve the illusion that he was polite company. She had been the recipient of a one-in-a-billion genetic lottery: a brilliant mind housed inside a vessel of epic beauty. Her black hair and porcelain doll's face alone could silence a room, but of all her abundant charms, her eyes were what captivated him most.

Actually, they hypnotized him. They were a piercing, crystalline blue that shot fireworks in his gut in a strange, primeval way, but still dark and stormy enough to hide secrets. And Grace had a lot of them – a scant few he knew about, but there were a lot more he didn't, and maybe never would.

They were sitting side by side in Adirondack chairs by the lake, sipping coffee in loose, easy companionship. She was cradling her very pregnant belly with one hand – a completely unconscious gesture, he'd come to realize – for support, comfort, or both, and her gaze was fixed on the still, flat plate of blue water in front of her. Even from the side, her eyes were compelling.

She wasn't wearing her Sig Sauer this morning, but the 9mm was resting on the arm of her chair, within easy reach, a jolting reminder that her dark past was still very much a part of her present, even in this peaceful bucolic setting. If anything, the pregnancy had heightened her defenses, made her more vigilant, if such a thing was possible.

There was a third chair for Charlie, but it was vacant. On this hot August morning, he had chosen a shady spot by his mistress's feet to snore off his Sisyphean squirrel chase.

'Do you think Charlie is ever going to get in the water?'

Grace reached down and ruffled the dog's wiry hair. The stub of his tail wagged a weak, sleepy acknowledgment, but other than that, he remained motionless. 'He's not a water dog. The vet thinks he's mostly terrier.'

'Ah. Rodent killers. That explains his obsession with squirrels. But his stats suck. In the few months I've had this place, he's zero and a hundred at least.'

'Entirely intentional. He's a pacifist.'

Magozzi smiled and watched a loon float by the dock, then dive for a fish snack. It felt like he had always lived there and nowhere else. He still owned the small house in the middle of the city where he'd spent most of his adult life, but everything about it – mostly bad things, thanks to his ex-wife – had faded from his memory, like a troubling dream. And, hopefully, he wouldn't own it for much longer. 'I think Johnny McLaren's going to put an offer in on the house.'

She turned to look at him, visibly surprised, a rare state for her. 'McLaren?'

'Said he wants to plant some roots, start a family, have some kids.'

'Is he putting the cart before the horse, or does he have a candidate in mind?'

'Gloria. He's been infatuated with her ever since he made detective.'

Grace was no longer visibly surprised, she was downright stupefied. 'Seriously?'

'It might not be such a bad match. He just has to talk her into it.'

'I don't think the Cerberus of Homicide can be talked into anything.'

'I don't know. They've got some kind of weird chemistry going. Every time he passes by her desk, he starts singing "Ebony And Ivory." And the crazy thing? I think she likes it. I *know* she likes it, because she always threatens him with grave bodily harm when he does it.'

'She's a charmer. Good luck to him – he'll need it.'

Magozzi thought about the one time Grace had come into contact with Gloria, two strong personalities butting heads in a big way. Both women were tough and street-smart, and under different circumstances, they would probably have appreciated one another. But at the time, Grace had been a person of interest in a multiple homicide, and Gloria gave no quarter to people like that. 'Guilty until proven innocent' was her personal mantra, and she had no qualms about making her disdain known. And Grace had no qualms about standing up to a challenge.

He reached over and placed his hands over hers, over their baby. He wouldn't have dared such an intrusion on her inviolate personal space eight months ago, but things were different now. He had a real place in her life, an irrevocable connection that hadn't existed before.

He felt a kick that he interpreted as a greeting to Daddy, and smiled. 'I'm making a prediction – two weeks. I'm putting my money on August twenty-fifth.'

She narrowed her spectacular eyes suspiciously. 'Do you and Gino have a running bet?'

'Totally busted.'

'What does he think?'

'He thinks eight days.'

She cocked a brow at him. 'Men never grow up, do they?'

'Never.'

'Well, may the best man-child win.' She patted his hands impatiently. 'Come on. It's time to go to work.'

Magozzi freed her hands, letting her reclaim her space. 'Ride together?'

'Sure. But I might stay in town for a couple days. Harley, Annie, and Roadrunner are almost finished with the database for our new software and they've been at it around the clock. They could use another working partner.'

'Monkeewrench doesn't offer maternity leave to one of its founders?'

'Are you kidding? Harley's been trying to get me on bed rest for the past seven months. I'm incubating precious cargo, you know.'

Magozzi chuckled. 'He actually said that?'

'Almost a direct quote.'

'Vintage Harley. But he has a point. It wouldn't hurt to take it easy until the baby comes.'

She waved a hand dismissively. 'Women used to work in the fields up until the day they gave birth.'

'Does that mean you'll mow the lawn tomorrow?'

'Anytime. Fortunately, you don't have a lawn. You live in the woods now.'

Magozzi settled more deeply into his chair and smiled. 'So what's this new database that everybody's so gung-ho about?'

'It's a freelance project. We've actually been working on it for a long time, but we're closing in on a finish.'

'That's vague. And slightly mysterious.'

Grace lifted a shoulder. 'Not really. Do you want me to bore you with the details?'

'Not the technical stuff I won't understand, but the general concept, yeah.'

'Generally? It's a prototype of an integrated anti-terror database and tracking system for local and state law enforcement, a repository of orphaned terror suspects under federal investigation or surveillance who don't have vigilant eyes on them anymore because of a manpower shortage or budget restrictions. It red-flags ongoing suspicious behavior via the Internet so the locals know whether or not to keep an eye on them when the feds can't.'

Magozzi felt his stomach squeeze, like he'd just eaten something a little off. Monkeewrench navigated the murky water between right and wrong, legal and illegal, all the time in their computer work, and he and Gino had been right beside them on some of those occasions, but he didn't like the sound of this. There was a fine line between privacy and national security – a little something called the Constitution. 'It sounds fantastic in theory, but it also sounds like something that could be wildly abused.'

'Not when it's constrained to the limits of existing law.'

Magozzi grunted cynically. 'And who do you trust to keep it constrained? The NSA?'

She gave him a bemused look, as if the answer was a

low-hanging, perfectly ripe peach he wasn't clever enough to reach up and pick. 'The program, of course.'

'The computer program?'

'Yes. It's very smart. We built in safeguards we can activate so it will only reference the FBI's existing watch list and mine accounts associated with active cases, not the population at large.'

'But it's basically an automated hacking program, right?'

'Federal cyber surveillance *is* legal hacking, Magozzi. The feds do this all the time, but right now, it takes hundreds of eyes-on hours to sort through the metadata their programs generate. Ours does it all by itself. Think of it this way. Right now, the feds are using a magnifying glass. This program is an electron microscope.' She assessed his troubled expression and apparently decided to take pity on him. 'Don't worry, Magozzi. The Fourth Amendment is safer in our hands than anybody else's. It's nothing to be afraid of, just something to hope for.'

Magozzi reached down to give Charlie a pat on the head. He was still unresponsive after his squirrel hunt. 'The feds do have over a thousand open terror investigations in all fifty states, and giving local law enforcement consistent, reliable access to their intelligence would be smart. Especially when you have some idiots on high telling you love, compassion and jobs programs are the only tools you need to combat a murderous global political ideology.'

'Exactly. That kind of attitude didn't work out so well for Neville Chamberlain and the rest of the world, did it?'

'No.'

'It's astounding, the human capacity to fixate on a maudlin concept, even if it's totally delusional and defies logic.'

'Emotion is the antithesis of logic. If somebody gets the promise of an easy happy ending, they'll buy it over reality any day. Snake-oil salesmen have job security forever. Washington D.C. is a perfect example – it grows Sophists faster than a Petri dish grows bacteria.'

Grace turned to look at him, giving him the opportunity to more closely examine her eyes. Yep – still crystalline blue, still hypnotizing, still shooting fireworks in his gut. 'I didn't realize you were a Socrates fan.'

'Yeah, we go way back.'

'Played football together, did you?'

'No, we were on the debate team.'

She granted him a sly smile, then stood up and Charlie sparked to life. Dogs were amazing that way. They could wake up from a stone-cold sleep and take a ten-mile run with you, just like that. 'Let's go. You're going to be late and so am I.'

Magozzi reset his mind to the here and now, to the things that were most important in this moment. 'What do you think?'

'About what?'

'Junior. When is he or she coming? Two weeks or eight days? By the way, you're welcome to throw some money into the pot.'

Grace looked out at the lake one last time before heading up to the house, a Mona Lisa smile playing on her lips. 'You're both wrong.'

Seven

Grace wanted to drive her Range Rover into the city, and Magozzi was fine with being a passenger. He was encumbered by some macho hang-ups, but always being behind the wheel wasn't one of them.

They were just entering the outer-ring suburbs when Gino called. 'Where are you, Leo?'

'About fifteen minutes out.'

'Good. The chief wants us at Gregory Norwood's house pronto. Suspected suicide.'

'Who's the vic?'

'Gregory Norwood.'

'Ouch.'

'Yeah. The chief is pretty ripped up about it. His tie was crooked when he called me into his office, and if that's not a tell, I don't know what is.'

To anybody else, that would have sounded like an inappropriate, smart-ass comment, but for anyone who knew the stoic, hyper-meticulous Chief of Police Malcherson, a hair out of place meant imminent doom, but a crooked tie was the definitive end of the world.

Magozzi rubbed his forehead. And to think the morning had started out so well. 'Of course he's ripped up about it. He was an old friend.'

'Media outlets are already reporting a nine-one-one call

to the address. It's going to be a frigging zoo there in an hour, if it isn't already, so put the pedal to the metal.'

'You got it. See you soon.'

'I'll be parked on Fifth, waiting for you.'

He hung up and looked over at Grace. 'Can you take me straight to City Hall?'

'Of course. What happened?'

'High-profile suicide. Suspected suicide,' he corrected himself. 'Gregory Norwood. He was an old friend of Chief Malcherson's.'

'I'm sorry. Please give him our condolences.' She adjusted her course to take him to downtown Minneapolis.

As promised, Gino was waiting for him in an MPD sedan when they pulled up to City Hall. He stuck his head out of the driver's side window, called a greeting to Grace and Charlie, then quickly shut the window against the escalating August heat and humidity. The one thing Gino hated more than cold and snow was heat and humidity. That left his touchy constitution with one or two comfortable months out of the year when he had to find something else to complain about.

Entering the sedan felt like going from the Amazon rain forest to Antarctica. Magozzi shunted the blasting vents away from his face and settled into the passenger seat. Co-pilot was apparently his role for the day. 'So what do we know?'

'Nine-one-one got a request for a welfare check at Norwood's address around nine this morning. The responding officers found him alone in the house, dead from an apparent self-inflicted gunshot wound to the head. Their words, not mine. Fucking cop-speak drives me nuts sometimes.'

'Who made the nine-one-one call?'

Gino made a sharp right and hit the freeway, maxing out the acceleration on the weak-hearted sedan. 'Robert Zeller.'

'The guy who's probably going to be our next governor?'

'The very same. And maybe the President someday, according to the political wags. They're fondling themselves over him. Anyhow, Zeller spoke to Norwood at around seven thirty this morning, then called nine-one-one an hour later, requesting a welfare check on the address.'

'So he figured something was up.'

'Makes sense. Zeller's firm has been Norwood's legal counsel since the nineties, and they're thick as thieves, always have been. Malcherson might be an old friend of Norwood's, but Zeller is a *consigliere*. Was. And today is the one-year anniversary of Trey Norwood's OD. And what does your best friend do on a tough day? Call to check in, make sure you're handling it. Which he obviously wasn't.'

Very briefly, Magozzi thought of his ex-wife Heather, a former defense attorney, champion of all the scumbags he and Gino risked their lives trying to put away. 'Nobody loves a lawyer until they're yours.'

'You know it better than anybody.'

'What about Norwood's family? Where are they in the mix?'

'His wife and daughter are in Aspen, but they won't be for long.' Gino let out a weighty sigh. 'Suicides are a bitch. Everyone loses.'

'Everyone loses in any unnatural death.'

'Yeah, but with a homicide, there's a chance to bring some kind of justice to the family and to the perp. With suicide, it's just over. We walk in, we make the call, and it's a done deal. We step out of the picture, do the paperwork, and the family limps away, walking wounded. It'll never make sense to them as long as they live.'

There were a lot of branches that the tree of this conversation could grow, but that morning Magozzi wasn't eager to pursue any more dialectics, especially since they hadn't even visited the scene yet. He changed the subject. 'Grace thinks we're both wrong.'

'About what?'

'The bet.'

'You *told* her about it?'

'Of course I did. She's the one who's carrying the baby so I thought I could get some insider info and screw you blind for twenty bucks.'

Gino's mouth broke a smile, all gloomy introspection temporarily suspended. He'd save it for later. 'Did you?'

'Hell, no. All I could get out of her was the general impression that we're both total idiots. In an amusing way.'

'Fair enough.'

Eight

Amanda White pushed her way to the front of the stage as Robert Zeller finished his closing statements, capping off what had been an impressive morning stump speech in front of several hundred supporters. She caught a few grumblings from her more docile colleagues as they parted, like startled sheep. When would they figure out that Minnesota nice didn't get you anywhere in the news business? Maybe never, which was why she didn't belong in this market. Her ambitions were far grander than covering local news, which seemed to breed resentment in her professional circles. Not that she cared.

She homed in on Zeller with shrewd eyes, trying to spot some exploitable fissure in his polished demeanor, but the man seemed like he'd come out of the womb ready for the political arena. He was a unique gubernatorial candidate for Minnesota: he was handsome, he was charismatic, and he actually seemed to have ideas and personal conviction. He didn't regurgitate the stale rhetoric of past politicians, who'd promised anything in exchange for votes, then got amnesia when they'd taken office. She categorized him as a populist in the vein of JFK, a man who told people a rising tide lifted all boats. In fact, that might be exactly how she would begin her piece on him.

But that wouldn't stop her trying to pick him apart while the cameras were on. 'Mr Zeller!'

He gave her a nod. 'Good morning, Ms White.'

'If you're elected, you inherit a weak economy and an immense budget deficit that you've promised to turn into a surplus in your first two years as governor. Can you be more specific about how you would do that without cutting crucial services or forcing a government shut-down?'

'It's actually quite simple, Ms White. Government accountability across the board. A shocking majority of taxpayer dollars goes to running an inefficient system that services only itself and its special interests through profligate, unmonitored spending of public treasury. There is an understandable amount of frustration among our citizens who have had to make difficult decisions and cuts in their personal budgets during these challenging times and so must the state of Minnesota. Prosperity is easily within our reach if we allow common sense to prevail.'

So like a politician to give such a bloated, silky answer that didn't address the question. 'Yes, but what would your targets be? *Specifically?*'

Robert Zeller gave her a fond smile. 'There are no specific targets, Ms White. I propose a five percent budget reduction across the board for all government agencies as a start.'

There were some murmurs from the crowd.

'Sounds shocking, doesn't it? That would be the largest, most comprehensive budget cut in the state's history. But allow me to put it into perspective. How many of you spend a hundred dollars a month at Starbucks?'

There were plenty of guilty chuckles.

'And would you be so horrified to learn that your coffee budget was suddenly decreased by five dollars? Perhaps.

But isn't the simple solution to make a pot of coffee at home once a month to absorb the loss? When people need to tighten their belts, then those who serve them must also. When governments and government employees are doing far better than the constituents who elected them to represent their interests – the very constituents who pay their salaries – then we are on the precipice of tyranny, a tyranny of an elite political ruling class.'

'But you're advocating tax cuts on top of that as well.'

'There is no better place for money than in the hands of hard-working Minnesotans, and tax cuts have never failed to stimulate a languid economy.'

Amanda noted the enthusiastic cheers from the audience. He was in his element, speaking a language people wanted to hear. And she recognized something of herself in him at that moment – ambition. Pure, unalloyed ambition.

The crowd suddenly went silent when Robert Zeller's omnipresent bodyguard – Conrad was his name – walked hurriedly across the stage to the dais and whispered in his ear. Zeller's expression remained impassive, but his voice was diminished greatly as he spoke into the microphone.

'I'm sorry to cut this short, but I must attend to some unexpected personal business. Thank you all for coming.'

Formerly meek reporters dogged his sudden departure with frantic shouted questions about his agenda, suddenly emboldened by the fact that Zeller wouldn't be able to respond, but Amanda slipped away quietly. The story wasn't here anymore. It was somewhere else – and she would find it.

Nine

The Norwood home was impressive, tucked into a large, wooded lot in a pricey, exclusive neighborhood that seemed largely disconnected from the city it was a part of. But it wasn't crazy over-the-top, as one might expect from a man who had built a Fortune 500 juggernaut from a regional, family-owned home-improvement retailer. By those standards, it was downright austere.

It was sheltered from the road and prying eyes by a wooded area; today that protection was vastly enhanced by a battalion of squad cars, emergency vehicles, and police barricades. Traffic had been temporarily redirected to keep out the curious and the media, but they would need more people and a more organized perimeter to keep the area under control as the word spread.

The two first responders were local constables for the wealthy enclave and both looked pale and shell-shocked. Back-up had come in from some of the MPD's comparatively grittier divisions, but they didn't look much better. Head shots were something that haunted you for the rest of your life, no matter what your experience in the field.

Magozzi registered their names when introductions were made, but they drifted out of his mind as he focused on the walk-through and their accompanying narrative.

No sign of B and E at any point of entry, nothing overtly out of place . . . House was empty, no family, staff, or guests present . . . No sign of a struggle ... We found him here ... Looks like his home office ...

Magozzi reentered the present when they arrived at a door being guarded by another patrol, this one a woman. She was young, but wore a seasoned poker face and had a military bearing. She nodded a respectful greeting and stepped aside crisply. Definitely military. And maybe she'd seen a lot worse than what they were about to.

Gregory Norwood's body was crumpled on its side on the floor by a large, wooden desk, a gun near his right hand. Blood and gore were splattered on the rug, on walls painted a soft cream, on the pale blue shades that covered the windows. He was dressed in a suit and tie and his face was largely intact, framed by his famously thick white hair, which had garnered him the sobriquet 'Silver Fox.' The back of his skull wasn't intact, not remotely.

The top of his desk was uncluttered – there was a desktop computer, a cell phone, an empty martini glass, and a nearly empty crystal pitcher of clear liquid sitting in a bucket of half-melted ice. Next to the keyboard was a single sheet of paper and an open collector's-edition box with a velvet insert shaped to snuggle a gun.

Magozzi gave the cops a solemn nod. 'Thank you, Officers.' He still couldn't remember their names, but he would always remember the relief on their faces as they made a hasty retreat from the room.

Gino walked over to the desk to get a closer look at the piece of paper. 'I was thinking maybe this was his note, but it's an itinerary. He was scheduled to fly a private charter to Aspen at four forty-five today.' He stuck his nose into the pitcher. 'This isn't water, that's for damn sure. If this pitcher was even half full when he started, his tox screen is going to be off the charts.'

'A pitcher of martinis at the crack of dawn would help you pull the trigger if you were leaning in that direction.' Magozzi pointed to the gun. 'It's a Colt Peacemaker. Collector's edition. Fits the box.'

Gino skirted the blood spray behind Norwood's head, then started scanning the walls and floor. 'I'm on board with that. I don't see a spent shell casing, which fits with the revolver. Shit, he got lucky, one shot, lights out. As far as suicide goes, that's a home run. A lot of people who try with a handgun make turnips out of themselves instead of taking the eternal plunge they'd been hoping for.'

Magozzi looked around the room, up at the discreet, ceiling-mounted security cameras. They were like the ones in Grace's city house. That would tell them everything they needed to know if there were any questions.

Gino followed his gaze, then walked over to a digital panel on the wall. 'Security is off.'

Or not. 'He didn't want his suicide to be recorded.'

'Damn twisted. Considerate enough to spare the family his own snuff film, but not considerate enough to refrain from blowing his brains out in the first place.'

'The suicidal mind doesn't make sense to anybody except the one who's planning to do it.' Magozzi bumped the computer mouse and woke up Norwood's computer. A password-protected screensaver of an autumn mountainscape appeared. There were most certainly answers lurking inside the circuitry – computers were often people's closest confidants and nobody worried about sharing their darkest feelings with a machine. The MPD's computer guru, Tommy Espinoza, would handle that, and help tie a black bow around a very sad case.

Magozzi knelt, slipped on a pair of gloves, and went over Gregory Norwood's body. The necessity of frisking corpses had always disturbed him, but it was amazing what pocket litter could reveal.

'Anything?'

'Just his wallet. But there's a travel bag in the cubbyhole under the desk.' Magozzi withdrew the leather valise and unzipped it. It was filled with crisp stacks of cash, neatly bound with paper strips that designated the value. Two thousand bucks a bundle. 'Twenty grand total.'

Gino eyeballed the money. 'Jeez, I usually just pack a toothbrush and some underwear when I travel to my second home.'

'Maybe he was planning to restock the family coffers in Aspen.'

'That's probably grocery money for a week. The Norwoods are pretty famous for their luxe dinner parties.' Gino, circling the room, focused on a ceiling-to-floor bookshelf that held a few leather-bound literary volumes but was primarily filled with framed photographs. Most were of family – an elegant wife, a beautiful daughter, with intense brown eyes, a handsome son, with an impish smile – but some were solos of Norwood at significant public appearances: cutting the ribbon in front of one of the buildings he'd restored and renovated during the North Loop renaissance; throwing out the first pitch at a St Paul Saints game in the new stadium he'd ponied up a lot of cash to help build; signing a check that would fund construction of the new wing of a children's hospital.

Magozzi joined him at the bookshelf. 'A vanity wall. Pretty modest for a guy like Norwood.'

'He did a lot of great things for the state. This isn't the half of it.'

Magozzi's eyes kept returning to the photograph of him signing the check for the children's hospital. He looked back at the sorry wreckage of a human being behind him, then again at the photograph.

'What?'

'Gregory Norwood is left-handed when he's signing the check. The gun is by his right hand. Guns don't jump.'

Gino chewed on his lower lip, then walked over to the body. 'No, they don't. But he could have been ambidextrous. I used to play tennis left-handed, but I write with my right hand. He could have been a right-handed shooter.'

'You played tennis?' Magozzi asked, trying to conceal his incredulity.

'It was a fleeting thing, back when I was ten.' He pulled out his notebook and scrawled in it. 'We'll check it out.'

'Yeah. Let's do a walk-through and make some calls while we wait for Crime Scene and the medical examiner to show up.'

Everything seemed to be in place inside the Norwood domicile, just as the first responders had reported. It felt macabre and voyeuristic, touring the magnificent home with its sumptuous furnishings and astounding collection of modern art while the owner lay dead in his office, but it was part of the job, just like frisking corpses, as odious as it all was.

After their morbid tour, they spent fifteen minutes working their phones and learned that the household staff had all been dismissed after his wife had left for Aspen last night; confirmed the Colt Peacemaker was registered in Gregory Norwood's name; and that the entire security system, including all cameras inside and out, had been disabled from the main control panel in his office at 6:05 a.m. From the vast majority of prima facie evidence, Norwood had emptied his house of people last night and gotten drunk this morning in preparation for his suicide on the anniversary of his son's death. But then there was the pesky issue of the gun by a southpaw's right hand.

Outside, they found another pesky issue – blood on the lawn by the pool deck. A lot of it, and it was fairly fresh. Magozzi pulled a pen out of his pocket and pointed to a mat of wavy brown hair, held together by a small piece of flesh. 'Looks like a chunk of somebody's scalp and it definitely doesn't belong to the Silver Fox.'

Gino stooped down for a closer look. 'Somebody either had a bad accident or got clocked big-time out here. And not that long ago. Maybe right around the time Norwood bought it. This could be another dent in the suicide theory.'

'I'll call the property manager again and have him double-check on the staff. Maybe Norwood dismissed the household workers but kept on maintenance.'

'Clumsy gardener dings himself on the head with a pruning saw, nothing to do with Norwood's brains all over his office, and we'll have the crime-scene tape rolled up by sunset. That would be good.'

Magozzi made his call as they walked the lawn slowly and methodically, looking for more blood. A drop here, a drop there, leading past a rose garden to a wooded area that buffered the back yard from the street. He finally reached the property manager, who confirmed that no maintenance personnel had been on site since yesterday.

'So much for the clumsy gardener,' Gino mumbled.

They looked up when a Bureau of Criminal Apprehension crime-scene van cleared the police cordon and drove up to the house. Magozzi was vastly relieved to see the head crime-scene guru, Jimmy Grimm, in that van because this case had just gotten a little more complicated.

While his crew unloaded equipment and got suited up, Jimmy walked over to greet them. 'You know, we ought to get together for beers sometime instead of always meeting over dead bodies.'

'If you're buying, I'm there,' Gino said.

'Likewise. Maybe that's why we never get together for beers.' Jimmy smirked, then looked over his shoulder at the house. 'A Norwood suicide, huh? You guys pulled another whopper. Just can't keep your pretty faces out of the news, can you?'

'We wish. This thing was a nightmare from the get-go, but it might get worse.'

'How so?'

'We can't dismiss homicide.'

'Take me for a walk, then.'

'You got this, Gino?'

'Got it. You go take a hike and make sure nobody's bleeding to death out in the woods.'

Ten

While Gino brought Jimmy and his crew up to speed inside the Norwood house, Magozzi expanded the outdoor search, following intermittent drops of blood into a woodland area that seemed staged. There was no dead wood, no buckthorn, no scrubby, noxious undergrowth: he was in the middle of a meticulously groomed suburban forest. He paused and wiped his forehead with the back of his hand. The gesture was a lost cause – he could already feel sweat collecting around his shirt collar and soaking it. Nothing evaporated in this kind of humidity. His phone rang and he saw Gino's number on the caller ID. 'What's up?'

'What's up out there? Anything?'

'More blood. Tell Jimmy to send some of his people out here to tag and bag when he can spare them. Learn anything inside?'

'Nothing we didn't already figure out, but I just talked to Malcherson. He belonged to the same gun club as Norwood, and they went shooting together every month or so. Norwood was definitely a left-handed shooter.'

'One more click up the homicide dial.'

'Yeah, but Zeller's nine-one-one call still supports suicide. By the way, we have an appointment with him at one.'

'You talked to him?'

'Malcherson did. Chief also did us another solid and

broke the bad news to the Norwood family. He wanted to do it personally. They're flying in from Aspen at two o'clock and they'll be available for us any time after that. Are you having fun in the woods? Because I could use your help.'

'I love it when you're needy.'

'Leo, get your ass in here.'

Magozzi hung up and started retracing his steps, then widened his perimeter. The blood trail had ended, but that didn't mean the trail itself had.

He almost missed the backpack, just a little innocuous thing concealed in the shade of a big oak, but wildly out of place in this pristine forest. In this day and age, it would have been appropriate to consider it a suspicious package if it had been sitting on a street corner or in an airport, but out here, in the groomed woods of Chez Norwood, Magozzi deemed it harmless and called Gino back.

'What – did you get lost?'

'Yeah, the birds ate my breadcrumb trail. Get out here, I might have something.' While Magozzi waited, he gloved up and started going through the contents of the backpack. There were expensive lenses and a camera body, a crumpled-up wrapper from a protein bar, press credentials, and some business cards that read: 'Gerald Stenson, Freelance Photographer and Journalist.' He called the contact number listed on the card, but it went to voicemail.

He kept digging and found a poignant Post-it note that told Magozzi Gerald Stenson was cherished by somebody. 'Love you to the moon and back, Sugar Bear,' it read. At the bottom of the bag, he found a wallet with a Minnesota driver's license that confirmed the owner as

Gerald Stenson. The photo showed a youngish man with curly dark hair – a good match for the piece of scalp he'd found on the lawn. There were three credit cards, some cash, and an in-case-of-emergency card, with the name, phone number, and address of a Kris Stenson. He called and left her a message, too.

Five minutes later, Gino was pacing tight circles around the backpack. 'Photographer sneaks onto the property, gets assaulted. Wouldn't be the first time the paparazzi got an ass-whopping.'

'So where's Stenson?'

'In the hospital getting his head sewn back together. Or maybe he's filing assault charges. Or maybe he's getting booked for trespassing.'

'That's one scenario.'

'The other scenario is Stenson hiding out in the woods, trying to catch a shot of his mark. He hears a gunshot, decides to be a hero and runs to the house, but he surprises the guy who killed Norwood. He gets bludgeoned and dragged off the scene.'

'Who would want Norwood dead? He was practically the patron saint of Minnesota.'

Gino scratched his jaw, finding a patch of whiskers he'd missed during his morning shave. 'Everybody has enemies, even saints. Money makes people crazy. And Norwood wasn't just rich, he was powerful. Influential. There may be a lot of people who wanted him dead.'

Magozzi's phone rang. He lifted a silencing finger and put it on speaker. 'Detective Magozzi.'

'Detective, this is Kris Stenson returning your call.'

'Thank you for calling back, ma'am. I'm looking for Gerald Stenson. Is he available?'

'No, he's on a job. Is something wrong?'

'We're just following up some leads,' Magozzi white-washed. 'We have reason to believe Mr Stenson may have been a witness to a crime we're investigating and we'd like to ask him a few questions. Have you spoken to him recently?'

'Not since he left this morning. My husband is a photographer and sometimes his work keeps him in the field for hours at a time and out of contact.'

'Did he mention what the job was?'

'He was working a freelance gig at Gregory Norwood's house . . . Why are you asking me these questions? You have our names and unlisted home number and you're looking for him . . . Tell me what's going on.'

Magozzi appreciated short and to-the-point. Kris Stenson was no idiot, but he had no choice but to treat her like one. 'Routine follow-up, ma'am. Would you have your husband call us when you speak to him?'

'Of course. I'll try to get in touch with him right away.'

'Thank you, I appreciate it.' Magozzi gave her his cell number and hung up. 'Let's go shake the trees for Stenson. He's the only potential witness we've got right now.'

Eleven

It didn't take long for Gino and Magozzi to find out that Gerald Stenson wasn't in any local emergency room getting his head checked. It took even less time for the cops on the street to respond to the BOLO – the 'be on the lookout' bulletin – and find his ten-year-old Honda CR-V parked a few blocks away.

'Nothing sexy, guys,' Jimmy Grimm announced, crawling out of the back of the Honda with some sealed evidence bags. He wagged them in the air, then plucked at his white protective coveralls, which were probably poaching him alive. 'Fibers for future comparison, if you need them, receipts, some desiccated French fries and loose change from under the driver's seat – the usual junk you'd find in anybody's car. We gave it the full spa treatment front to back, top to bottom. You ask me, this was a regular guy who drove to work this morning and went off to do his thing. He just didn't come back.' He looked around. 'I don't see any security cameras.'

'There aren't many around here,' Gino said.

'Funny. A ritzy neighborhood like this, you'd think it'd be loaded with them.'

'Ritzy neighborhoods like this aren't supposed to need them.'

Magozzi loosened his tie. 'What's your take on Norwood's scene, Jimmy?'

69

He shrugged ambivalently. 'Looks like suicide, but you've got a couple of curveballs with the right-hand-left-hand thing and Stenson. Suspicious, but not evidence of homicide. I'd keep an open mind while things shake out.' He passed his fistful of evidence bags to one of his techs. 'I'll be in touch as soon as I know anything. Good luck, guys. You might need it.'

'He's losing it,' Gino muttered, watching him climb into the BCA van. 'He usually tells us something we don't know.'

Magozzi looked at his watch, which was already closing in on noon. 'Let's check in with the neighborhood canvass, then go talk to Zeller.'

Apparently, the Zeller family didn't have the same hang-ups the Norwood family did about conspicuous consumption. To call their estate on Lake Minnetonka palatial was an understatement of the highest order. They also took their security a lot more seriously than the Norwoods. There was a gate and a gatehouse inhabited by two armed guards who possessed all the charm of North Korean border-control agents. The entire property was fenced, probably electrified, and there were cameras everywhere. And for every camera Magozzi saw, he knew there would be dozens he didn't.

Gino parked the car in a circular courtyard where an ostentatious fountain burbled merrily. 'Jesus, I thought Grace and Harley had tough security, but this is like a prison. I was waiting for those two clowns at the gatehouse to throw hoods over our heads and chuck us into the back of the van.'

'I'll tell you to duck if I see a red dot on your forehead.'

'Hey, joke all you want, but this is a little paranoid, don't you think?'

'Zeller's a very public figure now. Paranoia comes with the territory. Besides, if you own a shack like this, you damn well better have good security.'

Without further intervention from guards, snipers, or packs of frothing, man-eating wolves, Gino and Magozzi made it to the grand front door, which opened before they knocked. They were greeted by a sober older gentleman, with a hard, leathered face that seemed at odds with the nice, crisp suit he was wearing. He gave them a polite, subdued greeting and ushered them into an opulent entry foyer where two enormous muscular black dogs sat perfectly still and at attention.

'What kind of dogs are those?' Gino asked.

'Italian Mastiffs.'

'They're huge.'

'A hundred pounds each.'

'Not exactly family pets, are they?'

'They're quite gentle with the Zellers.' The man gave him a thin smile. 'They're also excellent watchdogs. They have the run of the property at night. Please, follow me.'

He led them down a marble hallway to a pair of ornately carved pocket doors. 'Have a seat, Detectives.' He gestured to a row of fussy, suede-covered side chairs perfectly aligned against the wall. 'Mr Zeller will be with you directly.'

Gino sat down and rolled his eyes. 'You've got to be kidding me. Was that guy supposed to be the butler or the bodyguard?'

'He didn't offer to bring us tea.'

71

'He wasn't packing, either.'

'I think the pair of monsters salivating on the floor in the foyer precludes the need.' Magozzi stuck both his hands in the perfectly equidistant spaces between the chairs on either side of him. 'Maybe he's the guy in charge of arranging the furniture.'

'I'm giving Zeller one minute,' Gino whispered harshly.

'Gino, give him a break. The man is in mourning.'

'Okay, I'll give him two minutes. We're in the middle of an investigation and the clock is ticking.'

As if on cue, the doors slid open to reveal their host. Robert Zeller, legendary lawyer, the probable future governor of the great state of Minnesota, and possibly the future POTUS, looked every bit the part. In fact, he was almost a caricature of the part: salt-and-pepper hair trimmed just-so, a fit build, and patrician features set on a face just tan enough to exude robustness without looking like he'd spent too much time on a yacht somewhere along the Côte d'Azur.

His suit had probably cost a few grand, but it wasn't so conspicuously flashy that it would alienate the hoi-polloi he was courting for votes. Yep, just a regular working stiff in a three-thousand-dollar outfit, looking out for the little guy. Smoke and mirrors. The fine art of politics. The only thing about him that seemed one-hundred-percent authentic was the pervasive sadness evident in his face and posture.

'Please, come into my office, Detectives.' He shook their hands and invited them to sit in two more fussy chairs across from his desk, these covered with hob-nailed leather instead of suede. 'Did Conrad offer you any refreshment?'

Actually, no. But Magozzi didn't feel particularly offended and he didn't see an endgame to pointing out Conrad's lapse in hospitality. 'We're fine, sir. And we're very sorry for your loss. Thank you for seeing us during this difficult time,' he offered respectfully.

Zeller gave a weary, measured nod. 'I appreciate that. This is such a terrible thing. Such a tragedy.'

'We agree. And we don't want to take up too much of your time so, if you don't mind, we'll get straight to the point.'

'Of course.'

'Can you tell us about your last conversation with Mr Norwood?'

His handsome features distorted in pain. 'I called to let him know he and his family were in my thoughts and prayers on the anniversary of his son's death.' He exhaled a shaky sigh. 'Gregory was never able to come to terms with Trey's death and, frankly, I don't know if such a thing is even possible. It plagued him. I think the guilt was eating him alive.' He shook his head remorsefully. 'Obviously it was.'

'He felt responsible for Trey's death.'

'Of course he did. If either of you has children, you understand.'

Magozzi found himself in the unique position of not just understanding but empathizing. 'How did he sound to you when you spoke?'

'He'd been drinking heavily, which wasn't like Gregory at all. And it was so early in the morning. I wondered if he hadn't been up all night drinking, and that alarmed me. I offered to come over, but he dismissed the notion.'

'What eventually made you call nine-one-one instead of going over there yourself?'

'After reflecting on our conversation and his state of inebriation, I decided that a welfare check might be prudent, but by then I was due to leave for a campaign event. I certainly never expected something like . . .' His voice trailed away and he studied his manicured hands.

'That's why you waited before you called nine-one-one?'

He nodded mechanically. He was on auto-pilot. Magozzi had seen it a million times when dealing with the grieving. You couldn't be entirely present when you were rehashing the past hours, days, months, years of your relationship with the deceased.

'It was one of the most difficult decisions I've made in my life. He was my best friend, and a very public figure, who struggled to retain some modicum of privacy. He was mourning the loss of his son on a difficult day. He trusted me. Calling nine-one-one felt like an enormous betrayal. As it turns out, my deliberation over making the call may have turned out to be the ultimate betrayal.'

Magozzi resisted the urge to tell him that when suicides made the final commitment it was almost impossible to stop them. They always found a way. But telling Zeller not to beat himself up seemed condescending and wouldn't do a damn thing to make him feel any better. The man was going to live the rest of his life agonizing over the what-ifs, no matter what Magozzi said to him. Unless their investigation revealed a homicide, in which case his grief would be redirected in another, equally negative, direction.

'So, prior to this morning, you were never concerned about his mental state?' Gino asked.

'He was extremely depressed about Trey, particularly today, but I've always considered him to be the strongest man I knew. However . . .' he looked down and pinched the bridge of his nose '. . . Gregory received some devastating news last week. Pancreatic cancer. He had less than a year to live.' He looked up with an expression of pure misery. 'His family doesn't know yet. He was waiting to tell them after Trey's memorial. I understand this must come up during the course of your investigation, but I would very much like to be the one to break the news.'

'Of course, sir. We'd appreciate it if you could let them know before we meet with them this afternoon.'

He nodded absently, his desolate eyes wandering around his magnificent office. 'I'm picking them up at the airport. I'll speak with them then. My God, I still can't believe this.'

'Do you think anyone else would have wanted to harm him?'

Zeller gave them an incredulous look. 'Are you considering something other than suicide?'

'We just want to be thorough before we close the investigation.'

'I can't imagine another living soul who would want to bring harm to Gregory. Of course, up until now, I couldn't imagine him killing himself, either. But what can a man truly know about another's demons?'

Magozzi stood. 'We won't take any more of your time. Thank you for speaking with us.'

He rose and shook their hands. 'I appreciate your compassion and attention to detail. Chief Malcherson holds you both in the highest esteem, and I understand why.' He stood, opened an engraved wooden box Magozzi had assumed held cigars, then handed them both cards. They were heavy stock and embossed with gold lettering, about as pretentious as you could get where business cards were concerned. His name was in a substantially larger font than the contact details below, as if it alone was enough to summon him. 'That's my private line, Detectives. Please don't hesitate to call if you need anything further.'

'What do you think?' Gino asked, as he pulled out of the driveway.

Magozzi rested his eyes on the lush canopy of old trees that stood like sentinels along the street. The foliage allowed intermittent spots of sunlight to splash onto the windshield as they passed through, creating a strobe effect. 'He made a pretty compelling case for suicide. Depression over his son, then a terminal cancer diagnosis? That double hit could send anybody over the edge.'

'Occam's Razor – the simplest explanation is usually the right one. Not that we ever get that lucky, but there's always a first time.'

'Any other insights?'

'Yeah. That Conrad guy is an asshole. He didn't offer us any refreshments.' Gino stepped hard on the brakes and Magozzi felt his seatbelt snap into strait-jacket mode, crushing his chest as momentum threw him forward.

'What the hell, Gino?'

He pointed at the skinny blond woman standing in the middle of the road, blocking their path. 'Fucking Amanda White. The woman's got a death wish. Let's put her in cuffs and request a psych hold.'

Magozzi staunched a smile. A few months ago, he and Gino had loathed Amanda White on the deepest level because she'd been making their work on a serial-killer case an absolute nightmare by threatening to obstruct the course of the investigation in any way humanly possible. But, at the end, she'd surprised them with a deep streak of humanity, and principles that seemed alien to any journalist in the modern era. They weren't exactly buddies with her and she was still as annoying as hell, but there was now a grudging respect between them and maybe even a little friendly competition.

She waved and smiled, then minced up to the car on needle-heeled shoes. 'Good morning, Detectives.'

'Jesus, what the hell do you think you're doing?' Gino shouted, out of his open window, more out of panic from near vehicular manslaughter than belligerence.

'It's hard to get your attention when you're working a case. Throwing myself in front of your car seemed like the only recourse. I was betting you wouldn't kill me.'

Gino grunted. 'That was a courageous gamble.'

'I was at Robert Zeller's presser when he got the news about his friend. I tried to catch up with you at the Norwood house, but I couldn't talk my way past the barricades.'

'Which is why we put them there. Have a great day.' Gino gunned the engine, which didn't sound nearly as threatening as he would have liked.

'Care to comment on cause of death?'

'Nope.'

'Or why you took such an interest in a photo-journalist's car?'

'It's for sale. I'm car shopping.' Gino swerved around

77

her and floored it until the next stop sign, which he largely ignored before picking his way out of the charming streets of suburbia and onto the freeway.

'That was kind of rude,' Magozzi observed mildly.

'I didn't run her over. That would have been rude.'

Twelve

Grace had always considered herself a person who wasn't particularly troubled by anything specific because she was troubled by everything. The reality was, the world was a dangerous place where bad things happened all the time, every second of every day. It was non-stop, and if you let yourself attempt to calculate the loss and tragedy that occurred in even a single hour, you'd be paralyzed. And insane. You just had to be prepared. And at this moment in her life, when she was about to become a mother, she felt more prepared than she ever had.

Some people described that world view as negative and anti-social; she called it realism. It was pointless and destructive to arbitrarily assign a glossy false reality to existing conditions. Nothing got done that way, with everybody living in their own fabricated fantasy land of false rhetoric. She'd learned that very young, which was why she'd run away from every foster home after the age of seven.

Still, she hadn't given up on the human race. Annie, Harley, and Roadrunner were partially responsible and, more recently, Magozzi. The man had infinite patience and fathomless love, and now he was the father of her baby. But he was more than that: she just didn't know what.

When Grace pulled into the drive of Harley Davidson's Saint Paul mansion, she saw the lord of the house himself holding a hose over the rose hedge he'd planted last year.

If there was ever a study in incongruity, she was looking at it – a physically imposing man in biker's leathers and jackboots, tenderly doting on his cherished pink blooms.

When he heard her pull in, he turned and gave her a wave and a big smile, a slash of white cutting through his coal-black beard. He put down the hose to let it continue irrigating his roses and walked over to greet her, but Charlie was first out of the car – always. His claws dislodged small divots of grass as he tore over to Harley, dropped and rolled, inviting a belly rub.

'Such a good boy, aren't you, Charlie? Good boy! What do you think about chicken tenders? I've got some waiting for you.' Charlie barked happily while Harley scrubbed his wiry fur, blabbering more smitten baby talk to him, then finally looked up to greet her. Humans were always second on the list when it came to Charlie.

'Hey, Gracie! You are looking ravishingly shiny and glowy and very pregnant. But I keep telling you, you shouldn't be working in your delicate condition.'

'I'll be sitting in front of a computer, not digging ditches, Harley,' she said, with fond exasperation.

Just then, Annie Belinsky stepped out onto the front walk, the very picture of a Southern belle, in an ornately embroidered linen dress with a matching sun bonnet. Grace had long ago determined that Annie was genetically programmed to be a Southern belle, even though she'd grown up in the squalor of a rural Mississippi slum.

'How are you, sugar? Lord, I've been missing you. You can't even imagine what it's like working alone with two barbarians and not a single speck of female common sense in the room aside from my own.'

Grace allowed herself a delicate chuckle, stifling the strange compulsion to laugh out loud. This was happening with alarming frequency lately, but she still found the alien involuntary reflex disturbing. 'I missed you, too, Annie. Is Roadrunner in the office?'

Annie nodded. 'I don't think he's left it in a week. Harley and I have been force-feeding him bananas and vegan cookies to keep him alive. Those are the only things he'll eat, poor soul.'

Harley shook his head sadly. 'We should have had an intervention a long time ago. I keep telling him his brain is going to disintegrate if he doesn't eat some real food, but it might be too late.'

'What's the progress report on the program?'

'The skinny guy is running a beta test right now and it's going pretty well. Listen, I need to fill you two in on a new development before we go upstairs. I talked to Roadrunner about it already, but this is something we all need to discuss. It's kind of urgent.'

Annie narrowed her eyes suspiciously. 'I do *not* like the sound of that. Every time you come to us with something urgent we need to talk about, we almost end up dead.'

Grace didn't like the sound of it either. 'Tell us.'

'Dahl paid me a visit this morning . . .'

'An official visit?'

'No. Not remotely.'

Annie sighed impatiently. 'Cough it up, Harley.'

'He thinks Minneapolis might be in the cross-hairs of a terror attack, but they're having trouble isolating the threat. You know how it is, it gets harder every day. Privacy and encryption software are open source, so anybody who knows what they're doing can use the architecture and go dark. Terrorists included. It's a problem.'

Grace felt something sinister and unwelcome unfurl inside her. The truth was, she never felt safe anywhere at any time, but a terror attack was usually far down on her list of potential personal threats. It was also the one thing that her Sig couldn't avert. Only knowledge could do that. 'Is this *imminent*?'

'He's pretty worried, and I wouldn't bet against it. Minneapolis does boast the dubious distinction of having the most ISIS recruits of any state in the nation. But whatever information he's getting, the feds can't trace it.'

'Can the program help?' Grace asked.

'Roadrunner can probably answer that by now, so let's go see what he has to say.'

Thirteen

Grace loved the Monkeewrench office on Harley's third floor, with its vast expanse of polished maple flooring and elegant, arching mullioned windows that let the morning sun flood in. In the Gilded Age glory days, this office space had served as a ballroom. It still hosted dances, but now all of them took place in front of a large bank of computers arranged against the back wall.

Roadrunner was at his station, folded awkwardly into his chair, long limbs jutting out, like the wings of a gangly butterfly. Harley had customized his desk to accommodate his six-foot-eight frame, but even with the adjustment, their skinny giant still didn't quite fit into his space. Not that he noticed any discomfort, big or small, as long as he was in front of his computers.

He spun around in his chair when he heard Charlie's claws clattering on the floor as the dog ran to greet him. A boy and his dog, Grace thought. Just like Harley. Both would probably get their own dogs when the horrible reality of Charlie's biologically limited lifespan finally came to pass, but Grace didn't want to think about that.

Roadrunner gave her a sheepish smile while Charlie swiped his hands with his long pink tongue. 'I think he missed me.'

'Of course he missed you. Tell us about the beta test.'

He nodded, his head bobbing on his neck, like a ripe

sunflower in a breeze. His Lycra bike suit showed off a ladder of ribs that made Grace want to feed him. Bananas and vegan cookies were no way to live. 'It's pretty amazing so far. There are kinks to work out, but we're on to something. Did Harley tell you about Dahl?'

'He did. Give us an update on the program and then we can talk about that.'

'I inputted some data we had on local persons of interest who aren't on the FBI's watch list anymore, then merged that into the search engine of the program. It takes all inputted information, collates it with archival information available anywhere on the Internet, and compares it with real-time activity from the Web. Our algorithm isolates keywords, names, addresses, whatever – anything that keeps popping up in unsavory data streams – finds links between them all, and analyzes them.'

Harley was beaming like a proud papa. 'It's like a stealth cyber GPS tracker. We can follow the bad guys wherever they go on the Web, no eyes-on, no manpower required. What used to take anti-terror cyber divisions months to sort through will take the program an hour. And the best part is, it automatically attacks encryption and hangs around until it finds a weakness to exploit. There's nothing like this out there. Nothing that can come close.'

'Just what we designed it for.'

'Damn right, Gracie.'

Roadrunner extricated himself from his elaborate origami pose and scooted his chair away from his flashing computer screen so everyone could gather around. 'Right now, it's scouring the Internet for potentially nefarious activity associated with the email accounts and phone numbers I fed it, like suspicious purchases, contact with known terror organizations and operatives, and just about everything else. Hell, it will even tell us if they bought underwear on Amazon and if they were boxers or briefs. Some of the accounts aren't active anymore, but some still are, and on those we're getting some hits already.'

Annie tapped a cherry-pink nail on her matching lips. 'What kind of hits?'

'The program is accessing something on the Web that's linked to the data I inputted this morning. It sent out its tendrils and cross-referenced.'

They all watched the monitor as it started scrolling through what looked like lists of addresses. Some turned red and began blinking.

'What's it doing now?'

'Remember when I said the program looked for repetitions in the data streams it accesses?'

Harley was squinting hard at the screen. 'Yeah. So it found something?'

Roadrunner hunched down, toggled through a few screens, typed in some commands. Eventually, he leaned back in his chair and let out a shaky breath. 'Oh, man.'

'What is it, Roadrunner?' Grace asked quietly.

'Well, it might be a glitch . . .'

'Spill it.' Harley's voice was sharp and impatient, but there was an undercurrent of panic in his tone.

'It's telling us that Minneapolis City Hall is a hot topic with terrorists.'

'Oh, good Lord,' Annie breathed. 'Like a target?'

He shrugged. 'I can't think of another reason why City Hall would turn up repeatedly in terror data streams.'

'But you know where it's coming from, right?'

Roadrunner toggled through a few more screens. 'Not exactly. This information isn't directly associated with my initial data input. It's extrapolated intelligence from somewhere in the ether.'

'Well, trace this and find the root source, for Christ's sake, so we can get it to Dahl,' Harley blustered.

Roadrunner shook his head uneasily as he scanned his monitor. 'It's not going to be that easy, Harley. They're using BGP hijacking to corrupt the Internet routing tables and spoof a gazillion IP addresses. The packet origin is shifting too fast to lock on and trace. We're dealing with pros who know how to hack and know how to hide.'

Harley straightened and rocked back on the heels of his boots. 'Son of a bitch.'

Fourteen

Gino was driving up the spiral chute of a downtown parking ramp that connected to the Chatham Hotel where Betty Norwood was staying. He wondered if she would continue to live in the family home once the crime scene was released. Biological remnants of a murder or suicide could be cleaned from rugs, curtains and furniture, but the event that had occurred there could never be erased from the minds of loved ones who had once shared that space with the departed.

On the fourth level, he found a sweet spot next to a glass-enclosed elevator vestibule. He parked and draped his arms over the steering wheel. 'You ready to walk into somebody else's nightmare?'

'Never.' Magozzi got out and looked around. Silent cars with unseeing headlight eyes sat under tons of concrete held up by pylons that seemed like toothpicks in comparison to the load they bore. It was one of the many reasons parking ramps took his thoughts down dark avenues.

'What?'

'Nothing. Just thinking.'

'About Genevieve Alcott.'

'Among other things, yeah.'

'That was one of our finer moments, Leo.'

Magozzi was suddenly back in the airport parking lot,

prying open the trunk of a black Chrysler with a crowbar. Genevieve Alcott wouldn't have survived another fifteen minutes – she was lucky to have survived her psychopathic husband's wrath at all. It *had* been one of their finer moments – homicide cops didn't usually get an opportunity to save a life: it was right there in the finality of the job description. But that eleventh-hour rescue still haunted him, because it drove home the reality that his job was to sort through the aftermath of a murder when it was already too late for the victims and their families. 'Let's do this.'

They walked in silence to the vestibule and Gino punched the button to call the elevator. 'Word is, they've got a great restaurant in this hotel, except they put the calorie count and nutritional information below every entrée on the menu. How stupid is that? Isn't the point of going out to dinner to indulge yourself without a guilt trip? I mean, if I'm ordering osso buco, I don't want to know how much fat or how many calories are in it. Are they trying not to make money?'

Magozzi appreciated Gino's attempt to lighten the mood before they walked into a vale of tears. 'They're catering to a narrow demographic, I'll give you that.'

'Yeah, supermodels and fitness freaks.'

The elevator pinged and the doors slid open just as Magozzi's phone rang. When he saw Grace's name on the caller ID, his hands turned clammy and he fumbled to answer. 'Grace. Where are you?'

He thought he heard a smile in her voice. 'Not on the way to the hospital, if that's what you're thinking.'

Magozzi let out a shaky sigh and shook his head at Gino,

who was looking on expectantly. 'That's exactly what I was thinking.'

'Listen, I know you're busy with a case, but I need a few minutes.'

'Of course, go ahead.'

While Magozzi took his call, Gino set free the waiting elevator car and occupied himself by examining a Plexiglas-encased map of the hotel and the connecting skyways. He'd never quite gotten the hang of the skyway system, which was a genius human Habitrail that allowed you to navigate above ground from building to building in down-town Minneapolis without ever setting foot on the street during winter. If they ever hooked one up to City Hall, his life would be complete.

Gino finally tired of the map and started wandering around the small vestibule. The tile floor was spotless and there were no cobwebs, no dirt gathered in corners. The elevator doors were polished, not so much as a smudge or fingerprint visible. It was a prime example of good house-keeping, which made sense in the holding area that would ultimately shepherd you to the priciest hotel in the city. He would never spend a night there unless he won the lottery, but he had to admit there was allure in imagining himself as a guest ready to check in instead of a homicide cop pass-ing through on a job.

Magozzi wasn't saying much, just listening, which meant Grace had something important and pertinent to say, or she would never have bothered him while they were working a case. It was intriguing, but it was also scary, because with Monkeewrench, you never knew what might be coming your way. But scarier was the look on Magozzi's face when he hung up.

'What? What's wrong? Is it the baby?'

'No. Monkeewrench thinks that City Hall might be a target of a terror attack.'

'*What?* Are they sure? How do they know?' Gino squeezed his temples. 'Oh, God, did I just ask that stupid question?'

'Grace just told me this morning that they've been developing a new program to isolate terror threats the feds might miss. I had no idea they were already running a beta test, and that's what the test came up with.'

'Is this imminent? I mean, do I need to call Angela and tell her and the kids to stay out of downtown?'

'The program is in its infancy so they don't know about the accuracy, but the feds and our Joint Terrorism Task Force are on it. But, yeah, I'd call Angela and tell her they don't need to be downtown.'

'And we're just supposed to mosey on along, business as usual, and City Hall might be a pile of cinders by the time we get back there? Are you kidding me?'

'We do our job, the dedicated task forces do theirs. We don't have anything to bring to that party, Gino. There are great people working this right now.'

Gino stabbed the elevator call button again. 'Christ. I thought we already got our bad news for the day.'

'There's a lot to go around. Come on, the Norwoods are expecting us.'

Fifteen

Betty Norwood answered the door. She was an elegant older woman, deeply tanned, perfectly coiffed, and dressed in a dark linen suit appropriate for mourning, but her skeletal frame was startling. In the modern era, you could never be too rich or too thin and they often went hand in hand, at least if you were a woman. Historically, it was just the opposite: being plump and pale indicated your status as a member of the landed gentry. It was weird how things reversed course.

The daughter, Rosalie, hovered behind her, equally well-dressed and coiffed, with brown curls arranged carefully to cascade over her shoulders. She was a more mature version of the beautiful young girl they'd seen in the family photos in Gregory Norwood's office, but the striking brown eyes that had stared at them from the framed prints hadn't changed. If anything, they had gathered intensity over the years.

In stark contrast to her mother, she was fit, well-built and still blessed with the ephemeral beauty of youth, but despair and disbelief weighed down her pretty features. Both women's eyes were red and swollen and their expressions utterly vacant, as if shock had leached away all capacity for emotion.

'Please come in, Detectives,' Betty said, as perfunctorily as an automaton, stepping aside.

'We are so sorry for your loss, Mrs Norwood, Ms . . .'

'Norwood, but please call me Rosalie.'

'Thank you for seeing us during this terrible time.' Magozzi repeated almost verbatim what he'd said to Robert Zeller, but the level of devastation here was a thousand times greater and the words fell flat.

'Thank you for coming.' Betty gestured to a pair of wing chairs by a large window, a stoic hostess in spite of the circumstances. She was renowned for her elegant dinner parties – gracious hospitality probably came as naturally to her as breathing. 'Please, sit.'

'Thank you.'

'Father didn't kill himself,' Rosalie blurted out, then started crying softly, defusing the room's air of formality in an instant. 'He would never do such a terrible thing. He would never leave his family, especially today of all days. We were going to spread Trey's ashes in the river . . .' Her voice faded away as tears dripped steadily down her face.

There was poignant honesty in her raw emotion, and Magozzi was reminded that grief was the cost of love and it pillaged everybody in exactly the same way, regardless of socio-economic status. It was the great equalizer.

Betty placed a tender hand on her daughter's shoulder and discreetly passed her a tissue. 'I have to agree with Rosalie, Detectives. Gregory would never have killed himself. Not because of Trey and not because of cancer. He was murdered. It's the only explanation.'

She'd spoken with effortless authority, and Magozzi had to concentrate to keep his expression neutral. This was a very different narrative than Robert Zeller's, who seemed resigned to the possibility of suicide. The challenge was figuring out which party really knew Gregory Norwood best.

Gino leaned forward and folded his hands in his lap. 'Mrs Norwood, it's understandable that your husband would be depressed on this day and his cancer diagnosis would have compounded that greatly . . .'

'No, Detective. I understand what you're asking and the answer is no. Gregory did not kill himself. We were married for over forty years and I would have known if he'd been having suicidal thoughts.'

Magozzi disagreed with her on that point, but he remained silent.

'Rosalie would have known, too,' she continued. 'She's been working very closely with her father in the family business for several years. She might even know his moods better than I do. Isn't that right, dear?'

Magozzi noticed a sudden shift in Rosalie's demeanor and expression. It wouldn't be remotely obvious to anybody who wasn't watching closely, but it was definitely there. 'Maybe from a business perspective, but you knew him best, Mom.' She sighed anxiously, mangling the tissue her mother had given her. 'You were there, Detectives. Can you tell me unequivocally that my father committed suicide?'

Gino gave her an apologetic look. 'I'm sorry, ma'am, but it's still too early in the investigation to make any unequivocal statements.'

Magozzi decided to alter the course of the ship. 'You both seem certain that Mr Norwood wasn't capable of taking his own life. Can either of you point us in a different direction?'

Betty shook her head. 'Who would want to kill him,

you mean? I can't imagine. He had no enemies. He's never had any enemies.'

'That we knew of,' Rosalie interjected, blotting her eyes. 'But there are less dramatic possibilities, Mom, like robbery or home invasion. Isn't that right, Detectives?'

'It's a possibility, but we don't think so. We found a large sum of cash in his office, which would have been the most obvious mark for a robber. Do you know anything about that, Mrs Norwood?'

She hesitated. 'Gregory always brought cash to Aspen to replenish the safe there.'

'Did he usually engage the home alarm when he was home?'

'Most definitely. He was very security-minded.'

'The alarm system wasn't armed this morning.'

Betty Norwood looked confused. 'It wasn't?'

'No, ma'am.'

'That's not like Gregory. Not like Gregory at all.'

'Could he have been expecting a visitor?'

Rosalie looked at her mother. 'Minerva? She might have been dropping something off for him from the office.'

The elder Norwood's face soured dramatically. 'Certainly not. Not this morning.'

'Who's Minerva?' Magozzi ventured cautiously.

'Father's personal assistant.'

'You might want to speak with her, Detectives,' Betty said, in a voice that chilled the room.

'We can promise you both we will, and we'll look at all possible angles.'

She seemed temporarily appeased. 'Chief Malcherson said you wouldn't leave a single stone unturned.'

'We're giving this our full attention,' Gino reassured her. 'Are there any other family members we might speak with?'

'Gregory and I were both only children,' Betty explained. 'It's just Rosalie and me now.' She lifted her eyes and gave them both measured looks. 'I suppose it's only natural to consider financial motivation when investigating the death of a man of Gregory's means, but nobody had anything to gain from it: Rosalie and I will inherit in equal measure. There's nobody else.'

'That was sad. And weird,' Gino commented, as they waited for the elevator to take them down to the parking garage. 'Betty Norwood got pretty frosty when Minerva's name came up. Maybe he was having an affair.'

'It's a place to look.'

Gino clucked his tongue. 'We've got Zeller crowing suicide, the Norwoods crying bloody murder, and we could go either way with what we've got so far. I don't like it. Something's off.'

'The daughter has something on her mind.'

'Yeah, I caught that.'

Magozzi turned his head when he heard a room door close down the hall. He put a finger to his lips and listened to the muted fall of footsteps approaching, the sound almost entirely absorbed by the plush carpet. Just as the elevator pinged to a stop at their floor, Rosalie Norwood came around the corner. She was carrying an enormous snakeskin handbag. If you were killing off a destructive, invasive species, why not capitalize on the effort and make handbags out of them? It was probably a lucrative cottage industry down in Florida.

'Do you mind if I take a ride with you, Detectives?'

'Please.' Gino held the doors open.

She stepped in and punched the lobby button. 'I'm glad I didn't miss you. I could have called but . . .' She fidgeted with the strap of her handbag and brushed imaginary lint from the front of her dress. 'Do you have a few minutes for a drink downstairs? There's a café, but I think I could use something stronger.'

Sixteen

Rosalie Norwood was nervous. She twirled her curls around her finger while her eyes swept the hotel bar in random patterns. In Magozzi's opinion, she wasn't looking for anything more sinister than a distraction from her anxiety. The room was mostly empty, so their drinks arrived roughly thirty seconds after they'd ordered – Scotch, neat, for Rosalie; two Cokes for Magozzi and Gino.

She took a deep drink and leaned back against the banquette. 'Thank you for speaking with me in private, Detectives. I didn't want to upset Mom any more than she already is.'

Gino and Magozzi nodded sympathetically and waited for her to start talking, which didn't take long.

'As she mentioned, I've been working side by side with my father for several years. He's been grooming me to take over the family business ever since Trey's troubles started.' She scoffed; bitterly, Magozzi thought. 'That's what we called them – his *troubles*. It was the only acceptable way to discuss the fact that he was a drug addict. As if words could alter reality.'

'Addiction is a difficult thing to deal with,' Magozzi offered. 'It's complicated.'

'It's not that complicated. The family suffers, their hearts break every day, and they wonder what they did wrong and what they can do to fix it. And always they fear the obituary that might be coming. Ours finally did.'

Magozzi thought she could just as well have been talking about suicide: the two were on the same continuum of misery where the toll it extracted from surviving family members was concerned.

She looked down into her drink for a moment while she regained her composure. 'But I'm going off-point. I want to tell you about my father . . . No, that's not exactly right. I want to tell you about Gregory Norwood the businessman and let you draw your own conclusions.'

Gino flicked a quick look Magozzi's way, then focused on Rosalie Norwood. 'Please. Go ahead.'

'We called my father the Savant at the office. Not in front of him, but that's what he was – a numbers savant. You could ask him about any transaction that had occurred in the business over the course of forty years and he could recite every single detail down to the last cent. He had this uncanny memory and a laser-sharp focus on everything he did, which was part of the reason he was so successful. None of us could hope to keep up with him, not even his most senior people. But something changed a few months ago.'

'How so?'

'He seemed wildly distracted. Totally unfocused, like I've never seen him before in my life. It was almost like he'd lost interest in his work. It was a complete departure from his personality. When things didn't improve in the short-term, I pressed him about it.'

'What did he say?'

'He finally admitted he was taking another look into

Trey's death. Well, actually, he'd hired a private detective to look into it. Father had gotten it into his head that Trey's death wasn't an accident. And, like everything else, he put all his energy into it.'

'But your brother did die of an overdose, right?'

'Yes. I know it doesn't make any kind of sense, but Father was adamant about it. He wouldn't tell me why. I know it's probably nothing more than a desperate father wanting to exonerate his son of causing his own death, but I wanted to mention it to you, for what it's worth. I imagine in your line of work, every piece of information can be crucial, no matter how insignificant it may seem.'

Gino nodded. 'We appreciate it. Did your father happen to mention the name of the detective he'd hired?'

She let out a frustrated sigh. 'I didn't think to ask. I wish I had.'

'That's all right, Ms Norwood,' Magozzi reentered the conversation. 'No reason you would have. Earlier, your mother said she didn't notice any mood changes in your father.'

'He wouldn't bring this sort of thing home, especially anything that was to do with Trey. His death destroyed her, but she'd finally come to some sort of peace with it. Father would never have done anything to cause her pain by reopening that wound.'

'But people in the office noticed his change in personality?'

'Yes, but not in the way I did as his daughter. Except Minerva. She's been his assistant for almost twenty years.'

'Your mother doesn't seem to have warm feelings for her.'

'That's a delicate way of putting it. No, she doesn't, although I have no idea why. Minerva is an angel, and

Father and I have always considered her family.' She looked at her watch, then drained the rest of her Scotch, wincing a little. 'I'm sorry, Detectives, I have to go. I promised Mom I'd pick up a few things for her and I don't want to leave her alone for too long.' She fished in her snakeskin bag and withdrew a slender business-card case, also made out of some kind of reptile. 'Call me anytime if you have more questions.'

Magozzi responded in kind, giving her his own card. 'And the same goes for you, Ms Norwood.'

Her brows dipped in consternation, maybe even in mild irritation. 'I can't convince you to call me by my first name?'

'It wouldn't be appropriate, ma'am.'

Gino nodded. 'It's out of respect to you. We're only on a first-name basis with criminals and hostile witnesses.'

She seemed intrigued by the answer, possibly relieved for a distraction from her immediate reality. 'So criminals and hostile witnesses don't deserve your respect?'

Magozzi was thrown off-guard a little. He'd never bothered to analyze the intricacies of proper salutation in law enforcement. 'Our personal opinions are irrelevant. Using first names is a way of encouraging cooperation and trust.'

'Does it work?'

'Sometimes. It depends on the circumstances and the personality you're dealing with. There are no hard-and-fast rules.'

She absorbed that with a mild look of satisfaction. 'Things aren't any different in the business world. Call it whatever you want – conversational prowess, interlocution, charm, the gift of the gab – whoever does it best wins. It's all just psychological exploitation in the end.'

'You're a born pragmatist.'

'Pragmatists are created, not born. Thank you for your time, Detectives.' She gave them a gracious nod and retreated into the lobby.

Seventeen

After Rosalie Norwood had left, Gino put his chin into his hands, pushing the flesh of his jowls up to his cheeks. 'That was an interesting coda to an interesting conversation. She's got an edge to her. I didn't see that coming.'

'Never underestimate the power of a glass of Scotch in the afternoon.'

'Or taking Betty out of the equation. So, Norwood thought his son was murdered and his wife and daughter think *he* was murdered. What are we looking at?'

'Rosalie Norwood is young and distraught, looking for answers that don't involve her father blowing his brains out. Just like Norwood was probably looking for another explanation for his son's overdose. Denial all around.'

Gino swirled the ice cubes in his nearly empty glass and downed the dregs of his Coke. 'Say somebody did kill Trey Norwood and the old man was getting close. That would be a great reason to kill him.'

'The kid was a known heroin addict who died from an overdose. Tough to prove murder in that case.'

Gino snuffled. 'Yeah. It's about as close to perfect as a crime could get. Except maybe for shooting a potential suicide in the head with his own gun. Tough to prove murder in that case, too.'

'All right. We've got two motives for suicide. Let's start looking for a motive for murder. Call Zeller and ask about

Norwood's will. Maybe there are other beneficiaries Betty and Rosalie didn't know about who wanted to speed up their payday. I'll get a hold of this Minerva. A personal assistant of twenty years might know him better than anybody.'

Magozzi had a hard time understanding anything Minerva Jones said because she was sobbing so hard when she finally answered her phone. He made arrangements to meet her at the Norwood office complex, a seven-story affair in Golden Valley that housed an empire now without its emperor.

'What did you get?' Gino asked, when he hung up.

'An appointment with an inconsolable woman.'

'Huh. Inconsolable like a mistress capable of a crime of passion, or inconsolable like a loyal employee of twenty years-cum-family member?'

'We won't know until we meet her. What did Zeller have to say?'

'Betty Norwood had it right – the entire residue of his estate after it gets gutted by the government is equal shares to her and Rosalie. That's a hell of an inheritance.'

'Don't even go there, Gino.'

'Hey, I'm just thinking out loud. It's part of the process.'

'Let's go talk to Minerva and pull together what we've got before we start jumping off ledges.'

Gino threw a twenty onto the table and stood up. 'Looking at the possible career ramifications of this case, I think I'd rather go straight for the ledge.'

*

One thing became starkly evident once Gino and Magozzi were inside the Norwood office complex: his employees from bottom to top were all in a state of shock and despair, and if there wasn't a warehouse of tissue boxes somewhere on the premises, all seven stories of the building would soon wash away in tears. Gregory Norwood had a lot of fans.

They found Minerva Jones in her office, crying quietly. Gino's suspicious mind and Betty Norwood's obvious dislike for the woman had seeded an image with Magozzi of a lean, leggy, ruthless *femme fatale*. But in reality she was a plump, matronly woman pushing sixty, by his estimation, and judging by the dozens of family photos in her office – most of them featuring young children – she was a proud grandmother of many.

She reiterated a common motif through her tears: Gregory Norwood was beloved by everyone, he would never have killed himself, neither would anybody have wanted to kill him, and he was the most compassionate, generous man who'd ever lived. Yes, she'd noticed his odd behavior over the past few months, but attributed that to stress over Trey's death and the upcoming memorial.

It was a difficult interview because she never stopped crying, not for a single minute. She obviously harbored love for and unquestioned devotion to Gregory Norwood, but there wasn't anything carnal about either. She was an unlikely candidate for dalliances with the boss, and there didn't seem to be a conniving bone in her body.

After ten minutes, she finally managed to gather herself enough to carry on a dialogue unbroken by emotion. 'I'm so sorry, Detectives, but I haven't been able to get a hold of myself ever since I heard the news. I just can't believe he's gone. Things won't ever be the same here. Not for me, not for anybody.'

'Did Mr Norwood have any business appointments this morning?' Gino asked.

'No, absolutely not. Today was meant to be a family day. Mrs Norwood made it very clear to me that he wasn't to have any distractions on such an important day. It was the one time I agreed with her.' Her eyes widened and her hand fluttered to her mouth. 'That came out wrong.'

Gino gave her a commiserative nod. 'It's okay, Ms Jones. I'm sure the dynamics could be pretty difficult sometimes. Your loyalty was to Mr Norwood and the company, and I'll bet that conflicted with the wishes of the family sometimes.'

Her shoulders dropped in relief. 'That's exactly how it was. Rosalie was part of the business and understood the demands, but Mrs Norwood could be . . . difficult sometimes.'

'How so?'

'Not to speak ill of her, she's had such a horrible time, but frankly, I think she was jealous of the time he spent working. Mr Norwood was always a workaholic, but it got to a fever pitch after Trey's death. He was hardly ever home, at a time when she probably needed him most. As I was Mr Norwood's proxy, she often took her frustrations out on me.' Tears started running down her cheeks again. 'I guess that was the way he dealt with his grief. We all do that differently, don't we?'

'We do,' Magozzi said softly. 'Thank you for speaking with us, Ms Jones. I know it was hard . . .'

'No, it was good to talk about Mr Norwood. And I know you'll find out what happened and do what's right.'

*

'Betty Norwood just got a little more interesting,' Gino mused, once they were on their way back to the office. 'You see somebody as polished and poised and rich as her and you automatically assume everything in her world is just one big cream puff. But pull back the ten-thousand-dollar curtains and you've got an angry, frustrated, sad human being, just like anybody else who's suffering.'

'She has reason to be all of those things. But she's not our killer.'

Gino nodded. 'Pretty hard to kill someone from a thousand miles away.'

Eighteen

Special Agent Dahl had spent half an hour briefing Special Agent in Charge Paul Shafer on what Monkeewrench had just told him – entirely leaving out his early-morning visit to Harley – and now he was enduring the discomfort of Shafer's agitated cross-examination.

The man was tall and thin, with an exaggerated jaw, a sharp hawk nose, and small eyes that were sometimes blue, sometimes gray, depending on the light. Right now, they were the color of wet stone. His temperament was normally as cold as his countenance, but he was hot that morning. Of course, having his greatest fear confirmed, that the city under his watch might indeed become an international story for all the wrong reasons, would try even the most imperturbable soul. More than anyone, his career hung in the balance and he was one bad decision away from involuntary retirement.

He was drumming his fingers on the edge of his desk, seeming not to care that it broadcast his anxiety level. 'This is very disturbing indeed, and I would be insincere if I didn't credit Monkeewrench for giving us a more specific location to focus our attention. My concern is the accuracy of the information and how they obtained it in the first place. To be honest with you, Special Agent Dahl, I've had occasion to deal with Monkeewrench several times, long before you were posted here, and I have my suspicions about their methods. They may be able to operate on the margins of the law, but we don't have that luxury.'

'I can't speak for them or to your experience with them, sir, but the times I've collaborated with them, I've found them to be beyond reproach. But, personal perceptions aside, I don't think anyone could argue that they haven't been strong, reliable partners.'

Shafer snorted out a sharp breath, making Dahl wonder what Monkeewrench had done to him in the past that had alienated him. He'd have to ask them one day. Not that it was hard to alienate Shafer – he was a rigid ideologue, and a simple disagreement on policy could become grounds for a lifelong grudge.

'Does Monkeewrench know this is accurate intelligence?'

'They don't, sir, and they were very upfront about that. They were simply running a beta test on some new law-enforcement integration software they've developed, using publicly available data on local terror suspects. Some have been under our surveillance in the past. Their program identified City Hall as an area of concern, which corroborates our own concerns for Minneapolis. Obviously, they felt it was their duty to inform us, even though the results were generated from a prototype.'

'And how does this program work?'

'I couldn't tell you that, sir.'

'Can it trace the source?'

'I couldn't tell you that either, sir. I imagine they would run into the same problems with encryption we're having on that front, but I know they would do everything they could to assist us if we asked them for support.'

Shafer's fingers stilled briefly, then found new, ardent

focus contorting a paperclip. 'Special Agent, we are treading very delicate territory here.'

Dahl straightened his spine as physical reinforcement. He couldn't push this much further, but it was worth at least one Hail Mary play. 'May I suggest we treat any additional information we might get from them as an anonymous tip? If someone called with the same information Monkeewrench might relay to us in the future, it would be our duty as law-enforcement agents to take it seriously and dedicate manpower to investigating a potential threat.' He cleared his throat. 'I might add that Monkeewrench's information would undoubtedly be as reliable, if not more so, than most anonymous tips the Bureau receives and acts upon.'

Shafer gave him an arid smile. 'Should I be concerned about a personal attachment to Monkeewrench? It seems you've become somewhat of an ambassador on their behalf. I'll remind you that any sense of impropriety on your part would be extremely deleterious to the Bureau and our mission.'

Dahl felt the blood rise to his face and his fists clench out of sight in his lap. 'With all due respect, sir, a terror attack in Minneapolis would also be extremely deleterious to the Bureau and our mission, especially if we didn't utilize any and all tools available to us. And I'd hate to think any partisanship or personal grievance might be grounds for us to abrogate our duty and jeopardize the safety of innocent civilians. Wouldn't you?'

Shafer abandoned his paperclip and all the toxic energy seemed to drain out of him, leaving his narrow, bony face as gray as his eyes. 'Partisanship and personal grievance have nothing to do with this. Legality does. We are sworn officers of the law. We uphold it, we don't break it. You would be wise to remember your oath.' His face pruned up, as if he'd just tasted something repugnant. 'I want a meeting with them immediately. I want to know more about this software.'

'I'm sure they'd be happy to oblige you.'

He let out another ugly snort. 'I doubt that. Task force meeting in an hour. Assemble your team and keep me posted on all developments. Especially those that have anything to do with Monkeewrench.'

Dahl closed Shafer's door quietly behind him and fingered the flash drive in his pocket, wondering what it would be like not to walk these halls every day. He might find out soon enough.

Once he was safely locked in his office, he retrieved the burner phone from his desk drawer and punched in Harley's number.

He answered on the first ring. 'Hey, Dahl, got anything for us?'

'Mr Davidson, I have a flash drive and thirty minutes. I can be there in ten.'

'I'll be waiting.'

As promised, Harley was there to greet him at the door. Even his considerable bulk seemed diminished by the size and grandeur of the foyer, but his presence usually compensated for that. Not now – his face was haggard and worried, and his eyes seemed to be searching for a focal point that didn't exist in this space but in his mind.

'Is there something wrong, Mr Davidson?'

'Our bad guys aren't novices. They're using onion routers, domain generation algorithms and BGP hijacking.'

'In English, please?'

'It means we're having a hell of a time tracing them, too. But we'll slice through the Gordian knot eventually. Come on in. You look worse than you did this morning, Dahl.'

'You're generous with your compliments. And I might say the same of you. I guess we're all a little depleted.'

'And we're all in the same boat.'

'Hopefully that boat doesn't have bars on the windows.'

Harley smiled, and with that smile, his presence returned to fill the vacancy in the foyer. 'I'm telling you, Dahl, there's a sense of humor in there somewhere.'

'I'm flattered you think so.' He withdrew the flash drive from his pocket and placed it in Harley's hand. 'Get rid of this as soon as you load it. It's all the intelligence we've mined on the local terror threat and everything is classified at the highest level. I hope it will help.'

Harley thumbed the piece of plastic concealing an electronic chip, then tucked it into the front pocket of his leather biker's jacket.

'Shafer wants to meet with you to discuss the program as soon as possible. Of course he knows nothing about our visits, and certainly nothing about what I just gave you.'

'We'll get back to you on that. What's happening on your end?'

Dahl checked his watch. 'We have a task force meeting at the top of the hour and we'll be dispatching people to help cover City Hall and monitor every suspicious character that ever existed in Minnesota. I haven't heard from the cyber division.'

'Then we keep working. Whatever happens, you're doing the right thing. We all are.'

'Let's hope it's enough.'

Nineteen

Dennis Fruetel was weeding what was left of his vegetable garden after a malicious family of gophers had laid waste to half of it overnight. The little bastards had stripped the roots and pulled down four fully fruited tomato plants, plus some squash and peppers. They were an evil lot, always working underground, so you couldn't shoot them, you couldn't drown them out with a hose because they would just dig another warren of tunnels, and he wasn't about to lay down poison and risk taking out the cats along with the gophers.

But that was country living. An hour outside the city and things were very different. You had to deal with a lot of things your urban counterparts couldn't even conceive of. And that was just fine with him. He'd grown up in the heart of the city, and the hardships and dangers there were a lot worse and more unpredictable than the wildlife he and Mary shared space with out here.

'How bad is it, Den?'

He turned around and saw Mary walking into the garden with a big wicker trug, still optimistic about bringing in some fresh produce for dinner, even though he'd warned her about the gophers.

'Bad enough that you probably won't need that basket to take what the gophers left us. You've got to get those lazy cats working.'

'They already killed three.'

'Gophers are like cockroaches. Where there are three, there are a hundred.'

'Then we probably need more cats,' Mary teased, as she walked around and surveyed the damage with increasing distress. 'They ate my habañeros, too?'

'Might be some consolation, thinking about their evil little butts on fire right now.'

His wife of twenty years, the sweetest soul on earth as far as Dennis was concerned – savior of feral cats and just about any other animal or human in need of food, care, or comfort – smiled a little wickedly and stomped her tiny foot on the ground. 'How do you like my habañeros now?'

They shared a laugh, then jerked their heads up when they heard a distant scream. 'Oh, my God, Den . . .'

Dennis gauged the distance and direction, then shrugged it off. It was coming from the state park adjoining their property, which was a wellspring of wildlife: not just gophers and assorted other rodents, but bear, coyote, fox, skunk, deer, and the occasional rattlesnake. He'd even heard about some recent bobcat sightings from Myron Nelson, who volunteered there on the weekends. 'It's coming from William O'Brien. Probably some weekend warrior looking to commune with nature and got a little more than they'd bargained for. It wouldn't be the first time.'

Mary shook her head forcefully. 'No, Dennis. That wasn't the scream of somebody who ran across a deer carcass or saw a bear or a rattler.'

There was another scream, this one truly primeval and filled with horror, and Dennis had to agree with her for a change. 'Call nine-one-one.' He grabbed his shotgun, which was at the ready in case a gopher dared pop its head above ground while he was weeding, and started jogging toward the park through their back field.

'You know what I like about this view?' Gino asked.

Magozzi cracked open his window a little, letting in some heat and humidity to alleviate the meat locker Gino had created inside the sedan. 'What view? We're on Fifth Street by City Hall.'

'Exactly. City Hall is still here. Minneapolis is still here.'

'Probably because half the bodies you see on the street are undercover feds or our joint terrorism task force people.' Magozzi pointed up. 'Those are two of our guys on the roof.'

'Which probably makes City Hall the safest place in the state right now, but I'm never going to feel the same way about walking through those front doors again. It's like my house just got burglarized, but a thousand times worse.'

'That's part of terrorism.'

'This really sucks, Leo.'

Magozzi's phone rang and he shaded the display from the sun with his hand so he could read the caller ID.

'Who is it?'

'Says Washington County.'

'Did you forget to pay your real-estate taxes?'

'I wish. Detective Magozzi here.'

Gino parked the car and started drumming his fingers on the steering wheel, trying to make sense of the conversation that was dominated by the person at the other end. Just like his earlier call with Grace, Magozzi wasn't saying much, but it didn't take long to figure out he was talking to another detective and there was a dead body involved.

'Gerald Stenson,' Magozzi said morosely, signing off. 'A hiker found him in William O'Brien state park on the bluffs by the river, broken up on the rocks. He had a camera around his neck, so the detectives on scene figured he took a nasty fall during a photo shoot. It happens there a couple times every year . . .'

'Son of a bitch. A body dump. A smart one. Who's going to notice a prior head wound when a guy is in pieces over some rocks?'

'Have a little faith in our colleagues, Gino. One of the detectives pegged him as potentially being our BOLO and ran his prints. Stenson did a stint with the Peace Corps so he was on record.'

'Did they take a look at the camera?'

'Of course they did. It was digital. No chip in it.'

'Shit. So, what's the status of the investigation?'

'Crime scene is almost finished and they'll copy us on everything they have. The body is getting transported to the ME here, and the Washington County detectives are en route to notify Kris Stenson. They asked us for a little time before we go talk to her, but they'll rough out some details and let her know we'll be paying her a visit this afternoon.'

'Oh, man. The poor woman. First she finds out her husband is dead, then that he's probably been murdered. And she gets the third degree from two different counties in the process. This is going exactly the way I hoped it wouldn't.'

'"Crime-scene tape rolled up by sunset." Isn't that what you said?'

Gino scowled. 'I was being extremely sarcastic.'

Magozzi's cell rang again and he cussed before answering sharply, 'Magozzi.'

'Man, you sound pissed,' Jimmy Grimm said. 'Is your better half around? I'm hoping he's in a sunnier mood than you are.'

'I doubt it, but I'll put you on speaker and you can judge for yourself.' Magozzi did, and passed the phone to Gino.

Gino leaned into the phone's speaker. 'Hey, Jimmy, give us some love.'

'Are you guys really that desperate?'

'Pretty much. Washington County found Gerald Stenson's body in William O'Brien state park, dashed over some rocks on the bluffs. Our number-one witness isn't talking, and probably wasn't the second he left the Norwood property.'

Jimmy paused for a moment, a brief silence for the dead. 'I'm sorry to hear that, guys. I was hoping there would be one happy ending in this mess. Man, you two really bought a headache.'

'Actually, it was free.'

'Well, I'm probably not going to make it any better, but I can tell you some things you didn't know. We finally found a slug buried in the woodwork in Norwood's office and it matched with the Colt. There was a full load minus one in the weapon.'

'We figured. What else?'

'No foreplay? Jesus, you two are tough customers today. Okay, Norwood was definitely a homicide. The gun was wiped clean. Not a single print. In my humble professional opinion, dead men don't wipe their guns, so start working up a shortlist of suspects.'

'In the pantheon of stupid criminals, this has got to be right up there.'

'Criminals are stupid. You guys are telling me so all the time. Probably the only reason two schlubs like you have such a great track record clearing cases. Listen, I have to run, but we'll be in touch. Call if you need anything.'

'Thanks, Jimmy.' Magozzi hung up while Gino rested his forehead on the steering wheel with a tortured groan. 'Are you passing out?'

'I'm just thinking. Norwood is officially a homicide now and so is Gerald Stenson. Two homicides, twice as easy to solve, right?'

Magozzi chewed his lower lip. 'If there's a personal connection between Stenson and Norwood, yeah, but I don't see those two running in the same circles. I think you were right when you said Stenson surprised the killer. We've got to focus on the primary right now, which is Norwood and motive.'

'It was personal. Crime of passion. There were no signs of struggle, so Norwood let whoever killed him into the house.'

'Home invasion,' Magozzi parried. 'His door was unlocked, his security system was disabled, and he was blind drunk. Anybody could have walked into the house. Norwood surprises him with his gun and the invader overtakes him, then shoots him.'

'I still like crime of passion. Minerva Jones is out of the picture, but that doesn't mean Norwood wasn't getting extracurricular with somebody else.'

'Distraught mistress realizes Gregory Norwood the Second isn't going to ditch Betty after all. That's your theory?'

Gino lifted his head from the steering wheel and bristled defensively. 'My theories are always intricate masterpieces of psychological insight and this one is currently in progress. We have a lot more legwork to do before I can start fleshing it out. Besides, I'm a flowchart kind of guy. I can't think right without visual aids.'

'Then let's get up to the office with a whiteboard and markers and, while we're at it, have a chat with Chief Malcherson about his friend.'

Gino unclipped his seatbelt and reluctantly left the frigid cocoon of the sedan while he ran a potential dialogue. 'Afternoon, Chief. We'd like to interview you, since you're now a person of interest in the homicide of your buddy.'

'I'm sure he'll appreciate our devotion to the job.'

Twenty

Rosalie Norwood let herself into her house and looked around at a space made chaotic by family heirlooms, artifacts gathered during a lifetime of global travel, and modern pieces her designer had used to stitch together what he had complimented as 'a beautifully untidy amalgamation of meaningful possessions.'

Or maybe it hadn't been a compliment. Maybe he'd really been inwardly appalled by her insistence on displaying things like a dinged-up teak table with ivory inlays that her grandparents had gotten for her in Bali, or the Tibetan singing bowls Father had picked up in China. Probably more horrifying was the collection of Dala horses she'd been given by her host family while studying in Sweden, and most definitely the tarnished brass bells hanging by the fireplace, strung with fraying pink cord – a gift from Trey after he'd spent some time in India, probably to indulge in the heroin that came across the northern border from Pakistan.

Hang this on a door, Rosie. It'll warn you when evil spirits are coming.

She dropped her handbag by the front door and walked into the living room. The last time she'd been there was a week ago. And so had Father and Mom and Uncle Robert, enjoying a cocktail before dinner. And now, just like that, one more person was erased from her mental photo album, just like Trey had been erased a year ago.

She sat on a chair near the hearth and ran a finger down those bells. They emitted a harsh, unmelodious clang, but it was strangely comforting to her. 'What happened to you, Trey? You were my perfect little brother until one day you weren't. What happened?'

He didn't answer, of course. He never did.

'Father? Daddy? What happened to *you*?'

No answer from him either. No spirits lurking around, evil or otherwise.

She closed her eyes for a moment and let herself succumb to a torrent of emotion. She might even have dozed off, because at some point she became aware that her eyes and cheeks were wet with tears and she didn't remember crying.

'Spirits, huh?' she muttered, grabbing the bells from their spot near the fireplace. They clanked obnoxiously as she walked them to the front door and hung them from a hook that had held a wreath last Christmas. 'Maybe you'll talk to me now.'

As she positioned them just so, her cell phone rang, startling her out of what was probably a semi-psychotic state of grief: who else would talk to bells and dead people?

'Hello?'

'Rosalie, dear, where are you?'

'I stopped at home to check on things. Is everything all right?'

'Robert is here to sit with us. Louise was hoping to join him, but she's been feeling unwell. Some kind of dreadful late-summer bug. Will you be coming soon?'

'Yes, Mom. I'll leave in a few minutes.' Rosalie hung up and thought about Louise Zeller – in her opinion a tortured soul if there ever was one. She wasn't suffering from a late-summer bug and everybody knew it. The poor woman was suffering from crippling, bipolar depression and had been for as long as she'd known her, which was a very long time. Even as a little girl, she'd understood there was something different and sad about Louise.

But things had gotten worse when Uncle Robert's political ambitions had begun to take shape – for a very private woman, the prospect of being thrust into an even more public life than she already endured was probably torture. And Rosalie got it, even if nobody else did. There were a lot of times when she wished she could just hole up in her house and not talk to anybody for a month.

She touched the bells again, and suddenly all the horrifying, speculative images she'd had of Trey in India revisited her memory: Trey left for dead on a filthy mattress in a festering slum, Trey getting killed on the border by a drug trafficker, Trey pushing a dirty needle into a vein and flooding his body with poison . . .

Rosalie shook away the awful visions. He'd made it home from India alive, thanks to Father . . .

She froze and took a deep breath.

I've hired a man, a private detective, who promised he would go to the ends of the earth to find Trey and bring him home.

A private detective. One who'd succeeded in an almost impossible task. It would stand to reason that Father would trust him and hire him again. She punched redial on her phone and waited impatiently for her mother to answer. 'What is it, dear?'

'Do you remember when Trey went to India?'

There was a long silence at the other end. 'Yes, of course I do.'

'And Father was so worried, we all were, and he hired a private detective to find him?'

'Rosalie, what does this have to do with anything?'

'Mom, do you remember his name?'

'I . . . Really, this isn't appropriate under the circumstances.'

'It might be important, Mom. He might know something.'

'Know something about what? Rosalie, are you feeling all right?'

'I feel fine. Please, Mom, think.'

She heard a sigh laden with anxiety. 'The only thing I remember is that he had a strange name. Melchi or Malachai, something like that. Something that sounded Biblical.'

'Thanks. I'll see you soon, Mom.' She hung up and found the card Detective Magozzi had given her.

Twenty-one

Chief Malcherson's tie was still crooked when Gino and Magozzi walked into his office, which neither of them took as a good sign. Worse yet, there was a general aura of mayhem hanging like smog in his immaculate, spit-shined space. Magozzi had seen him endure varying degrees of stress over the years, but his stoic, unyielding armor of propriety and authority had always remained intact. Today was different. He was weathering a storm on two major fronts – a possible terror attack and a personal loss – and seemed frayed to the limits of human endurance.

Magozzi's phone blatted in his pocket and he fumbled to silence it. It was Rosalie Norwood, but she was going to have to wait. 'Sorry about that, sir.'

He looked up at them with his scary ice-blue eyes and gestured for them to sit.

'Sir, what's the latest on the terror threat? We noticed men on the roof.'

'We are and will remain on the highest state of alert for the foreseeable future. Our joint terrorism task force team and federal agents cleared the building and there is an overwhelming presence outside, including aerial surveillance. Every precaution is being taken.'

Which didn't always ensure a positive outcome, Magozzi thought cynically. Gino was right – none of them were ever going to feel the same way again. 'That's good to know, sir. It sounds like the interdepartmental response is working well.'

'The task forces are. However, Special Agent in Charge Paul Shafer and I have different approaches and vision for the future.'

Gino nodded in commiseration. 'Law enforcement versus government bureaucracy. I feel your pain, Chief. Shafer's always been a monumental –'

'We all have the same goal, to keep our city and our citizens safe,' Magozzi interrupted, before Gino could say something really stupid, like call Shafer a prick or an asshole in front of the chief. Although, given that the chief had actually called out Shafer in front of them, maybe he would have appreciated a little profanity.

'Tell me about the Norwood investigation.' The chief changed the subject.

Magozzi tried to ignore his phone, which was vibrating insistently in his jacket pocket. 'Things just turned upside down. His death wasn't a suicide, Chief.'

'You think he was *murdered*?'

Gino, perennially oblivious to charm, détente, protocol, or any other extraneous fluff held in high esteem by the civilized world, told him straight up. 'No question about it. Got any ideas on who would want him dead? Because nobody else we've talked to does.'

Gino's inelegant comments earned him a deep scowl. 'Are you absolutely certain?'

'We just talked to Jimmy Grimm and evidence doesn't lie. The gun and entry wound were both on Mr Norwood's right side, which made us suspicious from the get-go, but the capper is that the gun was wiped clean. We also found evidence of a recent assault on a photo-journalist by the swimming pool near his office. Washington County just found his body in William O'Brien state park.'

What little was left of Malcherson's stoicism degraded visibly.

'His name was Gerald Stenson,' Magozzi added. 'He was on assignment, staking out the Norwood home. We figure he was on the property when Mr Norwood was shot and he surprised the killer.'

'Do you have any suspects?'

'No, but there are some moving parts right now. Gerald Stenson is one of them. And Rosalie told us her father recently became obsessed with Trey's death. He didn't think it was an accident and he'd hired a private detective.'

Malcherson frowned. 'He certainly didn't mention anything of that nature to me.'

'Rosalie said he was secretive about it.'

Malcherson swiveled his chair and briefly contemplated the view of the street outside his window. 'Murder seems impossible. Gregory was beloved. He had no enemies.'

'From the get-go, the Norwoods believed he was murdered. They were adamant about it.'

'Did they say why?'

'They wouldn't accept that he would take his own life. Turns out they were right, but they had no suspicions or ideas about a possible killer.'

'Suicide made horrible sense to me.'

'Mr Zeller thought suicide fit, too,' Gino said.

'If you were in Gregory's inner circle, you knew how tormented by grief and regret he was. You also knew he

would try to keep the extent of his agony from his family.'
He looked at his watch and finally straightened his tie. 'I
have a meeting with the mayor in ten minutes, but I want
to see detailed reports as soon as possible. Keep me
informed of any new developments. Now, go find your
killer, Detectives.'

Twenty-two

Magozzi was deep into the tedium of crafting a preliminary report while Gino worked on his computer, sucking down an unnaturally green energy drink, like it was the water of life.

'Malachai Dubnik,' he finally said, victorious, pushing away from his desk. 'Now that's a name for the record books. No real on-line presence, except for threads that mention him as part of bigger news stories. Left Hollywood Robbery-Homicide ten years ago and he's been operating as a PI in Los Angeles ever since. He's the go-to guy for the rich and famous. He'd be a top pick for Norwood, for sure, and like Rosalie said, if he hired him once and he got the job done, he'd hire him again.'

Magozzi dragged a hand through his hair, which reminded him he was supposed to have it cut today. 'Get him on the phone.'

'Dubnik doesn't advertise, referrals only, so we'll have to hunt him down. I guess he's so successful he can afford to be a pain in the ass.'

'Referrals only, huh? This guy is going to be a real prick.'

Malachai Dubnik wasn't a prick. On the contrary, he was polite, cooperative, and expressed sadness over the death of Gregory Norwood. Whether the origin was genuine sorrow or grief over hearing that one of his paying customers was on a slab, so that particular gravy train had hit the end of the tracks, Magozzi didn't know.

'I'll help in any way I can, Detectives. What do you need?'

'Can you send us your files?'

'I can do better than that. I'm in Minneapolis right now, following up on a couple leads for Norwood. Well, I was. If you want to meet up, I'll pass the baton to you.' He paused for a moment. 'Gregory Norwood was a fine man. Not the kind of guy I'd expect to have a target on his back. Rich people usually have more true enemies than true friends, and they can be a real pain to handle. They don't like to pay their bills and they make unrealistic demands. Norwood wasn't like that. I hope my files can help you out.'

Gino leaned into the phone. 'Hollywood Robbery-Homicide is pretty elite. Why did you leave?'

'It wasn't voluntary, but fortunes can turn on a dime, right? I pissed the wrong people off, simple as that. But then I found out there was life after HRH, and the sky's the limit as far as pay grade. If you two ever want to jump, call me anytime. Business is always booming in Lotus-Land.'

They arranged to meet Dubnik later at his hotel – ironically, it was the Chatham, the one where Betty and Rosalie Norwood were staying. His choice of lodging supported his reputation as PI to the rich and famous, the generous expense account and remuneration for services that went along with it. Dubnik hadn't been lying when he'd said the sky's the limit as far as pay grade.

After the call with Dubnik, Magozzi refocused on his report, until Detective Johnny McLaren interrupted, breezing into the office wearing a pair of Bermuda shorts, a golf shirt, and a big smile. His spiky red hair clashed with the orange plaid shorts, and the blue shirt was another fashion misstep, but the smile was nice.

Gino gave him a critical once-over. 'Please tell me you're on vacation.'

'You know I'm on vacation as of yesterday at five p.m. Damn lucky, too. I was next on the roster and, man, did I miss a shit storm by the skin of my teeth. First Norwood, now the terror scare.'

'How'd you hear about the terror thing so fast?'

McLaren rolled his eyes. 'Freedman. His fearsome visage may strike fear in the hearts of all who gaze upon him, but he's as gossipy as a clique of teenage girls.'

Eaton Freedman was Johnny's new homicide partner. He looked like an African American Incredible Hulk at six-five, carrying about two hundred and fifty pounds of solid muscle, but he was known to have a soft, caramel center. As unlikely as the pairing was – a scrappy little Irishman with a scary photographic memory and an intimidating street sergeant turned detective, McLaren and Freedman had formed a strong bond and working relationship straight out of the gate. It didn't surprise Magozzi that Freedman would keep him in the loop. 'Probably wanted to save your hide. You're kind of his mentor.'

'He could do worse,' McLaren said modestly, loading folders from his desk into a battered briefcase. 'So how's it going with the Norwood case?'

'Bad. We confirmed homicide, and the shit storm just turned into a shit maelstrom,' Gino carped.

McLaren's brows crept upward, punctuating his pasty white forehead with flame-colored frowns. 'Oh, man.

Give me a shout if there's anything I can do to help. I'm just golfing locally for the next seven days, but I'll take a call from you guys anytime if you need some back-up.'

'Thanks, but we wouldn't dream of messing with your game.'

'How's the chief taking everything? He got a double-whammy today.'

'He's in a meeting with the mayor right now, but if you see him, run the other way.'

'So it's like that. Damn crazy times. Don't get blown to Hell while I'm gone.'

Magozzi folded his arms across his chest. 'I thought you were going to make an offer on my house.'

McLaren gave him a mysterious smile. 'Getting my ducks in a row, friend.'

Gino snorted. 'Still trying to get Gloria on board with the whole domestic-bliss situation?'

'She requires finesse.'

'So how many more years is this finesse phase going to last?'

'Heaven can wait, Rolseth.'

A commanding voice, the aggressive clomp of platform heels, and the clickety-clack of beaded cornrows announced Gloria's presence before her corporeal form appeared in the cubicle. Magozzi briefly wondered if she'd been lurking in the shadows, eavesdropping on their conversation. If so, they were all in deep shit.

She tossed an admonishing scowl McLaren's way. 'I thought we got rid of you yesterday.'

'Oh, but parting was such sweet sorrow. The memory of your dulcet voice called me back, like a siren's song.'

She punched a hand into a generous hip and eyed his briefcase. 'You came back because you forgot your files, fool.' She slapped a stapled hand-out on each of their desks. 'New protocol for heightened alert. I sent an email with an attachment, too, but I knew none of you divas would look at it unless you had paper on your desk. Read it or not, I don't care, but Chief Malcherson does.'

'Put your head between your legs and kiss your ass goodbye?' Gino asked ingenuously.

Gloria didn't smile – ever – but she came close. 'This tells you exactly how to do just that.' She looked at McLaren again. 'Where are you going in that ludicrous get-up?'

'I'm golfing with Willy Staples.'

'Hmm. You and that fancy billionaire are getting awfully chummy. What does he see in a twerp like you?'

'I don't even know where to start, Gloria. My talents are so prodigious.'

Gino snickered. 'He's got a scary memory and he's fluent in about fifty languages, for one. Willy does a lot of foreign deals and, for some bizarre reason, McLaren is the only one he trusts to translate.'

McLaren shrugged modestly. 'Willy also appreciates my fluency in golf – under my devoted tutelage, his handicap has improved twenty percent.'

Gloria gave him an imperious look. 'Doesn't make up for your appalling wardrobe malfunctions. Are you color blind, McLaren?'

'No.'

'Well, I hope Willy Staples is.'

He gave her a mischievous smile. 'Do you like baseball, Gloria?'

'I hate baseball. It's the most boring, pointless sport on the planet.'

'That's too bad. Willy gave me two tickets to his private box for the Twins game tonight. It's pretty amazing – there's a big buffet and an open bar, and they wheel in a dessert cart that would blow your mind. I was going to invite you, but I guess I'll have to find somebody else.' He made a great show of looking at his watch. 'Gotta run or I'll be late.'

Gino cleared his throat to mask a laugh as McLaren sauntered away. 'I guess Willy Staples sees something in him you don't, Gloria.'

'Don't go there, Rolseth. Don't even think about it.'

Twenty-three

Jim Beam stopped the company van in front of 111 Washington Avenue and called his arrival into Office Dispatch. Not that it was necessary because the GPS tracked his every move all day. If he stopped to take a piss at a gas station on the way to a client, he'd get a call from his boss before he'd even zipped up. But being proactive earned him Brownie points with old Lloyd, and maybe, just maybe, by God, he'd see a little Christmas bonus at the end of the year for his excellent and loyal service to Lloyd's HVAC Systems.

'In your fucking dreams,' he muttered to himself, as he started off-loading equipment onto a dolly. By the time it was fully loaded, he was soaked in sweat down to his tidy whities and looking forward to going through those fancy glass doors into an air-conditioned lobby.

'Excuse me, sir.'

Jim turned around and saw a street cop standing a few feet away, watching him cautiously. Actually, the cop looked nervous, and that made Jim nervous. Ten years ago, he would have bolted, but those times were long gone and he had nothing to hide anymore. 'Hot day, Officer,' he greeted him, mopping his brow with the back of his hand. 'What can I do for you?'

'May I see some ID, please?'

Jim pointed to the laminated employee ID hanging

from the lanyard around his neck. 'My driver's license is in the van if you need something more than this.'

'Please get your driver's license, sir.'

Jim automatically lifted his hands, an unfortunate reflex from his darker days that he hadn't quite been able to kick. 'It's right in my wallet on the console.'

'Go ahead.'

Jim started sweating more heavily as the cop shadowed his every move as he reached into the van. He calmly and carefully grabbed his wallet and turned it over to the cop without opening it. 'License is right in front. Troubles today, Officer?'

The cop, not much more than a kid by Jim's estimation, opened the wallet, examined the license and then his face, then closed it and handed it back. 'Your license identifies you as Jim Beam. Is that your real name?'

Jim took a deep breath and steeled himself to answer the question he'd been asked a million times before, the same question that had cast a dark penumbra over him his whole life. 'Yep, that's my given name, says so right on my birth certificate. Not James, Jim. My father was a drunk, so he named me after his favorite booze. It killed the son of a bitch young, I'm not sorry to say.'

The young cop's face relaxed a little. There might even have been a little sympathy mixed in. 'Thank you for your cooperation. Have a nice day.'

'You, too.' Jim watched him walk away, feeling something dark and bad uncoil in the pit of his stomach. Something about the cop's demeanor bothered him. He'd been tight, on high alert, like he was expecting something to go down.

Or maybe it was just the heat and humidity messing with his head. It wasn't unusual in this day and age for a cop to stop a guy unloading equipment in front of a downtown commercial building, especially a building that was housing the Minneapolis FBI field office until their new state-of-the-art location in Brooklyn Center was finished. Lloyd's supplied HVAC equipment for that, too, but Jim couldn't make deliveries there because a background check was required to get within a light year of the construction site.

Jim finally decided he didn't really care if something was going down or not. The whole world was a damned powder keg, and if you thought too hard about it, or let paranoia get the better of you, you'd end up in a fetal ball in bed for the rest of your life. You had to focus on the good things in the here and now, like getting out of this hellish heat and humidity and pushing a dolly into an air-conditioned building.

He rejoiced internally once the cool blast of central air hit him in the face and started drying the sweat from his brow. He rolled his equipment up to the security desk and slid his manifest toward a chubby guard, who'd outgrown his uniform by a few Big Macs. 'Delivery from Lloyd's HVAC.'

The security guard gave him a sour look. 'Deliveries are supposed to come in and out through the service entrance in back, by the loading dock.'

Jim formed an instant opinion: he didn't like this fat, pompous rent-a-cop, but he wasn't getting paid to have opinions, he was getting paid to deliver equipment, and part of his job was to be courteous and accommodating and kiss whatever asses demanded kissing. It was the story of his fucking life.

He stole a quick glance at the guard's nameplate and swallowed his pride in a big, bitter lump. 'I'm just following orders from my boss, Mr Kramer. Take a closer look. Specific instructions are right there on the manifest: delivery to be made through the front entrance. A representative for TCG Construction will sign.'

The guard eyed him suspiciously with beady brown eyes that looked like dried-up raisins, then scrutinized the manifest. 'This is irregular.'

Jim never paid much attention to the details of his job, just did what he was told to do, but it suddenly occurred to him that this was irregular. He made a lot of deliveries to this building, always at the loading dock, and almost always to the TCG Construction super, Big Mike. 'I'm sorry, but that's what it says. Call Big Mike Guidry. He can probably sort this out.'

'Mike Guidry isn't here today.' He sighed irritably and picked up his phone. 'Let me make a call.'

Jim waited, digging deep for patience. He had six more deliveries to make today and this Kramer knucklehead was sucking up time. He was also making a point of being as unpleasant as possible, which really pissed him off. The fat fuck was sitting on his lard butt in an air-conditioned lobby while he was sweating his nuggets off, doing all the heavy lifting, and Kramer was the one with the attitude.

Fat Boy finally hung up and gave him a distrustful look. 'Take the service elevator to the lower level. Somebody will meet you.'

'Great. Thanks.'

'Sign in first.' He handed over a clipboard and Jim scrawled his name on the form, anxious to get away from the man and the building.

'Please note the time.'

Jim gritted his teeth and noted the time next to his signature. 'Everybody seems a little twitchy today. Is something going on?'

'It's the renovations. Lots of equipment and people coming and going all the time. The FBI field office is in this building and that makes them nervous, I guess.'

'Yeah, that makes sense. Service elevators are . . . ?'

'That way, on the west end of the building.'

Jim nodded an insincere thanks and headed toward the elevators reserved for dregs of the earth like him while suits and ties swirled around him. Nobody gave him a second glance, as if he didn't exist at all.

Once he got to the lower level, he was met by a beefy guy in a hard hat he hadn't seen on this job before. He was cordial enough, but he seemed tweaked as hell, like he'd just snorted his bodyweight in meth. His small, darting eyes made Jim uneasy. 'Delivery from Lloyd's HVAC.'

'Am I glad to see you! I've been waiting for this shipment for days.' He jumped on the dolly, like it was the Holy Grail, and started unloading boxes with frantic urgency.

'You might want to take a look inside, check to make sure the order's right.'

'Not necessary.'

'Are you sure? Big Mike always checks. He's a real stickler for details. Wouldn't want you to get in trouble.'

The man ignored him and kept unloading. What did

Jim care if he got in trouble? This guy was turning out to be a prick, too. 'Where's Big Mike today, anyhow?'

'He's around here somewhere.'

Jim's thoughts stuttered to a halt. Big Mike wasn't here today: shouldn't a rep for TCG know that? 'You're with TCG, right?'

'Yeah, why?'

'Uh . . . well, since I don't know you, I'm just making sure things are getting to the right place. Company policy and all that,' he said weakly, as sweat trickled down his spine. It suddenly occurred to him that maybe Lloyd, money-grubbing bastard that he was, had a little side deal going under the cloak of his very legitimate and respected business and this guy was a part of it. It was a preposterous thought, unless you knew something about the darker side of human nature; the darker side of man, more specifically.

See something, say something. The only problem with that public-service message was that Lloyd was his meal ticket: it was damn near impossible for ex-felons to find decent-paying work, and for some reason he'd never know, Lloyd didn't have a problem with ex-felons. But if Lloyd went down, he'd go down with him and end up pulling minimum wage in one of the few holes in the city that didn't care if you had a criminal record.

He realized the man was staring at him intently with those little, darting eyes. 'Something wrong?'

'Uh, no.'

He gave him a strange smile. 'Are you sure? You're not looking so good.'

Jim let out a breath and shook his head. 'Just a little

light-headed. Probably too much caffeine. And the heat, you know.'

'Too much caffeine, too much heat, not a good combination. Drink lots of water, you'll feel better.'

'Yeah. Are we done here?'

'We are. Thanks. And take care.'

Jim gathered his empty dolly and hot-footed it toward the elevator, anxious to get the hell out of there. For all his paranoia, he never anticipated the silenced bullet that hit him in the back of the skull and mushroomed into his brain, killing him instantly.

Kramer drummed his fingers on his clipboard while he scanned the lobby anxiously. The Lloyd's HVAC guy had been in the basement a long time. It wasn't unusual for delivery personnel to spend some time with the construction crews and walk them through the manifests, maybe shoot the shit a little, but it had been almost half an hour and he was getting nervous. If he didn't get a sign-out, his job wasn't just on the line, it was over, and he couldn't afford that right now.

He felt beads of sweat popping on his brow, even though the air in the building was cool and dry. He finally picked up the phone and called downstairs. 'This is Kramer at the front desk. Who's this?'

'Gus, with general contracting.'

'Okay, Gus, there was a delivery from Lloyd's HVAC a while ago. Have you seen the driver?'

'Yeah, he made his delivery, but it was all the wrong stuff. I told him to go back to the mothership and start over.'

Kramer started sweating more. 'Did you send him back up to the lobby?'

'Didn't send him anywhere. Like I said, I just told him to leave and get it right. Is there a problem?'

He clenched his fist around the phone. 'Yes, there's a goddamned problem. This is a secure building, and if you sign in at the front desk, you sign out when you leave. Find out where he went.'

'Don't see how that's my concern, but hang on, I'll check.'

Prick, Kramer fumed, as he heard muffled voices conferring before Gus came back on the line.

'I just talked to my guys. They saw him leave through the loading dock, said he'd be back before the end of the day.'

Kramer slammed down the phone and stared at his clipboard, rehashing his earlier conversation with the man.

Deliveries are supposed to come in and out through the service entrance in back, by the loading dock.

After a few moments of soul-searching, he scrawled a reasonable facsimile of the HVAC guy's signature in the sign-out box. But it didn't feel right, and the longer he thought about it, the worse it felt. All he could hope for was that this didn't come back to bite him in the ass later.

Twenty-four

Grace was standing in Harley's kitchen, resting her eyes on the blooming hydrangeas outside the bay window. Their heavy heads bobbed in cadence with a light breeze, reminding her of the broken metronome she'd once had. It had been a Christmas 'gift' from a foster mother, but even as a young girl, she'd understood that the metronome was useless, just a token hand-me-down piece of junk that nobody else would want. Just like nobody had wanted her.

She frowned and turned away from the hydrangeas. Lately, her mind had been randomly pulling pieces of her past out of the dark, exposing them, and it was unsettling. People near death supposedly summoned certain critical memories of people or events or even things from their distant past, and she supposed it was entirely possible the prospect of a new life engendered the same kind of introspection.

While she waited for the tea kettle to whistle, she pressed her hands against the small of her back. The pregnancy had been pulling her muscles out of whack lately, and she wondered if they'd ever snap back. She was still fairly young, but when you thought about the reproductive years of a human starting in the teens, the thirties, at least in biological terms, were ancient.

Suddenly she felt a sharp pain deep in her belly and braced herself against the counter, willing it to go away.

The life growing inside her was getting increasingly impatient to explore new horizons, but Grace wasn't all that eager to give up the euphoria that came with pregnancy. She'd read articles about the misery some women endured, but she had never felt better.

Maybe that's because you're not alone for the first time in your life. You'll never be alone again.

'You're looking awfully thoughtful, sugar.' Annie startled her as she sashayed into the kitchen.

'There's a lot to think about. A lot to worry about.'

'On multiple fronts,' she said knowingly, killing the burner under the tea kettle when it started to whine. 'Maybe you should call your doctor. You're in pain, I can tell.'

'It's just false labor, Annie. It comes and goes.'

'Are you sure?'

'Positive.'

Annie gave her a skeptical look, but abandoned the subject for the time being. You didn't push things with Grace. She was like a feral cat – they would come to you eventually if they needed something but, by God, don't try to put them into a pet-carrier and take them to the vet, because they'd just run away for good. 'What do you think about meeting with Shafer tomorrow morning?'

'It's a good start. We designed this program for law enforcement, so I'm glad he has a healthy curiosity about how it works and what its potential is.'

'It's not ready for prime time yet.'

'We're just selling him the concept. It's a powerful program, Annie. It's going to do great things one day.'

Annie tapped her nails nervously on the counter. 'Well,

I don't like Shafer or trust him, and he feels the same way about us. What if this is some kind of a trap? Personally, I'm convinced that man has been waiting for the chance to catch us doing something illegal so he can throw us all in prison.'

'There's nothing illegal about the program. And we all share a common goal: to stop terror attacks. He may not like us, but we're an asset and he knows it.'

Annie smoothed her hair, currently a sharply cut bob in platinum blond. 'I suppose I might be just a wee bit paranoid. I look terrible in orange, you know.'

The intercom crackled and Roadrunner's voice came over the speaker in the kitchen. 'Grace? Annie? You need to come upstairs.'

Annie looked up at the ceiling. 'Oh, Lord. I don't like the sound of that.'

Roadrunner was so deeply focused on his work at the far side of the room, he didn't even hear the elevator delivering Grace and Annie to the office, but Harley jumped up from his chair. 'You two have got to see this.'

Roadrunner turned in his chair. His hair was sticking out at odd angles and dark circles cupped his eyes. 'The program finally isolated the algorithm that was shifting those IPs, and I was just about to get into their account, then everything went black.' He pointed to his screen, which was empty, except for a blinking cursor. 'No data, no domain names, no IPs, no nothing. Everything disappeared.'

'A kill switch,' Grace murmured. 'They knew they were getting hacked and they pulled the plug. They're watching us.'

The screen suddenly sprang to life again and started

flashing a warning. Roadrunner muttered an oath and his fingers flew over the keyboard. 'They're not just watching us, they're trying to hack us back.'

'Arrogant pricks,' Harley seethed.

Grace took a seat next to Roadrunner. 'The only good thing about arrogant pricks is they always make mistakes. That's one thing in life you can always count on.'

Twenty-five

Kris Stenson was a pretty young woman, who had been damaged badly by Fate in the past few hours. If Magozzi and Gino had passed her on the street yesterday, they would have seen a carefree, Bohemian type in a gauzy, colorful dress, a woman who wouldn't have seemed out of place at a Grateful Dead concert or chanting in a sacred circle at a Wiccan ceremony. Somebody without a care in the world.

But today her Sugar Bear was gone and nothing was going to be the same for her. She would eventually repair her life, find a new path and somebody else to love, but the psychic scars of her husband's murder would be with her forever.

She was sitting in a papasan chair next to a bamboo table that held a framed photograph of the couple standing in front of the Eiffel Tower – a desolate reminder that life was fleeting and death assailed all without prejudice and on its own schedule.

The apartment was small and unmemorable, with the standard white walls of a cheap rental that had high turnover, but there were lots of rugs, wall hangings, and other thoughtful, decorative touches that made the cramped space seem like a real home.

'I can't believe this is happening,' she whispered, after Magozzi and Gino had detailed all the suspicious circumstances surrounding her husband's death. 'I can't believe it.

The detectives who were here earlier explained some things, but . . . what you're saying is . . . you're saying Gerry was attacked at Gregory Norwood's house, then kidnapped and taken to William O'Brien? To kill him? To dispose of his body?'

'Looking at the evidence we have right now, that's our conclusion.'

She nodded, glancing at the Eiffel Tower picture. 'Gerry would never leave his camera bag or his car, and he had no business at William O'Brien, so I guess that's right. But . . . who? Why? Everybody loved Gerry.'

'That's what we're trying to find out. Is it all right if we ask you some more questions?'

She regarded them both with bloodshot green eyes. The monsoon of tears had dried up – there probably weren't many more left to shed. 'Yes, of course.'

Gino and Magozzi went through the usual litany of questions they asked during a murder investigation to eliminate the obvious: enemies, recent arguments or strife in his life, erratic behavior or unexplained absences, and so forth. That left a possible connection to Norwood.

'Did your husband know Mr Norwood or have a personal relationship with him?'

She smiled ruefully. 'No, of course not. We don't know anybody at that altitude. Gregory Norwood was in thin air, we're just muddling by down here on Earth.'

'Did your husband tell you about his interest in Gregory Norwood?'

'He had no specific interest but there's a local gossip paper that does – the *Whisperer*. Gerry worked for them occasionally. Gregory Norwood and his family were always marketable to them, especially after his son's overdose last year.' Her lower lip quivered. 'I wasn't happy that Gerry worked with them. We even had some words over it. I don't approve of that kind of exploitation of a tragedy, and neither did he, but . . . there were bills to pay.'

She started wringing her hands together, possibly trying to rub away an existential crisis. Idealism and principles were all well and good until there were bills to pay. Welcome to the real world.

'He was just a good man who worked hard and did what he could to provide for us,' she said quietly, pulling a tissue from the folds of her dress and blotting her eyes.

Gino leaned forward in his facing chair. 'We will find out who killed your husband, Ms Stenson. That's a promise.'

She looked up gratefully. 'Thank you. I hope you can.'

'Could we take a look at his computer?'

She nodded and stood. 'I'll show you his office. We couldn't really afford a two-bedroom, but Gerry needed his own space to work.'

Magozzi's heart ached for Kris Stenson. She was offering an inconsequential detail of her life with her husband to complete strangers as she worked through her grief, and those were some of the most poignant moments he ever spent with surviving family members. They shared whatever was on their mind without hesitation or encouragement because they weren't living in the moment: they were living in the past. Magozzi had done the same thing at his grandma's funeral when he'd been seven years old.

Is there anyone else who would like to say some words or share some memories of Luciana Magozzi?

Uh . . . Grandma liked ice cream. Really liked it, especially rum raisin. And she made good pot roast with potatoes and carrots and turnips. I don't like turnips, but I didn't tell her. And she always had pretty flowers at her house. The ones outside are real, but the ones inside are fake. Unless it's Mother's Day, and then we send her roses. Real, not fake.

Thank you, Leo. That was very nice.

Magozzi dusted off his own memories as they entered Gerald Stenson's office, which was bereft of his wife's hippie influence. It was a simple, stark room with a desk, photography equipment, electronics, and hundreds of photographs on the walls, in folders, and spread out loose on every available flat surface. One particular image, framed and hanging on the wall, caught his eye – it was a black-and-white of snowy woods under a full moon. Shadows from the gnarled branches of oaks painted a striking overlay on the snow that looked like a network of veins.

Kris noticed Magozzi's attention to the print and tenderly touched the glass protecting it. 'That's my favorite. He called it "Life Blood of the Woods." He thought the shadows of the branches on the snow looked like veins on pale skin.'

'I was thinking the same thing.'

'Then you have a good eye. He won an award for this.'

'Impressive,' Magozzi said, meaning it.

Kris sat down in front of the computer and entered a password. 'All of his work-related documents are in these two folders. One is just photographs. The other is business correspondence and notes on projects. If there's anything here, it would be in that folder.'

Magozzi and Gino hunted and pecked for the better part of an hour, then searched other folders that Kris hadn't pointed out, but Gerald Stenson's computer yielded nothing more than precise schedules of gigs and possibilities for new ones, Norwood's included. There were a few notes on taconite mining in northern Minnesota, sketches on the wolf-to-moose population on Isle Royale, but nothing more than that. Stenson was heavy on the photography, and light on the investigative journalism.

The *Whisperer* wasn't exactly a lead, but they called the paper anyhow and spoke to the publisher, an unpleasant man named Corey Lefkowitz. He was defensive about his paper and explained that Gregory Norwood was as close to a celebrity as Minnesota got, since Prince was dead, and people bought papers to get a glimpse into a life they couldn't imagine, either because of money or tragedy or both. Everybody had to make a living, right?

They left Kris Stenson with a positive message about the justice they hoped to deliver, then left the house in the darkest of moods to head back to City Hall. Hopefully, Gregory Norwood's phone records would be waiting for them at the office and his computer would have been delivered to Tommy Espinoza. It was time to start the post-mortem dismantling of his digital life.

It should have been no surprise that Amanda White was there to intercept them on the sidewalk, where vehicular evasion was not an option. They could have taken off on foot, but that would have looked bad.

'I'm happy I caught up with you, Detectives.' She gave them a droll smile that showed a lot of blindingly white teeth. 'I'm sure you're happy to see me, too. Just guessing here, but I don't think Norwood killed himself. In fact, I believe you're working a double-homicide now, aren't you? Gregory Norwood and Gerald Stenson.'

Magozzi tried to keep his deteriorating mood in check. Gerald Stenson's name and cause of death hadn't been released yet, but of course Amanda White knew. She'd probably been staking out his house ever since she'd seen them going through his Honda that morning, and it wouldn't be hard to figure out what went down when two sets of homicide detectives showed up at the door.

'This is getting very interesting, isn't it, Detectives? Gerald Stenson working a gig at the Norwoods' this morning, then turning up dead in William O'Brien state park. Surely not an unfortunate hiking accident.'

Magozzi accepted the grim fact that bullshit was futile from this point on. Amanda White was smart and almost as connected as any cop. 'We haven't officially called homicide in either case.'

'Thanks for that,' she said sarcastically.

'Are you planning to run something along these lines?'

She lifted a shoulder. 'Is there any reason I shouldn't?'

'It's your career, Ms White,' Gino said, in a scary-calm voice. 'I'd hate to see you embarrass yourself by jumping to conclusions without all the facts.'

'I appreciate your genuine concern, Detective. Call me anytime. Especially if you feel it becomes necessary to control the message.'

Gino watched her strut away on her ridiculous heels. 'That woman is evil.'

Twenty-six

Grace didn't know why, but she felt compelled to call Magozzi. He answered immediately, as he always did, and she felt a little guilty that she had probably just launched him into another tail-spin of premature fatherly anticipation. 'I'm just checking in, Magozzi. I'm not giving birth at the moment, in case you were wondering.'

She heard Magozzi chortle and the mirthful sound made her smile.

'I'm always wondering about that lately. Any signs?'

'You're worried about your bet?'

'Desperately worried. I have twenty bucks on the line. But I win either way.'

'Nice recovery. What's happening at City Hall?'

'We're on high alert and all hands are on deck. The joint terrorism task force swept the building and cleared it, and there's ongoing surveillance inside and out. How about you? Any progress tracing the chatter?'

'We're getting closer. Right now we're waiting for somebody to make a mistake. That's how this kind of thing breaks sometimes.'

'Sort of like a homicide case.'

'Speaking of that, how's your case going?'

'It's going, but not in the direction we thought. It'll be a late night.'

'Same for us.'

'So you'll probably be staying at Harley's.'

'Not tonight. Harley and I are meeting with Dahl and Shafer tomorrow morning at eight to pitch an operational version of the program and I need to be fresh for it.'

'Huh. So do you want some company later?'

'Sure, but I'll probably be asleep.'

'I'll be sure to wake you up. Not with my snoring, I hope.'

Grace smiled to herself. 'Was that a tasteless, awkwardly delivered sexual innuendo?'

'I'm deeply offended you would even infer such a thing.'

'No offense intended.' Grace felt Charlie bump against her leg and reached down to pat his head. 'Magozzi, do you have anything from your childhood that you still think about?'

'A ton of things. My first tackle box. My Teenage Mutant Ninja Turtles pajamas. Hanging out with Granddad before he went into full-on dementia. Getting benched before the big Homecoming game when I was a senior in high school.'

'Why did you get benched?'

'Because I was a horseshit quarterback. And I may have been caught underage drinking with the coach's daughter, I really don't remember.'

'Uh-huh.'

'Why are you asking?'

'Idle curiosity. Do you ever wonder what pieces really matter?'

'They all do. But nothing matters more than the future. I learned that from Granddad even when his mind was almost gone.'

'Okay. I'll see you later.'

*

Magozzi hung up and thought what a strange conversation that had been. For most people, it would have been normal, but for Grace, it was anything but. She never delved into such waters: asking about somebody else's past opened the door for others to ask about hers, and it hadn't been a good one. But she was obviously revisiting some things, and it was troubling her mind. Or maybe this was how she was freeing herself from old shackles so she could start fresh.

He felt glad that he'd passed along Granddad's little pearl of wisdom that the future was more important than the present or the past, even if you didn't know what it would bring.

'How's Grace?' Gino asked.

Magozzi stirred from his reverie. 'Good.'

'Why do you have a funny look on your face?'

He shrugged. 'She asked me if there was anything I still thought about from my childhood.'

'Ah, that's where the Teenage Mutant Ninja Turtles pajamas come in.'

'Don't tell anybody.'

Gino's mouth quirked up in a funny half-smile. 'I had a pair myself. So Grace is doing a little soul-searching. Perfectly natural. She's at a big crossroads.'

'Yeah, she is.'

'When Angela was pregnant with Helen, she did the same thing, decided to start scrap-booking so the kid would have a detailed history of her parents when she was older. She filled up five albums with stuff I didn't even know she still had, like the corsage I got her for senior prom and a really embarrassing picture of me doing a beer bong in Ryan Waite's parents' backyard after graduation. I had to censor the damn things page by page. It took me forever.'

'I'd pay good money to get my hands on that picture.'

'Dream on. I torched it, along with the photo of me puking my guts out in the Waite family shrubbery after aforementioned beer bong. Women should never be allowed to get their hands on a camera, remember that.'

Magozzi chuckled. 'And eighteen-year-olds should never be allowed to get their hands on a beer bong.'

'You make an excellent point.'

'Anything pop in Norwood's phone records?'

Gino shifted back in his chair and held up a thick sheaf of papers. 'Do you have any idea how many calls Norwood made and received every day? It's insane, and this only goes back six months. We could spend a year parsing through this.'

'Fortunately, you're a highly skilled parser. You have something, I can tell.'

'Maybe. I've eliminated most of his legit contacts – friends, family, business associates – but there are some anomalies over the past few months, incoming calls from numbers that have no association with any person or business he was in contact with. And they're untraceable.'

'Untraceable, like from a throw-away phone?'

'You got it. And each untraceable number is different. If it was the same person calling, they used a new phone every time.'

'Did you try calling the numbers?'

Gino scowled. 'What a supremely insulting question. Of course I called the numbers. They're all out of service.'

'That's fairly suspicious.'

'So is the fact that one of these calls came in this morning before he got killed.'

'You think Norwood was into something?'

'A murder, mysterious phone calls, and a bag of cash in his office? Takes the mind on some alternative paths, doesn't it?'

Magozzi settled back into his chair and processed what Gino had just told him. 'Rosalie said her father got obsessed with his son's death a few months ago. That's when these calls started.'

Gino picked up his phone. 'I'm calling Tommy Espinoza. Maybe he can track down these numbers. It's a long shot, but not unheard of.' Tommy answered and Gino gave him a quick run-down, then hung up and looked at the wall clock. 'Let's go meet Dubnik. He might have some answers.'

'Right, so be nice to him.'

'I'm nice to everybody. Unless they piss me off.'

Twenty-seven

Gary Juneau squinted as his boss hunched over his shoulder at the dispatch desk, withering him with raw-onion breath from whatever lunch he'd eaten. Probably a *gyro* from the Greek bodega down the street. It was a decent place with decent food, but second-hand fumes from anybody else's meal were revolting, especially when they were getting exhaled straight into your face.

As a rule, he didn't entirely dislike Lloyd – he was a leathery old curmudgeon and a skinflint, and he had an unpredictable, salty temper that came up like a loud and sudden storm, but usually faded just as fast. If you overlooked those negative qualities, he was a decent employer who always made payroll on time and didn't dig too deep into your past. But the old man was going full-on nuclear now, pummeling him with hysterical questions, and his opinion of Lloyd started dropping way down into subterranean territory.

'What do you mean the transponder's off?' Lloyd shrieked in his ear.

Gary recoiled and poked a finger at the screen. 'See there? It's off. And I haven't been able to raise him by radio or phone.'

'So we don't know where my fucking truck is?'

'No, sir. The last place the transponder was functional was at one-eleven Washington Avenue, one of Jim's scheduled delivery stops.'

Lloyd uprighted himself, and started pacing the dispatch room, cussing under his breath, then launched another onion-scented assault. 'So you're telling me that son of a bitch took off with my truck and my equipment?'

Gary clenched his jaw. 'I don't know what happened, Lloyd. I'm just telling you what the computer's telling me. The transponder on his unit is dead and I can't raise Jim.'

Lloyd craned his skinny turkey neck to get closer to the computer screen. 'Did he log in his delivery on Washington Avenue?'

Gary started tapping his keyboard. 'I think so . . . Yeah, at three oh five. Ten minutes later is when I lost contact.'

Lloyd took a few deep breaths. Or else he was hyperventilating, Gary wasn't sure. 'Keep trying to raise him. I have to do damage control on the rest of his deliveries.'

Gary hesitated. He'd worked with Jim for five years and he was a stand-up guy, a friend. Sure, he was an ex-con, but half the guys here were, including himself. He wouldn't just disappear with Lloyd's truck. No way. Besides, what would be the point? 'You think he got truck-jacked or something?'

'That better be what happened to him.'

'Should I call the cops and report it?'

Lloyd puffed up like a blowfish and red blotches flared on his bony, sunken cheeks. Gary had always wondered if the old man wasn't just one meltdown away from a heart attack. Maybe today was the day.

'I don't want you to do a goddamned thing except the job I hired you to do, Gary. I've got ten other trucks and drivers on the road you need to watch. I'll handle the situation with Jim.'

'Got it.' He watched Lloyd storm to his office and slam the door, then tried to raise Jim again. He would have called his house, but he lived alone and, as far as he knew, there wasn't a lady in his life. In fact, there wasn't much of anything in his life except his job and his AA meetings.

Lloyd Nasif sank into his office chair and pressed his temples, trying to squeeze away the sharp pain behind his eyes. Son of a bitch. He should have listened to his gut. He'd had a bad feeling about this whole transaction, but it had been such easy money, and sending his most reliable man to make the delivery had seemed like an iron-clad plan. But maybe Jim wasn't so reliable. Maybe Jim had finally had enough and was fencing the rest of his equipment before he made a run for the border.

His arthritic hands were trembling as he dug into his desk drawer for the untraceable phone he kept for times like this. Just in case.

Gus answered on the first ring. 'This better be pretty fucking important, Lloyd. I'm in the middle of something.'

'It is pretty fucking important. Where's my truck and my driver? He logged in his delivery with you and disappeared.'

'How the hell should I know?'

Lloyd paused to rattle out some antacids from the bottle on his desk. 'You got the delivery, right?'

'Yep. And you got the cash, so we're done. Your driver and your truck are your problems now. But if I were you, I wouldn't call the cops.' Gus laughed and hung up.

Twenty-eight

The Chatham's posh bar was much livelier than it had been earlier in the afternoon. It was filled with a mélange of chic young partiers wearing designer mating plumage, businessmen and women in suits drinking away the ardors of the workday, and tourist types in flip-flops, shorts, and sundresses. It was an interesting cross-section.

It suddenly occurred to Magozzi that they might run into Rosalie Norwood here and wouldn't that be awkward? Thankfully, she was nowhere in sight, but Malachai Dubnik was, conspicuous to them even at a far corner table as the only character who truly stood out in this varied but predictable human stew. Nobody else seemed to notice him – superficially, he fit in well here in his fine suit, and any jagged edges from his past career in Hollywood Robbery-Homicide had been smoothed by his time working in the more rarified environment of private for-hire. But he retained the unmistakable edge and demeanor of a tough, seasoned cop and his impressive build suggested he hadn't let his gym membership expire. He was totally bald, with a shiny, smooth scalp, not a hint that there had ever been a single hair sprouting from it.

He saw them approach and stood with a subdued smile. 'Detectives, nice to meet you both. Have a seat. Whatever you're drinking, I'm buying. I recommend the passion-fruit caipirinha. It's nothing I'd ever order as a cop, but I'm not a cop anymore, so I drink what I like.'

'Thanks for meeting with us,' Magozzi said, shaking his hand. It was impossible not to notice that Dubnik's head wasn't the only part of him that was hairless – there wasn't an eyebrow or eyelash in sight. It was startling, like looking at an unfinished person.

'Alopecia universalis,' he explained. 'They think it's an autoimmune disorder where your body attacks all your hair follicles. I like to be upfront about it, because it's pretty damn hard to ignore. Of course I've gotten a lot of mileage out of it, too. Especially in the interrogation room. It's not too hard to get some brainless dirtbag thinking you've been in a nuclear accident and developed super-powers, like mind-reading.'

Gino broke out in a grin. 'That's good.'

'You've got to make the most of what the Lord gave you – or didn't give you for that matter – right?'

A server appeared and took drink orders: Magozzi requested a bourbon, neat, and Gino got on board with the passion-fruit caipirinha.

Dubnik passed a thick folder across the table. 'This is everything I have on the Norwood case, including the time I chased down his son's sorry ass in India a few years ago. That was the first time I dealt with Norwood.'

'Why was he in India?' Gino asked.

'He was a drug tourist. Half dead by the time I found him and not a piece of paper on him – he'd been robbed blind. I had to smuggle him out of the country on a private plane.'

Magozzi had initially liked Dubnik, but now he was afraid they were dealing with a spinner of yarns, a self-aggrandizing purveyor of the tallest of tales. 'That's a little above and beyond the call of duty, isn't it?'

Dubnik shrugged. 'Norwood didn't want information, he wanted his son back in the country, period, whatever it took. I was compensated accordingly. Ask me some questions, I'll tell you what I know. I've got half an hour before I have to head to the airport.'

Magozzi opened the folder and skimmed through it. 'Why was Gregory Norwood suddenly so convinced his son was murdered when he'd clearly OD'd?'

'Because a guy named August Riskin contacted him and told him so. Said he had details, but it was going to cost him.'

Magozzi and Gino shared a look as things clicked into place. 'So he was being conned.'

'Yeah. Pretty low, right? Call a rich, grieving parent, tell them you know who killed their kid, then string them along and make them pay for info they don't have. Nobody wants to believe their kid OD'd, even if that's what the coroner's report says.'

Gino took a tentative sip of his drink. 'No offense, but why would Norwood hire a PI instead of going straight to the authorities?'

'I asked him the same thing. All he told me was he wanted to keep the whole thing on the down-low, and he wouldn't answer any of my questions. He made it clear my only job was to find Riskin, and I haven't been able to do that. A couple years ago, his trail went stone cold, like he dropped off the face of the earth, so I started digging deeper.'

'What did you learn?'

'There's a family connection. His parents were the managers and part-time caretakers at the Norwoods' properties in Aspen until his older sister Clara was murdered. Bludgeoned with a piece of wood. She was fourteen.'

'Jesus.'

'This world is a sick place, but I don't have to tell you two that.'

'No, you don't.'

He let out a heavy sigh. 'The Riskins packed it up after the trial, moved to Kalispell, Montana, and the family fell apart. And I mean really fell apart. His mom ate a bottle of Oxy a few years later, and when Gus turned eighteen, his father hanged himself.'

Gino shook his head. 'Not a real surprise the kid didn't turn out so great. Was there a conviction in the murder trial?'

'Yeah, it was short and sweet, a slam-dunk. Pitkin County nailed some drifter, a Richard "Kip" Kuehn. History of violence, substance abuse, and severe mental illness. They found him passed out near the crime scene and his DNA was all over her body and the piece of wood he'd killed her with. He'd rolled into town a few months earlier, floating himself as a handyman, taking odd jobs for cash. Did some work for the Norwoods.'

'Norwood doesn't exactly strike me as the kind of guy who'd hire a violent, mentally ill drifter to work his property,' Gino commented.

'Norwood didn't. The Riskins did. That was their job as managers. In places like Aspen, where there are a lot of part-time owners who only pop in every few months, it's not unusual for property managers to subcontract on the cheap, then give their absentee employers falsified invoices. They usually do it in collusion with the subcontractor and split the profit. Hell, if you're worth a few hundred mil or a billion, who's going to notice ten or twenty grand? At least, that's the theory behind it, but it's a flawed theory, because some people do notice.' He spread his hairless hands on the table. 'Look, I'm not saying that's what the Riskins did, I'm just telling you like it is. Half my work is this sort of thing. I'd be on food stamps without it.'

'Do you know what happened to Riskin after his father killed himself?'

'From what I could piece together, he left Montana and headed to sunny So-Cal. He got cozy with the Hessians and had some scrapes with the law for assault. If you don't know, the Hessians are one of the nastier West Coast biker clubs that excel in drug distribution. Evil sons of bitches, every last one of them, they'd douse a box of puppies with gasoline and set them on fire to stay warm. And that's all I know.'

'You said you were in town chasing down some leads. What are they?'

'Did I say leads? I meant one lead. A meth head named Milo Parr. Former Hessian, did some time in San Quentin for felony possession and manslaughter, pled down from murder two. I have a source in Orange County who told me Riskin and Parr used to run together before he got thrown into the Q. Thought it was worth checking out.'

'Parr is in Minnesota now?'

'Yep, living back in his home town of Rush City. He

doesn't answer his phone, but his address is in the folder. If you pay him a visit, keep your eyes wide open. He's built like a Sherman tank and he's a total sociopath. Once a meth head, always a meth head.' He checked his Patek Philippe and casually tossed a hundred onto the table. 'Sorry, but I have to get to the airport. Call me anytime.'

Twenty-nine

'So, what do you think?'

'I think this passion-fruit caipirinha is the bomb. You want a sip, Leo?'

Magozzi released a long-suffering sigh. 'I'm talking about what Dubnik said.'

Gino chewed the end of his straw while his eyes wandered around the lively room. 'This case just got a hell of a lot weirder, along with Norwood's behavior. Hell, he knew who was squeezing him for cash. He had a name. Any rational person would have gone straight to the cops, not taken things into their own hands. And, seriously, what was his plan once he found Riskin? Kidnap and torture him?'

'The fact that Norwood didn't want this to see the light of day is a good place to start. Let's go talk to the family about it, then pay Milo Parr a visit.' He called Rosalie and she answered on the second ring.

'Good evening, Detective Magozzi. Do you have some news for us?'

'We're in the area. Do you mind if we stop by?'

'Of course not. I'll tell security we're expecting you.'

'Hotel security?'

'No, we have somebody at the door. See you soon.'

Magozzi hung up. 'They have security now.'

'I would, too. They thought all along Norwood was

murdered. Why take the chance that he was the only Norwood on the hit list?'

Gino and Magozzi were both a little taken aback when they approached Betty Norwood's room and saw Conrad, the same man who'd escorted them into Robert Zeller's house, standing guard at the door. He still looked like a tough-guy butler, but this time he was definitely carrying.

'Detectives.' He nodded politely and pushed open the door for them.

'Do you have any refreshments?' Gino couldn't help himself.

Conrad didn't take the bait. 'I'm sure the Norwoods can offer you something.'

Magozzi gave Gino a sharp nudge as they walked into the suite, reminding him to keep it cool. He could be Prince Charming, but he was a brawler at heart – a commendable trait, but one that had to be checked occasionally.

The suite looked more lived-in now, with an array of half-eaten, half-drunk food and wine on the dining-room table. The overall atmosphere was of a wake, which, essentially, it was. The only surprise was Robert Zeller, which explained Conrad guarding the door.

Betty greeted them as politely as before, but she had a little more color in her hollow cheeks and seemed slightly less dolorous. Maybe she'd had some wine. 'Thank you for stopping by, Detectives. You've met Robert, of course.'

He greeted them cordially but impersonally, like they were constituents at a town-hall meeting. 'Detectives. I can't tell you how much we all appreciate your attentiveness. How are things progressing with Gregory's case?'

Magozzi turned to Betty Norwood. 'We're investigating your husband's death as a homicide, ma'am.'

She was silent for a long moment, then nodded. 'I'm glad to hear that. I won't ever believe Gregory took his own life and I'm counting on you to get to the bottom of this.'

'He was murdered?' Zeller asked in disbelief. 'Are you certain?'

'Yes.'

'My God. Do you have any leads?'

'We've been following up on several things. One was a photo-journalist named Gerald Stenson, who was assaulted on your property this morning, Mrs Norwood. His body was found in William O'Brien state park this afternoon. We wanted to let you know before the media got a hold of the story.'

Her hand fluttered to her mouth. 'That's horrible.'

'I know his name, Detectives.' Zeller's voice was chilly. 'He was a photographer who made regular contributions to a disreputable local paper called the *Whisperer*. I've filed several cease-and-desist orders over the years for libel against the Norwood family. Corey Lefkowitz is the publisher, and he is unequivocally a despicable human being.'

'We spoke with him this afternoon and got the same impression,' Gino said. 'Did anything stick in court?'

'No. We all have First Amendment rights, and the *Whisperer* was clever enough to keep their chicanery within those boundaries. I certainly hope you're considering him as a person of interest. He is rapacious and, morally, one short step away from causing any kind of calamity he could profit from.'

A door opened and Rosalie appeared, now dressed in workout clothes. Magozzi wondered how many rooms there were in a suite at the Chatham. Hell, maybe one of them was a gym. He would probably never know without a search warrant.

'Do you have any new information, Detectives? Were you able to reach that Malachai or Melchi person?'

Zeller's unnaturally smooth brow puckered. 'Who is Malachai?'

'A private detective.' She took her mother's hands and squeezed them gently. 'Mom, Father believed Trey was murdered. He hired the detective a few months ago to look into it.'

Betty bristled and released her daughter's hands. 'That's ridiculous. We all know how Trey died and your father wouldn't do something so foolish.'

'We just spoke with the detective,' Gino said. 'He confirmed.'

'Well, he didn't share this with me. And neither did you, Rosalie. Why on earth not?'

'Father asked me not to say anything. He didn't want to upset you and neither did I.'

'Did you know about this, Robert?'

Zeller seemed genuinely bewildered. 'No. Gregory never said anything to me.'

Betty's eyes locked onto Magozzi's. 'What does this have to do with your murder investigation?'

'We're trying to find out if it does. A man named August Riskin had been in contact with your husband recently . . .' Magozzi paused when all three of them froze, their mouths simultaneously forming stunned Os.

'Gus Riskin?' Betty finally asked. 'The son of our caretakers?'

'Yes, ma'am. He told him he had information that Trey had been murdered, and we believe your husband was paying him to try to get that information.'

Betty covered her mouth and sank to a chair. Rosalie's big eyes got even bigger, and Zeller's face turned a dark shade of crimson. 'That's sick . . . twisted. Cruel. And after everything Gregory did for the family.'

Gino lifted a questioning brow. 'What did he do?'

'Gregory paid for the Riskin family's relocation after Gus's sister was murdered. They couldn't bear to stay in Aspen after what happened to Clara, but they had no property of their own to sell to cover the expenses.'

Rosalie shook her head. 'This doesn't make any sense. The last time any of us saw Gus Riskin he was ten years old. Why would Father believe him?'

Betty pulled a lace-trimmed handkerchief from the pocket of her dress. She wasn't crying yet, but it seemed like a preemptory move in case the faucet turned on unexpectedly. 'Because he wanted to, Rosalie. He needed to. If Trey was murdered, there would be a chance of justice for him and exoneration for us.'

Magozzi saw Rosalie's jaw set stubbornly. She wasn't going to let this go, and that was a good thing, if for nothing else than to give her something to focus on that would help deflect her grief. 'Or maybe he had a reason to believe him. What if Gus and Trey reconnected at some point after Aspen and he really does have some information –'

Zeller interrupted her with a tender pat on the arm. 'Rosalie, what happened to your brother, it was a terrible tragedy, but it wasn't murder. We need to focus on who killed your father, and the detectives are doing that.'

'Is he a suspect in my father's murder, Detective Magozzi?'

'He's definitely a person of interest. If any of you think of something that might be helpful, please let us know as soon as possible.' He looked at Rosalie. 'As you mentioned earlier, every piece of information can be crucial, no matter how insignificant it may seem.'

She nodded in resolve. 'Trey and I used to be very close. I'll look through all his old emails tonight. Maybe I can find some kind of a clue in them.'

Thirty

'They were all totally clueless about Riskin,' Gino commented, as they hiked it back to the parking garage.

'Yeah. But Rosalie said something interesting about Trey and Riskin hooking up at some point after Aspen. Riskin was in So-Cal running with a gang that distributed drugs and Trey did them. He could have been his dealer.'

'Maybe. But I don't see how that gets us any closer to Norwood's killer.'

'Norwood gets killed on the one-year anniversary of his son's death, a couple months after Riskin got in contact with him. The guy has a criminal history and he was conning him. Maybe things went sour and Riskin is our guy.' Magozzi buckled himself into the passenger seat and opened Dubnik's folder. 'Head north. We're looking for Flamingo Terrace Trailer Court in Rush City.'

Gino shook his head. 'Bad things happen in trailer courts, Leo.'

'Hopefully not tonight.'

Gino leaned over and peered at the folder. 'Are you kidding me? Is that Parr's mugshot?'

'Yeah.'

'Dubnik wasn't fooling. The guy's a monster. I mean, he doesn't even look human. He could probably pinch our heads right off our necks.'

'Not much else to do in prison except throw iron.'

'Christ. Call the locals and make sure there's back-up available.'

The brutal heat and humidity had already peaked for the day by the time Magozzi and Gino arrived at Flamingo Terrace Trailer Court, but it was still in the nineties and the air was so heavy with moisture that Magozzi felt like he was drowning each time he took a breath. Gino's face turned instantly red the minute he stepped out of the air-conditioned sedan and he rattled off a litany of complaints.

'You complain more in the summer than you do in the winter. You should be enjoying this. It won't last long.'

Gino snorted. 'I won't last long either if this weather doesn't break. And I don't complain more in the summer – I loathe extreme temperatures whatever side of zero they're on.'

Magozzi looked at the decrepit trailer that was supposedly the humble abode of Milo Parr and pointed to a gasping window air-conditioner. 'You're in luck – our felon friend's got AC.'

'That thing couldn't cool down a shoebox on a good day.'

'We'll see.'

If Milo Parr's trailer had seen maintenance in the past century, that was news to Magozzi. What little was left of the siding was shredded, pockmarked with hail dents from storms over the years, sagging and ready to take the plunge into the uncut crabgrass lawn to join the rest of its brethren that had already made the fall. Nobody had bothered to clean up, and he wondered why the neighbors, who had relatively tidy domiciles on either side, didn't complain. Maybe Milo Parr wasn't somebody you complained to. His history and mug shot supported the theory.

They mounted crooked, pulpy wooden stairs that led to the front door. It was nothing short of a miracle that the rotting structure didn't collapse beneath their combined weight.

'Jesus!' Gino barked, when a malnourished pitbull exploded around the corner and got yanked just short of his ankle by the thick chain around its neck.

The dog's incessant barking was part snarl, part desperation. Gino backed away from the snapping jaws, reached into his jacket, and pulled out a granola bar. The dog went instantly silent, settled onto its haunches, and whined. 'Poor thing,' Gino mumbled, unwrapping the bar and tossing it to the dog.

The dog gobbled it down in a single bite, then whined again, looking up at Gino expectantly with sad brown eyes.

'Let's go kill this fucker and take his dog.'

They had their hands firmly on their weapons when they rapped on the bent, flimsy aluminum door of the trailer and announced themselves. They were waiting for the beefy thug whose mug shot had shown a hungry, sneering grimace, like he was ready to eat the person behind the camera. And maybe he had. But the hollow-eyed, physically wasted man who appeared at the door in boxers and a sweat-stained tank wasn't that guy.

Once a meth head, always a meth head, Dubnik had said, but aside from his wretched physical appearance, he wasn't showing any of the tell-tale tweaks or tics of an active user.

'Milo Parr?'

He gummed the cigarette sticking out of the side of his mouth. 'Who's asking?' he rasped, then expelled a sickening, liquid-sounding cough along with the lit cigarette. He stooped to pick it up, then stuck it back in his mouth.

'Minneapolis Police.'

His watery eyes narrowed as he looked them up and down through a screen patched with duct tape. The smell of marijuana was drifting out of the trailer in a massive, putrid wave, which explained his mellowness. 'Don't look like cops to me.'

'That's because we're homicide detectives,' Gino snapped back. 'You know a little something about homicide detectives, don't you, Milo?'

'Fuck,' he muttered, pushing open the door to let them in and more marijuana miasma to escape. 'Whoever's dead, I ain't got nothing to do with it.'

'We'll see about that. So you are Milo Parr?'

'Affirmative, Chief. The one and only. I'd ask you to make yourselves comfortable, but I don't really give a shit if you're comfortable or not.' He kicked a teetering stack of mail, old newspapers, and bags of empty beer cans out of their path, a grandiose gesture of hospitality if Magozzi ever saw one. Milo really did give a shit, beneficent soul that he was.

He sank into a ratty corduroy sofa and dropped his spent cigarette into a beer can that was tucked between the cushions. It sizzled for a moment, then died. 'Whatever you got to say, make it quick 'cause I got radiation in an hour. A fucking year of that shit and they keep telling me it still might work. I don't see it working, do you?'

Magozzi didn't, and it wasn't breaking his heart, seeing an unrepentant, violent felon a wispy shadow of his former bad-ass biker self. His body was shrunken; his hair and beard were lank and gray. His tattooed arms looked like deflated balloons, distorting the images in ink that had been etched into his skin while he'd still had hams on the bones that showed now. But there was still something sinister about what was left of Milo Parr – his empty eyes, his indolent demeanor. 'Our murder victim had cancer, too, but he didn't get a chance to try radiation or chemo because somebody shot him in the head.'

'Lucky fucker. If I had any brains, I'd shoot myself in the head.' His eyes skittered to a cluttered Formica table that listed in the corner of the trailer, like a drunk. 'Just so you know, there's a loaded gun on that table. If I went for it right now, would you shoot me?'

Gino pulled his gun. 'You want to find out, asshole?'

Magozzi's heart was slamming in his chest as he retrieved a nice Smith & Wesson 629 and emptied the chamber. 'You are one stupid son of a bitch, aren't you?' he seethed. 'Maybe you forgot felons can't possess firearms.'

'It's not my gun.'

'I know it's not your gun. Where'd you steal it? It's a little too nice for a street piece, so I'm thinking burglary.'

'Hey, it's not stolen, it's my old lady's. She likes big guns.' He let out a crackling chuckle.

Gino re-holstered his weapon. 'It's in your house. That's good enough to throw you back in.' He sniffed the air. 'Cancer's a bitch. That's why you smoke pot, huh?'

'Doctor's orders. I got a slip.'

'Bullshit. Medical marijuana in Minnesota is limited to pills and tea. Looks like your day is getting worse by the minute.'

'Uh-huh. So two homicide detectives are here to bust my dying ass over a gun and a joint?'

'Your dog dying of cancer too?'

'Not my gun, not my dog.'

'Let me guess: it belongs to your old lady. You might want to tell her to feed it once in a while.'

'We're here to ask you some questions about Gus Riskin,' Magozzi interjected.

'Don't know any Gus Riskin.' He looked back at Gino. 'She's not feeding the dog?'

'The dog's skinnier than you and tied up on a chain. I didn't see any water, either, and it's really fucking hot and humid outside. In addition to the gun and the pot, we could cite you for cruelty to animals, but we might want to cite you for something else, like murder, so let's say we let the little things slide for the time being.'

'That stupid bitch.' Milo eased himself from the sofa with evident pain, then hobbled to the kitchen. Magozzi kept a sharp eye on him, kept his hand on his gun, but there was nothing more nefarious going on than Milo filling a plate with store-bought rotisserie chicken and filling a bowl with water. 'I didn't kill anybody.'

'You sure?' Gino asked.

'I gotta take care of the dog,' he muttered, juggling the two items as he headed for the front door unsteadily.

'Sit your ass back down. I'll handle the dog.' Gino took the dishes from him.

While Milo and Gino had an animal-welfare moment, Magozzi looked around the hot, sad, foul-smelling room. Gino was right – the window air-conditioner couldn't cool a shoebox on a good day, and they were essentially in a shoebox fitted poorly for human habitation. The humidity had seeped into every crevice, warping cheap paneled walls, and the odors of marijuana and deep-fry oil were heavy in the wet air, penetrating everything.

There were cheap, lighted beer signs tacked up on the trailer's walls, several faded, curling posters of biker babes suggestively straddling Harleys in bikinis, and a single framed and matted piece that looked wildly incongruent in a decaying dump like this, even though it was a simple rendering of a tattoo: the word 'angel' in classic tat-Goth lettering, with nice shading on a flesh-colored background. The former artist in him noted the refinement of the work, the high-quality paper, the mahogany frame, the precisely cut matting. It was definitely as hot as the gun.

'That's a fine-looking piece,' Magozzi said, when Milo sat down on the sofa and lit another cigarette.

His hazy eyes drifted up to the print and he smiled, displaying his misgivings about dentistry. 'I like it.'

'Looks like it's worth something.'

'I paid a hundred bucks for it.'

'Where'd you buy it?'

'From a friend of mine.'

'Gus Riskin?'

'I told you already, I don't know any Gus Riskin.'

Magozzi got up and examined the print more closely, saw a signature and date in the bottom right corner and no print number. It was an original. 'You got the frame and everything for a hundred bucks?'

'Told you, the guy was my friend.' He stretched out the flaccid skin on his biceps to reveal a tattoo that read 'Angel' in the same Gothic lettering. 'Got this when I was fifteen. He gave me a deal because the picture matched my tat.'

'Thoughtful friend. So what brought you back to Minnesota after you did time in California?'

'Wanted to get as far the fuck away from California when I got cut loose from the Q. I grew up here, figured it was as good a place as any. Don't know why I stuck around, though – the weather sucks.'

'Are you still using, Milo? Besides the pot.'

'Shit, no. I'm clean. Got a lot of chemicals in my body, courtesy of the doctors who are fucking me up worse than the cancer.'

Magozzi almost believed him. 'So you don't know Gus Riskin?'

'Christ. No. Doesn't matter how many times you ask me, the answer's gonna be the same.' He squinted through a fog of cigarette smoke as Gino walked into the trailer with a satisfied look on his face.

'Milo here says he doesn't know Gus Riskin.'

Gino rubbed his chin thoughtfully. 'Huh. We heard different.'

Milo gave him an ugly sneer. 'Well, whoever told you that is full of shit.'

'Yeah? Let's talk about what happens to you if you're withholding information and obstructing a homicide investigation. On top of parole violations.'

While Gino led Milo down a different path, keeping his

paranoid, shriveled brain busy, Magozzi took the opportunity to wander around the trailer in small, innocuous circles, soaking up every detail he could. He expanded his perimeter to the back while the cockroach tried to stumble his way through the increasingly combative questions Gino was asking him.

Sounds and a movement outside caught his eye through an open window with threadbare, dusty bedsheets tacked up with nails as curtains. A straggly, bleached-blond, black roots halfway down to her ears, was stumbling through the yard, barely able to keep upright. The tank top she was wearing didn't cover her loose, wobbly breasts or stomach; likewise, her ragged cut-off jean shorts didn't cover her loose, wobbly behind. At least, not enough of it. Milo's 'old lady.'

As he watched, the sad, skinny pitbull on the chain started going nuts, thrashing against its chain tether, barking. The woman dropped to her knees beside the dog and tried to find its head to pat it. Her motor skills were lacking and so was her speech, but he could make out some of her mostly incoherent words.

'Gussy, buddy, how's my boy? How's my Gus Riskin?'

Son of a bitch. 'Hey, Milo, your dog's got an interesting name,' Magozzi called, then moved to the next window near the very back of the trailer to get a better look at the action outside. He stopped dead when his nose started to burn. It didn't take him long to figure out why. 'Shit,' he muttered, quickly retreating to the front, where Gino was increasingly in Milo's face.

'You got your own chemo suite in the back?'

Milo jerked his head away from Gino and gave Magozzi

180

a startled look. 'What kind of shit talk is that? You making fun of me?'

'I wouldn't make fun of a dying man, just giving you the benefit of the doubt, because you've got some kind of chemicals cooking back there.'

His bony shoulders slumped and he shook his head in defeat. 'Stupid bitch.'

Thirty-one

'Milo, we don't care about the meth, that's not our problem. What we care about is Gus Riskin. You named your dog after him.'

'Get it off your chest, Milo,' Gino snapped. 'We're the least of your problems right now. We can make things better for you or we can make them a lot worse, your choice.'

Magozzi couldn't be sure, but it looked like Milo was actually getting a little emotional. 'Knew him in California. He was part of the brotherhood.'

'The Hessians.'

'Yeah. He was a righteous dude. Took care of things for me when I went in. Visited me a few times, then disappeared. Never saw or heard from him again. I'm pretty sure he's dead. He's gotta be dead or he would have come back to visit me.' Milo pinched his nose and blew snot onto the floor in the absence of any tissues.

Gino looked at Magozzi. 'This guy's a real charmer, isn't he?'

'In a Cro-Magnon kind of way.'

'Well, that wasn't so hard, was it, Milo?' Gino cooed. 'If you'd been upfront with us, we wouldn't have found your chem lab and you wouldn't be looking at dying in prison. Not a smart move, Milo.'

He wiped his nose with the back of his hand. 'I got a target on my back, *Detective*. People still want me dead.

I didn't come back to this shit-hole town because I grew up here. I came back because it's a good place to hide. And when you're a walking bullseye, you don't talk about your past. To anybody.'

Magozzi thought of what Dubnik had told them earlier about Parr's rap sheet. 'Your plea deal to manslaughter – you turned state's evidence, didn't you?'

Milo gave him a black, partially toothless smile. 'Somebody gets it. Everybody I ever knew is dead, and I'm next. The only good thing about cancer is that it'll probably get me first and those cock-suckers won't have the pleasure.'

'Did you know Trey Norwood?'

'Yeah, right, we joined the same country club.'

'Gus Riskin may have been his dealer,' Gino pressed.

Milo got a funny look on his face. 'Gus didn't deal. Worked construction most days, and when he had time off, he was our grease monkey, kept our bikes running.'

The bleached-blond had somehow made it to the front door of the trailer. She stumbled in clumsily, tripped over a bag of empty beer cans, then gasped when she saw the intruders in her corrugated-metal palace. Her face reddened, screwed up in fury, and she gave Milo a withering look that drifted from one side of his face to the other, never quite finding purchase on his eyes. 'What the fuck, Milo, you stupid fuck?'

Gino stood up and twirled an arm authoritatively. What he lacked in stature he made up for in presence. 'Minneapolis Police. Outside, both of you, before this place blows.'

The woman didn't hear Gino: her unfocused eyes were still trained in the general vicinity of Milo. 'You stupid fuck! I told you not to let anyone in here!'

'Stupid bitch,' Milo retorted. 'Stupid fucking bitch.'

'Outside,' Gino said more forcefully, herding out his pathetic flock.

'That was truly heart-warming, wasn't it, seeing a relationship based on mutual love, trust and respect? I felt like I was living a romance novel in a *Breaking Bad* sort of way, and look at them now, riding off into the sunset together in the back of a patrol car.'

Magozzi smirked. 'I guess our friend's going to miss his radiation treatment today.'

'Maybe somebody should have told him cooking meth in a trailer can cause cancer.'

'Who would bother? I'm more worried about what's going to happen to the dog.'

Gino started up the car. 'Got it covered. Animal Control and a pitbull rescue organization are on their way. That dog's finally going to have a life.'

'Happy ending all around, then.'

A patrol walked up to their car, carrying the angel picture in a clear plastic evidence bag, along with a chain-of-evidence sheet. 'Just sign, here, Detective, and it's yours.'

'Thanks, Officer.'

Gino cocked a brow. 'If you were going to steal some of Milo's art, you could have taken one of the biker-babe pictures.'

'This *is* art and it's stolen.'

'How do you know?'

'This is a Ruscha. An original.'

'What's a Ruscha?'

'He's a famous artist. I think Parr got it from Riskin, and I think Riskin stole it from Trey Norwood.'

'Whoa, back up.'

'The Norwoods collect art and I noticed a lot of Ruschas in their house. Maybe Trey Norwood inherited the family passion for modern art, or at least had some of their pieces hanging in his place in Hollywood.'

'So you think Rosalie was right about Trey and Riskin hooking up in California?'

'It seems more probable now.'

'Yeah, but what are we going to do with it? We already knew Riskin is connected to the Norwoods and Milo Parr.'

'It might be important down the road. Even if it isn't, we can return it to its rightful owner. A piece like this has provenance so we'll be able to figure out if it belongs to the Norwoods.'

Gino sighed and pulled out of Flamingo Terrace. 'Riskin is a lynchpin. He could even be our killer. We've got to find him, dead or alive.'

'Nobody seems to be having a lot of luck finding him in the present, so let's look for him in the past, go back to the time when things fell apart on him.'

'Good idea. I'll drive, you dial. No reason to waste an hour just relaxing and enjoying the scenery. Not that there is any scenery. Just jack pines and meth labs.'

'At least we shut one down tonight. And we saved a dog, too, proving that bad things don't always happen in trailer parks.'

'I think this was a one-off.'

Thirty-two

Gary Juneau had cleared the last of the trucks for the day and checked them into the lot out back, but he was taking his time with the paperwork, hoping to hear from Jim. At first he'd been mildly uneasy about the whole situation, but as the clock had ticked down the hours to quitting time, his mood had darkened until he felt a full-blown doom.

He maybe wasn't the sharpest knife in the drawer, but he knew how the cops worked because he'd spent a few years trying to evade them. They would have taken seriously a report of something like this, as a possible jacking or a theft on Jim's part, and there would have been cops here long before now asking questions.

The only possible explanation, at least in his mind, was that Lloyd hadn't called the cops, and that didn't wash. As things stood now, Lloyd was out a truck and some equipment, which probably added up to a hundred grand, maybe a little more. The old man wouldn't take that sitting down. He should have been running around, screaming at the top of his lungs and punching his fists through walls. The fact that he wasn't was a pretty clear indication Lloyd knew more than he was saying, and in that instant, Gary knew Jim was in trouble. The thought made his stomach clench.

Gary looked up when he heard Lloyd's office door creak open. His boss stuck his craggy, scowling face into the space between the door and the jamb, and shouted, 'I'm leaving in five, and if your paperwork's not done by then, don't bother coming in tomorrow morning.'

Gary bit his tongue to stifle a nasty retort. 'Almost finished. What did the cops say?'

'The fuck? They're looking for that piece of shit right now. Not that it's any of your goddamn business.'

'Right,' he muttered under his breath, tapping in his final entry. 'Finished. I'm outta here.'

Lloyd just looked at him with squinty pig eyes, then slammed his office door.

Gary put some distance between himself and Lloyd's HVAC, walking under the hot sun until his shirt was clinging to him like a leech. He didn't mind the heat or the humidity – it reminded him of living in Florida, which had been the best part of his life, back when he'd had a decent future ahead of him and a brand new bicycle. That segment of his existence had been short-lived, from birth to the age of thirteen, but he still had fond memories of it.

He stepped into a dark pub and pulled up a squeaky stool at the bar. The two other customers perched there gave him laconic looks, then refocused on the drinks in front of them without so much as an acknowledgment. That was the kind of place Mario's was, and that was why Gary liked it.

It was a dive, with greasy floors, cast-off furniture, and sagging booths with tears in the red vinyl upholstery that exposed dingy puffs of fill. If you wanted to rack a game of pool, you'd have to play three balls short. If you wanted food to soak up the alcohol, you'd have to go someplace else. But popcorn was free, and that was good enough for Gary.

Mario came out of the back, a lumbering man with curly salt-and-pepper hair and a fleshy face pocked with acne scars. He didn't need a bouncer because he could scare you off with a look, but he was actually a jovial old Italian, who still clung to his accent, even though he'd been in the country for fifty years.

'What'll you have, Gary?' he asked, shaking his hand with his big bear paw.

'The usual, Mario. Just a pint of Guinness.'

'That's as good as a sandwich.'

'Better. So, I never asked you, what's a wop like you doing running an Irish pub?'

He gave him a dour look. 'I'm half Irish.' He executed a fine pour, placed the glass carefully on a coaster along with a basket of popcorn, then erupted in boisterous laughter. 'Just sheeting you, Gary. Not a drop of Mick blood in me, so I guess I can't answer your question, except to tell you the Twin Cities is full of Irish and they like their pubs.'

Gary gave him a weak smile and took a sip, licking the foam from his upper lip.

'Something on your mind?'

Gary shrugged uncomfortably. Keeping your mouth shut was a survival mechanism, but with Mario, it was different – he wasn't a friend exactly, but he was the closest thing to a confidant he had. Besides, bartenders had heard it all, a lot worse than what he had to say. 'My buddy's missing and I'm not sure what to do.'

'I see.' His tone was confidential and quiet. 'Well, if somebody's missing, you call the cops. Simple.'

Not so simple if you were an ex-con sneaking around

behind your employer's back. The fallout was unknown, but one thing was certain: he'd lose his job, either because Lloyd was into something and would end up in jail or because Lloyd would find out he was the one who'd made the call. Gary had never been one to grapple with morality, so his current quandary was like being on an alien battlefield without a light saber. 'It's a long story.'

Mario gave him a shrewd glance. 'So you don't want to call the cops but you do. He's your friend, right? You worry, you want to help?'

Gary nodded miserably.

Mario had a way of rubbing his perennially grizzled jaw circumspectly. It was one of his trademark gestures and it could have any number of meanings, depending on the situation. 'Hmm. Maybe I have a solution for you.'

'What's that?'

'Call from the phone here, make an anonymous tip. No worries, no troubles. Cops get anonymous tips all the time. I turn my back, you make the call, I never saw you.'

Lloyd closed the outside office door and fumbled for his key-ring with shaking hands. He'd eaten half a bottle of Tums today, but his sour stomach was still repeating, sending acid up into his throat. Goddamn Jim Beam goes missing today of all days, and what a jackass he'd been, hiring someone named after booze.

As he shoved the key into the lock, he heard a sound behind him and felt a prickling sense of dread creep up his spine. He turned slowly, sluggishly, like he was executing a clumsy pirouette underwater, but there was nothing to see except his truck in the parking lot and some crows fighting over an empty McDonald's bag that had blown in from the street.

Paranoia will destroy you. The sentence popped into his head and started running an agitating loop. He didn't know where it had come from – an old song, maybe, or something he'd read, but it was persistent and loud in his mind.

He turned back to the door and thought about going inside to get the gun that was locked in his office drawer. Paranoid or not, you never knew what kind of shit could happen in a city, especially during a heat wave like this one. Tempers ran as high as the mercury, which brought every single crazy son of a bitch scuttling out from under their rocks.

He jumped when he heard a string of firecrackers popping in the distance. Or maybe it was gunfire. It was hard to know in this fringe neighborhood that was on the cusp of an uncertain fate – the gangs and the city planners bent on gentrification were in the middle of their own turf war right now. None of that really mattered, though, because he'd made his decision: he was definitely getting his gun.

As he pushed the office door open, he felt something heavy hit him from behind and sailed back into the office with outstretched arms, thinking bizarrely that paranoia didn't destroy you after all – other people did.

Gus walked past 111 Washington Avenue and felt the most amazing sense of freedom and exhilaration. Things were finally coming full circle. He didn't know how his journey would ultimately end but, with luck, he'd be someplace very far away by this time tomorrow.

Two blocks ahead, he saw the archaic red-stone bulk of City Hall. It looked out of place, looming in the shadows of modern steel and glass skyscrapers, and he wondered if it would eventually be razed, like the rest of the old buildings that had been sacrificed in the name of progress in the last century.

As he approached the light rail station in front of City Hall, he was surprised by a heavy police presence, and not just uniforms but a lot of plainclothes and definitely some feds. Maybe they weren't obvious to the average person, but to him they were glaringly apparent, with their furtive, watchful eyes and rigid postures.

Apparently Abdi had fucked up somewhere along the way because law enforcement had clearly had some kind of a heads-up on what they were planning at City Hall. They were all there to prevent the tragedy. Weren't they going to be so goddamned surprised?

He took a seat on a bench on the platform to wait for his train. It was an excellent vantage-point to safely view the low-level panic outside City Hall. He was a little disappointed that his train came so quickly, but he boarded and found a seat in the back, where there were no other passengers, just a discarded Starbucks coffee cup, an M&Ms wrapper, and a morning newspaper opened to the headline: GREGORY NORWOOD, MINNESOTA ICON AND PHILANTHROPIST, FOUND DEAD IN HIS HOME.

That was just a damn shame.

Thirty-three

Roadrunner had disassociated a possible terror attack on Minneapolis from the work he was doing now, the work they were all doing. It was important to compartmentalize to keep focus, keep going, and his entire youth had been a boot camp in that survival strategy. It had evolved over the years, but most of the time, and especially right now, his world was an endless stream of zeros and ones that shielded him from anything bad.

He was vaguely aware that the Monkeewrench office was unusually quiet. The hum of the large bank of computers was always so omnipresent in the room that it barely registered with any of them, and the occasional soft tap of fingers on keyboards seemed faint and distant. Even the deep aches in his lower back and shoulders hardly seemed to exist. His awareness was sharp and singular, focused on the agonizingly slow movement of the progress bar at the top of his monitor as the program processed the data input from Dahl's flash drive in the hope they could pinpoint the location of the terrorists through that.

Time seemed like it was moving through sludge that got more viscous with each passing second. They were asking a lot of a prototype, and none of them were entirely sure the program could get through all the encryption they were hitting, which was why they were all working manually on the hacks while they waited – even Annie, the most skittish of the four of them when it came to crossing questionable lines. But there weren't any lines at all when it came to the possibility of saving lives, and she knew that better than any of them. She'd stabbed a man to death to save her own when she was seventeen.

We have to think of a name for the program. The ridiculous, insignificant thought briefly interrupted the rapid-fire calculations that were consuming his mind. Somehow a name seemed important, even though Minneapolis was potentially on the verge of a tragedy they might or might not be able to prevent. Everything depended on what was happening in the tiny circuitry housed in the far wall of the office, and to a certain degree what happened in the circuitry housed inside their brains.

He stole a glance at Harley sitting next to him, his eyes lasered on his screen. Grace and Annie were at their own stations, equally focused. His leg started pumping up and down as if the motion would speed things along. But what was happening couldn't be rushed. The sources of the data Dahl had given them were hidden in the vast, unfathomable labyrinth of Tor, an onion router with layers of anonymity that made it virtually impossible to trace where traffic was coming from. They had to wait until somebody made a mistake they could exploit.

Virtually impossible, but not entirely impossible. People made mistakes all the time.

A half-hour later, his computer suddenly trilled an alarm and he jumped, feeling a prickly, hot rush of adrenaline shoot through his long limbs. Harley rolled his chair over while Grace and Annie simultaneously strode from their stations to gather around him expectantly. Even

Charlie joined the group, his pink tongue lolling from his mouth, panting in anticipation of some grand proclamation he probably hoped would result in more chicken tenders from Harley.

Roadrunner clicked to enter the alarm screen and jabbed a misshapen finger at the message there, which was flashing a simple, bold display in red letters: TARGET BREACHED, ACCESS GRANTED. He looked up at all of them, catching their stunned, disbelieving eyes before he said, 'We broke the encryption and got through Tor. We've got access to our bad guys. Now we just have to hunt them down.'

Thirty-four

Robert Zeller felt weariness and sorrow sinking deeper into his bones as Conrad pulled the Town Car up to his downtown office building. A cluster of media was loitering on the sidewalk, microphones and cameras ready to violate. They'd been tailing him most of the day and had generally been respectful, but they were getting bolder and more impatient now. The very short half-life of media consideration had apparently expired and now he was fair game again. It was sickening and infuriating and intolerable, yet he had to tolerate it. It was his job.

'Are you sure about this, sir? I can divert now and go into the parking garage. At least it's secure and that way you wouldn't have to deal with them.'

'That's a tempting proposition, Conrad, but my presence is important right now.' He took a deep breath, prayed for forbearance, then stepped out of the car and into a relentless blizzard of camera flashes. The reporters knew well enough to give Conrad a wide berth and maintain an appropriate distance, but that didn't stop them shouting idiotic questions as if Robert were deaf.

Will you be canceling tomorrow's fundraising dinner in light of Mr Norwood's death?

How is the Norwood family handling this sudden shocking loss?

Are you satisfied with the MPD's investigation so far?

Are you concerned the MPD hasn't issued an official statement on cause of death by now?

Each question fueled his ire more than the last, until he heard Amanda White's unmistakable shrill voice rising above them all: 'Do you believe there's a connection between Gregory Norwood's death and the death of a photo-journalist assigned to his home this morning?'

He couldn't ignore that. Such an irresponsible, outrageous statement was exactly the type that fueled salacious gossip and detracted from the tragedy. 'Speculation is pointless at this time, and almost always harmful, Ms White. Let us not lose sight of the fact that a great man has been taken from us, and many are deeply devastated. I will say that the police are conducting a thorough, highly competent investigation, and a statement will be forthcoming when it is appropriate. Now, I implore you all to respect my privacy and, more importantly, the privacy of the Norwood family during this terrible time. I have no further comment. Good night.'

He escaped into his building under the protective shadow of Conrad, shaken by the encounter. 'There is no shame and not a single shred of human decency between the entire lot of them,' he hissed.

'I agree, sir, but you handled it well.'

'Thank you, Conrad. Now you understand why I asked you to deliver me to the front door instead of using the garage. There is great value in being present and showing strength during difficult times. That's leadership, and I don't think it will go unnoticed.'

'That was very clever, sir, and it won't go unnoticed. Even Amanda White didn't have a follow-up.'

'Oh, she always has a follow-up, but she's a chess player,

always thinking several moves ahead. She'll wait for another opportunity somewhere down the line. She's one to watch, Conrad. A true snake in the grass.'

The lobby was empty, save for the guard at the front desk. Normally Robert relished the solitude of the building after hours, but tonight the absence of human bustle felt lonely and surreal, even with Conrad at his side. He walked up to the counter and greeted a man he'd known for years. 'Good evening, Kramer.'

'Good evening, sir, although it's not a very good one, is it? I'm so sorry about Mr Norwood. I met him a few times when he came to visit you at your office and he was a kind man. A good man. He had time for everybody, even somebody like me, just a guard at the desk.'

'Thank you for your condolences.'

He scowled at the doors. 'The minute I saw the media show up, I tried to chase them away, but they kept coming back. I'm sorry I couldn't do more.'

'It's a public sidewalk so there's nothing you could have done, Kramer, but your consideration is always appreciated. You're here late, aren't you? You don't usually work the night shift.'

'I'm pulling a double tonight. Bought myself a fishing boat this spring and I'm trying to keep up with the payments. It was probably a stupid thing to do, but I sure enjoy my weekends on the water.'

Robert signed in, then passed the clipboard to Conrad. 'That's what counts. Happiness is always worth sacrifice. That's why I'm working a double tonight, too.'

Kramer grinned. 'It's probably why your poll numbers are so high. Congratulations, sir, you'll make a fine governor.'

'Thank you, Kramer, but we don't want to get ahead of ourselves. November is a long way off, especially in the political arena. Anything could happen.'

'Well, you have my vote. Have a good night, sir, and if you need anything, I'm here until eight tomorrow morning.'

'Thank you. And, actually, I do need something.'

'I'm at your service.'

'As you saw for yourself, the media is getting aggressive. They're relentless, following us everywhere, and won't give us a moment's peace. I promised the Norwoods I'd be available to attend to them at any time, and I can't have the media tailing my every move and causing even more distress to the family than they're already enduring. Protecting their privacy is paramount.'

'I can see the problem. It's terrible, sir. What can I do to help?'

'I was wondering if we might be able to use one of the back service entrances, just for this evening, so Conrad and I are free to come and go if necessary without alerting the media.'

Kramer hesitated, then started squirming in his chair. Robert knew he was thinking about his job, his boat payments, the possibility of his instant termination if anybody found out. 'No one is supposed to access the service doors after five p.m., sir. It's against building policy. I could lose my job.'

'I wouldn't let that happen, I can promise you. Given the extenuating circumstances behind my request, any actions on your part would be entirely defensible and I would vigorously litigate on your behalf.'

Kramer was far from happy, but he seemed to relax a

little. 'Well . . . under the circumstances, I guess I could do that for you. If it's only for tonight.'

'Only tonight.'

'Okay. Consider it done.'

Robert gave him a grateful smile. 'I can't tell you how much I appreciate it. How much the Norwoods appreciate it.' He tipped his head, rubbed his jaw thoughtfully. 'Let me know if you're ever considering a job change. You can't imagine how difficult it is to find competent, loyal people in the security industry, so we're always looking for new team members. You would be a welcome addition, and the compensation would be such that you wouldn't have to worry about making your boat payments anymore.'

'I . . . I'll do that, sir. Thank you, sir.'

Once they got up to the office, Robert withdrew a key and a slip of paper from his jacket pocket and handed them to Conrad. 'You know what to do.'

Conrad took the key and put it on the Town Car's fob, then read the numbers on the paper. 'Yes, sir. Are you sure this is the current security code?'

'Positive. Be careful.'

'I will.'

Thirty-five

Rosalie was sitting in front of her home computer, drinking a second glass of wine, which made her feel only slightly less furious about hiding in her house like a criminal. But the media had been skulking around earlier, so she'd parked a block away and snuck in through the back. The only light on in the house was the small desk lamp in her interior office, invisible from the street. The media had eventually left, but she was still locked away behind the closed door, agonizing over the confounding pieces of puzzle surrounding her father's murder and how they might fit together, if they did at all. She hoped Detectives Magozzi and Rolseth were as clever and competent as the reputations that had preceded them.

She returned her attention to her computer. She had hundreds of saved emails from Trey and she'd been studying them for almost two hours, looking for something, anything. After the first fifty, she knew they probably wouldn't reveal anything significant, but reading them was a reconnection to him and gave her some sense of purpose, of movement at a time when her world had simply stopped.

Some of Trey's emails were beautifully written – he had been the artist in the family, equally adept at writing, art and music – and some made no sense at all, obviously composed when he was deep in the throes of his addiction.

She'd spent years agonizing over why her little brother

had succumbed to drugs. They were privileged rich kids, there was no question about it, with unlimited access to ridiculously large, irrevocable trust funds when they each turned twenty-one. But Trey's darkness had started long before he'd had unfettered access to the money, around the time he was sixteen. That was when some awful switch went off in his mind. At first he was just moody and angry, but then he'd withdrawn from the family and life in general. The medications hadn't helped, the psychiatrists hadn't helped, and the family couldn't help, though the Lord knew they'd all tried in a million different ways.

Her mind drifted back to her sophomore year in college. She was walking to class on a beautiful autumn afternoon, listening to the crunch of leaves beneath her feet, when Father had called with the news that Trey was in the hospital. That was the first any of them knew of how Trey had been coping with his silent suffering; and after that, their formerly idyllic family life became a low-level hell.

She pulled up an email from last year, just days before his overdose.

Hey, Rosie girl,

Start treatment again next week. I'm nervous because I know I can't live this way anymore. I can die this way, but I can't live. I just want these demons to go away and I'm afraid they never will. I see bad things all the time, Rosie. People doing horrible things, unimaginable things. They seem so real sometimes. I think they are real sometimes.

I'm so sorry for what I've done to you. I understand now that my pain is your pain and always has been. I don't know if I'll ever be able to forgive myself or if I even should. I don't expect you to forgive me, and I'm okay with that. Know I love you.

Your little brother,
Trey

Rosalie grabbed a tissue and blotted her eyes, but the tears kept coming as she tried to comprehend what kind of psychic pain had driven him to such despair. 'I wish you'd talk to me, Trey, goddamnit.'

And then she heard the faint tinkle of bells, which launched her out of her chair. She didn't believe for one second that Trey would ever talk to her through those bells, as fanciful and attractive as the notion was. She also knew a breeze couldn't have disturbed them because the air-conditioning was on and the house was shut up tight. Those simple realities led to one stark, terrifying conclusion: somebody was in her house.

She reached for the Walther she kept under her desk and checked it to make sure there was a loaded clip, listening carefully as she disengaged the safety and took a few steps toward the office door.

Nothing. The house was silent.

You're losing your mind . . .

And then she heard the front door slam and Trey's bells clanging a sharp warning.

She had never felt anything like it before: her heart thrashed, the blood in her veins turned to ice, yet every pore in her body seemed to open all at once and gout sweat. The fight-or-flight response. She had nowhere to run, so flight was out.

It seemed like an impossible task, but she held on tight to her weapon and started walking to the office door on rubber legs. The gun wobbled in her shaking hands, but it was still a gun with bullets, and she hoped she still had the presence of mind to pull the trigger if she had to.

Or else you'll get somebody else's bullet to your brain before you even know what hit you, just like Father, and maybe you're a target, too . . .

Time lost all meaning, seeming to fold and warp, like melting plastic, but somehow she made it through the adrenaline psychedelia to the door and the security pad next to it. Her finger seemed strange and disembodied as it pressed the button with the police shield on it – and Father's voice suddenly came back to her, loud and clear, admonishing her for her lax security practices.

I don't care what time of day it is, Rosalie, I don't care if every door and window is locked, when you're in your house, engage the security system. That's why it's there.

She cringed when the siren started wailing, then crept slowly toward the front door, gun waving in front of her, which was a brave and stupid thing to do. An extended weapon could easily be knocked out of your hand, and what happened after that wouldn't be good.

She was panting with fear when she reached the foyer, elated that she hadn't been killed yet. The door was unlocked, which was wrong, so wrong.

The bells were silent. But they were still swaying gently on the frayed pink cord as the motion from their disturbance slowly wound down.

Thirty-six

The humidity-hazy Minneapolis skyline was just coming into view as the sun sank behind the buildings, a giant orange ball that left a riot of bold, streaky colors that could only work on Nature's palette.

Gino tapped the windshield. 'Check that out. Have you ever seen a sunset like this, Leo? It's like the city's on fire.'

'It's pretty.'

'Pretty spectacular is what it is. They say that molecules and small particles in the atmosphere, like pollution or smoke or humidity, scatter the light rays and make all the colors.'

'Then you shouldn't complain about the humidity.'

'Maybe not.' Gino pulled off the freeway and into the parking lot of a Kwik Mart. 'We need to fill the car's tank and I need to fill mine. Do you want anything?'

'Get me one of those shriveled hotdogs that's been rolling under a heat lamp all day. Mustard, no ketchup.'

'Coming right up.'

While Gino was inside, Magozzi decided to call Grace. He knew Monkeewrench was inundated, and so were their computers, but things were at a relative standstill while they waited for callbacks, and those callbacks might not yield anything.

'Hi, Magozzi. Where are you? I hear traffic noise.'

'We're on our way back from Rush City. What's the news on your end? Is City Hall going to be there in all its dark, forbidding, Gothic glory when we get back?'

'It's not Gothic, Magozzi, it's Richardsonian Romanesque.'

'I don't even know what you just said. That's too many syllables for my brain right now.'

'It doesn't matter. Just remind me to take you on an architectural tour of the city one day.'

Magozzi thought he heard a chiding lilt in Grace's voice, and suddenly meth trailers and dead bodies transformed into rainbows and sunshine. Not really, but he felt a little better about himself and the world at large. 'I can't wait. You didn't answer my question.'

'Because I don't have an answer yet, but we finally had a break-through. Roadrunner thinks we'll have some solid information to give to Dahl soon. After that, it's in the feds' hands.'

'That's fantastic.'

'It is, and we're happy, but there's still a lot of work to do. What about you? You and Gino didn't drive all the way up to Rush City for the scenery.'

'We were chasing a lead.'

'Did it pan out?'

'It's hard to say. It didn't answer any questions, but it brought up more. Grace, I know you're slammed . . .'

'What do you need, Magozzi?'

'We're trying to track down a guy named August Riskin, formerly of Aspen, Colorado, Kalispell, Montana, and California. We're waiting on callbacks and Tommy Espinoza's working it, too, but we could really use an extra hand with this.'

'I take it August Riskin doesn't want to be found?'

'No. He's kind of a cipher, went off the grid two years ago and nobody can pick up his trail.'

'Send us everything you have on him and we'll get to work.'

Magozzi hesitated. 'I don't want to reroute any computing power that might be saving that not-Gothic monstrosity I work in.'

Grace made a soft sound that could very well have been a chuckle, a foreign sound coming from her and one he'd heard her utter only a few times before. 'The new program has its own dedicated equipment and server, so we've got some computing power to spare.'

'Thanks, Grace.' His phone beeped an incoming call alert and he looked at the display. It was a Colorado area code.

'Take your call, Magozzi. See you later?'

'I'm planning on it.'

Grace hung up and looked at Harley, who had come into the sitting room next to the office while she'd been on the phone. He was stretched out on a chaise across from her, reading a worn book of poetry and drinking a beer; Charlie was curled up next to him, his hind leg twitching occasionally. He was probably dreaming about the unattainable squirrels at Magozzi's lake house. 'You're taking a breather, good for you.'

Harley closed the book and set it on the side table. 'Actually, Roadrunner kicked me out of the office. You know how Boy Wonder can get sometimes when he's cracking something.' He reached to pat Charlie's head. 'Besides, our buddy here needed a little *mano-a-mano* couch-potato time. What did Leo have to say?'

'They want us to help them find someone.'

Harley sat up and cracked his knuckles, careful not to jostle Charlie. 'Fantastic. I'm getting bored already.'

'I don't have much information yet, just a name and a few locations. Magozzi will send us more when they get back to the office.'

'Better yet, a challenge. Of course, anything after today is going to seem like a cakewalk.'

She gestured to the book. 'I didn't know you were a poetry buff.'

'I ran across an old box of stuff from when I was a kid. I forgot I even had this. Brings back good memories.' He smoothed his hand on the cover.

'Where did you get it?'

'From Miss Lizzy. Elizabeth Daltry.'

'Who is she?'

'Was. She was a very special old woman, who taught me to love poetry and probably saved my life.'

Grace cycled through her mental index and couldn't recall an Elizabeth Daltry or a Miss Lizzy. 'You never told us about her.'

'I will one day.'

Thirty-seven

Gino came out of the Kwik Mart fifteen minutes after he'd gone in, carrying a frighteningly large bag.

'Should I even ask?'

'Hot dogs, assorted chips, some pizza slices, and a six-pack of Coke. Candy bars for dessert. That should keep us fueled for the night.'

'While you were inside hunting and gathering, you missed a callback.'

Gino buckled in and gave Magozzi a disappointed look. 'Who?'

'Aspen. The Pitkin County sheriff himself.'

'So what did he have to say?'

'He doesn't know anything about what happened to the Riskin family after they left Aspen, but he was sitting when Clara Riskin was murdered, and he confirmed what Dubnik said. The evidence against Kip Kuehn was a slam-dunk. The bastard was stalking her – the cops found a hidden encampment on the Norwood property near the caretaker's house where she lived.'

'So she was killed on Norwood property?'

'Yeah, and the Riskins filed a civil suit against the Norwoods because of it.'

Gino was quiet for a long time. 'That makes Gus Riskin look even better as Norwood's killer.'

'Gus Riskin was a ten-year-old kid when his sister was

killed. I can't see a ten-year-old forming opinions on a murder, then fomenting a years-long grudge that ends in homicide.'

'It could be simpler than that. Maybe he just plain hated the Norwoods because his sister was killed on their property, so his little-kid mind blamed them. And their perfect life just kept going along like nothing had happened while he went to Hell. I could see a grudge forming over the years if you had the right psychological make-up.'

'That would be ironic, considering the Riskins were the ones who hired her killer on the cheap and brought him onto the property in the first place.'

'Yeah, and then they take their daughter's murder and try to turn it into a lottery ticket. That's pretty slimy.'

'That's essentially what the sheriff said. Apparently, Norwood was furious when he found out they'd hired the guy to work for him, but by then it was too late. He found out about it when everybody else did, during the investigation. But what's he going to do? Fire the family whose daughter was just murdered?'

'Bad optics,' Gino agreed. 'Still, it must have stung to get slapped with a lawsuit. Talk about biting the hand that feeds you. So what happened with the civil case?'

'It was settled out of court and they were paid through an umbrella insurance policy, which explains the very nice Montana ranch the Riskins bought for cash after they left Aspen. Sorry recompense for a lost child, but Norwood's insurance company gave them a nice payday.'

'Huh. So he didn't really pay for their relocation, his insurance company did after he got sued.'

Magozzi shrugged. 'That's why rich people carry umbrella policies.'

'Yeah, I suppose. Man, they really had Norwood between a rock and a hard place. Norwood couldn't fire them and he couldn't fight the civil suit without looking like Satan incarnate.'

'That's probably why it was settled out of court. There was already enough ugliness in everybody's world, and I'm sure Norwood was anxious to close the lid on the whole thing.'

Gino dug into the Kwik Mart bag and started pulling out his cache of junk food. 'What else do you know about the Montana ranch?'

'When old man Riskin died, Gus sold it for five and some change.'

Gino peeled the foil away from his hotdog and started eating while he drove. 'Damn nice nest egg, plenty to start a new life in California or anywhere else. He could have done a hell of a lot better than hooking up with the Hessians.'

'He's damaged goods. They don't always make the best decisions.'

'So we follow the money trail.'

'There isn't one. August Riskin paid the taxes and took the rest in cash. And then he disappeared.'

Thirty-eight

Tommy Espinoza didn't even notice Gino and Magozzi as they wended their way through a maze of document boxes stacked up in his office. He was entranced with his computer, clattering away at his keyboard while robotically shoving mini pretzels into his mouth. Magozzi had always thought he and Roadrunner were kindred spirits, except for the stark difference in diet: Tommy lived and died by junk food and soda and Roadrunner was a gluten-free health fanatic, who drank Kombucha and biked about a thousand miles a day.

Gino nudged a box with his toe. 'Did you get fired or something?'

Tommy jerked his head up, dislodging a hank of black hair from his forehead. He had his Mexican father's coloring, his Swedish mom's blue eyes, and a build on the chubby side of stout that publicized his nutritional preferences. 'Hi, guys. I didn't even hear you come in.' He smiled apologetically. 'Sorry about the mess. I'm just clearing out some paper. Nobody needs it anymore and I can save some trees.'

'What happens when your precious cloud crashes for all eternity?'

'You are such a Luddite, Rolseth. Come on in, make yourselves at home. Sorry there's no place to sit, but I can grab you some chairs.'

'No need,' Gino said, inspecting the wreck of Tommy's

desk for snack food, even though he had a big Kwik Mart bag of his own. He was like a Serengeti predator, ready to gorge on whatever was available in preparation for the seasonal famine. 'Pretzels, that's all you got? That's damn near diet food. Where are the Cheezy Puffs?'

'I ate them all. Pretzels are the only thing left, unless you want to make a run to the vending machine.'

'I checked it on the way in and you cleaned it out. What do you know?'

Tommy pushed back from his desk and rubbed his eyes as he yawned. 'Those numbers you asked about, the ones that called Norwood, all belonged to burner phones, for sure, but I managed to track down local points-of-sale on two of them. Whoever was calling him bought them at a Best Buy in Roseville. Surprise, surprise, they were both cash sales made in April and May of this year.'

'Good work, Tommy. What about Norwood's computer?'

'From what I've gone through so far, it's definitely a window on how the other half lives. Norwood has more money in more accounts than the International Monetary Fund. I'm staying away from the business stuff – if you're looking for any monkey business there, you'll have to hire a platoon of forensic accountants.'

'What about personal financials?'

'Almost as Byzantine, unless you can give me something specific to look for.'

'Large cash withdrawals or transfers. Norwood was being fleeced and we need to find the guy who was doing it.'

'I hate to tell you, but that's not very specific in Norwood's case. Just eyeballing the ledgers, he moved a lot of big money around all the time.'

'Look at the past year and see if you can find any anomalies, especially around the time Norwood got the calls from the burner phones.'

'Got it.' Tommy scratched down a few notes on a pad. 'What about emails, correspondence?'

'That's a bust. His personal stuff isn't all that personal. Email and written correspondence about business travel, his charities, meetings, dinners, parties, things like that. No family stuff, nothing that hinted at a mistress, no lockbox on his hard drive where he hid a journal filled with deep, dark secrets.'

'That's weird.'

'Not really. I think Norwood was smart and kept his personal stuff on a different device, not on his home-office computer. This one is linked to the business – any IT tech at his company would have access if they wanted it. I'd start looking for a laptop.'

Thirty-nine

Magozzi and Gino were pleasantly surprised to see Eaton Freedman at his desk when they entered the Homicide cube farm. The only downer was that he wouldn't have been there unless a dead body was somewhere else.

His pay grade didn't synch with the nicely tailored tan suit he was wearing, but when you were built like Freedman, you couldn't just grab and go off the rack. The original Incredible Hulk didn't have that problem – he just busted out of his suit until he was half naked and turned green.

'Looking sharp, Freedman.' Gino high-fived him as they walked to their desks. 'What brings your pretty face here at this hour?'

'Some poor sucker bought it in a delivery truck on the north side. It was stripped right down to the tires, but they left the body. Mighty considerate.'

'What was it carrying? Gold?'

'Construction equipment – HVAC equipment, to be more specific. Doesn't have to be gold on the north side.'

'Construction equipment's worth something, too.'

'Sure it is, but robbery wasn't the motive. The driver had a gunshot to the head, but there was no evidence of the crime in the truck. The perp killed him somewhere else, then dumped the body and the truck where he knew it would get stripped. The driver worked for Lloyd's HVAC. You know it?'

Gino and Magozzi nodded. Almost everybody on the force knew about Lloyd because he was one of the few employers who gave cons a second chance with responsibility and decent pay. MPD had sent plenty of candidates his way.

Freedman took a noisy sip from the bottle of water on his desk. 'So this ex-con driver – his name was Jim Beam, if you can believe that – is the one who ends up getting rolled and killed, working an honest job for the first time in his life. Had five years in, clean as a whistle. It's a damn mean twist of Fate, this. It just doesn't seem fair.'

'Life has a different definition of fair,' Gino observed sagely, as if reciting from the *I Ching*. 'So what are you thinking? Past came back to bite him?'

'Not from his sheet. He was just a punk, as far as crime's concerned.'

'What does Lloyd have to say about it?'

'I'm trying to track him down, get a bead on Beam's schedule for the day, see where his travels took him. His killer's in that timeline somewhere. The thing is, he was on somebody's radar – MPD got an anonymous tip that he was missing around five thirty tonight.'

Magozzi frowned. 'I wonder why anonymous.'

'Don't have an answer for that yet.'

'You will.'

Gino pulled Cokes out of the Kwik Mart bag and tossed him one. 'Have a Coke and a smile.'

Freedman showed them two even rows of nice white teeth. 'Thanks.'

'Sounds like you're doing okay on your first solo flight.'

'It's a good thing for a man to test his wings without his patron leprechaun. What's up with your case?'

'Don't ask.'

'That bad?'

'Worse. We've got two connected homicides and we're pushing the crime lab to their limit. And now you had to bust in with another case. McLaren is the only guy who's going to be getting any sleep for the next week.'

'Luck of the Irish. Let's hope it rubs off on all of us.'

'Amen.' Gino settled into his chair and cleared off his desk, which meant throwing stuff he didn't need on the floor. 'Where do you want to start, Leo?'

'I'm going to send Monkeewrench everything we've got on Riskin. They said they'd take a look for us. Then let's go back to the Norwood hacienda and look for a laptop.'

Magozzi had just pressed 'send' when his phone started jingling a tinny, sacrilegious rendition of 'The Girl From Ipanema,' a ring tone he most certainly had not selected, and wouldn't ever, even under threat of death. No great music should ever be debased in such a way. 'Did you screw with my phone, Gino?'

'No, and FYI, mine does the same thing. There's some flaw in the software. You bump the phone the wrong way or whatever and suddenly your ring tone changes to something really stupid. Or maybe we're being hacked.'

It was Rosalie Norwood, and Magozzi didn't like the news she passed on. Apparently it showed on his face, because Gino was suddenly hovering over him with an anxious expression when he hung up.

'What?'

'Somebody broke into Rosalie Norwood's house while she was home.'

'Is she okay?'

'Yeah. Rattled, obviously.'

Gino rolled his head back and Magozzi heard his neck crack. 'Oh, shit. Remember when I said why take the risk that Gregory Norwood was the only Norwood on the hit list?'

'I do, and I'm hoping you weren't right.'

Forty

Rosalie Norwood's house was surprisingly modest, just off Minnehaha Parkway. This particular thoroughfare had a network of excellent recreational trails that followed the Minnehaha Creek, and plenty of bikers and dog-walkers were enjoying a hot summer night, along with some free auxiliary entertainment they hadn't bargained for. They slowed as they passed to gawk at the four lit-up patrol cars parked outside and the cops coursing the lawn, but they didn't stop. Minnesotans were too polite to stare too long at anything out of the ordinary.

Magozzi and Gino were about to intercept one of the officers when they heard a familiar voice behind them. 'Hey, guys, hold up.'

He and Gino turned around and saw McLaren jogging toward them on the sidewalk. He was still wearing the bad Bermuda shorts he'd had on earlier but had changed his shirt for something slightly more complementary with them.

'What the hell are you doing here? Sick of golf already?' Gino gave him a soft slug on the shoulder.

'No way, but I was listening to the scanner on my way home from the course – three below par today, my personal best, in case you're interested – and I heard the call-out. I know who lives here, so I stopped by to see what's up, figured I'd run into you two. This case is getting curiouser and curiouser, huh?'

'What have you heard? We just got here and all we know is breaking and entering.'

McLaren scrubbed his spiky red hair thoughtfully. 'Suspected B and E, but no sign of it according to the guys I talked to. No sign of an intruder at all. They've got a full-on canvass going but, so far, nobody saw anything.'

Magozzi looked at the substantial foot traffic on the trails. 'Lots of potential witnesses. Something might turn up.'

McLaren followed his gaze. 'You know what people do when they're supposedly out enjoying nature? They don't pay attention to anything except their heart rate or how their quads look when they're pushing their bike or running, or their dog's stopping by a shrub to eat rabbit shit. If they get bored with that, they're on their Twitter accounts. You're looking at a pack of self-centered urban zombies who'd probably trip over a dead body and keep going.'

'That's a unique world view. Slightly misanthropic. Gloria would probably appreciate your perspective. You should share.'

Gino snickered. 'Hey, Johnny, you want to jump on board with us while we have a chat with Rosalie Norwood just for the hell of it? I know you're dying to get a piece of this.'

'Fuck, no. You two are on your own.' He gave them a twinkling, elfin smile. 'Besides, I've got a date tonight.'

'No way. Gloria actually took the bait?'

He rubbed his hands together, inordinately pleased with himself. 'Yep. I think I had her at "dessert cart."'

'Well, that's one way to get the girl. Let us know what happens.'

McLaren moved in closer and kept his voice low. 'It's

not all play. Willy Staples knew Norwood pretty well. And he's a big donor for the Zeller campaign. I'm going to massage him for a little info tonight. Who knows? Maybe he's got an inside angle.'

'You're the best, Johnny. By the way, Freedman pulled a case. He's at the office right now.'

McLaren looked distraught. 'Does he need my help?'

'He's doing just fine on his own. Besides, if he found out you cancelled a date with Gloria to go to work on your vacation, he'd pound you into applesauce. Have fun tonight.'

'I'm counting on it.'

'Well, shit, I guess miracles can happen,' Gino mused, as Johnny hurried away.

'It's a baseball game, not a trip to the altar.'

'Same thing in my book. I took Angela to a baseball game when we were dating and I proposed two weeks later.'

'Did she accept?'

'No. It took me another year to break her down.'

'I think Johnny's already proposed to Gloria fifty or sixty times.'

'It wouldn't be the first marriage by attrition.'

'You're a full-blown romantic and I never knew it.'

'Come on. Let's see what Rosalie Norwood has to say about her break-in.'

A uniform escorted them through the front door to the living room, which was a surprise to Magozzi. The exquisite appointments and design in her parents' home were pure *Architectural Digest*, no doubt conceived and executed by one of the world's most venerated designers. Yet the place had seemed oddly generic in its subdued splendor.

By comparison, Rosalie's décor was quirky and charming, and seemed very personal – there were unquestionably some very fine pieces in the room, but there were also items that were clearly of little monetary value, but of great importance in their careful placement as focal points. Not that Magozzi wasted any time thinking about interior design, but he'd made the mistake of hiring a designer a while back in an attempt to woo Grace and had learned a few things during that unfortunate experience.

Rosalie was sitting on a sofa by a fireplace, watching with dull eyes as police came and went out of her front door as if it was an everyday occurrence. Robert Zeller was sitting next to her, a watchful guardian and elder companion; Conrad was standing at attention near the back of the room, keeping his eye on Zeller and making sure none of the police were commandos in disguise, here to whack him before he got elected.

She stood eagerly when she saw them, as if she was anxious to get away from the hovering specters in her life. As a child of privilege, she'd probably had a lot of them growing up, and they were still gnawing around the edges of her life as an adult. Magozzi figured that kind of incessant hand-wringing and helicoptering could be frustrating for an independent young woman anxious to make her own mark and her own decisions.

'Detectives, I'm so glad you came. I was in my office when it happened. Let me take you there and tell you about it.'

Zeller stood too, but Rosalie gave him a fond pat on the arm. 'It's okay, Uncle Robert; I won't be a minute, and I certainly don't need a lawyer.'

Zeller smiled uncomfortably and sat down again on the sofa, like a very wise man who understood the prudence of acquiescence when it came to the wishes of the women in his life. 'I'd like to have a word with you before you leave, Detectives.'

'We'll find you.'

Rosalie led them to her office and settled into her desk chair. 'I was right here, going through some of Trey's old emails, when I heard the bells on my front door ring. They're hung inside, so somebody had to be in here to make them ring that loudly. I think those bells saved me.'

'So, your security system wasn't engaged at the time?' Magozzi asked.

'No. I only set it when I go to bed at night.'

'Was the door locked?'

'My door is always locked when I'm home.'

'Are you sure it was tonight? The responding officers haven't been able to find any evidence of breaking and entering, like a damaged lock, for instance, or an open window.'

'I'm positive. When I got home tonight, there was media loitering out front, so I let myself in through the back. I never went near the front door, and I armed the security and locked up on my way out this afternoon.'

'What happened after you heard the bells?'

'I heard another loud noise – I think it was the door slamming. That was when I activated the alarm.'

'Anything out of place?'

'Nothing.'

Magozzi eyed the Walther sitting on her desk. 'You were afraid enough to get your gun.'

'I was terrified. Somebody was in here, I'm telling you, but I don't think anybody else believes me. The police keep explaining to me that there is no sign of breaking and entering. To be frank, I get the feeling they think I'm a hysterical woman, crazy with grief, and I shouldn't be taken seriously. But somebody was in here, Detective Magozzi. Will you and Detective Rolseth take me seriously?'

'We *are* taking you seriously. And so are the other officers. They're just doing their job, trying to understand what happened here.'

'Does anybody else have a key to your house?' Gino asked.

'No. Well, Mom does, of course. But it obviously wasn't her.' She looked at them both with wide brown eyes. 'Do you think this has something to do with my father's murder?'

Gino gave her a sympathetic look. 'We won't know until the police finish their investigation. They're doing a neighborhood canvass now to find out if anybody saw anything.'

Her brows furrowed, dimpling her forehead. 'There's a lot of waiting in police work, isn't there?'

Gino nodded. 'More than people realize. Are you planning to stay here tonight or go back to the hotel, Ms Norwood?'

'I think I'll go back to the hotel to be with Mom. Uncle Robert said he'd put somebody outside our door tonight.'

'Good. We'll keep a police presence around, too, just in case.'

Magozzi nodded at her computer. 'Did you find anything in your brother's old emails?'

'Not really. They were mostly just sad and reminded me that his life started to fall apart when he was only sixteen, and none of us could ever figure out why. He was just a normal kid up until that point. Well, he wasn't exactly normal,' she corrected.

Magozzi raised a brow at her. 'What do you mean?'

She let out a sigh. 'He was extraordinary. Brilliant – much smarter than me, but in a different way. He was creative. And sensitive, in the way artists are, you know? He probably could have been a great one.'

'So your brother liked art?'

'He loved it. And he loved books, the outdoors and animals, especially animals.' She frowned down at her lap. 'He had such deep empathy for all living creatures. When he was eight, one of the neighbors in Aspen shot an elk. Trey was playing in the woods and ran across him while he was field dressing it. He came home crying. He wouldn't stop – he was inconsolable. He couldn't understand why somebody would do something like that, kill such a magnificent animal. That was the real Trey, not the heroin addict.'

Magozzi felt a pervasive gloom settle over him. Sensitive people sometimes didn't shoulder this pitiless world easily. 'Did anything happen when he was sixteen that might have been a trauma?'

'At that age, anything can be a trauma. I got into a fight with my best friend when I was sixteen and I thought the world had ended.'

'So that would be about twelve years ago that your brother started exhibiting a change in behavior. Two thousand and six.'

She nodded.

Magozzi did some quick math in his head. 'That was when Clara Riskin was murdered.'

'Yes, and it was a horrible thing, a traumatic thing. We were all affected by it – the whole community was – but none of us really knew Clara, or her parents for that matter. Our family's reaction was one of shock, empathy and compassion, of course . . .' She shook her head in frustration. 'That probably sounds monstrous.'

'No, it doesn't. Murder is very different when it affects you on a personal level.'

'Exactly. My father was just murdered, but I'm not going to spiral into heroin addiction.'

'Was Trey having difficulties with substance abuse before that?'

'No. Well, he got caught drinking a few times, but there were no signs of anything beyond that. Like I said, he was just a normal sixteen-year-old boy who snuck into his parents' liquor cabinet every once in a while. I'm just as guilty of that.'

'Did your brother collect art, Ms Norwood?'

'I wouldn't say he was a collector, not in the way my father was. But, as I told you, he loved art and I know he had several pieces he was very proud of. Why?'

'We have an original Ruscha that we think may have belonged to him or your family.'

Her mouth dropped open. 'What? How is that possible?'

'It's a long story. Is the name Milo Parr familiar to you?'

'No.' She squeezed her eyes shut, trying to think. 'Trey had one original Ruscha that I know of. It says "angel" in tattoo-style lettering. He called me when he bought it – he was so excited.'

225

Even though Magozzi had posited the possibility to Gino, the confirmation still stunned him.

'Is something wrong, Detective?'

'That's the piece we have.'

'Oh, my God . . .' She covered her mouth and tears shone in her eyes. 'Where did you find it?'

'Milo Parr had it.'

'Where is it now?'

'In evidence. We figured it had been stolen.'

She gazed up at the ceiling, as people did when they were trying not to cry, as if the gesture could defy the gravitational force that would eventually pull the tears from their eyes. 'Will we get it back?'

'We'll have to have it verified, but if it belonged to Trey, you will. Definitely.'

'I don't know what to say.' She looked at them expectantly. 'You're making progress on the case, aren't you?'

'We hope so.'

'Thank you.' She stood up and started pacing tight little circles. 'Detectives, am I in danger? Is my mother in danger?'

'I'm sorry, but we can't say for certain. The safest thing is to assume you are until we can solve this.'

She eyed her gun. 'Then I'll be taking this to the hotel. I have a conceal-and-carry permit.'

'That's a good idea. Ms Norwood, did your father have a laptop computer?'

'Of course. He traveled quite a lot.'

'We didn't see one at his home.'

'It might be at the office.'

'He would have taken it to Aspen, wouldn't he?'

'Definitely. But he might have planned to stop at the office to pick it up on his way to the airport. I can check if you'd like. Minerva would know.'

'We'd appreciate that.'

Five minutes later, Rosalie Norwood hung up her phone. 'Minerva said he took his laptop home with him when he left the office last night. It should be there.'

Forty-one

Magozzi and Gino found Robert Zeller in Rosalie's kitchen, pouring himself a mug of coffee. Conrad was really falling down on his hospitality duties.

'Mr Zeller, you wanted a word?'

'Yes.' He lowered his voice. 'I don't think I have to tell you how disturbing this is, and I'm deeply concerned about Betty and Rosalie. They're very vulnerable right now, and this ... this incident, it's maddening and quite frankly, scary. Has the canvass yielded any witnesses?'

'The Third Precinct is handling this and they'll be forth-coming with any new information as soon as they have it.'

He let out a frustrated sigh. 'It's the paparazzi. I'd stake my life on it. They're such depraved, disgusting parasites, stalking a grieving daughter hours after her father's murder.'

'You think that's what happened here?'

'It makes perfect sense. Rosalie simply forgot to lock her door and some vile photographer let himself in, hoping for a shot of her in private mourning.'

Gino lifted his brows. 'That's pretty bold, even for a depraved, disgusting parasite. It's also illegal.'

'Worse deeds have been committed for less. You don't know these people like I do. They'd sell their own mothers into bondage for a scoop.'

'It's an interesting theory,' Gino said, helping himself to a mug of coffee. 'Does Conrad take milk or sugar?'

Zeller looked confused. 'I don't think so.'

'We'll keep our hands in this, Mr Zeller. The timing is suspicious – we'd be fools to think this wasn't related to Gregory Norwood's murder, paparazzi or otherwise.'

'Have you had any luck locating August Riskin?'

'You know we can't answer that. We'll be in touch, Mr Zeller.' Gino exited the kitchen with his coffee.

Magozzi shook Zeller's hand, seconded Gino's promise to stay in touch, and followed him out to the living room, where Gino was offering the coffee to Conrad. 'You look like you could use a refreshment. Mr Zeller said you liked it black.'

Conrad narrowed his eyes and took the coffee without a word.

Gino seemed exceedingly pleased with himself as he stepped outside and lifted his nose, like a dog, to test the sultry night air. 'Conrad doesn't have very good manners, didn't even say thank you.'

'Conrad's seriously pissed off. For future reference, you should probably only annoy unarmed people.'

'Conrad's a punk. So Zeller has a pathological hatred of the press, but to tell you the truth, it's not the craziest scenario.'

'It is, if her front door was really locked. Come on, let's go back to the Norwood house and look for Gregory's missing laptop.'

'If we overlooked a laptop in that house, then we're totally losing it and should retire tomorrow.'

'We didn't miss it because it wasn't there. But we still have to check it out.'

'What are we missing, Leo, besides a laptop?'

Magozzi looked up at the sprinkling of stars that had replaced the sunset. 'Trey Norwood, a normal, sixteen-year-old boy. He starts to nosedive around the time Clara Riskin was murdered. I agree with Rosalie, it was a traumatic event for everybody, but it wasn't personal. Even if it was, we know better than anybody that people learn to cope with murder every single day. But the timing bugs the hell out of me.'

Gino's brows crept up his forehead in increments while he considered. 'Maybe it *was* personal for Trey. Maybe he killed her.'

Magozzi gaped at him. 'A kid who cries over a dead elk taking a human life? God, Gino, that's pretty far off the reservation, even for you.'

'I'm not talking premeditated, I'm talking a privileged, handsome kid, who's sixteen and horny as hell. He gets a little lit one night on Daddy's booze and puts the move on the caretaker's daughter. She fights back, the situation gets out of hand, and he accidentally kills her. Daddy covers it up. Trey can't live with the guilt, and that's a great explanation for his death spiral.'

Magozzi scuffed his shoe on the rough sidewalk. Flecks of quartz sparkled in the pool of light from the streetlamp. 'The DNA doesn't match. The Pitkin County sheriff said the evidence against Kip Kuehn was irrefutable and evidence doesn't lie.'

'Yeah, but people do. We need to take a look at the murder book. And talk to Kuehn. Something started back then and I have a feeling it isn't finished.'

Magozzi watched two of the squads pull away from the curb. They were finishing up at Rosalie Norwood's house. 'I'll call Pitkin County back and have them send it.'

'Detectives!' They heard Amanda White's voice calling from behind. 'May I have a word?'

'Oh, God.' Magozzi groaned. 'We almost made a clean getaway.'

She strode up to them, looking ready for prime time in an obnoxious fuchsia skirt suit. Her blond hair was perfectly arranged, but so stiff with gel, mousse or hairspray that not a single strand ruffled in the hot night breeze.

'Good evening, Detectives. You two have certainly been busy today. First Norwood, then Stenson, then a trip up to Chisago County. Interesting that an investigation into the death of the esteemed Gregory Norwood the Second brought you to a Rush City meth lab. Perhaps something to do with Trey Norwood?'

'Leo and I are moonlighting in Narcotics in our spare time,' Gino snarked.

She forced a tolerant smile and gestured broadly to Rosalie's house. 'And now this. I can't help but think the break-in is related to her father's murder. You're obviously thinking the same thing, or you wouldn't be here.'

Amanda White was enjoying herself too much, and Magozzi was getting pissed off. 'People break into other people's houses every day. We felt compelled to visit this scene for obvious reasons. As it turns out, it doesn't look like there was a B and E, but it's not our case, so you'll have to talk to the officers on scene if you want answers.'

'Care to comment on why Milo Parr is part of your investigation?'

Gino was getting impatient and snappish. 'He's not. He was just a lead that didn't go anywhere, kind of like what you're experiencing now. As it turns out, the guy just happened to have a meth lab in his trailer, so it was a free-bie for us.'

She made a sulky *moue*. 'Can you give me *anything*?'

'Come on,' Gino said irritably. 'There hasn't even been a press conference yet. If you promise to leave us alone, we'll give you first dibs on anything we can share with the media. As much as it pains me to say it, we owe you one.'

She tapped a dark green fingernail on her lips, then sighed in resignation, which was undoubtedly for show. 'All right, Detectives. Thank you. Have a good night.'

She clicked away on her skinny heels, and Gino's eyes followed her suspiciously. 'That woman's got something up her sleeve, I can tell. No way she strolls off without busting our balls more than that. And why the hell is she wearing dark green nail polish? It makes her look like a zombie.'

'That's a mystery we'll never solve. Don't waste any brain cells on it.'

'Are you kidding? I don't have any brain cells left.'

Forty-two

Magozzi ended his second call of the night with Pitkin County just as Gino pulled up to the curb in front of the Norwood house. The ubiquitous garlands of yellow crime-scene tape that surrounded the property fluttered in the night breeze, the only sign of movement in this otherwise silent, sleeping neighborhood.

'What did the sheriff have to say?'

'He cheerfully reminded me that it's past midnight and he'd been asleep for two hours.'

'Whiner.'

'He seemed a little annoyed that we wanted to look at Clara Riskin's murder book, but he agreed to copy us. We won't be scoring an interview with Kuehn, though. He was serving time in Florence Super Max in Colorado and got dusted by his cellmate over some contraband.'

Norwood's body was gone, but the pervasive stench of death wasn't. Its malignant presence had even penetrated the upstairs rooms in the big house. There were companies that specialized in sanitizing the aftermath of crime scenes – 'trauma cleaning' was the polite term for it – but Magozzi had always wondered if it was possible to scour a place entirely of death's effrontery.

He finished searching the fifth and last bedroom and

caught up with Gino in the hallway. 'We've been over every inch of this place twice. There's no laptop.'

'Yeah. Let's go.'

'I want to take one more look in his office and see if we can find some physical files. Norwood was old, and old people are old-fashioned. He might have hard copies of everything that was on his laptop. He probably didn't trust the cloud any more than you do.'

Gino's nose crinkled at the prospect of spending more time in the most polluted room in the house, but he walked downstairs without comment or complaint, which disturbed Magozzi, because Gino was usually never without either.

The big oak filing cabinet seemed like an obvious place to start, so they began systematically shuffling through drawers and folders, all meticulously labeled and alphabetized. After a few minutes, Gino pulled out a thick manila folder labeled 'Aspen' and started flipping through the pages.

'Norwood wasn't just a neat freak, he was a saver,' Gino said, in a nasal voice, breathing out of his mouth. 'There's stuff in here dating back to the late nineties.'

'What did I tell you? Old people are old-fashioned.'

'Let's take it and get the hell out of this abattoir. I need some fresh air.'

'We've got two more drawers to go.'

'Unless you see a file labeled "Enemies", I think this is a good start.'

'Go get some air. I'll meet you outside.'

'I'm not going to argue with that.'

Gino was standing by the car when Magozzi finally emerged from the house. He was looking up at the sky and gulping air, like a landed fish.

'You okay?'

'I shouldn't have eaten that hotdog.' He nodded toward the folder Magozzi was carrying. 'What else did you find?'

'It's labeled "Trey." You want me to drive? You still look kind of green.'

Gino tossed him the keys and hopped into the passenger seat. He spent most of the drive back to City Hall with his face stuck out of the open window, trying to clear his nasal passages.

Magozzi kept stealing glances at him. No matter how long you'd been on the job, you never got used to crime scenes, but you did get inured to them, simply in the interest of self-preservation. But there were times when a certain scene or sight or smell hit even the most seasoned detective like a rookie, and it was usually when you were so exhausted you could no longer shoulder the ponderous mental fortress that separated your work from your life. 'We're both zombies. We need to grab a few hours' sleep.'

Gino fiddled with the vents, directing the chilled air to his face. 'Drop me at the office. I'll drink a pot of coffee, go through Norwood's files, then grab some Zs there. You go spend some time with Grace. She's close to giving birth, for God's sake. Leo, this is a moment in your life you might get to live again, but maybe not.'

'I'm not going to cut and run on you. I'd never hear the end of it.'

'Leo, just go. Trust me on this. There are some moments you shouldn't miss and they might never come back to you.'

Forty-three

Grace was floating in a calm blue sea, staring up at the sky. Keening seabirds flew overhead, then tumbled and dove acrobatically toward the water, plucking up fish. She felt seaweed tickle her toes, then tangle around her ankles. She tried to kick it off, but it was persistent. She kicked harder, but it seemed to be tugging her now, pulling her down. She rolled over and tried to swim away, legs flailing, and then she saw a small, pale, oval face looking up at her from below the clear water. And in that instant, the world tipped. Everything went silent and calm. Grace. Grace . . .

'Gracie, wake up, sugar.'

Grace jolted upright, disoriented, blinking at her computer screen. She smelled gardenia perfume and looked up at Annie, who had a gentle hand on her shoulder and a very concerned look on her face. 'I hated to wake you, sugar, but we just hit the jackpot and I thought you'd want to know.'

She was still groggy, but awake enough to be embarrassed and slightly horrified, like all people who are caught sleeping at inappropriate times. 'What's happening?'

Harley spun in his chair, an ecstatic smile carving a broad swath of white through his black beard. 'Roadrunner just located the source of origin of the threats on City Hall. Our beautiful cyber-athlete monster of parallel processing just earned its first gold medal. This is huge, Gracie.'

She was wide awake now. 'Where is it coming from?'

'An apartment complex in Roseville. The place wasn't even on the feds' radar, and neither were any of the residents, according to Dahl,' Roadrunner said proudly. 'The program just accomplished something in a day that might have taken a year. Or it might never have happened at all if we hadn't started the beta test.'

Harley jumped up and started pacing, trying to burn off his adrenaline buzz. 'It kept pulling in millions of data packets related to the threads we were trying to follow and trace, and analyzed them instantaneously. With all that data it gathered, it finally found a way through the last layer of encryption. We're into one of these assholes' computers right now, only this time he doesn't have a clue. We are totally stealth, midnight marauders, and we have full access to his hard drive. Damn good thing, too.'

Grace felt weightless as she rose from her chair, like an untethered helium balloon, even though she was anything but. She joined the rest of them at the main computer hub and placed her hand on Roadrunner's shoulder. 'This is amazing. Show me.'

Roadrunner stabbed a finger at his monitor, which was displaying several thumbnails of architectural drawings punctuated by red dots. 'These are the original building plans for City Hall. And there are multiple schematics in here for bombs.'

'What are the red dots?'

'Proposed areas to plant explosives.'

Grace felt her heart squeeze. The baby apparently felt it, too, because it started to shift and kick. She knew that City

Hall had been swept earlier, but it was an old building and these were original blueprints; blueprints that showed all the little nooks and crannies in the structure that might have gone unnoticed by the JTTF because they'd been walled off during a century of renovation.

She almost jumped when Annie's hand alighted on hers. 'Don't worry, sugar. Dahl is getting a team ready to raid the apartment building, and a bomb squad is doing a second sweep of City Hall with the blueprints we sent them. Now you have *got* to go home and get some rest. I'd bet my shoe collection that you've never fallen asleep in front of your computer in your life, and I don't think I have to remind you that you're eight months pregnant and that little munchkin in there needs all your energy. We've got everything under control here, and law enforcement is doing its job.'

'We still have to find August Riskin.'

Harley nodded. 'And we will. The search is already in progress, fair lady. Go home and get some rest. You and I have a date with the feds tomorrow morning.'

Dahl was in the back of the tactical van where his men waited for the order to move in. The air was stifling, rank with the smells of gun oil and flop sweat. Weapons and gear rattled softly as the SWAT team shifted anxiously in place, like racehorses in a gate waiting for the bell.

He felt a steady dribble of sweat running down his cheek, his breath coming faster as seconds ticked by in slow motion. The screen in front of him showed surveillance footage of the apartment complex and the forward reconnaissance team crab-walking in the shadows along the sides of the building, weapons raised. Ninety-nine percent waiting, one percent terror . . .

There was a sudden flash of movement on the screen and then a voice shouting in his ear-bud. 'Suspects on the move, GO GO GO!'

Forty-four

Grace let herself into her house, Charlie first, and followed him to the kitchen, where he did a comical dance in front of his empty food dish. 'Starving, are you? Even after all that people-food Harley thought he was sneaking you today?'

Charlie sat down with an anxious whine and wagged the stub of his tail.

'You think I didn't know about that?' She filled his bowl with kibble and poured herself a glass of apple juice while she pondered her immediate future, when she would have another non-verbal being in the house to talk to. It was both thrilling and terrifying to anticipate the upheaval and chaos to come, almost impossible to comprehend change on such a profound level.

There had been times when she'd silently fretted about being a mother – how could you be a good one when you had absolutely no benchmark, no guidelines, no tutelage? But then it occurred to her that she knew exactly what *not* to do, and wasn't a bad example just as instructive as a good one?

While Charlie dined, she wandered into the tiny spare bedroom that had been transformed into a nursery, with Magozzi's help. It was simple – practically austere compared to the grand Rococo 'infant salon' Harley had created at his house – but this felt cozy and right. She trailed her fingers along the Shaker-style oak crib, ran them through the silky faux-fur of a giant teddy bear Annie had given her, then settled into an antique rocking chair with a worn leather seat that Gino had insisted she take.

You need a rocking chair, Grace. Don't ask me why, but Angela says so, and we're passing it on.

Grace closed her eyes and smiled, crossed her hands protectively over her belly, then let the easy rhythm of a chair that had succored generations of mothers lull her into a dreamless sleep.

When she woke up again, Magozzi was standing over her, one hand soft on her cheek.

'You looked so peaceful, I hated to wake you.'

She stood, took his hands, and gave him a light kiss. 'I'm glad you did. I need a softer chair.' She led him to the sofa in the living room, curled up under a blanket, and mumbled something, then fell asleep again.

Magozzi laid his head down so his cheek was against her belly. He could feel the movement of life within, a slow unfurling of limitless possibilities and dazzling hope. It suddenly occurred to him that every child had a grand destiny: it was only life's circumstances that whittled down the options once it was born.

He closed his eyes, understanding with absolute certainty that all of life's victories, milestones, and joys up to this point were hollow by comparison. This brief sliver of time, meaningless to the universe, was an ultimate, defining moment of bliss for him; just the two of them on the sofa together in utter contentment, anticipating the birth of their baby and their own rebirth as human beings. There was no past anymore, just the future. Gino was right – there were some moments you just couldn't miss, moments that might never come back to you.

Grace's breathing was the deep, even sound of sleep, but she stirred a little and her fingers moved through his hair. It wasn't seductive, because she wasn't conscious, but he chose to interpret it as a subliminal gesture of love in lieu of the words that had yet to find their way into her waking lexicon.

He closed his eyes and smiled, then murmured, 'I love you, Grace,' as sleep came crashing down on him.

He had no idea how long he and Grace had been asleep on the sofa when his phone jarred them awake. He wanted to smash it and go back to Grace, his cheek on her belly, her fingers in his hair, but it was Gino calling.

'How long have I been gone?' he answered groggily, feeling a skulking guilt over his dereliction of duty.

'Only an hour, and I hope it was a great hour. Sorry to wake you, buddy, but we've got some shit going down you need to be here for.'

Magozzi looked longingly at Grace, who was quite possibly even more beautiful with tousled hair and sleep-foggy eyes. 'I'll be there soon. Just let me grab a cup of coffee so I don't drive into the ditch. What's up?'

'Freedman's case – the dead delivery driver who worked for Lloyd's HVAC?'

'Yeah?'

'I just talked to Jimmy Grimm. He printed the delivery truck, and guess whose prints were all over it?'

Magozzi tried to squeeze a cogent thought out of his slothful brain. 'I don't know. I'm still asleep.'

'August Riskin. The son of a bitch is right under our noses.'

Forty-five

When Magozzi entered City Hall through the parking garage, he ran into Barney Wollmeyer from the Bloomington Bomb Squad, which shot tracers of dread through his raw nerves. 'Jesus, Barney, tell me you're here on a scheduled routine sweep.'

His mouth was set in a grim line. 'This wasn't scheduled, but we got a call to do another sweep. Some new info came in and the chief wanted us to double-check a few areas. A little scary, getting the call at one in the morning.'

'Yeah. So what do you see?'

'Nothing so far, but we just got here an hour ago. It's a big building.'

'Shit.'

'That's one way of putting it.'

Magozzi wasn't surprised to see McLaren at his desk – he wouldn't miss a twist like this, not for vacation, not even for Gloria. He was dressed like a normal person for a change – jeans and a button-down, his date clothes, presumably. He was scrutinizing his computer screen while Gino and Freedman paced the tight space between their desks, phones glued to their ears.

There was a taut frisson of energy in the air that seemed almost like an entity in itself. Magozzi wanted to ask how the date with Gloria had gone, but the sense of urgency in the room seemed too weighty for small-talk right now.

'Bring me up to speed, Johnny.'

He leaned back in his chair and raked his fingers through his red hair. 'I don't know if I should be happy or pissed that your person of interest was at our scene. You guys have a mess on your hands, and now it's our problem, too.'

'Be happy that we've got four heads in the game. Be pissed that you're here on your vacation.'

McLaren rolled his head back. 'Fair enough. Four heads in the game, it'll be a breeze, right? Only we got nothing to offer right now. Riskin is still way off the grid, except his prints aren't. They're on record for assault and battery in California and all over Lloyd's HVAC truck.' He nodded at Freedman, who was still on his phone. 'Eaton's been trying to track Lloyd down, but the guy's not answering. We got two cars en route, one to his office, one to his house.'

'Did Willy Staples have anything to say about Norwood at the ball game?'

'Just what a great guy he was. Everybody loved him, even his business rivals, and he couldn't believe he was dead.'

'Gloria?' Magozzi asked, pleased by the natural segue into the juicy stuff that had nothing to do with death.

McLaren wouldn't give him any more than a grin.

Gino hung up and sagged into his chair. Purple haloes shadowed his eyes and Magozzi felt a renewed guilt over getting at least an hour of sleep. 'That was Pitkin County. They're scanning Clara Riskin's murder book now – we should have it by morning.'

Magozzi glanced at Norwood's open files on Gino's desk. 'Anything in there?'

244

'The Trey folder was just plain sad, Leo. Mostly stuff from when he was a kid, mementoes of his childhood. Drawings, poems, scraps of writing, every Father's Day card Norwood ever got from his son. Nothing from the later years. It was like Trey just ceased to exist.'

'In a way, that's exactly what happened. What about the Aspen file?'

'Bills, receipts, ledgers, tax and real-estate documents, what you'd find in anybody's house files. There was something, though.' Gino handed him a single sheet of paper. 'That's a letter of termination to the Riskins. Drafted by none other than Robert Zeller on behalf of the Norwoods, no surprise there.'

Magozzi scanned it. 'He was going to fire them.'

'Yeah, three weeks before Clara Riskin was murdered. Norwood knew about them hiring Kuehn before that and he was pissed about it, which was the basis for their termination, clean as a whistle. The sheriff told you Norwood only found out during the murder investigation, so I just asked him about it again, and that's still how he remembers it.'

'Curious, maybe, but it doesn't mean anything. It was a long time ago. I'm sure the sheriff's had plenty of paper cross his desk over the years, and he's not going to remember every single detail of a twelve-year-old case.' Magozzi scrutinized the signature. 'This is an original. Norwood never sent it. I wonder why.'

'I don't know, but if he had, Clara Riskin might still be alive. The Riskins would have lit out of Aspen with their tails between their legs, and the scumbag who killed her wouldn't have had his mark.'

Every child has a grand destiny until life's circumstances take it away. And who would Clara Riskin have become? 'We'd better follow up with Zeller.'

'I left him a message when I found it.'

Freedman startled them by letting out a strident curse as he signed off his call and rapped his knuckles on McLaren's desk. 'Lloyd Nasif was murdered. Shot in the head in his office with the same caliber gun that killed Jim Beam.'

'Son of a bitch.' McLaren jumped out of his chair. 'We'll keep you posted,' he called over his shoulder, as he and Freedman hustled out of Homicide.

Gino clucked his tongue. 'This whole thing stinks, Leo, and Riskin is in manure up to his eyeballs.'

'So you think he killed the driver and Lloyd, too?'

'We've got Riskin indirectly connected to three murders here. Well, actually four, including Gerald Stenson. That's not random and it's not coincidence, and right now, that's good enough for me. We just have to find the fucker. I put in a call to Tommy and Monkeewrench when I got the news about the prints in the truck and dispatched a be-on-the-lookout on his mug shot. His days in the shadows are numbered.'

'We'd better hope.'

Gino's phone rang. He picked up and put it on speaker. 'Thank you for calling back, Mr Zeller. Sorry to disturb you so late.'

'Not at all. I was just getting Betty and Rosalie settled in for the night. Do you have any news on the break-in?'

'No, but we do have a question about a document you drafted for Mr Norwood. A letter of termination to the Riskins.'

Zeller was quiet for a moment. 'That was a long time ago.'

'Twelve years.'

'I'd have to consult my files to accurately answer any questions about it.'

'Actually, sir, I'm looking at the original document right now. It cites breach of contract for hiring unauthorized personnel to work on the property. The drifter who killed Clara Riskin. Except this was drafted three weeks before her murder and Mr Norwood never sent it. Do you have any idea why?'

'I'm sure he had his reasons, but he never shared them with me.'

'The Pitkin County sheriff remembers that Mr Norwood was shocked to learn that they'd hired the drifter when it came out during the investigation of Clara Riskin's murder. We're just trying to get the timeline straight, sir.'

'Of course, and I'm sorry I can't help you, but I don't recall any details. I'll consult my files in the morning and see if I made any notes that might be useful.' He cleared his throat. 'With all due respect, a twelve-year-old boilerplate legal document seems irrelevant and rather inconsequential in light of the matters at hand.'

Gino nodded. 'Sorry to disturb you so late, sir. Thank you for your time.' He hung up and shrugged. 'No stone unturned, that's what the chief promised.'

Forty-six

After the previous frenetic day, the Monkeewrench office was downright peaceful, except for the occasional grunt or oath from Harley whenever he hit a wall or stumbling block.

Roadrunner pushed himself out of his chair and stretched with a yawn, then walked over to Harley's station. 'No luck yet?'

'No. This Riskin son of a bitch doesn't want to be found.'

'I wonder what sent him into hiding.'

'He did time in California, so he probably made some enemies. The problem is, if he was running in unsavory circles, he could have gotten himself a decent new identity with a stolen social security number from some underground shop and started fresh once he got out of prison. Hard to track down that kind of illegal activity.'

'Did you hack his state records?'

'That's what I'm doing right now. For future reference, the government of the great state of California has shit firewalls.'

The doorbell rang and Harley stuffed a wad of bills into Roadrunner's hands. 'That's the pizza. You fly, I'll buy. Give him a twenty for a tip. Deliveries stopped an hour ago, but I called my regular guy for a favor.'

By the time Roadrunner returned with two fragrant pizza

boxes, Harley had full access to every documented move August Riskin had made in California while he was still August Riskin.

Harley started the printer and abandoned his computer for his Carnivore Special. He selected a huge, greasy slice and took a lusty bite. 'You don't know what you're missing, Roadrunner,' he mumbled, around an enormous mouthful. 'That gluten-free, vegan-cheese crap you're eating is an abomination and shouldn't be called pizza.'

Roadrunner gave him a nasty look. 'I'm gluten-intolerant and I don't eat animals.'

'What's the problem with eating animals? Animals don't have problems eating other animals. You ever have a cat? Those suckers are the sweetest, most adorable little bloodthirsty killers in the world.'

'A lot of animals are vegetarians, too.'

'Whatever. I got into California and I'm printing everything on Riskin. If nothing pops, I don't know where else to go. Drives me crazy, thinking there might be a dead end in all those pages.'

'Have we ever hit a dead end?'

'Come to think of it, no. You want a beer?'

'I don't drink, you know that.'

'Because the last time you drank, you had too much pink champagne and felt like shit for three days. If you're not a drinker, champagne hits you like a ton of bricks. Beer isn't like that.'

Roadrunner shrugged ambivalently. 'I don't know . . .'

'No animals in beer.'

'Okay. Why not?'

While the two of them enjoyed pizza and a beer, quite

possibly the holiest of holy grails for male bonding, they started doing the yeoman's work of going through the printouts. August Riskin had had his share of past shenanigans, but even his records before he'd disappeared were few and far between. His only permanent address in California had lasted six months, and that was an apartment in Tustin, down in Orange County. When he was picked up on assault and battery, he was living in a trailer in the desert with no running water, no electricity and no address.

'This is like looking for a phantom,' Roadrunner commented, his speech slightly slurred. 'Is it possible to get drunk on half a beer?'

Harley chuckled. 'It's possible to get *buzzed* on half a beer, if you're a lightweight. Should I cut you off?'

'No way, I feel great.'

A half-hour later, Harley was finishing his fourth piece of pizza, deliberating on a fifth, when Roadrunner ruffled a sheet of paper at him. 'Harley, look at this. It's a notarized application for a name change and a signed order from a judge.'

Harley took the paper and studied it. 'Damned if you aren't right, Roadrunner. August Riskin legally became Gustav Holst two years ago. Clever. He could still be Gus, if he wanted to be, but the baggage that came with his last name disappears.'

Roadrunner started laughing.

'What's so funny?'

'Gustav Holst was a famous early-twentieth-century English composer. He wrote *The Planets*. You've probably heard parts of it a million times.'

'If it's not opera, I don't know it. So he's a smart-ass who likes classical music, but I don't give a crap about his name selection. Why didn't the PI or Leo and Gino find this before now?'

'Because it's a sealed record – says so right there on the cover. They didn't have a reason to dig that deep until Riskin's prints showed in the truck.'

'Like Witness Protection?'

'No. That would be federal. This is state. He must have made a compelling argument to the judge to get this buried. With his background, it probably wasn't hard to do. He was running with some nasty characters. He probably gave a few up.'

Harley gave him a hearty pat on the back. 'Good catch. I'll give Leo a call. And if you're sober enough, start looking for a Gustav Holst in this century.'

Forty-seven

'There is no public record of any Gustav Holst in Minnesota,' Gino said in disgust, pushing away from his desk. 'No driver's license or vehicle registration, no property records, no arrests, not even a parking ticket. I'm waiting on the warrant for utilities records.'

'Did you try California? Maybe he's just passing through here to kill a few people.'

'Of course I did. Nothing there, either. But you know what's really bumming me out? Just because he changed his name a few years ago doesn't mean that's the ID he's using now. He could be anybody.'

Tommy Espinoza toddled in carrying a Red Bull and a scrap of paper. The whites of his eyes were bloodshot, which had turned his irises a surreal shade of blue. 'I finally found something.'

Gino raised his head upward in a silent hallelujah. 'Show us.'

Tommy placed the paper on Gino's desk and pointed out a series of numbers. 'Here are the unusual cash withdrawals you were looking for, taken from a bank account with just Gregory Norwood's name on it. Twenty K every month from April to August of this year. A hundred K total. It piqued my interest because there was no precedent for this kind of cash withdrawal from the account prior to this year, going back three years. The timing synchs with the phone calls from the burner phones.'

'Thanks, Tommy.'

'You're welcome. By the way, I'm zeroes on Gustav Holst, but I'll keep trying.'

Gino gave him a fist-bump. 'You're the man. Be in touch.'

Magozzi looked up at Tommy. 'These transactions should have triggered reporting by the bank. Do you know if they did?'

'Norwood had an exemption as a regular business customer, filed by his bank to the IRS yearly. If he needed big chunks of his own cash for whatever reason, he got it, no questions asked, no Bank Secrecy Act triggered.'

'I don't suppose there's some kind of money trail, any additional wires to accounts in those increments?'

'No, just the cash.'

After Tommy had left, Gino got up from his chair and paced around his desk, no destination in mind. 'How did Norwood get the cash to Riskin?'

'Some kind of dead drop. Probably a safety deposit box somewhere. Or a lot of different safety deposit boxes. That's what I'd do.'

'A hundred grand is a lot of money to pay out for information that's dubious at best, but for some reason, Norwood kept shelling it out. He had to have had another reason to play the game.'

'You think Riskin had something on him?'

'That's what I'm wondering.'

Roadrunner pushed away from his computer and rubbed his eyes. 'Hey, Harley, I just got into Xcel Energy. I've got the utility records pulled up.'

Harley rolled his chair over. 'Good job. Who needs to wait for warrants?'

'You shouldn't even say stuff like that out loud. Can you spell me? My eyes are on fire and I need a break.'

'Go. Get on the treadmill or do some t'ai chi or yoga or something. You're hunching over like a ninety-year-old man.'

'Actually, I was thinking of taking a walk. You want something from downstairs when I get back?'

Harley eyed his half-empty bottle of Heineken. 'Yeah, bring some more beer.' When Roadrunner had left, he started scrolling through the list of Xcel Energy customer names, hoping Gus Riskin-slash-Gustav Holst wasn't living off the grid in a van down by the river and had been stupid enough to keep his California alias and entrust it to a utility company. Five minutes later, he hit paydirt, polished off the rest of his beer in celebration, and called Magozzi.

'Hey, Leo, I just found Holst.'

'You are a god among men. Do you have an address for us?'

'Yep, it's . . .' Harley squinted at the monitor and rubbed a deep crease between his brows that hadn't been there that morning.

'Something wrong?'

Harley enlarged the screen, not trusting his eyes. 'You tell me. Gustav Holst lives in the same Roseville apartment building the feds raided a couple hours ago. The building we traced the terror threats against City Hall to.'

Forty-eight

Gino careened down a deserted Roseville street while Magozzi tried Dahl for the fourth time. He had absolutely zero hope he would answer his phone, but it didn't hurt to keep trying. 'Dahl, this is Detective Magozzi again. I know your hands are extremely full, but there might be a murder suspect in the building you raided, unit twenty-four, Gus Riskin a.k.a. Gustav Holst. He's armed and very dangerous.'

Tires squealed as Gino made a sharp right. 'Dahl's in the middle of an anti-terror op, which I'm really thrilled about, but our murder suspect is way down on his priority list right now.'

'For all we know, Riskin is part of it.' Magozzi grabbed the door handle as the car leaned dangerously into another turn. 'Jesus, Gino, get us there alive.'

'The raid could have flushed him out. He's a slippery bastard.'

'Or he could be sitting in a room somewhere getting interviewed by the feds.'

The red meat of the raid was winding down when they arrived, but it still looked like a war zone. There were dozens of FBI vehicles, from sedans to SWAT units to Evidence Response Team vans and K-9; the outer perimeter that encircled them was made up of multiple MPD squads that splashed red and blue into the darkness.

Heavily armed men and women patrolled the grounds and exited the building in a steady stream, carrying out boxes of evidence.

They got through the MPD cordon and pushed through federal agents with their shields extended to save everybody the time and hassle. They were met with stern, sometimes suspicious glances, but nobody seemed to have the will to engage, probably because they had more important things to do than abuse two MPD detectives who didn't belong at a terror raid.

They found Dahl pacing by a crime-scene van, his head down, phone pressed to his ear. He was having an animated conversation with whoever was at the other end of the line, but they garnered his undivided attention when he looked up and saw them. His expression shifted between confusion and mild shock before he finally spoke. 'Detectives. What are you doing here?'

Apparently, he hadn't gotten the messages. 'We've got a murder suspect listed as occupant of unit twenty-four in this building and we need to get in there. August Riskin a.k.a. Gustav Holst.'

'Do you have a warrant?'

'We have exigent circumstances. We think he killed Gregory Norwood and three others, and there's a possibility the surviving Norwoods might be in danger, along with anybody else who gets in his way.'

The cheap, hollow-core door of unit twenty-four gave easily to the FBI SWAT agents Dahl had co-opted for the job. Gino and Magozzi watched in awe as the team breached and cleared the apartment, like deadly dancers executing a perfectly choreographed ballet. 'Clear!' one finally shouted, stepping aside to let Dahl, Magozzi and Gino into the apartment.

It didn't take long for the bad news to sink in. If August Riskin-slash-Gustav Holst had indeed ever lived there, he was gone without a trace. The only things left behind were a few pieces of cheap furniture and a half-dozen eggs.

'Fuck,' Gino muttered, slamming the last kitchen cabinet shut before joining Dahl and Magozzi in the living room. 'We missed him. And not by much. I can still smell coffee and burned toast.'

'Any way he knew you were on his tail?' Dahl asked.

'No. We didn't even know we were on his tail until an hour ago. He cleared out way before that and way before your raid. It was part of his plan, whatever the hell that is. For all we know, he's on a flight to Zimbabwe right now, if Zimbabwe's even still a country.'

'I'm sorry you didn't get your man tonight, but I'll brief my team on his name and alias and include it as part of our ongoing investigation.'

'We owe you one.'

'And we owe Monkeewrench one, so let's call it even. We took six men into custody tonight. We believe they were part of the plot against City Hall, but we're missing a key person of interest. Ahmed Abdi. His specialty is bomb construction.'

'We're not letting our guard down. The bomb squad was back at City Hall when we left.'

Dahl nodded morosely. 'The entire city will be on high alert for a while.' He looked around the empty apartment. 'One day, I'd like to hear how an investigation into Gregory Norwood's murder led you to a federal anti-terror raid.'

'It was a twisted path. Do you believe in coincidences?'

'No.'

'Neither do we, so have your crime-scene people go over this place with a microscope and ask your suspects about Riskin.'

'I will.' Dahl checked his buzzing phone. 'I'm sorry, but I have to take this.'

'You've got a job to do,' Magozzi said. 'We'll slink out of here and leave you to it.'

Dahl started hustling toward the door, then turned around. 'You need to talk to the landlord.'

'We have questions for him, but I'm sure your people are keeping him busy right now.'

'They are, but he's still on site and, depending how it goes, he might not be for long. I can get you five minutes. Does that work?'

George Crenshaw, the landlord of the Roseville apartment complex the feds had trampled, was on the wrong side of middle age, with a badly receding hairline and a protruding gut that strained his Minnesota Twins T-shirt. He was wearing floral board shorts that would have looked stupid even on a twenty-year-old surfer. Worse yet, they revealed fleshy calves that were covered with a startling amount of wiry gray hair. Magozzi thought, Slob, when he first met him, but now he was feeling a little sorry for him: the guy seemed genuinely terrified. And who wouldn't be? It wasn't every day the feds came to raid your building in the middle of the night. The shock alone would have been bad enough, but he had the feeling the feds had been giving him the full-on interrogation treatment – as they should – and this was his five-minute reprieve from the wrath of Dahl's minions.

When he spoke, his voice was an octave or so higher than it probably was normally, and it was shaky. 'All I can tell you about Gustav Holst is that he paid his rent on time in cash. He was a good tenant. No troubles. But it was the same with the Somali guys that got taken away tonight. They paid their rent on time, too, no troubles with them, so I guess you never know about people. Are they really terrorists?'

'That's not our case, Mr Crenshaw. Our only concern is Gustav Holst. How long did he live here?'

'Since April, I think. I'd have to check in the office to know for sure.'

'Do you have a vehicle for him on record in the lease office?'

George looked genuinely baffled. 'No, why would I? People come and go, they change cars, that's their business.'

Magozzi tried to tamp down his disappointment as one easy lead disintegrated. 'Do you know what kind of vehicle Holst drove? Maybe you saw him in the parking lot, leaving or coming home, something like that.'

He thought for a minute. 'Actually, no. I never saw the guy except on the first of every month when he dropped off his rent in cash. I don't even know if he had a car, to tell you the truth. He kept to himself.'

'Was he employed?'

'I don't know that, either, but I'm assuming he was. How else is he going to pay rent?'

Magozzi's disappointment was slowly being usurped by growing frustration. It was truly stunning how unobservant

259

most people were. 'Well, did he wear a suit and a tie, for instance? A uniform of some kind?'

He shook his head. 'No, nothing like that. He wore jeans, T-shirts, sometimes a heavier workshirt, like a Carhartt. If I had to guess, I'd say he was in the trades, construction, you know. He had rough hands and he was pretty well-built. Muscular, like a laborer would be.'

Gino pushed a copy of Riskin's California mug shot across the desk. 'Do you recognize this man?'

Crenshaw studied the photo for a long time. 'This guy is a lot skinnier than Holst. And his hair is long and blond. But put some meat on his bones and shave his head, then, yeah, I'd say it's him. Jesus, this is a mug shot.'

'It sure is.'

'What did he do?'

'It doesn't matter.'

'Jesus,' he muttered again. 'I never had any trouble with Holst, I swear. You never know about people,' he repeated.

Forty-nine

Gus Riskin was on top of the world as he pulled into Flamingo Terrace Trailer Court. Milo had a different car for him and a sofa he could crash on until things blew over. Then he could get the hell out of Minnesota. In return, he'd give him a little cash to help with his medical bills. Cancer was a nasty bitch.

He turned a sharp bend in the road and his heart started slamming in his chest when he saw all the lights – Klieg lights, strobing patrol car bubble lights, bouncing flashlights. Crime-scene tape was festooned around Milo's trailer, like birthday crepe paper, while cops and techs were crawling all over the damn place. There were four squads parked out front, along with a crime-scene unit and two Haz-Mat vans.

Keep driving, nice and easy. Don't lose it now.

He slowly made the loop around the trailer park, then jumped back onto the freeway and headed north at exactly the speed limit, trying to keep his panic in check. Son of a bitch, what was he supposed to do now?

He didn't have any real fear of the cops because there was no way they could connect him to Milo or anything else. And if by some miracle they did, Milo couldn't hurt him because he didn't know anything. But he needed a different car – he couldn't take any chances at this stage in the game. The only reason he was here now was through an abundance of paranoia and caution. Preparation. Care.

So why the fuck didn't you think of plan B while you were being so careful?

Goddamnit, he needed a place to think, a place to rest for the night, a place to plan how he would start over this time.

After fifteen miles of driving a dark, desolate stretch of interstate, the beams of his headlights picked up a blue information sign that announced there was food and lodging at the next exit. It seemed unlikely, because all he could see along the freeway were pine trees and swamps, but he took the exit and followed the signs to the Hitching Post Motel, a small, depressing, cinderblock eyesore that squatted on the side of the lonely road under a weak sodium vapor lamp. It would only be memorable to any passers-by because of its ugliness, like a boil waiting to be lanced.

A partially lit, weakly flashing neon sign in a smudged window read: 'Vac n y.' No shit. There was only one other car in the lot, an old Toyota Camry, and it probably belonged to the night clerk. The place was a dump, but it had two things going for it: it was private and it was empty. A great place to come up with plan B.

Gus didn't know how such a thing was possible, but the lobby was even less inviting than the exterior, with torn carpet that might once have been gold, salvaged furniture that had probably come from a garbage dump, and buzzing fluorescent light fixtures that cast a stark, sickly hue on everything, including the kid who was manning the counter. A plastic wall clock in the shape of a fish loudly ticked away the minutes to three a.m. The most charming thing in the room was a cracked plastic display stand that held faded brochures aimed at fishermen. He wondered if anybody had killed themselves there. If you were headed in that direction, the Hitching Post Motel would take you the rest of the way.

'Good evening, sir,' the kid said politely. He was wearing a crisp blue polo shirt with a nametag that said 'BEN', and Gus immediately felt sorry for him. What was a clean-cut, polite young man doing in a shithole like this?

'Hi, Ben. I need a room.'

'No problem.' He pushed a piece of paper across the counter. 'If you could just fill out this form, then I'll get you set up.'

Gus wrote in the name John W. Harris and the Tustin, California, address that matched his vehicle registration and plates. 'There you go.'

Ben looked at the form and got a wistful look on his face. 'You're from California?'

'Yep.'

'Is it as nice as everybody says?'

'It's got something for everybody.'

'I've always wanted to go to California. What brings you to the most boring place on earth?'

Careful, careful, lay the ground work, use the cover story. 'I work construction here in the summer. My job just finished, so I thought I'd see some sights before I head back to California.'

Gus slid his eyes toward the rack of brochures. 'Do a little fishing.'

'That's about all there is to do here. Unless you want to go to the Arcola Sculpture Park. Some farmer welded together a bunch of old tractor parts and other machinery into dinosaurs. It's kind of cool. People seem to like it.'

'I'll keep that in mind.' Gus was getting impatient with

the idle chit-chat, but Ben was clearly bored out of his mind and probably lonely, too. And a little human kindness never hurt. Sometimes, it could really make a difference in somebody's day. 'You get a lot of traffic here?'

'It's pretty dead during the week, but summer weekends we can fill up with fishermen, like yourself.' Ben went to a pegboard and grabbed a room key. 'This is our biggest room and there's a vending machine right outside the door. Oh, and there's a twenty-dollar deposit.' His eyes drifted toward the door and Gus followed his gaze. A squad car was pulling into the lot.

Jesus Christ.

'I hope there's no trouble,' Gus said calmly, trying to ignore the hard lump that had formed in his stomach.

'Oh, no, that's just Deputy Marlin. He stops by once or twice when I work the graveyard shift. It's pretty remote out here, so he likes to check in.'

'Isn't that the great thing about a small town?' Gus said, with forced brightness, nodding at the deputy when he walked in.

'Young Ben. Sir.'

Suspicious eyes, suspicious face, looking for trouble, just like every cop. Middle-aged, thinning hair, trying to keep in shape but losing the battle.

'Hi, Deputy Marlin,' Ben said cheerfully. 'I got my first and only customer of the night. Mr Harris here is from California.'

The deputy eyed him up and down. 'Whereabouts?'

'Tustin. Orange County.'

'I've got a cousin in Irvine. Passing through or are you planning to fish?'

What was it with these people and fishing? 'I'm definitely planning to fish. A buddy of mine told me the lakes up here are great.'

'Your buddy is right about that. Best walleye fishing in the state.'

What the fuck was a walleye?

'That's just what he said.' Gus weighed his options. You didn't offer up anything you didn't have to, but people around here liked to talk and he didn't want to stand out as a sullen Auslander. 'Have any secret spots you're willing to share with an out-of-towner, Deputy?'

The deputy eyed him again, then smiled and grabbed a brochure from the rack.

Fifty

Gino finished his fast-food breakfast biscuit and tossed the crumpled wrapper into the empty bag on the console of the car. 'Goddamnit, we were so close to nailing that son of a bitch. All we've got now is Riskin maybe had a car, maybe worked construction, and he paid his rent in cash.'

'He's also on the run, exposed, and vulnerable. Every cop in the five-state area has his mug shot. He won't last a day.'

'That hour of sleep did wonders for your optimism.' Gino pointed out of the windshield at the lightening, pink-hued sky above City Hall. 'Look at that. The sun's already rising. Didn't we just watch it set?'

'About ten hours ago.'

They stepped out of the car and listened to the relative quiet of the awakening city for a moment. It was almost peaceful, if you ignored the grind of garbage trucks making early-morning pick-ups or the engine noise of the first wave of commuters filtering onto the streets from the suburbs. You could even hear birds singing.

'Still humid as hell,' Gino observed, lifting his face to the rising sun. 'I thought this heat was supposed to break.'

'It will.'

'Good morning, Detectives.'

Gino cringed, then turned to face Amanda White. 'You're up bright and early.'

'I didn't sleep last night and, by the look of you two, neither did you.'

'Flattery will get you nowhere.' Gino looked her up and down. She was wearing a different skirt suit this morning, but her helmet-hair was a little limp. 'At least you got a chance to change your clothes. Still stalking us, huh?'

She gave them a thin smile. 'That's my job. Care to comment on why you were at an FBI terror raid early this morning?'

'Nope.'

'I'm sure it's not connected to your case, just like Milo Parr isn't connected to your case.'

'That's exactly right. We asked a buddy tonight if he believed in coincidences.'

She arched an over-plucked brow. 'And what did he say?'

'He said no. But sometimes coincidences happen. Us being at the raid was just a coincidence.'

She let out a petulant sigh. 'You obviously have a person of interest in the Norwood murder.'

'Unfortunately, there's nothing obvious about this case,' Magozzi said, thrilled that his phone chimed at that moment with a text alert, saving them all from any more pointless conversation. He grabbed Gino by the arm and steered him toward the doors. 'We have to go. Have a good day, Ms White.'

'One more thing before you go.' She gave them a toothy, shark smile that telegraphed her next question would be the zinger that brought them, weeping, to their knees. They would then disclose every detail they had on the case and Amanda White would solve it, be a media hero, and go national within a week. 'Care to comment on your interest in August Riskin?'

Gino and Magozzi didn't fall to their knees weeping, but they didn't say anything either.

To her credit, she didn't look smug, just inquisitive. 'Don't look so surprised. You put out a BOLO on him. It wasn't hard to backtrack to the Norwoods.'

'If you tip our hand now, this whole thing could blow up in our faces. Yours included,' Magozzi said carefully.

She deliberated for a moment. 'How much time do you need?'

Magozzi sensed that Gino was about to explode next to him. Part of him wanted to let him do his worst; the more rational part of him understood the benefits of a symbiotic relationship with a media mouthpiece. 'However much time it takes to get him into custody. Ms White, we're at critical mass with this. If Riskin's name gets out to the public right now, we could lose him.'

She nodded grudgingly. 'I won't tip your hand, but now you really owe me. I want an exclusive.'

'We'll give you that.'

'Thank you. Good luck.'

'I don't trust her,' Gino fumed, once she'd left. 'Goddamnit, she's like a nippy little Chihuahua, snapping at our heels.'

'At least she's not a depraved, disgusting parasite, which is more than I can say for some of her colleagues. Besides, she doesn't know Riskin changed his name. She'll be floundering around for a long time, just like we were.'

Gino grunted. 'Like we still are, you mean. Who texted you?'

268

Magozzi checked his phone. 'Pitkin County. Clara Riskin's murder book is waiting for us.'

McLaren looked up from his computer with weary, blood-shot eyes when Gino and Magozzi entered Homicide. 'Bomb squad cleared the building an hour ago.'

Gino grabbed a donut from the box on McLaren's desk. 'The feds made some arrests this morning.'

Freedman walked in with a cardboard tray of coffee. 'We know. It's all over the news. Where have you guys been?'

'Chasing Riskin. He cleared out of his apartment before we got there.'

'Sorry to hear that.'

'Any progress on your homicides?'

'Lloyd Nasif took a bullet to the head, just like Jim Beam, the delivery driver. Same caliber, probably the same gun. We're waiting on ballistics, we're waiting on prints.' Freedman slurped his coffee, scowled, then dumped in a plastic container of creamer and three sugar packets. 'We tracked down the driver's last delivery before Lloyd's dis-patcher lost contact, to one-eleven Washington Avenue. He reported the delivery to Dispatch and the guard at the front desk confirmed he signed out of the building. After that, the transponder on his truck went dead and Jim Beam disappeared.'

'Point of contact with Riskin. Who took the delivery?'

'TCG Construction. They're doing some big renova-tions on the building. We've got a call in.'

Magozzi's thoughts stuttered. 'We think Riskin was in construction. Freedman, get somebody on the line from that company now. I don't care how you do it. Go break down doors and roll people out of bed if you have to. Find out if either Gus Riskin or Gustav Holst is on their payroll. If he is, take it from there. We need a vehicle, contact numbers, anything they have on him.'

'You got it.'

Gino looked at Magozzi. 'One-eleven Washington Avenue. That rings bells.'

'It should. It's where the feds live. We've been there a few times.' He looked up at the wall clock. Seven thirty-two. Grace and Harley were probably on their way now to meet Dahl and Shafer.

'No, it's something else.' He pulled out his wallet and started digging through it while McLaren looked on curiously.

'You don't have to pay for the donut, Rolseth.'

'Never crossed my mind.' He pulled out a business card and waved it at Magozzi with a flourish. 'Zeller's card. Guess where his office is?'

Magozzi felt a tickle in the furthest recesses of his brain as tumblers started clicking, but none slotted into place. 'One-eleven Washington Avenue.'

Gino nodded and started gnawing the end of a pen. 'Something's coming together, but hell if I know what.'

'Pull up Clara Riskin's murder book.'

Fifty-one

Rosalie Norwood was in bed, staring up at the dark ceiling of her hotel room. For all the vast comforts the Chatham offered – posh mattresses, Pratesi sheets if you asked for them, goose-down pillows and aromatherapy kits – she hadn't slept more than an hour all night. And what little rest she'd managed had been a thrashing and disturbed one, haunted by home intruders and vague, terrifying images of violence. There was just no point in trying any longer.

The sun was barely up when she got out of the shower. As she combed her hair, she heard a soft rap on her door.

'Rosalie, dear?'

'I'm up, Mom.'

'I've ordered some coffee and pastries.'

'I'll be right out.'

She pulled her wet hair into a ponytail, threw a robe on over her T-shirt and shorts, and entered the living room of the suite. The window shades were partially drawn, letting in the muted gold of the rising sun. Sitting in a chair by the window, the unflappable Betty Norwood was weeping softly. Dawn's light turned her tears into prisms that played on the sharp planes of her face, and Rosalie suddenly realized that she'd only seen her mother cry once before, at Trey's funeral.

She knelt down beside her and took her hand. The skin

was soft, but as thin as parchment and knobby with bones. 'It's going to be okay, Mom. We'll get through this together.'

Betty cupped her daughter's face in her hands. 'Promise me I won't lose you, too.'

'I'm here. I'll always be here.'

'I want to believe that, but I'm afraid more horrible things are going to happen, Rosalie. Trey first, then your father, and last night an intruder at your house. Who knows what their intent was? And what next?'

'Don't think that way, Mom.'

She sighed and delicately blotted her tears. 'I miss him. Your father was such a good man and I'll always be so proud of him. Everything he did was always for us. For the family. Don't ever forget that, no matter what.' She gazed out of the window at the street below, which was slowly filling with pedestrians and vehicles as the city came to life. 'Do you think about Trey much?'

Rosalie sat back on her heels, more stunned by that question than she had been over her mother's unfamiliar display of vulnerability. She never brought up the sacro-sanct memory of Trey, and Rosalie didn't know how to respond, except honestly. 'I think about him all the time. I miss him every day.'

'So do I, Rosalie.'

'But you never talk about him.'

'That's wrong of me, I realize that now. Selfish. He deserves to be remembered always, no matter what the cost in pain.'

'You weren't being selfish, Mom. Grief visits everyone in different ways.'

'Yes, it does.'

'What do you think about when you think of Trey?' Rosalie ventured, hoping the question wouldn't slam the door shut on a conversation that had barely begun.

'I think of what a tender, loving heart he had, especially when he was young. Do you remember?'

She nodded. 'Last night I was thinking about the time he found the elk, how upset he was. For days.'

'That was dreadful. This world is no place for fragile hearts. I'm convinced that's what ruined him.'

'Heroin ruined him, Mom.'

'In the end, it did. But you saw how he reacted to the elk. Just imagine what it was like for him when Clara Riskin was murdered. When your heart is broken, the love inside the shattered pieces never dies. It can lift you up or it can drag you down.'

'What are you talking about? Trey didn't even know Clara Riskin existed.'

'He was in love with her, dear. He was only sixteen, but he wanted to marry her.'

Rosalie felt a dark emptiness fill her, an irrational sense of betrayal emanating from every direction of her family. 'Trey and I were so close. Why did he tell you and not me?'

'You were already in college then and worlds apart. And there are some things you only confide to your parents.'

'Then why didn't you tell me? Maybe I could have helped him.'

'I don't think so. When he found out Clara was murdered, he told me he wished he'd never been born. That was what we were up against. We didn't want to burden you.'

'Burden?' She felt a sob hitch in her chest. For her lost

273

brother, her lost father, her lost mother, who was facing her failure with the same maddening reticence that had always defined her character. But she still couldn't believe a teenage infatuation had shattered her brother in such a dramatic way. There had been something else, there must have been. 'What did you and Father say when Trey came to you about Clara?'

'Childhood crushes are one thing, marriage is entirely another, and we certainly couldn't support such ridiculous youthful folly. He would have come around to our way of thinking eventually, but then Clara was murdered and unfulfilled love is the only perfect love. It never becomes soiled and it never betrays.' Her face hardened. 'We were so afraid she'd destroy him, Rosalie. But even dead, she destroyed him. Destroyed our family.'

Rosalie gaped at her. 'Mom, she was *killed*.'

'I'm sorry, that was a terrible thing to say. Pain does that. When you have children of your own someday, you'll understand.'

'What aren't you telling me?'

And then, just like that, the public Betty Norwood suddenly re-inhabited her body. The familiar Betty poured coffee and carefully arranged croissants and cinnamon buns on plates with a pair of silver tongs as breezily as if they'd just been discussing the weather.

'Eat something, Rosalie,' she admonished gently. 'You're too thin.'

Fifty-two

Magozzi rubbed his eyes, drained the last cold dregs of his insipid, Homicide-brewed coffee, then returned his attention to his computer screen. Clara Riskin's murder book was thick, rife with the longhand, chicken-scratch language every detective used to record initial observations and the potential theories that emerged throughout the course of an investigation. Most of these notes never made it to a final report because the hard evidence that came later rendered them irrelevant.

There were also timelines, interviews, court transcripts, witness statements, and photos of the crime scene that enraged and sickened him. Clara Riskin had been beaten to death with a piece of wood, and there would never be justice for a savaged fourteen-year-old girl whose life had ended before she'd had a chance to live it.

But from what he'd read so far, there was no magic here – something he had to admit he'd been hoping for, foolish as it was. So far, it looked like Pitkin County had conducted a solid investigation. Richard "Kip" Kuehn had been found near the scene, half dead from a cocktail of drugs, still holding the piece of lumber he'd used to bludgeon Clara Riskin.

But that was how homicides were. You chased any dangling thread, hoping it would bring you home. Sometimes it worked out, others it didn't.

'This seems pretty tight, Gino. I'm not seeing anything. How about you?'

Gino looked up from his own computer with bleary eyes. 'Not really, but I haven't gotten to the court transcripts yet. Right now I'm looking at the witness list. Robert Zeller is on it. He was in Aspen with the Norwoods when the murder happened, along with his wife Louise, and Conrad Jarvick. The asshole.'

'Makes sense. Zeller doesn't seem to go anywhere without him.'

'What are you looking at?'

'I'm about to crack into the coroner's report. Did you look at it yet?'

'Hell, no. I don't do coroners' reports until noon. It's bad luck.'

'Since when?'

'Since right now. I need more coffee. You want some?'

'Yeah, thanks.' Magozzi handed him his mug and delved into the cold, antiseptic language of the coroner's report, which seemed completely disassociated from the actual victim and the crime it detailed. Reading the words 'blunt force trauma' was an entirely different experience from studying the crime-scene photos that showed what blunt force trauma actually looked like.

A call from Rosalie Norwood interrupted him, a reprieve from a depressing task. 'Good morning, Ms Norwood.'

'Good morning, Detective Magozzi. I hate to bother you with something that seems inconsequential . . .'

'Remember, nothing is inconsequential in a homicide investigation.'

'That's why I'm calling. I remember you asking if Trey

experienced a traumatic event when he was sixteen. I disregarded Clara's murder as a cause at the time, but my mother just told me he was in love with her. He wanted to marry her. I still can't believe that's what sent him down such a dark road, but I thought you should know. I guess that was never your mystery to solve.'

'I appreciate your call.'

'Did you ever find Father's laptop?'

'No, we didn't. We went back to the house last night, but it wasn't there. Whoever killed your father took his computer.'

'But you said there were no signs of robbery.'

'That might be the only thing that was taken.' Magozzi heard an apprehensive sigh at the other end of the line. 'Is there something else?'

'There's probably sensitive information on that computer. Account numbers, passwords. I have to call our banker, Detective. Goodbye.'

Gino returned from his coffee-gathering odyssey and set a freshly filled mug on Magozzi's desk, along with a chocolate éclair. 'Thank McLaren for the donut, thank me for the coffee. I had to brew a new batch because the sludge that was sitting in the carafe was toxic slime mold. Whatever happened to coffee-room etiquette?' He brushed some powdered sugar off his shirt. 'Who was that?'

Magozzi told him about Rosalie Norwood's call.

'Huh. Not to sound callous, but doesn't that seem like a little bit of an overreaction, destroying your life over a high-school crush?'

'That's essentially what she said.'

'Well, it's a sad story all around. Kind of like a modern version of *Romeo and Juliet*. I hated that play.'

Magozzi decided to abandon the grisly coroner's report until his éclair had had a chance to settle in his stomach, which gave him an opportunity to call Grace. Just hearing her voice smoothed the jagged edges of his frustration and exhaustion, and temporarily alleviated his misanthropy.

'Hi, Magozzi. How are you?'

'Great. I'm talking to you, I just ate an éclair, and I'm on my fourth cup of coffee.'

'Did your case break?'

'We're breathing down Riskin's neck. Are you still meeting with Dahl and Shafer this morning? They had a pretty busy night.'

'As far as we know. Harley should be here any minute to pick me up.'

'You're meeting them at their office?'

'Harley doesn't want Shafer in his house. He said it would be like inviting a vampire in.'

'Fair analogy. Since you're going to be a few blocks away, stop in for a minute before you go home. Gino and I could stand to see some friendly faces.'

'I'll call you when we're finished.'

'How's baby?'

'Active.'

'How active?'

'Marathon-running active. I'm glad you came over last night.'

'I'm sorry I had to leave.'

'Your case will be over soon and you'll be bored to tears.'

'But I won't know I'm bored because I'll be asleep.' Magozzi heard Harley's voice in the background, making a fuss of Charlie. 'Sounds like your ride's there.'

'He is. See you later, Magozzi.'

He hung up and went back to his computer, thinking it was just wrong to follow up a conversation with the love of your life and the mother of your baby with a coroner's report.

Five minutes into reading, his eyes stuttered over the primary cause of death. 'Hey, Gino. Clara Riskin was beaten, but not to death. Official cause is strangulation. The trauma wasn't enough to kill her.'

Gino's coffee mug froze before it hit his lips. 'Sick bastard. Literally. Kip Kuehn was a disaster waiting to happen. He beat his twelve-year-old sister with a paperweight when he was seventeen, caused brain damage. He was institutionalized for two years after that, but they obviously should have thrown away the key.'

Magozzi kept scrolling through the report. 'There were no ligature marks or embedded fibers in her neck, which meant it was a hands-on, manual strangulation. But there were no fingerprints, either.'

Gino frowned and rubbed the whiskers that were sprouting from his chin. 'Seems a little clean for a disorganized, certified loony-tune on drugs. But the evidence against him is unimpeachable. Her blood was all over him, his DNA and prints were all over her.'

'Except on her neck, which means her killer was wearing gloves or some kind of protection. That doesn't synch with his profile or how sloppy he was.'

'He went to prison for it, so there's a reason Defense didn't score on that. I'll start looking.'

Magozzi went back to the coroner's report, took some notes, and his eyes froze on the computer screen. In the end, an investigation was simply a collection of tiny pieces that eventually filled a mosaic; tiny pieces that could steer you in an unexpected direction; tiny pieces that could easily be overlooked if you weren't careful. Magozzi stared at his monitor for a long time before he spoke. 'Gino. Clara Riskin was pregnant. And I think we know who the father was.'

Fifty-three

Deputy Frank Marlin was at the station, finishing his shift by officially logging the night's thrills into his office computer – after his detour to the Hitching Post Motel to check in on Ben, he'd ticketed two speeders, arrested one drunk driver, and had responded to a deer versus car. He'd had to put a young doe out of her misery, which would haunt him for a while. When he got to the scene, she was flailing in a ditch, trying to run on broken legs. She probably had fawns somewhere out in the woods and he hoped they would survive.

He finished his last report, which explained the discharge of his firearm – three bullets just to make sure the doe didn't suffer – then rubbed his eyes. They felt sandy and raw, and his whole body ached from sitting in his squad all night. He liked the job enough, just not the butt-time. But the shift was finally over and he'd catch a quick breakfast at the Pineview to see Kayla's sweet face and ripe curves. Maybe he'd ask her to go fishing or to see a movie this weekend. They'd been spending some time together since his divorce and she was an easy companion, who could bait her own hook and bake a perfect lemon meringue pie.

He flipped over to the bulletin screen and scrolled through it, not because he wanted to but because it was department policy to check any new BOLOs before signing off. He paused when he saw a California Corrections mug shot of a skinny, long-haired man with empty eyes. Presumed to be somewhere in Minnesota, armed and dangerous. August Riskin, a.k.a. Gustav Holst. The longer he stared at the shot, the more he thought it bore some resemblance to Mr California from the Hitching Post, but he'd run the plates before he'd left the motel and they'd checked out clean. John W. Harris from Tustin, in Pine County for some fishing.

He looked at the mug shot again, then printed out a copy. The shot was only a few years old, but this was obviously a young man. John Harris had some wear and tear on him, a lot of bulk, and the deep creases that came with time. You didn't age ten years in three. Still, it was worth checking out. He'd just swing by the Hitching Post on his way to the Pineview and have a chat with him about fishing, get a closer look.

He glanced up when Randy Morrow walked into the office, ready and eager to start his shift. He was a new hire, fresh out of the academy, and his enthusiasm hadn't yet been dulled by the realities of the job. It was refreshing for a veteran such as Frank, and he liked him. 'Hey, Randy, you want to take a ride with me?'

'Sure, Frank. What's up?'

'I'll fill you in on the way.'

Gus jerked awake in the sprung-out bed at the Hitching Post Motel to the sound of gravel crunching in the parking lot outside his door and the indistinct chatter of a police radio.

FUCK, FUCK, FUCK! his mind screamed. They'd found him. Somehow, they'd found him.

Impossible, his mind stubbornly resisted. *It's just Deputy Marlin, stopping to check in on Ben.*

He heard a sharp rap on his door, the cop calling, 'Mr Harris?' and at that moment he knew something was very wrong. And there was no way in hell he was going to let all his work go up in flames in a shitty motel in the middle of nowhere.

With a frantic heart, he slid out of bed, crab-walked to the bathroom and shut the door quietly. On hands and knees, he ripped open the zipper of his duffel bag and clawed wildly through bundles of cash, grabbing the cell phone. He saw the gun and grabbed it, too, but suddenly it felt alien and wrong in his hand as a bright, strange truth was revealed to him: he didn't want to die. And he didn't want to kill anybody else. His fight was almost over, and the only thing that mattered was finishing it, whatever the consequences.

His hand was shaking badly as he began punching numbers into the phone to start the sequence earlier than he'd planned. There was an hour on the timer, and he wanted so badly to be watching TV when it happened but apparently it wasn't meant to be. No matter, he supposed. What was important was that Gus Riskin was finally going to make his impact.

The rapping on the door grew more insistent, the cop's voice louder. 'Mr Harris, this is Deputy Marlin. Can I have a word?'

'Just a minute,' Gus called, slipping on a pair of jeans and shoving the gun into the back waistband.

Fifty-four

Gino was pacing around his desk, demolishing a third donut. 'Clara's pregnancy and the lack of fingerprints on her neck never came up in the trial. I went through every frigging word.'

Magozzi shook his head. 'That's rotten to the core.'

'Damn right it is. And nobody's going to convince me Trey Norwood killed her, along with his own kid. And it doesn't look like Kuehn killed her either, so we're looking for a third party.'

'I suppose you have a theory.'

'Of course I do. Clara tells Trey about the baby, and Trey's in love with her so he wants to do the right thing. Happily ever after. He goes to his parents for help and their blessing. But the bad news that he'd knocked up the fourteen-year-old daughter of the help didn't sit well with them. That could have been a little tarnish on the sterling. Maybe even a major inconvenience and a problem the Norwoods needed to solve.'

'Please do not tell me you're saying Gregory Norwood killed her.'

'Hey, I'm just laying down some fresh tracks. Walk with me and don't panic.'

'I'm not panicking.'

'I don't see Norwood getting his hands dirty. But maybe he found somebody who would for the right price. Conrad Jarvick comes to mind. I told you he was —'

'Yeah, yeah, an asshole. But a homicidal one? I get where you're going, but you're speculating about pure evil.'

'And what's so weird about that? We see it all the time. A reputation, a fortune, and the future of an only son were at stake. And, don't forget, Clara Riskin was holding all the cards. What happens if there's a lovers' spat and she turns on the family, goes to the press? Maybe Gregory Norwood didn't want to leave it to chance.'

'That's crazy.'

Gino grunted. 'It's not the craziest theory I've ever come up with, not by a long shot. Try this on for size. Norwood never sent the letter of termination to the Riskins, and when we asked Zeller about the timeline, he got amnesia, right?'

'It was twelve years ago. I don't remember what I had for dinner last night.'

Gino batted away the interruption, sending a piece of donut flying. 'You had a Kwik Mart hotdog. So let's say Norwood's about to send the letter, then Trey shares the news he's going to be a daddy and wants to get married. Norwood wants to get rid of Clara and her family, but he doesn't want any loose ends, so he holds back the letter to keep her around until he figures out what to do with her.'

Magozzi let out an irritated sigh. 'Norwood wasn't going to jettison his son's pregnant girlfriend and her family. That would have opened up a lot of vulnerabilities.'

Gino persisted: 'Norwood already had knowledge that the Riskins had hired a druggie nutcase. What a perfect storyline, what a perfect candidate for a violent homicide. Kip Kuehn works the property, gets obsessed with a pretty young girl: who's *not* going to buy him as the doer, especially with the physical evidence?'

'Kuehn beat her. Norwood didn't set that up.'

'Maybe Kuehn didn't. He could have been framed from the get-go for everything. But they forgot to put some of Kuehn's prints on Clara's neck. Sloppy, but it got past the court. Or the court was bought and paid for. Gus Riskin pulled it together and decided the only justice he was going to get was killing Norwood. We had him figured for the murder anyhow. And you know damn well Zeller was in on this – he had to be – and so was Conrad.'

Magozzi felt a hollowness start to swallow him. What Gino was saying was horrific and outrageous, but in a very sick world, it made sense. 'This is all conjecture. Wild conjecture.'

'We wouldn't solve a case without it. Conjecture always leads to greater things.'

'Yeah, like evidence. Which we don't have. And if there's even a grain of truth in what you're saying, how would Riskin figure this nightmare out? He was ten when it happened.'

'He was there, Leo. Maybe he saw something. Maybe something that didn't make sense when he was ten, but makes sense now.'

'Like what?'

Gino rolled his tongue around his cheek. 'Could be something his parents had, something he found after they died. Or it could be that Zeller's face has been plastered all over the media ever since he decided to throw his hat in the ring for governor. And Conrad never leaves his side. Maybe that rang bells big-time for Riskin.'

Magozzi rubbed at the sharp pain that was burning in his temples. 'Norwood and Zeller as co-conspirators to the murder of a pregnant fourteen-year-old girl, Conrad as hitman, and Riskin as Norwood's killer. It's a great screenplay, Gino, but if that's what happened, there is no way in hell we're ever going to prove it.'

'That's where you're wrong. If we start hitting Zeller with this angle and he knows something, super-lawyer or not, he'll paint himself into a corner eventually.'

'You want to go after Zeller.'

'I want to question him. And the Norwoods. Betty, in particular.'

Both their phones jumped to life, ringing and clamoring with alert tones. Gino grabbed his first and answered. He listened, asked a few questions, then slammed it down. 'Getting closer, Leo. That was Pine County. Riskin shot two cops. He's on the run.'

Fifty-five

Gus hadn't wanted to use the gun again, but it turned out his survival instinct was more powerful than he'd ever realized. At least he hadn't killed either cop, just wounded them to buy some time. And he hadn't hurt Ben at all, at least not physically. And he wouldn't. He was just a kid with his whole life ahead of him. Besides, he needed a driver and a car while he thought things through. He had a very small window of time to figure out his next move and he couldn't give that important task the attention it demanded while driving and looking out for cops on his tail at the same time.

He needed a car. What had happened back at the motel wasn't hard to figure out, even for the hayseeds up here. There was definitely an APB out on Ben's Camry, and he was on law enforcement's radar, as unbelievable as it seemed, because the cops had recognized him. He'd seen the unmistakable flash of shock, then certainty in their eyes when he'd opened the door, as if they'd just been waiting to see his face, waiting for confirmation. Deputy Marlin had been clueless last night, so something had happened between then and now.

'How fast are you going, Ben?'

'I – I'm going the speed limit, like you said. I have it on cruise control.'

'That's good.' The poor kid was drenched in sweat and

his hands were shaking on the wheel. Gus was sorry for what he'd put him through and was still putting him through. He could smell the rank odor of urine in the car, emanating from the dark patch on the front of the boy's jeans. He'd pissed himself the second he saw the gun.

Ben needed to relax. Ben needed to trust him. 'I'm not going to hurt you, I promise you that.'

'Thank you, sir,' he said, in a wobbly voice.

'You're polite, that's a rare thing nowadays. What do you do with yourself when you're not working at the Hitching Post?'

'I . . . Well, I'm in school part-time. To be an electrician.'

'That's smart. It's good to have a trade. Like I told you, I work construction and do some mechanics on the side. A little electronics, too,' he added modestly. 'There's always work if you have a trade.'

'That's – that's what my dad says.'

'Your dad's a smart man. Listen to him.'

'Do you want me to drop you off somewhere, sir?'

'That's a nice idea, except the second you do, you'll call the cops. And I understand that, I really do.'

'No, I *promise* I won't. Or . . . you could just drop me off and take my car.'

'And you'll still call the cops. The outcome is the same either way, so it's best we stick together for now. But we need a different car.'

'Why?'

'The cops are looking for yours right now, Ben, I guarantee it. Do you know where we can find another?'

He shook his head and started crying. 'No. Please don't kill me.'

289

'I'm not going to kill you, Ben. I already said I wasn't going to hurt you and I meant it. How about we take the next exit and drive the back roads for a while?'

He sniffled and nodded. 'Somebody might have a car for sale at the end of their driveway. You see that a lot up here.'

'That would be good. I have cash to pay for it. And you can keep your car, Ben.'

'Thank you.'

'No thanks required. It's yours, and you need some wheels to get you back and forth to work and school. I want you to succeed, I really do. Tell me more about school.'

Ben gave him a brief, panicked glance, then returned his eyes to the road. 'It's – hard. But I like it. The challenge.'

'It must be pretty expensive if you're only going part-time.'

'It is. That's why I work at the Hitching Post. It helps with the bills.'

Gus pulled two five-thousand-dollar bundles out of the duffel bag at his feet and ruffled them casually. 'This might help you go full-time so you can finish up and get yourself into the workforce.'

Ben eyed the money in disbelief. 'What did you do? Rob a bank or something? Is that why the cops are chasing you?'

'I didn't rob anybody. I would never do that. What I did was make things right, but only when it could never happen any other way. You know the saying that Lady Justice is blind?'

He swallowed hard and nodded.

'Well, I don't think that's true. I think Lady Justice sees just as well as you and I and chooses to be blind when it suits her.'

'I guess . . . well, I guess I don't know . . .'

Gus sighed. 'Guys like you and me, Ben? We're nothing, just small fry struggling in a stream, trying to stay alive. The bigger fish eat us. That's the way it is. But we can still make a difference.' He tossed the money onto Ben's urine-stained lap. 'Take this and get a head-start on your life. I want you to have that chance. My sister never did. Neither did her baby.'

Fifty-six

Eaton Freedman startled Gino and Magozzi with a loud shout from the other side of the room. 'We got a bead on Riskin-Holst. TCG Construction confirmed Holst as an employee at one-eleven Wash.'

They felt as much as heard his heavy footfalls as he made his way to their cubicle. Then his colossal presence filled their realm. 'We got a car, too. The construction supe told me he drove an old silver Hyundai rust bucket with a smashed rear bumper. Johnny's putting out a BOLO right now.'

Gino nodded. 'Good work. What else do you know?'

'Riskin didn't show for work this morning, but he clocked in on-site yesterday at seven a.m. sharp and punched out when his shift was over at two.'

Magozzi pinched his eyes shut while he worked a time-line. 'That doesn't synch with Norwood's death. Riskin was at work when he was killed.'

'It's no alibi for Norwood's murder,' Freedman said. 'Riskin was a runner, spent as much time off the job site as he did on.'

Gino was staring at the ceiling, gnawing on his lower lip. 'So he offs Norwood, offs Gerald Stenson, runs the body out to William O'Brien, which is a two-hour round trip from the city, and nobody misses him? It doesn't add up.'

Magozzi scowled, as a roulette wheel of possible scenarios spun through his mind. He hadn't slept in over twenty-four hours, minus the hour he'd caught at Grace's, so he wasn't expecting a blinding moment of lucidity, but what Gino had just said cleared the mist a little. 'We always assumed Riskin was working alone, but as it stands now, we're still looking at him for Norwood, Stenson, Jim Beam and Lloyd Nasif. That's four people yesterday. If we're right, no way he's solo unless he's got a doppelgänger.'

'Unless he didn't do them all.'

Magozzi's phone rang and he scattered papers on his desk, looking for it. He found it buried under a copy of the last report they'd sent Malcherson about forty years ago. Or maybe it was just yesterday. 'Hang tight, guys, it's Jimmy Grimm, listen in. Hey, Jimmy,' he answered. 'I've got you on speaker. What's up?'

'Nothing good.'

Magozzi didn't like the darkness he heard in his voice; neither did anyone else, judging by their expressions. 'Go ahead.'

'We're just sorting and processing all the crap from Milo Parr's trailer. Jesus, that place was a nightmare. Haz-Mat was there all night and we were all chewing our nails down to our finger bones, just waiting for the place to blow. Praise Jesus it didn't, because Milo Parr wasn't just cooking meth in there, he was cooking bombs.'

Magozzi felt his throat tighten. '*What?*'

'Yeah. Haz-Mat found some empty containers of precursor chemicals and IED components. I won't get into the details, but there's no mistaking a meth operation for a bomb operation, and those guys know their way around both. The bad news is, there aren't any bombs there, just evidence that they were getting put together.'

'Jesus Christ,' Gino muttered. 'Are the feds there?'

'Crawling all over the place now. Not our problem, we've got our own jobs to do, right? So I'm doing mine, and guess what? That guy you're chasing down, August Riskin? His fingerprints showed up again, all over that damn trailer. Looks like you've got a domestic terrorist on your hands. For the first time in your lives, be thankful the feds are involved. They're putting the screws to Milo Parr right now.'

There were times when cases were solved slowly and methodically, with little fanfare; other times evidence and information coalesced into a burst of sudden revelation; but this was the first time in Magozzi's career that a slow-motion movie of the past twenty-four hours stuttered through his mind in blinding clarity until it reached a hor-rifying, impossible conclusion.

Norwood, Zeller, Aspen, Clara Riskin, Lloyd, Jim Beam, Milo Parr, Gustav Holst, terrorists in Roseville, bombs, one-eleven Wash-ington Avenue. And then there was Gino's voice saying just a few minutes ago, 'He was there, Leo. Maybe he saw something. Maybe something that didn't make sense when he was ten, but makes sense now.'

He looked up at the wall clock again. It was eight seven-teen. 'I think he's after Zeller. Riskin couldn't get close to him because he lives in a fortress, but he could bomb his office. One-eleven Washington Avenue is under renova-tions. He was working it. It's the perfect set-up.'

Freedman gaped at him. 'You want to tell me how you got there in the past two seconds, Magozzi?'

Maybe it had been only two seconds, but it seemed like an eternity. 'No time. Grace is there now,' he said, in a strange, strangled voice that didn't belong to him, that had never belonged to him until now, and suddenly he was on his feet, sprinting.

'You and McLaren call Dahl and tell him what you know!' Gino barked, as he ran after Magozzi.

Fifty-seven

Grace was sipping mineral water in an inauspicious waiting room outside Dahl's office. She'd only been to 111 Washington Avenue once before to visit the feds and, if anything, the dreary environment had deteriorated. She imagined the other floors of the office building that housed architects, accountants and law firms held substantially more charm. She supposed it was some consolation that a federal agency supported by taxpayer dollars wasn't wasting money on décor.

Harley was sitting next to her, reading a copy of *National Academy Associates* while he gulped coffee, courtesy of an apologetic assistant. Neither Dahl nor Shafer had arrived at the meeting yet, called or texted, but after the events of last night, that was no surprise. They had bigger things to deal with than a discussion about potential software upgrades. That could be handled later. There was no point in waiting any longer.

'I don't think we're going to see Dahl or Shafer today, Harley. They have their hands full.'

'I think you're right. Let me send Dahl a text and tell him to reschedule when things cool down. Then we can blow this place and get some real coffee. And breakfast. We can bring Gino and Magozzi donuts or something.'

Grace stood up and felt a sudden, sharp cramping in her stomach that flashed stars in her eyes and doubled her over. The first contractions of early labor – she'd spent a lot of time reading up on what to expect – this was just a preview before the main attraction, which would be much worse. But, damn, it still hurt.

Harley's expression was half panic, half glee. 'Holy shit, is it happening, Grace?'

If she hadn't been in so much pain, she would have laughed. 'It's just starting, not happening.'

'I got you, sweetie,' Harley said, hugging her against him and helping her toward the door. 'I'll get you to the hospital.'

'It's not time yet, don't worry. Just distract me. Walk me around, take me out to breakfast. This could go on for hours. I'll let you know when it's time to go.'

'I'm going to call Leo.'

Grace nodded, then cried out when another sharp pain racked her body. For all the research she'd done, she really had no idea what to expect, and neither did the experts. All they could do was give you guidelines, make far more educated guesses than she could, guided by experience, and they could diagnostically determine if things weren't right. Was this right? Was this normal?

Something's not right.

She took some deep breaths and tried to relax, sagging into Harley's calming bulk as he rubbed her back.

'Grace, forgive me, but you're going to the hospital right now, end of story.'

She let Harley guide her toward the elevators outside Dahl's office. He jabbed the call button mercilessly while she leaned against him, like a boneless puppet, floppy and weak from the pain.

'Are you okay, Grace?' he asked frantically. 'Can you wait for the elevator or do you want me to carry you down the stairs?'

'I'm okay, Harley,' she tried not to wince, 'and I definitely don't want you carrying me down the stairs.'

His breathing was heavy and fast and there was a sheen of sweat on his forehead. 'Okay, okay, just stay calm, don't panic.'

'I might say the same thing to you.' Grace simultaneously heard sirens wailing in the distance and her phone ringing in her pocket, as if the two were connected, which, of course, they weren't. She reached for it, but Harley had already grabbed it. 'I'll take it, Grace, you just relax. Talk about great timing, it's Leo. Leo!' he answered. 'I'm taking Grace to the hospital. She's having contractions. Hennepin County is closest ... Not yet, we're waiting for the elevator ... Yeah, outside Dahl's office.'

As she got through another spasm of pain, she heard Magozzi's voice shouting so loudly, she thought it would shatter the phone's speaker.

'GET OUT OF THAT BUILDING RIGHT NOW! DON'T TAKE THE ELEVATOR, TAKE THE STAIRS!'

Magozzi felt fire in his lungs and in his legs as he ran toward Washington Avenue, dodging and swerving to avoid people, cars, bikes. His heart and his feet pounded in equal, crazed rhythm as he raced past emergency vehicles angrily blatting their horns as they tried to navigate the snarl of morning rush-hour traffic. He'd probably beat them all, which was why he was on foot. Gino was somewhere behind him in a car, probably stuck in traffic, like everybody else on four wheels.

The sirens were deafening, amplified by the echo chamber the downtown buildings created, but the pounding of his heart was louder, thudding in his ears in a steady but manic cadence. He barely registered other ambient sounds — shouts, car horns, and a scream as he careened against the side of a building and re-launched his flight, knocking a woman to the ground. He'd feel bad about that later, but not now.

He veered onto Washington Avenue, his legs pumping harder, fueled not by any physical ability but by sheer adrenaline. The building was in sight now, just a few blocks up. He was going to make it, Grace and Harley would be safely outside, and this was probably just some crazy false alarm his sleep-deprived brain had manufactured. Nothing bad was going to happen.

His thoughts splintered as the violent concussion of an explosion rocked the ground beneath his feet and sent him stumbling, falling to his knees. Within seconds, screaming, crying people were running toward him against the sinister backdrop of an angry fireball, writhing in columns of black smoke, as if the earth had opened up and let Hell in.

Fifty-eight

McLaren and Freedman instinctively dropped to the floor and covered their heads when the explosion rocked City Hall. They waited breathlessly, listening to shouts and screams, sirens and phones ringing all at once in hysterical concert, which meant the 911 call centers were already inundated; cell coverage would soon be jammed by overload and down for the foreseeable future, if it wasn't already. There would be an immediate city-wide call-out that would drain law-enforcement personnel, and probably a state-wide one soon. Depending on how bad things were, it would extend far beyond Minnesota. A terror attack was the worst, most crippling thing that could happen to a city, and it had finally happened here, in pretty, peaceful, law-abiding Minneapolis in the heart of flyover country.

When the building didn't come crashing down on them, they finally got up and looked around – it was no worse for wear than it had been a few minutes earlier. Freedman gave his partner a dark, worried look. 'I don't think we got hit, Johnny. But I think one-eleven Washington Avenue just did. It's only a few blocks away.'

'Magozzi was right. Jesus, Mary, and Joseph. Pray to God Grace and Harley got out.'

'I'm doing that right now.'

Gloria ran into Homicide, her platform heels pounding the floor. She looked bewildered and frightened, not emotions McLaren or anybody else who knew her had ever expected to see on the face of their tough girl. 'What happened? What's happening?' she asked breathlessly.

'A terror attack is what happened.'

'But not here?'

'No.' Malcherson's voice and sudden appearance made them all jump. 'I just got confirmation from the FBI that the attack was on their building at one-eleven Washington Avenue.'

'Oh, my God,' Gloria whispered, covering her mouth.

McLaren reached out and bravely touched her arm – he took it as a good sign that she didn't slug him. 'Are you okay, Gloria?'

She swallowed, then shook her head. 'My sister works in that building.' She pulled her cell phone from a pocket in her blinding yellow dress and started dialing frenetically.

'Gloria, the circuits are already jammed,' Malcherson said gently. 'You won't be able to get through. There's nothing we can do right now except stay here and provide support and logistical help.'

McLaren elevated his diminutive stature by puffing out his chest and standing up to his full height. 'I'll take you there, Gloria. We'll find her.'

'Give space to the first responders, Detective McLaren.' It wasn't a request, it was an order. 'It's their job to save lives and they're the victims' best chance.'

'The chief is right,' Gloria said quietly. Her lower lip was trembling.

McLaren conceded with a miserable nod and helped her to his chair. 'It's going to be okay, Gloria, I promise. Chief, we need to tell you what's going on.'

Fifty-nine

Grace slowly regained consciousness sense by sense. She registered the metallic taste of blood; smelled smoke, acrid and foul; saw the faint red glow of an exit sign punctuating darkness; felt concrete and steel that should have been cold but were hot, and an all-encompassing, throbbing pain that radiated so completely through her body, she couldn't identify a source. But she heard nothing, nothing at all, not even the moan she felt rising in her throat. The only thing that was loud and clear were her thoughts, and Magozzi's voice.

GET OUT OF THAT BUILDING RIGHT NOW! DON'T TAKE THE ELEVATOR, TAKE THE STAIRS!

This building hadn't even been on their radar as a target. They'd missed it somehow, but at the last minute, Magozzi had known. She thought about City Hall: what if they'd missed something there, too?

Panic temporarily subsumed everything else and she struggled to sit up. A torrent of pain washed over her and she felt her fragile tether to consciousness start to slip. 'Harley?' she called out weakly, groping in the dark. She felt chunks of drywall, pieces of rebar, then recoiled when her fingers met with sticky liquid she knew was blood. A lot of it. 'Hang on, baby, it'll be okay,' she whimpered, rubbing her belly, then everything went black again.

*

Magozzi pushed against the wave of crying, hysterical people fleeing the burning building, oblivious to the thick haze of dust and the foul black smoke searing his oxygen-starved lungs. The sounds of pandemonium were earsplitting – sirens and more sirens, infinitely multiplying; shouts, screams, cries for help; the guttural roar of fire chuffing out a taunting devil's laugh.

Shards of broken glass glittered on the ground, like freshly fallen snow, and piles of steel and concrete littered the sidewalk. Fire trucks were massed on the street amid mangled cars, their hoses gushing water toward the building, while emergency personnel of every stripe descended on the scene. Stretchers and gurneys carrying the injured had started to come out of the building, and he frantically checked each one, all the while futilely dialing and redialing Grace's number, even though all the circuits were jammed and would be for hours.

'Sir, get back . . .'

He felt a strong hand on his arm and spun around, snarling, 'I'm a cop, goddamnit!'

'Magozzi?'

He couldn't see the person behind the fire helmet and face shield, but he recognized the voice of a friend and a fierce broomball opponent. 'Freddie Wilson?'

'It's not safe here, Magozzi. Just step back and let us do our job. It's bad in there and we need clearance.'

'Grace is in there, Freddie,' he said, choking on a combination of smoke and emotion. 'I think she's in labor. Harley is with her, too.'

'Oh, Jesus Christ, any idea where they might be?'

'In a stairwell. They were at the FBI office on the seventh floor.'

'I've got it covered. Stay put, Magozzi, I mean it. Don't fuck with me and don't fuck with your life. Your baby needs a daddy.'

Those last words kept Magozzi frozen in place as he watched Freddie spin around and run into the burning building, dodging flaming chunks of debris and the sheets of black water that were raining down from where the fire trucks were focusing their spray as they tried to extinguish the conflagration.

I want you to have this, Harley.

But it's your favorite book, Miss Lizzy.

It's our favorite book now, isn't it? And I won't have much use for it soon.

Why not?

I'm getting called to the other side. My husband Henry, he visits me now. He'll be taking me there.

What do you mean?

You see, Harley, when your time comes, people you've loved and lost come back to you in your dreams. Sometimes you even see them when you're awake. They're your shepherds. They help you, they guide you, they walk with you to the Pearly Gates and let you in.

Are . . . are you dying, Miss Lizzy? Please, you can't die . . .

Don't cry, son. I'm an old, sick woman who's enjoyed a blessed life. And you know what my greatest blessing is?

No.

You. Take this book and remember me, Harley. What's your favorite poem?

'Invictus.'

Why?

Because at the end it says 'I am the master of my fate: I am the captain of my soul.'

That's exactly right, Harley. That's exactly right. You are and so am I. Don't ever forget it. And when it's finally your time, I'll be coming down to guide you, too.

Harley jolted up and felt a searing pain in his left leg. He couldn't feel the other one at all. 'Grace? Gracie?' he called, into an echoing darkness that smelled acrid and deadly and felt hellishly hot. Magozzi had told them to take the stairwell out and then there had been an explosion, that much he remembered, but not much else.

He struggled, tried to stand up, but couldn't. 'Grace!' he kept shouting, but heard no answer above the din of mayhem outside the stairwell. At least they'd gotten this far, thanks to Magozzi.

He let out one last powerful shout: 'GRACE!' Then the effort and the pain in his leg overwhelmed him. He lay down again and let his eyes flutter shut.

When it's your time, I'll be coming down to guide you, too.

'It's not my time, Miss Lizzy,' he groaned. 'Please, I have things to do.' He rolled his head to the side and felt it rest on hard concrete that was tacky with blood. He could smell it now, and he could feel it growing cold on his left leg, stiffening the fabric of his jeans. 'Not my time yet,' he murmured.

When he opened his eyes again, he saw a wobbling light, which terrified him. *Go to the light.*

'NO!' he shouted, kept shouting, until he realized he was looking at the beam of a flashlight.

Sixty

'Leo!' Gino was running across the street, dodging debris, police, and firemen. 'Leo, Jesus, are you okay?'

Magozzi didn't know how he was holding it together, how he was just sitting on the hood of a squad while an emergency medical technician bandaged a nasty cut on his face. His suit was covered with dust and ash and blood. The EMT said something about shock, and maybe he was in shock, a surreal place of calm that shunted your blood to your organs and flooded you with endorphins. He couldn't leave this strange place, he didn't dare – if he did, he would simply disintegrate into a million pieces. He felt like a dying animal, curled up in the woods, blessedly anesthetized by brain chemicals while it waited for the end. 'Freddie Wilson went in for them, Gino.'

They didn't look at each other, didn't say anything, just stared at the open maw of the building, waiting. Time passed as turmoil swirled around them at dizzying speed; they sat as immovable as two boulders in the middle of a furious, engorged river.

'MAGOZZI!' somebody shouted, and he turned around slowly. Annie and Roadrunner were shoving their way through the panicked confusion, and God help anybody who got in Annie's way. But Annie didn't look like herself, not this morning – her clothing was as chic and impeccable as always, but her normally sleek bob was disheveled and mascara was trailing down her cheeks in sooty runnels. Roadrunner was as white as a sheet of paper and his sharp Adam's apple bobbed up and down in his throat.

'We didn't know what else to do, Magozzi,' she said, then started sobbing, sharp tremors shaking her body. He took her hand and held it tight and the four of them together held their collective breath as they watched a horror movie unfold in front of their eyes.

He didn't let go of Annie's hand until he saw Freddie Wilson jogging out of the building, clearing the way for two gurneys, and at that moment, everything that had been coiled so tightly inside exploded in a fierce discharge of violent energy.

'Grace!' he shouted, covering the distance in seconds. 'Grace!'

His breath stopped when he reached her side. Her beautiful face was bloody and her right arm was at an odd angle, but her eyes were open and somehow, they found his in the midst of all the chaos. She mouthed his name, but no sound came out.

He felt tears stinging his eyes for the first time in decades as he walked beside her toward a waiting ambulance, his hand on her cheek, wanting so desperately to touch more of her, but without any knowledge of her injuries, he knew he didn't dare. 'You're going to be okay, Grace. You and the baby are going to be okay. I'll be right behind you.'

He thought she gave him a faint smile, then her eyes closed as they loaded her into an ambulance. As it pulled away, he felt a hand on his shoulder and turned to see Freddie Wilson's soot-blackened face. Trails of sweat had washed away some of the grime, leaving pale streaks, like war paint. '*Is* she going to be okay, Freddie?' he asked, not recognizing the desperation in his own voice.

'She's going to be fine. Keep the faith, friend.'

Magozzi read ambiguity in Freddie's response, but deflected it because he couldn't face an alternative answer. 'What about Harley?'

'Looks like his left leg is broken. They're both pretty cut up from flying debris. I don't know what the hell they were doing in a stairwell or how you knew about it, but it probably saved their lives.'

Sixty-one

Rosalie and her mother had been sitting in front of the television ever since they'd heard and felt the explosion. There were no details yet, but plenty of speculation. Terrorism was always the first assumption, but the reporters had to restrain themselves and present alternative possibilities. One of the theories was a gas leak caused by a construction project. That had happened at a school just a few months ago and three people had died. But she didn't believe that theory, and she didn't think any of the reporters did either.

'This is just horrible,' Betty said, eyes fixed on the billowing plumes of smoke filling the TV screen. 'I can smell it. It must be close. I wonder where.'

'They'll tell us soon.' Rosalie switched channels and they watched and waited as information dribbled in. Details were sketchy so early on, but eventually a breaking news flash confirmed the location of the blast – the Lakota Building at 111 Washington Avenue – the building where Uncle Robert's offices were. And that was when her mother let out a startling, gut-wrenching keen of agony.

Rosalie took her hands and squeezed them. 'Mom? Are you all right?'

She shook her head vehemently. 'Robert.'

Rosalie withdrew a little, uncertain what to do. That stoic Betty Norwood was starting to unravel was clear, and it was difficult for Rosalie to wrap her mind around this new, emotionally fragile mother. Not that she didn't have every right to be unraveling: it was just disconcerting to witness her ongoing distress when she'd only seen her cry for the second time that morning. 'Uncle Robert wouldn't go to the office this morning. He was coming right to the hotel and he probably stopped at church to light a candle for Father. Just stay calm and I'll make some calls.'

'You won't be able to get through to anybody. The news said all the circuits are jammed.'

'The landlines still work. I'll call their house from the hotel phone.' She reached for it on the end table next to her and dialed the Zellers' home number. It rang and rang and rang, then finally went to voicemail. 'Nobody's answering, Mom, but I'll keep trying.'

Her mother looked down at her frail hands, listless in her lap. 'I knew something else horrible was going to happen, Rosalie. Didn't I tell you?'

'You did, and you were right. But let's not think the worst about Uncle Robert. We don't know anything yet.'

Her mother looked at her with vacant eyes. Her pupils were dilated and her gaze couldn't seem to settle permanently on anything. 'So much loss. I don't think I could bear another one right now.'

'There won't be any more loss, Mom.' She poured her a fresh cup of coffee, smeared a croissant with jam, and passed her the plate. Injecting caffeine and sugar into a distraught person was probably a horrible idea, but it was a minor distraction for both of them. What she should have been offering was a selection of tranquilizers, but she didn't have any, and if her mother did, they weren't working. 'I'll check on my computer, see if there's any more on-line about this.'

Betty nodded and sipped, then tore a small flake off the pastry. It took an expeditionary journey to her mouth, but she dropped it before her lips made contact. 'That's a good idea, dear. Thank you.'

Rosalie paused halfway to her bedroom door. 'Mom, do you know where Father's laptop might be?'

'He always had it with him. I imagine it's somewhere in the house.'

'It isn't. The detectives checked.'

'I'm sure they'll find it eventually.'

Robert Zeller was kneeling at the altar of the Basilica of St Mary, murmuring the Act of Contrition softly as he prayed the rosary.

O, my God, I am heartily sorry for having offended you. I detest all my sins because of your just punishment, but most of all because they offend you, my God, who are all-good and deserving of all my love. I firmly resolve, with the help of Your grace, to sin no more and to avoid the near occasion of sin.

When he was about to begin the ninth station of the cross, he heard the soft echo of footsteps behind him. He opened his eyes and turned to see Father Demestral walking down the center aisle. His broad shoulders were sloped this morning, his gait stiff and slow, his face worn with worry. He was an old man, but had never shown his age before, not like this. Robert found it disturbing and somehow ominous. 'Good morning, Father Demestral.'

'Praise be to God you're here, Robert. Praise be to God.'

He frowned. 'Is something wrong, Father?'

'I've just learned of dreadful news. Absolutely dreadful news. There's been an explosion – a terror attack, they're saying – at your office building. There are many injured, and I fear there will be fatalities.'

Robert blinked and opened his mouth, but no words came out.

'You're here and not there. Your faith spared you. I believe God has plans for you, Robert.'

Sixty-two

Magozzi would never forget the agony of waiting as he paced the floor of one of the intensive-care unit's family rooms – a cruelly deceptive term used to describe a special place in Hell where stricken friends and family idled helplessly, endlessly, awaiting word of their sick or injured loved ones. In a level-one trauma center like this, these walls had probably absorbed a lot of bad news, which was why Magozzi couldn't stop moving. If he did, the bitter reality of the situation might catch up with him and dispel the fog in his mind that was keeping him sane.

Gino, Annie, and Roadrunner were pacing, too, and it was probably a miracle they hadn't collided by now as they performed an anxious, shell-shocked minuet in front of an audience of upholstered chairs and softly colored landscape prints that were meant to be soothing. All of them were silent as their feet worried the carpet because there was nothing anyone could say to make it better.

A wall-mounted television droned the ever-breaking news in the background. The national affiliates had taken over the local news and a cavalcade of pundits was speculating about the terror attack. There hadn't been any official confirmation yet, but that would come soon. He kept waiting to see Amanda White on the screen.

He watched morosely as cutaways of reporters on the ground tallied casualties and fatalities as they were confirmed. So far, three were dead; dozens more were injured, Grace and Harley among them. Names weren't being released yet.

It suddenly occurred to him that nobody had more information about the potential source of this attack than himself and Gino, and the core of the cop that still lived inside Magozzi's devastated psyche couldn't ignore that fact. He reached out to Gino and grabbed his arm in mid-pace.

'Gino, get back to the office and finish pulling this together with McLaren, Freedman, and Dahl, if he's still alive.'

'It's already pulled together enough for them to know Riskin is responsible for every dead body in Minneapolis these past couple days. McLaren, Freedman, and the feds are on him big-time, and if he's not already in custody, he will be soon. Your only job is here and I'm staying to wait it out with you, period, end of story.'

Magozzi felt the sludge in his mind clear a little. Gino was right, of course, but it still didn't stop the manic compulsion to do something, anything, but wait. A shrink would probably tell him he was trying to fill the vacuum that fear, uncertainty, and helplessness had carved out of his soul. Denial, avoidance, displacement behavior – whatever the term, he was in the thick of it.

Annie stopped pacing and gestured to the television, which was showing grim pictures of the scene on Washington Avenue. 'Wait. Are you saying that August Riskin was behind this?'

Magozzi shrugged. 'We think so.'

Roadrunner settled into a chair, shaking his head in

confusion. 'How does a terror attack connect with Norwood?'

'It's a long story, Roadrunner, and we're not at the end yet.'

Roadrunner seemed to accept the non-answer and returned his attention to the television.

Magozzi had no idea how much time had passed before a doctor finally entered the room and introduced himself. Annie, Roadrunner, and Gino clamored around him, like kids at a free ice-cream stand, but Magozzi froze, suddenly realizing that he was no longer in a holding pattern where possible outcomes were indefinite. It was wheels-down time now, and the plane was either going to crash or it wasn't.

The doctor's words came in a roaring surf, at least in his mind, although he suspected that, in reality, they were calm and measured and delivered with compassion. Harley would recover from a badly broken leg; the orthopedic surgery to pin him back together had been successful, and he would be ready for visitors soon.

'Grace MacBride?' Magozzi asked, before anybody else had the chance. His voice was shaking, and it was all he could do to keep from shouting.

The doctor appraised him. 'Are you Detective Magozzi?'

'Yes.'

He smiled. 'Ms MacBride is stable . . .'

Magozzi let out a rush of breath and almost collapsed in relief.

'. . . but because of complications, we had to perform an emergency C-section. Congratulations, Detective. You have a healthy, beautiful baby girl to meet. Follow me.'

'I *told* you it was going to be a girl,' he heard Annie upbraid Roadrunner, as Magozzi let the doctor lead him down the hall.

She *was* beautiful, impossibly beautiful – tiny, red-faced, wrinkled, with a cap of fine black hair. But the mental snapshot he took as he entered Grace's room and saw her cradling such a precious gem took his breath away and reached a place in his soul that hadn't existed until now. At this moment in time, there was nothing else in the world except the three of them – not the cuts and bruises on her face, not the monitor flashing Grace's vitals above her head, not the array of IV lines sprouting from her arms, like unruly plastic vines, feeding off bags that hung from metal trees behind her bed. The cruel simile of a garden no one should ever have to walk through simply wasn't there.

He sat down on the bed and met his daughter for the first time, took her in his arms and felt the love in his heart expand infinitely, reaching far beyond the limits of mortal understanding. Then he held them both close, silently communicating everything he'd comprehended and become in the past minute or so. He felt like his life had always been leading up to this perfect moment in an imperfect world.

Sixty-three

An hour later, Gino walked out of the hospital, as buoyed by joy as he was crushed by despair. The city was in crisis, and in mourning for lost lives and lost innocence. Although the bomb hadn't been as lethal as initially feared, there were still fatalities and dozens more injured, and this morning's tragedy hadn't finished wreaking havoc – it would continue to radiate outward, like a poison cloud, to smother countless more.

And then there was the bright counterpoint of life – a beautiful new one – and affirmation that Harley, Grace and many others were going to be okay. It was a stubborn, unyielding conundrum that offered no reconciliation of such a stark chasm between dark and light. It was the mysterious yin-yang, the ancient continuum of misery and joy co-existing as reliably as the tides. It didn't have to make sense, it just was.

'Detective Rolseth?'

He closed his eyes when he heard Amanda White's voice. Of course she was there. Of course she'd found him. He turned around slowly, wondering how he would gather the strength to deal with her invasive presence without losing his mind.

But when he laid eyes on Amanda White, she seemed like a very different person from the one he'd seen countless other times – the reporter who mercilessly dogged him, dogged Magozzi, hungry for a scrap or a bone that could eventually become a scoop. There was none of the feral energy or aggression in her demeanor that he was so used to, and her eyes were glassy and rimmed in red. 'Ms White. I probably don't have to say it, but no comment.'

The pained look his remark elicited made him feel like an A-1 jackass. 'I'm not asking for one. I just want to know if they're okay.'

'Who?'

She shook her head in frustration. 'I'm not talking to you as a reporter right now, I'm talking to you as somebody who cares. Grace and the baby and Harley. Tell me they're okay.'

It took a while, but Gino finally found a smile for her because he believed what she said – he had no reason not to. As much of a nuisance as she could be, she had earned his and Leo's trust over the past year, had actually become a strange ally in the way cats and dogs might. 'They're all going to be okay. And Grace and Magozzi have a new baby girl.'

She smiled back. 'Out of darkness, let light shine.'

'That's a good way of putting it.'

'I can't take credit for it, it's in the Bible. In so many words, at least.'

'I didn't take you for the religious type.'

'When something unimaginable, something horrible, happens, like it did this morning, people either find their religion or lose it.' She held his gaze. 'I can't imagine how August Riskin ties into all this, but I look forward to hearing the story. Thank you for telling me about your friends, Detective. I'm so glad for them. I'm so glad for you all.'

As she started to walk away, Gino reached out to touch her arm. It was a small gesture, and a strange one he would never be able to explain, but today was unlike any other and a reminder that, without human connection, the world was a pretty bleak and meaningless place. 'Do you like Minneapolis, Ms White?'

'I love it. I love it more than ever now.'

Gino shoved his hands into his pockets and looked around at the milling crowds, the film crews and news vans behind barricades, the ambulances still pulling into the emergency entrance. Things would settle eventually, but the ghosts of this day would linger forever. 'That's too bad. When you get your exclusive from us, you're not going to be here for long. I'd start packing for New York.'

She gave him a strange look. 'You know where to find me when you're ready.'

Gino watched her walk away, then looked around, trying to remember where he'd parked the car. He blinked, then rubbed his eyes when he saw an apparition that looked like McLaren and Gloria, rushing toward the hospital entrance hand in hand. He had to get some sleep before he started seeing flying monkeys.

Sixty-four

Rosalie flinched when she heard the knock on the hotel-room door, then let out a shuddering sigh of relief when she heard Uncle Robert's voice. 'Betty? Rosalie?'

She ran to the door, flung it open, and hugged him. 'Oh, thank God you're all right. We didn't know what happened to you.'

'God is exactly who you should thank. I was in church when it happened.'

She heard a strange squeak behind her and turned to see her mother standing there, weeping for the second time today. Uncle Robert went to her, gathered her in his arms, and held her close as her tiny body shook. 'It'll be okay, Betty,' he soothed her.

Rosalie wasn't sure anything was going to be okay, and in her ragged emotional state, it was disconcerting to see her mother in the arms of someone other than her father. Come to think of it, she'd never seen her mother cling to her father like that, not even after Trey died. There had always seemed to be some barrier between them, an invisible morbidity that was a repelling force, she just hadn't realized it until now. She saw Conrad, standing dutifully in the hall, and gestured him in. 'Please, Conrad.'

'Thank you, ma'am, but my place is out here.'

Zeller turned and shook his head. 'Not today, Conrad. Come in.'

'What about Louise?' Rosalie asked, thinking of the poor woman alone in her giant house while her husband comforted somebody else. 'Does she know you're all right?'

'I was finally able to get through to her. She wants us to be together, all of us. Pack your things and we'll go to the house. She's waiting for us.'

Betty Norwood nodded and reluctantly peeled away from Robert's embrace.

'All of our things?' Rosalie asked.

'Everything. You'll be our guests. I don't want either of you anywhere near downtown.'

It was strange to walk through the lobby, which was filled with people, but absolutely silent – everybody was held captive by the televisions in the open lobby bar. When someone finally caught sight of the favorite gubernatorial candidate, murmurs started to ripple through the crowd. Uncle Robert did exactly the right thing by joining the somber gathering and speaking with his future constituents, listening to them, reassuring them, offering prayers. It was a demonstration of compassion, strength, and unity during a terrible time and just what a politician should do, but Rosalie still found it distasteful. Then again, she'd always found politics distasteful.

He finally excused himself and she watched as admiring eyes followed his departure. He'd made a personal connection and they wouldn't forget it.

No one seemed to notice the grieving Norwood women or Conrad pushing a large brass luggage trolley out to Uncle Robert's Town Car. Rosalie wondered how long it would take the city to find some semblance of a normal rhythm again, or if it ever would.

She stood under the portico and watched mindlessly as Conrad loaded their bags into the trunk. The streets were empty, except for police cars and emergency vehicles; the air was choking and thick with a bitter miasma held close to the ground by humidity; sirens were still wailing in the near distance. A funereal pall had settled over everything and everyone.

Conrad closed the trunk with a thud and she was startled out of her melancholy trance, suddenly missing her purse. 'I'm sorry, Conrad, would you open the trunk again? I forgot I put my purse in my overnight bag.'

'Of course.' He opened the trunk and gestured. 'Which one is it, ma'am?'

'I can get it, thanks.' She reached into the very back of the trunk and retrieved her purse, then took a seat next to Mom. No one spoke, because what could they say? Car rides were for small-talk, and that would have been offensive. Any deeper discussion remained bottled up in all of them, waiting for time, distance and a different environment to smooth the raw edges and make what had happened to her father yesterday and to Minneapolis this morning acceptable topics of conversation.

But the silence in the car was oppressive, the view out of the window depressing, so Rosalie turned inward and distracted herself by rummaging in her purse, getting out her wallet, checking her phone, putting on lip gloss – normal things on a steamy, hot, post-apocalyptic morning, twenty-four hours after her father had been killed.

It wasn't until they were halfway to the Zellers' that she finally depleted all the distractions the purse had to offer, zipped it up, and placed it at her feet. She looked down at her lap and noticed a reddish-brown smudge on her dress where the purse had been resting. She tried to brush it away, but it smeared, leaving an unsightly blotch on the cream silk. Perhaps it was her old-fashioned father sending a message that she should be wearing black.

Tears burned her eyes. She *should* be wearing black – her mother was. But this morning's mayhem had distracted her from her personal loss and she'd given little thought to dressing.

'What's wrong, dear?'

'Everything. Nothing. I just picked up some dirt and I don't know why it's making me cry.'

'Because you're sad, Rosalie.' She placed a hand on her knee and examined the stain. 'It looks like clay. You probably picked it up in Aspen – you know how red the soil can be there.' She reached into her purse and pulled out a package of wet wipes. That was the wonderful thing about mothers' purses – no matter how many useful things you kept in yours, they always had more. 'Thanks, Mom.'

'You should keep these on hand when you travel. They're meant specifically for clothing and they'll take out any stain.'

And there it was – the purest distillation of Betty Norwood: the staunch pragmatist, the quintessential queen of avoidance, staking her claim to a fantasy where the soil in Aspen was somehow important in the face of her husband's murder and a terrorist attack; where a wet wipe was the panacea to any ill or misfortune.

Betty Norwood blotted the stain on her daughter's dress delicately, with motherly care, and just like magic, it started to fade. 'See? They work wonders.' She sat back in the seat and looked out of the window. Her job was done. Even though the world, their world, was crumbling, a pricey cream silk dress had been saved.

Rosalie looked down at the used wipe. She blinked a few times, then stifled the strange sound rising in her throat. That was the funny thing about blood. When it was old or dry, it looked brown. But when it was reconstituted with moisture, it turned red again.

Sixty-five

Gus Riskin hadn't expected the cops this soon. The optimistic part of him hadn't expected them at all. He and Ben had bought a rust-eaten pick-up truck for five hundred bucks, ditched the Camry, and were almost halfway to the Canadian border. They blended into the rural landscape perfectly, where battered pick-ups were plentiful, and empty back roads provided safe passage for fugitives.

He kept his eyes on the side mirror. There must have been a dozen squads trailing a short distance behind, pacing them but not making a move. Their lights were on but the sirens were silent, as if they were all part of a funeral procession.

It had been a good day so far – maybe the best he'd ever had. He would never be able to describe the thrill of hearing a somber radio announcer talk about the explosion in Minneapolis. Last count, there were five dead, and he knew one of those fatalities would be Robert Zeller – he'd carefully situated the bomb in the ductwork that ran directly behind his office and the man was there at six a.m. seven days a week. He was sorry for the others, but his careful placement had been meant to minimize collateral damage.

Yes, it had been a good day so far, but good days eventually came to an end. He probably wouldn't ever see that little place in the desert with the chickens and a dog and a lady friend, but that was okay. He'd made his mark in the world: he'd rebalanced the scales of justice.

'What should I do?' Ben squeaked, his hands trembling on the steering wheel.

Gus took a deep, cleansing breath and felt the serenity of accomplishment; the serenity of acceptance. His fight was finished and there was no reason to prolong the inevitable. And Ben was really starting to fall apart. It would be cruel to put him through any more strain.

'Pull over, Ben, and be calm. Keep your hands on the wheel and do what the cops tell you. Keep that cash if you can. Stuff it in your drawers right now. If they find it, tell them you just sold your car.'

'But they'll know that's a lie,' he blubbered miserably.

'I really want you to go to school full-time.' He pulled another ten grand out of the duffel and added it to the bundles already on Ben's lap. 'I won't have any use for this now, so I want you to have it. Do what I said and hide the cash, then slow down, put on your signal, and pull over to the shoulder.'

Ben obeyed, shoved the cash down the front of his pants, and put on the signal light. 'You won't shoot anybody else, will you?'

'Nah, no point now. Nice and slow, Ben, that's right, then stop and put it in park. Remember, keep your hands on the wheel and do exactly what the cops tell you to do.'

'Wh-what are you going to do?'

'I'm going to be a good citizen and cooperate.'

Sixty-six

Magozzi was woken from a sound sleep by his ringing phone and it took him several seconds to remember where he was – on the sofa in Grace's hospital room. Earlier, the nurse had taken the sleeping baby to the nursery so mother and daughter could get some rest.

Childbirth is as much a trauma for the baby as it is for the mother, even more so after a C-section.

Magozzi had been slightly offended that she hadn't mentioned anything about dads being traumatized, especially dads who'd seen the mother of their soon-to-be-born baby being taken out of a burning building on a gurney. To make matters worse, she'd then shooed him out of Grace's bed for the same reason. He had been about to lay the bossy nurse out with a few choice words about ripping a newborn from its mother's arms and breaking up a family, but before he really stepped in it, he realized the nurse was right. Grace had a lot of healing to do and you couldn't heal without rest.

She was snoring softly in bed, which made him smile. Even perfect people snored, which made him feel a little better about being a mere mortal in the presence of a goddess. Her black hair was fanned out on the pillow and her beautiful face, even bruised and battered, was as still and serene as he had ever seen it. The sight was so mesmerizing he almost forgot someone had called.

Reluctantly, he snuck out of the room, found a seat in one of the dreaded family rooms, and pushed redial.

Gino answered brightly: 'Leo! How goes it?'

'Terrific. Grace is sleeping and so was I.'

'Good. I didn't want to disturb you, but I knew you'd pistol-whip me if I didn't give you an update.'

'You're right. What's going on?'

'Let me start you out with a little *amuse-bouche* – we have a potential new lead from Norwood's next-door neighbor, who's a paranoid surveillance nut with twenty-five trail cams covering the outside of his house. He and his wife were in Seattle yesterday, so they missed the canvass, but when he got home, he checked out the footage. One cam has a partial view of the Norwoods' yard. He says, around eight ten yesterday morning, a car pulled into the driveway. It left fifteen minutes later. That fits the timeline of Norwood's murder perfectly.'

Magozzi felt his pulse speed up. 'Did he make out the car?'

'Unfortunately it was an almost non-existent view, obscured by trees, a rose hedge and some pergolas covered with vines. He's compressing the file and sending it, for what it's worth. Tommy's going to try some enhancement. It's not much, but it's something, which is why this was an *amuse-bouche*.'

'What's the main course?'

'The feds have August Riskin in custody. Caught the bastard on the back roads halfway to Canada. Dahl said he's toast, but we didn't hear that from him.'

Magozzi felt the knots in his shoulders melt a little. 'He's good for the attack?'

'And then some. I don't know many details, but from what I do know, we might as well save taxpayer dollars, skip court, and put him right on Death Row.'

'When do we get a shot at him?'

'Sooner than you'd think. This big fucking mess is all connected. They know it, and they want what we've got. Besides, our buddy Special Agent in Charge Paul Shafer is too political to hamper an investigation into Norwood's death.'

'I want a piece of this.'

'You've got way more important things to do than interrogate some scumbag terrorist, Leo.'

'He almost killed Grace and our baby, and Harley, and he did kill a lot of other innocents, and not just in that building. I have to be there. Just hold me back.'

Gino was quiet for a moment. 'I get it. I'll come pick you up when you're ready.'

Magozzi was suddenly struck by the absence of any ambient sound in the background, and he knew damn well City Hall was bedlam right now. 'Where are you? There's no noise.'

'I'm hiding out in an interrogation room. City Hall is one big staging area, wall-to-wall cops everywhere, and the decibel level around here is somewhere between a fighter-jet launch and a Howitzer. My eardrums were starting to bleed and I sure as hell couldn't hear myself think, let alone make a phone call.'

'Thanks, Gino. I'll get back to you soon.' Magozzi hung up, thinking it was damn strange that what had started out as the absolute worst day of his life had turned into the absolute best.

Grace was barely awake when he walked back into the room. 'Did somebody call?' she asked groggily.

He walked over to her and took her hand. 'Gino.'

'A break in your case?'

'A big one.'

'You should be there.'

'I know. But I don't want to leave you or the baby. Ever.'

She squeezed his hand. 'We're not going anywhere.' Then her eyelids fluttered and closed.

Magozzi stopped to check in on Harley on his way out. Annie and Roadrunner were still in chairs at his bedside but he was semi-alert now, sitting up and enjoying his captive audience. He looked like crap in every way, with a bandaged head, two black eyes, and his leg in traction, but there was a funny smile on his face that carved a lopsided crescent in his black beard. 'Leo!'

'Hey, big guy, good to see you awake. Last time I was here you were zonked out and snoring like a lumberjack with adenoid problems.'

Annie turned and gave him a long-suffering look. 'That was when the morphine was fresh. Now he's just as high as a giraffe's backside, trying to grope me seven ways to Sunday.' Her voice sounded huffy, but the relief in her eyes told a different story.

'What else is a red-blooded American male supposed to do in the presence of such an astounding Rubenesque beauty?' Harley reached out a hand, which she slapped away.

'Hmm, let me think. Maybe pretend your gene pool didn't stop evolving sometime during the Paleolithic age?'

Magozzi smiled, comforted by the normalcy of Annie's

and Harley's bickering. Things were going to be okay. 'How's the leg?'

'Feels great,' he slurred. 'I've never felt better in my life.'

'Morphine will do that,' Roadrunner said archly.

'And what do you know about morphine, Roadrunner? You don't even eat animals or drink. At least until last night.'

'Enough to know you should probably lay off the clicker for a while.' Roadrunner looked at Magozzi. 'I told the doctor not to let him self-medicate.'

Annie bobbed away from Harley's wandering hand, like a boxer ducking a roundhouse. 'I think anything that will render him unconscious again is a fine idea.'

Harley's mischievous, crooked smile became sentimental. 'How are Gracie and the baby?'

'They're both gorgeous, both resting. The nurse tried to kick me out of the room earlier, but I charmed her into letting me stay.'

'Sure you did. You've got a pretty face, Leo. And you've got a gun. How did you get a gun into ICU?'

Magozzi showed him his shield. 'A cheap piece of metal can open doors and soothe even the most savage nurse. Rest up, Harley, you have a leg that needs to mend. I hear you've got enough pins in you that you'll never make it through airport security for the rest of your life without a shitload of paperwork.'

Annie reached out and gave Magozzi's arm a squeeze. 'You look like you're on your way somewhere, darling.'

'Taking a quick run to go pound the sorry life out of Gus Riskin.'

'Yeah!' Harley raised his arms, then winced. 'Go get

'em, Tiger. Grrrr . . .' He started to giggle, then his head fell back on the pillow and he was snoring again.

'Some company.' Annie rolled her eyes. 'On his best day, Harley's emotional age is somewhere around sixteen, but the morphine turned him into a five-year-old.'

Roadrunner snickered. 'Annie and I will keep an eye on Grace for you while you're gone.'

'Thanks, guys. See you soon.'

Sixty-seven

Rosalie hadn't seen Louise Zeller in three months, so the decline in her appearance was shocking. As always, she was perfectly dressed and made-up, but she looked ravaged and gaunt, with haunted dark eyes and skin so pale it seemed almost bloodless.

There was a specific aura of hopelessness unique to the very depressed and Louise was wreathed in it. She always had been. There was also a glassy detachment in her eyes, probably a result of her medications. But she put on a brave face and hugged her hard. 'I'm so sorry about your father, Rosalie. This is such an awful time and you're in my thoughts and prayers the most.'

Rosalie hugged her back and kissed her cheek. It was perfumed by cosmetics, her breath by wine, courtesy of the open magnum of Montrachet on the kitchen counter. If there was ever a time to get tipsy before noon, this was it. Uncle Robert didn't look particularly happy about it, which suggested this was an ongoing point of contention, but she didn't seem to notice. Or else she didn't care.

Louise finally broke away and greeted Betty with equal warmth, then caught her husband's eyes. 'God called you this morning, Robert. He saved your life.'

Rosalie didn't remember Louise being particularly devout, just religious in the way church-going Catholics were, but she'd certainly had her share of tribulations.

Perhaps faith was sustaining her during a particularly difficult time as she stared at the likely prospect of becoming the First Lady of Minnesota.

He gave her a light peck on the cheek. 'Father Demestral and I prayed for Gregory and the souls lost today. Shall we all go down to the gazebo? I can't think of a more grounding, peaceful place where we can mourn and reflect together.'

'Please go ahead. I'll join you all in a bit. I just want to make sure Betty's and Rosalie's luggage gets to their rooms and everything is in order. Andrew?'

A young man in chef's whites walked out of the catering kitchen. 'Yes, ma'am?'

'There's been a change of venue. Would you lay out lunch at the gazebo, please? And, Conrad, please bring the Norwoods' luggage up to the guest wing. I'll show you which rooms.'

'I'll follow you,' Rosalie said. 'I'd like to change and freshen up before lunch.'

Louise looked pleased. 'I've put you in your favorite room, dear.'

Conrad trailing behind them, Rosalie and Louise went up a broad marble staircase and into a large bedroom filled with rich tapestries, intricate mosaic tile work, and Moroccan furniture. All the guestrooms had different themes, but this one was the most exotic and Rosalie had always liked it best. Conrad placed her bags carefully on an ornate antique camel saddle, the perfect luggage stand for the room, then excused himself.

Louise called after him, as she fretted over a brass urn of lilies, 'Put Mrs Norwood's bags in the Colonial Room, would you?'

'Thank you, Conrad,' Rosalie added, as she watched Louise obsess over the apparently troublesome cluster of flowers that looked perfect to her. There was a controlled mania to her movements.

'I was so terrified for you when Robert told me somebody tried to break into your house last night. Have the police found them?'

'Not yet.'

Louise gave her a grave look. 'There are bad things happening, Rosalie,' she whispered. 'I've seen evil in visions before, but now they're happening. I know it means something, but I can't make sense of it. Be careful.' Her eyes drifted to the spot on Rosalie's dress. 'Oh, my, would you like me to soak that for you? If you send it to the cleaners like that, they'll ruin it.'

'I'll take care of it, but thanks.' She hesitated. 'How are you, Louise?'

She considered carefully. 'Lonely. Robert is hardly home anymore. Of course, I'm not the best company these days.'

She *was* alone, isolated, and not just because her husband was occupied with other things. Those closest to her still insisted on couching her struggles in maddening euphemisms, as if there was inherent weakness and shame attached to the truth, which was therefore something to be ignored. It was exactly how Trey had been treated. Real lives sacrificed for appearances.

'But now isn't the time to be melancholy over never having children,' she mused, with bizarre levity. 'I've got you and you've never been less than a daughter to me.'

'Louise, I'm here for you if you ever want to talk. I understand. More than you know.'

'Thank you, dear. Maybe we'll have lunch sometime, just you and me.' She gave her another hug, then left the room, tossing a carefree little wave over her shoulder.

As she walked away, Rosalie considered the grim possibility that Louise might have reached her breaking point and was beginning to deteriorate. It was a new sorrow to compound the old. Bad things *were* happening.

She closed the door and locked it, then carried her overnight bag into the bathroom and tipped it upside down on the vanity. There was a reddish-brown patch on the leather and when she wiped it with a damp tissue, it turned red, just like Mom's wet wipe had.

There was a perfectly plausible reason for there to be blood in the trunk of Uncle Robert's Town Car: Conrad had cut himself. It was as simple as that. Nothing sinister about it. But blood anywhere outside a person's body was disturbing. Blood in a car trunk was worse by half because of the steady diet of mob movies Hollywood fed the populace. When movie mobsters got whacked, they were thrown into trunks. 'You're being an idiot,' she chided herself.

'Rosalie?' She heard her mother's voice on the other side of the door. 'Is everything all right?'

'Uh . . . sure, I'm just changing, Mom.' *Out of my bloodied dress.* 'Freshening up.'

'There's a lovely lunch down at the gazebo. Please join us.'

'I will, Mom, in just a few minutes.' She stashed the bag and her soiled dress in a cupboard, slipped on a black linen shift, then checked herself in the mirror. She looked normal, except for the dark circles under her eyes that advertised a sleepless night and profound stress, which was apparently causing pathological paranoia. Or maybe Louise's was

336

contagious. And then she heard bells, which made her heart jump.

They're not bells, they're wind chimes. You are losing your mind, seeing things, hearing things, imagining things, 'out damned spot' . . .

But they sounded just like Trey's bells, which no rational person would take as a message from beyond, but she was not rational today, not by a long shot.

Rosalie walked over to the French doors that led to a veranda overlooking the lake. Wind chimes hung from the railing, tinkling in a light breeze. No carousing evil spirits, no malevolent presence hulking in the shadows of the eaves, like a gargoyle, waiting to drain her life force.

She could see her mother and Uncle Robert sitting in the gazebo at the bottom of the broad, gently sloping lawn, Conrad at attention a few yards away, flanked by the two giant mastiffs that helped guard the property. They were drinking wine and, by God, that was exactly what she needed right now.

She went downstairs and poured herself a generous glass of white Burgundy from the open magnum on ice, inviting her to partake in its mind-numbing potential. Her mother's purse was sitting on the kitchen counter next to it, the package of wet wipes protruding from the open top, reminding her of just how strange life had become in the past twenty-four hours.

After a few fortifying sips, she wandered the vast main floor of the house, as familiar to her as her own or her parents'. She paused in the Great Room, a spectacular space with vaulted ceilings and a dramatic stone fireplace that had been sourced from the multi-colored rock on their Aspen property. She and Trey had spent hours playing there as kids and he'd always loved that fireplace – it reminded him of the stones in the Roaring Fork River, where his ashes should have been scattered yesterday. At some point, she and Mom would return to Aspen and release the ashes of father and son: they could take the journey downstream together.

Eventually, she found herself in the front foyer. She peered out of the sidelights of the big double doors and saw the Town Car still sitting in the motor court. On a table by the door was a set of keys. A quick check of the trunk and she would realize the blood hadn't come from there and she could bring her lunacy to an end once and for all.

Keys were funny things, she thought, as she picked them up and held them in her palm. They were mostly generic in appearance. You could tell a car key from a house key, but beyond that, they all looked pretty much alike, unless you had a very particular kind of lock that required a very particular kind of blank, one that couldn't be duplicated without the original paperwork and serial number.

Like her house key, which was just like the one on this fob.

Detective Magozzi's voice sounded in her head.

Does anybody else have a key to your house?

No. Well, Mom does, of course.

But these weren't Mom's keys, and somewhere deep inside her, she understood that something was very wrong. She just couldn't grab hold of it.

A home intrusion that wasn't. No evidence of B and E. Maybe because it hadn't been a break-in.

She backed away, retreated to the kitchen, and began rifling through her mother's purse. Her pulse was pounding in her ears and her hands shook as she felt the cool metal of keys and withdrew the ring. All accounted for. Except her house key.

Her mind didn't go beyond that, didn't speculate or try to rationalize. She simply walked back to the foyer, pressed a button on the Town Car's fob, and watched the shiny black trunk lid rise, completely unaware of Louise Zeller watching her from the veranda.

Sixty-eight

Magozzi and Gino took seats around Dahl's ad hoc desk in the temporary location the feds had set up after their former domicile had been blasted to smithereens. All three looked equally bad, but Dahl didn't smell of smoke, which would give him a slight advantage if some sadist were to hold an impromptu beauty contest.

'Gus Riskin is done.' He pushed two folders across the cluttered surface, displacing several others. 'Jackets on what we've got so far. Based on hard evidence alone, he'll never see the light of day again.'

'Is he cooperating?' Magozzi asked, skimming through the pages.

'Beyond our wildest dreams. He hasn't lawyered up yet, he's talking, and he doesn't seem remotely concerned about the consequences. Of course, he is a psychopath, so the verity of his statements is questionable.'

'Give us a short version of what you know.'

'He claims a long-standing relationship with the Roseville suspects through unnamed associates in Orange County, California, which we're looking into. He told me they were working together to attack seats of justice everywhere, including City Hall, "because the scales must be evened." But he won't talk about the venue change to one-eleven Washington Avenue, and the Roseville suspects deny any knowledge of it. We assume the attack was aimed at our FBI office, and the construction on the building made it more convenient than City Hall.'

Magozzi closed the folder. 'We think he was trying to kill Robert Zeller.'

Dahl lowered his head, squeezed his temples. 'You two have a lot of explaining to do.'

'We will, but give us Riskin first. We might be able to fill in more blanks after we've talked to him.'

He looked Magozzi straight in the eye. 'I have a request.'

'What?'

'Don't kill him. Because if I were in your shoes right now, I'd be damn tempted.'

'I'm not going to kill him. I want him to rot in prison.'

Dahl nodded. 'I thanked God a few hundred times when I heard Grace and Harley were going to be okay. Congratulations on the baby, Detective. That was the best news I've heard in a long time.'

In spite of everything, Magozzi felt a smile form on his lips. 'Thanks, Dahl.'

'Go do your thing. I'll be watching.'

If you passed August Riskin on the street, you wouldn't give him a second glance. And if you weren't used to dealing with psychopaths, you certainly wouldn't know him for the hideous monster he was. But his eyes were a dead giveaway. If he'd ever had a soul, it was long gone.

Magozzi let Gino take the lead because he didn't trust himself. All he could focus on was the fantasy image of his hands wrapping around Riskin's throat and watching the life seep out of his blank eyes.

Gino didn't waste much time on preliminaries and got right to the point. 'We know why you did it, Gus.'

'Did what?'

'Come on. You're in such deep shit with the feds, you might as well tell us your personal story. It's not going to hurt you, that's for damn sure. You might think you're sitting here with us, but you're already on Death Row. Even if you hired the greatest lawyer on the planet, the best you'd do is skate into prison with about a thousand consecutive life sentences. And even that scenario's iffy.'

'I don't have a story. I just did what I had to.'

'Yeah, yeah, yeah, and nobody understands, the devil made you do it, right? So far you killed five people today in that building and injured dozens more.'

'I'm not proud of that, but there was no other way.'

Gino snorted. 'Oh, you're one prince of a guy, aren't you? And how about the four you killed yesterday? Was that just a warm-up for the main event?'

'I didn't kill four people yesterday.'

'Tell us your story, Gus. I'm in a real bad mood and my partner here has a serious personal beef with you. I'd hate to see what would happen to you if I decided to leave the room.'

'I told you, I don't have a story.'

Gino paused and took a sip of coffee from the white Styrofoam mug Dahl had given him. 'Tell us your sister's story, then. That's what this is all about, isn't it?'

Riskin's face stilled.

'We know about Clara, we know you were scamming Gregory Norwood, and we know you were trying to kill Robert Zeller. How about we start with why you killed Norwood?'

Riskin's eyes widened in genuine surprise. 'I didn't kill Gregory Norwood. Why would I? He'd been living in hell ever since his son died and he was paying me good money. I told him I knew who killed his son, which is pretty funny. Everybody knows Trey overdosed.'

'That's hilarious.'

'Of course, Trey may have had some help.' He smiled. 'Oh, and I told him I knew Zeller covered Trey for Clara's murder, and that's what really got him,' he said proudly.

Gino propped his elbows on the table and got into his face a little. 'I guess the joke's on you now.'

Riskin scowled. 'What are you talking about?'

'You think Trey Norwood killed your sister?'

'I know he did. That worthless piece of shit got her pregnant, but she wasn't good enough for him, so he killed her and Zeller covered it up.'

'Who told you that?'

'I figured it out.'

'You figured wrong. Trey Norwood was in love with your sister. He wanted to marry her.'

Until this point, Riskin had been a pretty cool customer, like psychopaths and sociopaths always were until you derailed their flimsily constructed delusions. That was when they got agitated. 'That's not true!' he shouted, thrashing against his shackles.

'You saw him kill her?'

'No! But I know he did.'

'You don't know shit,' Gino snapped.

Riskin's face started to turn a livid red. 'Robert Zeller and that fucker who's always tailing him covered it up and faked the evidence, pinned it on that nutcase who worked for us. I saw them at the scene, only I didn't know who he was back then.'

'And you never thought about going to the cops.'

'They threatened me and my family! I was just a kid! Besides, I didn't figure out what was really going on until way later, after my parents died and I went through their stuff. Found out Clara was pregnant and everybody was trying to make her get an abortion, but she wanted to keep the baby. Then Zeller started showing up all over the TV. I recognized him and his watchdog, and then I knew.'

'So you killed Norwood and blew up a goddamned building.'

'What was I supposed to do? Go to the cops?' he sneered. 'My word against Zeller's or the Norwoods'? That's a fucking joke. And I told you, I didn't kill Norwood. I thought about it, trust me, because he was all part of it. But watching him suffer was better.' His lips curled in a chilling smile. 'He was really starting to fall apart at the end. If he'd lived a few more days, I think he would have cracked up. Maybe even spilled his guts. In my opinion, he had a real guilty conscience.'

Magozzi felt a cool, slow rage building deep inside. 'Let's say we believe you. How does killing a lot of other innocent people make up for your sister? And don't tell me it's collateral damage or I'll smash your face in.'

'Zeller was never going to pay for it unless I made him. And I'm telling you straight up, I didn't kill Norwood.'

Gino slammed his hand on the table and Riskin jumped. 'I'm getting sick of looking at your face and listening to your bullshit. You killed Gregory Norwood, then you killed Gerald Stenson.'

'Who's Gerald Stenson?'

'And you tried to kill Rosalie Norwood last night, but her alarm scared you off.'

'I got no problem with Rosalie Norwood.'

'Jim Beam and Lloyd Nasif. I suppose you didn't have a problem with them, either.'

Riskin frowned. 'I don't know Jim Beam.'

'Yeah, you do. The delivery driver . . .'

'Oh. Yeah. I didn't have a choice with him. He knew something was up.'

'Lloyd Nasif?'

Gus shrugged. 'I had a big problem with him. I paid him to get my stuff in the building in his deliveries. He was a loose end. I guess the way things turned out, I could have let him live.'

Gino's face was almost purple and he slammed the table again. 'And then you blew up a fucking building to kill Zeller, but guess what? Zeller's alive. He wasn't in the building when you lit it up. You probably should have double-checked on that, Gus.'

'He's not dead?'

'No, but you're as good as.'

'Son of a bitch!' he screamed, and started thrashing again, then suddenly stilled, bowed his head, and covered his face with his hands. For a minute of wishful thinking, Magozzi thought he was going to break down, but then he jerked his head up and looked at them, his face contorted in frenzied glee. 'But this is all going to break wide open now, isn't it? Yes, it is.'

Magozzi wasn't surprised he answered himself. He obviously had a robust dialogue running inside his wrecked mind.

'Yes, it is,' he repeated with satisfaction. 'People are finally going to listen to Gus Riskin, and when they do, Zeller's political career is dead. And it couldn't have happened any other way. It wasn't my initial vision, but this might be even better.' He giggled, and the sound was pure madness. 'And, for the last time, I didn't kill Gregory Norwood. Looks like you two still have another murderer to find.'

Dahl was waiting for them on the other side of the glass. 'I don't understand half of what went on in there, but you two owe me a story when this is all over.'

Magozzi ran a hand down his unshaven cheek. 'Pencil us in for a weekend in Vegas – it'll take that long to lay it all out.'

'Are you finished with him?'

Gino shook his head. 'Not by a long shot, but Leo and I need to cool our heels. That guy's a fucking lunatic, and if either one of us had spent any more time in there, we *would* have killed him.'

'Do you believe him? That he didn't kill Norwood?'

Gino scowled. 'I don't believe anything that comes out of his mouth. Like you said, he's a raging psychopath and psychopaths don't know how to tell the truth. But he didn't seem to have a problem confessing to mass murder. I don't know why Norwood would be any different.'

'I've spent two hours with him so I have a baseline on his particular brand of insanity. I don't think he was lying about that, for what it's worth.'

'Maybe he didn't kill him, Gino,' Magozzi said quietly. 'And we're never going to find out who did unless Tommy can do something with that surveillance footage.'

Sixty-nine

Rosalie ran her hand along the black pile that lined the Town Car's trunk. It was damp and smelled like shampoo. Of course, nothing would dry completely in this humidity.

Who shampoos their trunk?

She found a tiny dark spot at the very back where her bag had been sitting and rubbed it, then jerked her hand away and looked at it. It was red. Diluted from the shampooing, but still unmistakably blood.

'What are you doing, Rosalie?'

Rosalie slammed the trunk of the Town Car and hid her bloody hand behind her back, thankful she'd changed into black. 'Uncle Robert! You scared me half to death.'

'I'm sorry. I've never been accused of being light on my feet, but I guess there's a first time for everything. Your mother sent me up to look for you. We're hoping you'll come down to the gazebo.'

'I will, I plan to, I was just looking for . . . an earring. One of the diamond studs Mom and Father got me for college graduation. I was thinking maybe it fell into the trunk when I was getting my bag earlier. I've looked everywhere else.'

'No luck?'

'No.'

'That's terrible, losing something of such sentimental value, especially now. We'll keep our eyes out for it.' He tipped his head and his eyes went straight to her earlobes. 'Are you sure you lost it? You're wearing two diamond studs now. I couldn't help noticing them glinting in the sun.'

Her clean hand fluttered up to her earrings. *Stupid, stupid, stupid.* Of course she was still wearing them and now she had to cover one lie with another, which was when people got into trouble.

And what are you so worried about? Why are you lying? This is Uncle Robert.

She tried to put on a smile, but it was weak and so were her knees. 'I . . . put in another pair when I realized I'd lost one of the others. I didn't want Mom to know. She'd be heartbroken.'

'I think you're right about that. It's important to protect the people we love, and some things are better left unsaid, aren't they?' He winked at her. 'This will be our little secret.'

'Thanks.'

He offered his hand. 'Come down to the gazebo.'

'I'll be right down, Uncle Robert. I just have to check in with the office first. They've been leaving messages non-stop since the cell phones started working again.' *Lie number three. Three's a charm.*

'We'll be waiting for you.'

Rosalie followed him into the house and watched him walk down to the gazebo, then took a deep breath and ran upstairs.

She almost screamed when she flung open her bedroom door and saw Louise sitting on her bed, sipping a glass of wine and working on a laptop.

'Oh, dear Rosalie, I've given you a shock, I'm so sorry.'

'That's okay, I just wasn't . . .' She tried to stop her voice trembling.

'Expecting anyone, I know.' She patted the bed. 'Come have some wine. I need your help.'

Louise's eyes were glittering strangely and her speech was halting. Not just from drinking – it couldn't be just from drinking. 'Maybe you should lie down for a bit first.'

'Oh, I will soon,' she slurred. 'I took some anxiety medication and it makes me so sleepy. But, first, look at this.' She swiveled the computer and showed her a password-protected screen with an autumn mountainscape. 'I can't seem to get into my computer.'

Rosalie frowned. 'That's a picture of Aspen.' *The same photo Father has on his laptop.*

'Why, yes, it is, now you mention it. That's odd. I don't remember putting that picture on my computer.'

'Are you sure it's yours?'

She tapped a finger on her lip. 'Hmm. Maybe not. Silly me.'

'Where did you find this, Louise?'

'Oh, I don't know. It was lying around. In Robert's office, I think. I'll go look again. Will you wait for me?'

Rosalie gave her a brittle smile that felt like it would splinter off her face if she moved. 'Of course.'

'Good. There's something I need to show you. Did you find what you were looking for in the trunk?'

'Oh. I lost an earring but I didn't find it.'

'That's a shame. I'll be right back.'

Rosalie waited until she heard her footsteps fading down the hallway, then frantically punched her father's username and password into the computer and watched in despair as it logged into his home page.

There was a reasonable explanation for this too, of course there was. This was just some computer mix-up, some mistake. *But don't think too much or you may come up with conclusions that are simply unacceptable . . .*

Whoever killed your father took his computer.

She chugged what was left in Louise's wine glass, willed her mind blank, and tried to distract herself by reading the titles of the folders on his desktop. Trips, events, photos – the standard fare of anybody's personal computer – but one folder caught her attention, one simply called 'ROBERT'.

Rosalie's finger hovered over the touch pad for a long time before she finally opened it. There was a single file listed: 'GOODBYE OLD FRIEND'. A final missive before cancer took him? A suicide note he'd never had an opportunity to use? This wasn't meant for her eyes, and maybe she didn't want to know what was in that file. As she tried to gather the courage to open it, Louise startled her. She stood in the doorway, swaying unsteadily, another laptop in one hand and a fresh bottle of wine in the other.

'Rosalie, what's wrong? You look terribly upset.'

She jumped up and helped her to the bed, then settled her in, propping her head on the ridiculous mountain of silk pillows that covered half of it. 'I'm just a little confused.'

Even in repose, Louise deftly refilled her empty wine glass. 'I understand exactly what you mean. Things *are* getting so confusing. Nothing feels real anymore.'

Rosalie sat down next to her and showed her the laptop. 'This is my father's computer, Louise.'

'It is?'

'Yes.'

She giggled. 'No wonder I couldn't get into it.'

'Do you know why it's here?'

'No. You'll have to ask Robert about that.' Tears started running down her cheeks, but she seemed unaware of them.

Rosalie was afraid she was witnessing a final breakdown, a final collapse, as Louise's personality disjointed and shifted from motherly to childish to desperate. She took her hand. 'Tell me what's wrong and maybe I can help you.'

'That's so sweet of you, my darling Rosie, but I don't think anybody can help me. Or any of us.'

They jolted up when they heard Robert's voice. 'Rosalie? We're waiting to start lunch. Is everything all right?'

Louise looked at her with panicked eyes. 'Please don't go.'

'Go ahead, Uncle Robert, you and Mom start without us. I'm just helping Louise with some computer problems.'

'Oh. Well, that's very kind of you. I hope we'll see you both down at the gazebo soon.'

Rosalie sat down, grabbed Louise's hands and looked into her vacant eyes. 'Tell me what's happening,' she whispered.

'It's the devil. You can't outrun him forever.'

Seventy

Tommy Espinoza jumped out of his chair when Gino and Magozzi walked into his office. 'I just finished the enhancement on the surveillance footage from Norwood's neighbor. I did what I could and it's not much, but come take a look. See if anything pops for you.'

Magozzi and Gino crowded around his computer. 'Show us what you've got, buddy.'

Tommy clicked his mouse and started to roll tape. A black-and-white image of Norwood's house came into view. Trees, hedges, vines, and the pergolas definitely obstructed the view of the driveway, but in the tiny spaces between the foliage, the hulking shadow of a car came into view. Tommy paused the image briefly. 'Here's the car. Can't see much, but even though the profile's broken up, you can tell it's a bigger car, a sedan.'

'It's not Riskin's silver Hyundai,' Gino commented.

'No. Now pay close attention. This looks like two people getting out, doesn't it?'

Magozzi shrugged. 'Kind of. But it's like the car – just vague images and hidden shadows.'

'Keep watching. See, the shadows both disappear from the frame, but before they do, they're going in different directions. I don't know the layout of the Norwood place, but I'm thinking one went inside the house and one stayed outside. From the time stamp, they don't show up again for fifteen minutes. One gets in the passenger seat, one goes to the back of the car, but what happens there is almost totally obscured by a rose hedge.'

Gino rocked back on his heels and looked at Magozzi. 'Loading up Stenson's body?'

'Couldn't prove it from this. It's great, Tommy, but it doesn't do it. We can't make the car, we can't make the players.'

'Hang tight, keep watching.' He froze the screen again. 'Look in between the roses. You get a partial profile of the guy in back for just a second.'

Magozzi and Gino both squinted. 'Roll it again, Tommy.'

They watched it several more times before Gino pounded his hand on the desk and shouted, 'Fucking hell! That's Conrad, I'd bet my life on it. And if that's Conrad, what do you bet the other guy is Zeller?'

Louise Zeller sniffled and wiped her eyes with the back of her hand. 'I didn't know what to do, Rosalie. With Robert being gone all the time, I thought he was having an affair.' She lifted the lid of her laptop and pulled up a screen that listed multiple dates and locations. 'I put a tracker on his car, so I could follow him everywhere. I'm quite proud of myself for figuring it out, but you're the only one who knows. Look here.' She pointed to a time stamp from yesterday. 'Why was he in a park? There was no campaign event there. I checked. There's no other reason why he would have been in a park way out in the middle of nowhere unless he was meeting someone. I think it's his campaign aide,' she seethed. 'That little bitch.'

Rosalie felt acid creeping up into her throat as she saw William O'Brien State Park under the heading 'Location.' 'Oh, my God,' she whispered.

'I'm sorry, I know this is difficult for you, too. Robert has always been your second father, and to know he betrayed me is like a betrayal to you, isn't it?'

But Rosalie didn't answer because her eyes were fixed on the entry from yesterday morning, just above the park entry, where her parents' address glared at her in evil pixels. Yesterday morning, when her father was killed.

She was horrified into complete shock and immobility. Even her mouth didn't want to move. For a moment, all she could do was sit motionless, watching Louise's bleary eyes try to focus on hers as her head lolled back and forth. This wasn't happening, this couldn't be happening . . .

'I'm so tired, Rosalie, and I just don't know what to do about all this. That's why I wanted to show you.' She sagged against the pillows.

'Lie down, Louise. You need to rest, okay?'

'Your voice is shaking. I've upset you.'

'It's okay, Louise. I have to make a phone call, but then I'll come right back.'

'Promise?'

It was a wounded child's plea, so pitiful, so heartbreaking, and she suddenly hated herself and everyone around her for deserting this sad, destroyed woman. She bent and kissed her forehead, which was hot and damp. 'Yes.'

'Thank you,' she murmured, closing her eyes.

Rosalie grabbed the two computers and ran to the

window. Uncle Robert kept looking up at the house worriedly and her heart started slamming in her chest. She shoved the computers in a closet behind extra blankets and pillows, grabbed her phone, and punched in Detective Magozzi's number.

Seventy-one

Magozzi and Gino were hurrying down the hall toward the chief's office when Rosalie's call came in. They ducked into an interrogation room and Magozzi put the phone on speaker. 'Ms Norwood.'

'Detective, you said a photo-journalist was injured on my parents' property – how do you know?'

They both frowned. She was out of breath, almost panting, and she was also whispering.

'We found his blood and . . . well, to be blunt, a piece of his scalp by the pool deck. He was hit hard.'

'And his body was found in William O'Brien State Park?'

'Yes.'

'And you believe whoever killed my father killed him?'

'That's the working theory. Are you at the hotel, Ms Norwood? We could stop by and chat with you –'

'No! I'm at the Zeller house and something's wrong. Horribly wrong.'

'Take a deep breath and tell us.'

'Father's computer is here.' The words tumbled out of her mouth in a breathy rush. 'And there's blood in the trunk of Uncle Robert's Town Car. It got on my luggage and my dress and I have proof his car was at my parents' house yesterday morning and my house key is on the fob . . . Oh, God, I don't know what I'm saying, I don't know what to do, but I think he killed him and that's crazy.'

Gino and Magozzi bolted out of the interrogation room and started running toward the parking garage. 'Rosalie, did you talk to anybody about this?'

'No. But Uncle Robert caught me looking in the trunk. I told him I'd lost an earring, but I don't think he believed me. He keeps coming to check on me.'

'We're on our way, Ms Norwood. Can you do something for us?'

'Yes.' Her voice came out as a squeak.

'I want you to tell everybody that Detective Rolseth and I are on our way right now with news. Tell them Gus Riskin is in custody and we think he killed your father. Can you do that?'

'I can do that.'

'Is there still blood on your luggage and dress?'

'Yes.'

'We need those two things and your father's computer, too. Can you keep them safe?'

'I hid it all in a cupboard.'

'We'll be there as soon as we can.'

'Jesus Christ,' Gino hissed, weaving through traffic and sailing through a yellow light. 'This whole thing is blowing up and we don't dare move on it until we have it so tight the sun will never get through. I hope to hell Rosalie Norwood's evidence is good.'

'It could make this case, Gino.'

He grunted. 'So what are we going to do when we get there? Zeller already knows something's up and he'll probably have his dogs turn us into fish food and throw us in the lake.'

'I'm a little more worried about Rosalie right now. If Zeller did kill his best friend, I don't think he'd have a problem offing the daughter if he thinks she knows something. He's got a lot to lose.'

'He'll buy what you told Rosalie to say. No way somebody as arrogant as Zeller thinks he could be outsmarted by two dimwit cops.'

Rosalie couldn't breathe, couldn't stop shaking as she watched Uncle Robert walking toward the house. She felt like she was trapped in a bad dream, the kind where you were paralyzed, helpless to do anything but watch the nightmare unfold, except she wasn't going to wake up from this nightmare. He was coming to get her. And now she had to perform as if her life depended on it because maybe it did.

'Uncle Robert!' she shouted, through the screen door of the veranda.

He looked up, startled. 'Rosalie, we're really starting to worry about you. Is everything all right?'

'I'm on my way down right now. I have some good news.'

As she made her way to the gazebo, she felt a sudden disconnect between mind and spirit and body, a complete break from reality. Maybe this was how Louise felt all the time, like a hollow shell of flesh putting one foot in front of the other, unaware of anything but the simple act of walking.

'Rosalie, where have you been?' her mother admonished, when she heard her approach, then faltered: 'What's wrong, dear?'

'I just talked to the detectives. They're on their way

358

here. Gus Riskin is in custody and they believe he killed Father.'

Her mother looked like she was going to faint. Uncle Robert looked relieved. 'Finally some closure, some peace for us all. Justice will be served. Conrad, will you go to the gatehouse and meet the detectives?'

'Yes, sir.' He gave the dogs a silent command with his hand and they followed him obediently, tongues lolling against the heat.

'Where is Louise?' Robert asked.

Rosalie couldn't look at him. 'She's not feeling well. I'll go check on her.'

'No, sit and eat something. I'll look in on her.'

'I have to send some documents to the office anyhow,' she said, hoping she didn't sound as desperate as she felt. 'There's been an ongoing issue with the distribution center in Denver and things are coming to a head.' Another lie on top of so many. She wondered if she'd ever be able to recognize the truth again.

'Can't you just sit for a minute and have some lunch with me?' her mother asked peevishly.

'This really can't wait. We're in damage-control mode right now and the Denver office is closing in an hour. I'll be back as soon as I can.'

Louise was still asleep – or passed out, she wasn't sure which – when she crept into her Moroccan guest room and unearthed the two computers from the closet. Even with a racing heart and trembling, sweat-slick hands, it didn't take more than a few minutes to transfer files from Louise's and her father's computers onto a flash drive. For good measure, she uploaded them onto her own computer and sent those to two of her email addresses.

'Rosalie, you came back,' Louise said groggily. 'Come, sit with me.'

She put the computers back in the closet and sat down next to Louise, brushed her hair off her forehead. 'Just for a minute. The detectives investigating Father's murder are coming and I have to meet them.'

She nodded in resignation. 'I heard you speaking with them.'

Rosalie's throat closed, trying to remember what her end of the conversation sounded like. Not good and half hysterical, that much she knew.

'Just bits and pieces, though. I was drifting in and out. Did you think about what I should do?'

'I think you should rest some more.'

'No, I mean about Robert.'

'Louise, I don't think he's having an affair.' *It might be so much worse than that.*

'That's not what I'm talking about anymore.'

She frowned. 'What *are* you talking about?'

Her eyes wandered the room and finally settled on some faraway point. 'This is all my fault. I understand that now. I could have saved her. I could have saved us all. And if I had, none of this would be happening now.'

'Saved who?'

'I used to love taking walks in the woods when we visited you in Aspen. It was so beautiful, so peaceful, especially in the evenings and at night. The smell of pine, the sound of the river. I always thought it sounded like it was chuckling, but not on that night.'

360

Rosalie realized that Louise wasn't in the present anymore. She was just a time traveler now, entering her strange world of delusions rooted somewhere in the past, and Rosalie wondered if she would ever come back this time.

'It was awful. All I could hear were moans and I found her, that poor pretty thing, beaten so badly. It was horrible.' Louise covered her mouth. A tear escaped her eye and rolled down her cheek. 'But she was still alive when I left her.'

Rosalie grabbed her hands. 'Louise, what are you talking about?'

'I was terrified. I ran away, back to your house, and I told Robert and Gregory to call an ambulance, call the police. But they never did, they just disappeared. For hours.'

Rosalie felt something inside her drain away, something she understood, on a very elemental level, would never be recovered. 'Are you talking about Clara Riskin?'

She nodded. 'She was pregnant, you know. You could have had a niece or nephew. But I guess nobody wanted that, except Trey and Clara.'

Seventy-two

Gino pulled up to the Zellers' open gate where Conrad was waiting with his panting dogs. 'What did I tell you, Leo? Fish food.' He rolled down his window. 'Hi, Conrad. Your dogs look like they could use refreshment. I know I sure could.'

Conrad kept his composure but he was terse. 'Park in the motorcourt. Everyone is down at the gazebo.'

'Motorcourt,' Gino scoffed, as he sped up the driveway. 'I can't wait to see that prick fry.'

'Actually, he's been pretty tolerant of your abuse.'

'Yeah, well, he's still a killer in my book and so is his boss.' Gino slammed the car into park beside the ridiculous fountain and behind the Town Car. 'The warrant to impound that thing better come in soon before Zeller decides to get rid of it. So what's our plan in the meantime?'

'We're going to lie our asses off and keep Zeller cool, convince him that Riskin is our man. Then we get Rosalie the hell out of here along with her evidence.'

As they got out of the car, the front door of the house swung open and Rosalie Norwood stepped out, or at least what was left of her. Right now nothing about her resembled the vibrant young woman he and Gino had met yesterday. There was nobody home behind those devastated eyes, as if her soul had simply taken flight from the ugliness that had descended on her life. Her posture was slumped and her voice a dead monotone when she spoke.

'I did what you said, Detectives. They're waiting for you down at the gazebo.'

Magozzi approached her and offered his hand. 'I'm very sorry, Ms Norwood.'

She took his hand and walked unsteadily down the front steps, then reached into the pocket of her dress and withdrew a flash drive. 'There are two files on this you need to see. I made extra copies just in case. One is a letter my father wrote to Uncle . . . to Robert.' She dropped the familial designation. 'I haven't had a chance to read it and I don't know if I want to, but I think it might explain some things.'

'And the other file?'

'Data from a GPS tracker Louise Zeller put on the Town Car that places it at my parents' house yesterday morning. And at William O'Brien after that. My bag and dress are upstairs and so are both computers.' She let out an anguished sigh. 'Louise told me something else, too.'

'When we're finished, we'll take you home and we can talk. You can't stay here.'

'I can't wait to leave.' She looked down and tangled her fingers together. 'What's going to happen now? Will you arrest him?'

'First we have to put together our case and we have to be very careful. When we pull the evidence you give us together with ours, we'll bring him in for questioning, and things will probably move pretty quickly after that. But, for now, it's just like we told you. Gus Riskin is in custody and he's our only suspect. Will you come down to the gazebo with us?'

'It would seem suspicious if I didn't, but it's going to be the longest walk of my life.'

'You can do this.'

She nodded, straightened her shoulders, and Magozzi saw a little of the old Rosalie return, which said a lot about her endurance and resilience.

The terraced stone walk down to the gazebo on Lake Minnetonka was very different from the rugged, moss-covered path down to the dock on Magozzi's little lake, and he wouldn't have traded places for anything. Robert Zeller and Betty Norwood watched their progress anxiously from a large, gray-shingled gazebo. As they closed in, Zeller stood and shook their hands. 'Thank you for coming, Detectives. I understand there's been a break in Gregory's case and August Riskin is in custody.' He passed them each a bottle of water from a sweating silver bucket filled with ice.

'Yes, sir.' Magozzi let that hang, hoping to annoy him right off the bat, but it didn't have the desired effect. Good lawyers and successful politicians were better actors.

'I commend you both on making such fast work of this. Rosalie said you believe he killed Gregory.'

'We do.'

'Did he confess?'

'Not yet, but we're confident he will. Our evidence is pretty damning.'

'So this will all be over soon?' Betty asked. 'We'll be able to lay Gregory and Trey to rest?'

'Yes, ma'am.'

Zeller touched her shoulder. 'Gregory will finally have justice. Do you have any idea why Riskin would do such a thing?'

'He's a pretty unbalanced individual, Mr Zeller,' Gino said. 'Delusional, actually. He blames Trey Norwood for his sister's death and, by extension, Mr Norwood.'

Magozzi caught a barely perceptible shift in Zeller's expression. Just a tiny tic, nothing more. He hadn't liked hearing that. 'My God, he is unbalanced. So it was some warped form of revenge.'

'Something like that.'

A gunshot suddenly shattered the breathless summer air and Gino and Magozzi started running toward the terrible sound while Rosalie screamed, 'LOUISE!'

Seventy-three

Gino and Magozzi stood in the shade of a big maple tree, watching the coroner's hearse pull away with Louise Zeller's body. Another stately home despoiled by violent death, cops and squad cars, another family destroyed, all against the backdrop of a city in shock. Her suicide wasn't their case, and the locals had taken over, but it had probably been an indirect result of it.

'This is so goddamn sad, Leo. This whole mess started with a suspected suicide and ended with a real one, and it's going to get way worse once the lid blows off this thing. The Norwoods are never going to get over it.' He kicked at a landscaping stone that had migrated to the lawn.

Magozzi thought about that. He wasn't sure Betty would, but he knew Rosalie would find a way to survive. She already was. Right now she was waiting for them at her house with a police escort, ready to answer their questions and probably ask a lot of her own.

After Zeller, Betty Norwood and Conrad had spoken with the police, a squad took them to the Chatham Hotel to mourn another life. He'd seen nothing but shock and devastation in their faces, scarcely an acknowledgment that they were being displaced by another crime scene and the accompanying horror. But Gino was right: it was going to get worse. They just didn't know it yet.

A wrecker pulled into the motorcourt. The warrant

had finally gone through on the Town Car and it was here to collect it. Magozzi directed the driver, Gino signed the paperwork, and they watched as another nail in Zeller's coffin was lifted onto the flatbed trailer and disappeared down the idyllic, tree-lined drive. Getting to the end of a homicide was usually an uplifting moment, and this should have been one, but the case had too many dark, ugly, tragic shadows that would never be dispelled, not even by justice.

'Come on, Gino, let's go pull the final pieces together.'

While Gino drove to Rosalie's house, Magozzi uploaded the files from the flash drive Rosalie had given them, then opened GOODBYE OLD FRIEND, Gregory Norwood's final epistle to his killer.

Robert,

You have been my dearest and most loyal friend for over four decades, my rock and stalwart companion, and no words can express my gratitude for everything you've done and been for me.

I'm writing to you not just as a friend but as a man who has very little time left on this earth. A death sentence engenders deep introspection and reflection on the life you have lived. What have I accomplished? What is my legacy? How will I be remembered?

Imminent death also forces us to recognize our subjugation under a power beyond our control, whether that be mortality itself or a higher being. It also underscores the arrogance of man for disregarding it. In my case, I dismissed the existence of Heaven and Hell and worshipped position and money and appearances above morality, above life itself.

I have never spoken of this or written it down until now, but you and I committed a most heinous, unforgivable act on that night in Aspen. What made us think that it was remotely justifiable? What made us believe we had the right? We became abominations that night, and I have endured some punishment, through crippling guilt, the loss of Trey, and perhaps even through cancer, but it is not nearly enough to make up for that grievous sin. She was just a young girl carrying a precious life, and it was our moral duty to save her and save her baby, Trey's baby, yet we did not.

And we destroyed and ultimately ended another life that night by transferring our sin, as if our own lives were worth so much more than Richard Kuehn's; worth so much more than Clara's and her unborn child's. You and I and Conrad deserve Hell, and if there is one (of which I'm still not entirely certain), we will all meet again. But justice should not have to wait for afterlife.

After much careful deliberation, I realize I can no longer shoulder this vile burden. I have considered taking my own life many times over the years, and especially now, but I realize that such an act would only bring more suffering and pain to my family than they have already endured. And the situation with August Riskin has made me realize our wicked secret is no longer safe. And why are we looking for him but to silence him? I cannot be party to the taking of another human life.

Robert, the truth will eventually prevail no matter what actions we take, and I believe the only way for me to preserve even a shred of honor is to atone for what I've done and beg for forgiveness and mercy before I die. That is the only act by which my family might actually find some solace amid their horror and disgrace, as infinitesimal as that solace might be. Please consider what I've said and ask yourself if it is worse to live with shame or die with it. As a man of religious conviction, I'm certain you have your own perspective. We will discuss this further. And if something happens to me before we do, goodbye, old friend.

Yours always,
Gregory

'This letter was written two weeks ago, Gino. Zeller obviously got it and acted on it.'

He shook his head and parked behind the squad in front of Rosalie's house. 'It's like he was begging Zeller to kill him. He knew damn well he wouldn't let him make his deathbed confession and ruin his life and his political career.'

'Maybe he was. In a twisted way, it was probably Norwood's ideal outcome. He didn't have to waste away in agony from cancer, he didn't have to take his own life, he didn't have to confess to his family, and I'm sure in his mind there was always a good chance this would never come out and everybody could move on with their lives. Zeller would be governor and the world could mourn the late great Gregory Norwood, finally resting in peace.'

Gino shut off the car. 'If Rosalie hadn't given us Dubnik's name, it might not have come out. That's a cruel irony, because this letter is going to shatter her if she reads it.'

Magozzi looked out of the window at her charming house on the creek where brass bells guarded the door and fine art mingled with tchotchkes, and the smart, talented young woman inside was trying to cope with unimaginable betrayal. 'I think she probably already has.'

Epilogue

Magozzi was sitting on Grace's sofa, cradling his baby girl, who was without question the most beautiful child ever born. He made faces, cooed, babbled incoherently – it was funny how babies could transform even the most dignified adults into shameless goofballs. Grace was sitting next to him, smiling down at the tiny heart-shaped face while she stroked the downy hair of her head.

It was strange to be in a state of such supreme contentment and bliss when the recent memories of multiple sorrows were still roiling around them, around the city.

'I can't tell whether or not she got your hair or mine.'

Magozzi shrugged. 'For her sake, I hope she borrowed most of her DNA from you. You have a lot more to offer than I do.'

'Don't sell yourself short.' She suddenly arched her brow at him and those amazing blue eyes narrowed. 'Speaking of short, I believe I'm forty dollars short right now.'

'What?'

She wiggled her fingers at him. 'Fork it over.'

Magozzi suppressed a smile. 'I don't know what you're talking about.'

'You're a terrible liar. The bet. You and Gino were both wrong, just like I told you.'

He scratched his jaw pensively. 'Hmm. I don't seem to remember you buying in.'

They played chicken with their eyes for roughly thirty seconds before they both cracked and started laughing. Magozzi pulled out his wallet, careful not to disturb the baby, and handed over two crisp twenties. 'Diaper money.'

Grace took the cash with the cutest expression of smug satisfaction. 'We need a name, Magozzi.'

They did need a name, and it seemed like the most daunting, impossible task he'd ever confronted. How did you pick a name for such a perfect, precious creature? 'Nothing's good enough. Except maybe Grace Junior.'

'What about Elizabeth?'

Magozzi rolled the name around in his mind as he gazed down at the piece of Heaven that had somehow magically fallen to Earth and into his arms. 'A name with a fine pedigree. Does it mean something to you?'

'Harley told me it was the name of an old woman who saved his life.'

'Anybody who saved Harley's life deserves to be honored.'

'That's what I was thinking.'

'I like it. We need a middle name, too.'

'Te Amo,' Grace said resolutely.

'I love you?'

'I want her to know that she's always been loved, right from the very beginning. That she always will be.'

'I think that's perfect.' He leaned down and kissed the soft forehead of their little girl. 'Elizabeth Te Amo, welcome to the world.'

She yawned and blinked up at him.

'I think she approves.' Grace released a contented sigh and rested her head on his shoulder. 'Is Robert Zeller going to survive to stand trial? I just heard about the suicide watch.'

Magozzi had never been able to keep up with Grace and her arcane mind, which could jump so quickly from a happy thing to a dark thing without any recalibration. He would always be ten steps behind her, for the rest of his life, he hoped. 'He'll gladly survive to face the jury. He thinks he'll come out of this without anything more than a dent and a scratch. Suicide watch is just a precaution.'

'He's that arrogant?'

'Yeah, he is. He's subverted the law for so long, he can't conceive of an ending to it.'

'Is it possible he'll be acquitted?'

'Not a chance. He's got the A Team in his corner, but his cabal is gone and he's totally alone. He just doesn't realize it yet.'

Elizabeth started fussing and Grace reached out to take her, both of them finding comfort in one another. 'I always thought I'd seen the darkest side of people, what they were capable of, but I was wrong.'

Magozzi kissed both his girls. 'There's more light than dark, Grace, remember that. I'll be back soon. Gino and I just have one last thing to do.'

The heat wave had finally relinquished its chokehold on Minneapolis to the relief of all, especially Gino, and curtains fluttered lazily in Rosalie Norwood's open windows, inviting the cool, fresh breeze inside.

She smiled sadly when she opened the door to the tinkling of bells that hung on the inside – the bells she said had saved her. And maybe they had.

She looked thin and exhausted. 'Detectives, it's good to see you.' She eyed the paper-wrapped package in Magozzi's hand. 'I wasn't expecting a gift.'

'We're just returning something to its rightful owner.'

'Come in. Please.'

Magozzi and Gino followed her inside. There were several pieces of luggage stacked by the door. 'It looks like you're taking a trip.'

'Mom and I are going to Aspen tonight. We're finally spreading Trey's ashes along with Father's. Strange that this whole thing is ending the way it began.'

'How are you?'

'Most days, horrible. On the other days, worse. I try not to think about things, but it's impossible not to – not to dwell on the fact that people you've loved and trusted with all your heart are monsters. I've made peace with some things, others I never will.' She let out an anxious sigh.

'How is your mother?'

She looked away. 'Heavily medicated. She'll probably be that way for the rest of her life. She barely speaks anymore. She won't talk to me about anything. So much damage,' she said bitterly. 'So much loss. I've always thought you could get through anything, but I don't believe that anymore.'

Magozzi reached out and touched her arm. 'You'll get through this, Rosalie. It doesn't seem that way now, but you will. You're a strong woman. Always remember that.'

Her sad brown eyes lifted. 'You finally called me by my first name. I appreciate that.'

'We've been through a lot together.'

'Yes, we have.'

'Remember. You're strong.'

She nodded. 'I'll try.'

'This might help you.' Magozzi placed the package on her dining-room table and watched her unwrap it carefully. Her eyes filled with tears when she saw the 'angel' piece – the Ruscha Trey had been so proud of. 'Thank you.'

'I'm afraid the piece has lost most of its value.'

'Was it damaged?'

'The appraiser said it had been defaced, but we disagree.' Magozzi slipped on gloves, carefully removed the art from the frame, and turned it over. On the back, a large heart drawn in marker enclosed the words 'CLARA AND BABY.'

She sank into a chair. 'Trey's angels,' she whispered. 'Now I understand why he was so happy when he bought this. It was for them.'

They all turned their heads when the bells on her front door started jingling.

Just the wind, Magozzi thought.

Acknowledgments

Enormous thanks to Joel Richardson at Michael Joseph/ Penguin Random House, and his entire, talented team for their continued enthusiasm and faith in P. J. Tracy. High fives and much appreciation to Matthew Martz and his colleagues at Crooked Lane Books, all of whom jumped on board with gusto and expert attention. Writing is a solitary endeavor, but it takes an extended family to produce a book.

And endless gratitude to Ellen Geiger at Frances Goldin Literary Agency. She is not only a brilliant agent, but a dear friend. Many thanks also to the charming David Grossman of David Grossman Literary Agency.

The internationally bestselling
Twin Cities crime series by P. J. Tracy

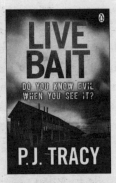

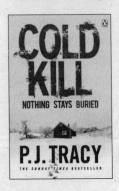

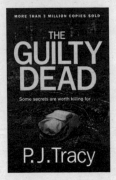

**See where it all began in *Want to Play?*,
the first gripping thriller in the Twin Cities series**

The slaying of an old couple in small-town America looks like
a one-off act of brutal retribution. In Minneapolis, teams of
detectives scramble to stop a sickeningly inventive serial
killer striking again in a city paralysed by fear.

When the two separate investigations collide, decade-old
secrets begin to fall away. It seems an old killer has resurfaced.
Yet their real identity remains dangerously out of reach . . .

OUT NOW

P. J. Tracy was the pseudonym for the mother-and-daughter writing team of P. J. and Traci Lambrecht. Together P. J. and Traci were authors of the brilliant best-selling Twin Cities thrillers. P. J. has now sadly passed and Traci continues to write the series.

Want to discover more killer crime books, drama and film?

Sign up to the Dead Good newsletter at
www.deadgoodbooks.co.uk